Nicole Helm grew up wit[...] dream of one day becomi[...] few failed career choice[...] she g[...] dream—writing down-to-earth contemporary romance and romantic suspense. From farmers to cowboys, Midwest to *the* West, Nicole writes stories about people finding themselves and finding love in the process. She lives in Missouri with her husband and two sons, and dreams of someday owning a barn.

Janie Crouch writes passionate romantic suspense for readers who still believe in heroes. After a lifetime on the East Coast—and a six-year stint in Germany—this *USA Today* bestselling author has settled into her dream home in the Front Range of the Colorado Rockies. She loves engaging in all sorts of adventures (Triathlons! Two-hundred-mile relay races! Mountain treks!), travelling and surviving life with four kids. You can find out more about her at janiecrouch.com

Discover more at millsandboon.co.uk

FATAL DECEPTION

NICOLE HELM

PROTECTIVE LAWMAN

JANIE CROUCH

MILLS & BOON

First Published in Great Britain 2025
by Mills & Boon, an imprint of HarperCollins*Publishers* Ltd
1 London Bridge Street, London, SE1 9GF

www.harpercollins.co.uk

HarperCollins*Publishers*
Macken House, 39/40 Mayor Street Upper,
Dublin 1, D01 C9W8, Ireland

Fatal Deception © 2025 Nicole Helm
Protective Lawman © 2025 Janie Crouch

ISBN: 978-0-263-39738-3

1225

MIX
Paper | Supporting
responsible forestry
FSC™ C007454

This book contains FSC™ certified paper and other controlled
sources to ensure responsible forest management.

For more information visit: www.harpercollins.co.uk/green

Printed and Bound in the UK using 100% Renewable Electricity at
CPI Group (UK) Ltd, Croydon, CR0 4YY

FATAL DECEPTION

NICOLE HELM

For all the reluctant helpers.

Chapter One

Audra Young didn't mind having the whole ranch to her-self, even if it meant working from sunup to sundown. She didn't mind the quiet, the solitude. She didn't even mind making her own meals.

If her neighbor, Natalie Kirk, didn't send over leftovers, Audra baked herself silly and subsisted off brownies and breads. Either worked for her.

Which was good because she was losing roommates left and right. First, her second cousin, Vi, had gotten married and moved into town with her daughter and new husband. Then, just last week, her sister, Rosalie, had gone and mar-ried Duncan Kirk and jetted off on a long and well-deserved honeymoon.

Which just left Audra's *other* cousin, Franny Perkins. But Franny was at a writer's conference that would culmi-nate in spending a few weeks in Washington with her folks.

Audra was well and truly on her own for at least three more weeks. The first few days had been fun. She got to do everything her way, which included none of Rosalie's messiness or Franny's distracting conversations.

Moving into week two of *just her*, it felt a bit lonely. She walked up to the mailbox, her usual post-workday but pre-dinner routine, thinking some company would be nice.

Maybe a dog or two to trek around with her. But Franny was terribly allergic to dogs, so it didn't seem right to get one.

Maybe she could hire on a hand. No doubt she could find a woman who wanted a little work in exchange for room and board.

But that was the problem. Audra couldn't offer much more than that. She was still digging out of the hole her parents had left her four years ago, and keeping the ranch just breaking even meant not hiring anyone on.

She paused when she opened the door to the mailbox, surprised to find a package inside. She wasn't expecting anything. Probably Rosalie sending something from Italy just because she knew it would give Audra a thrill.

Smiling at the thought of that, and her sister happily married to her absolute perfect match, Audra pulled everything out, then took the long walk back to the house.

Nothing much had changed there in the last thirty years. Her parents had never been ones for *improvements*.

Audra patched up what she could when necessary, doing everything in her power to avoid the expense of hiring someone to fix things. But that porch was starting to sag, and come spring, she'd need someone to check on the crooked gutter.

And she'd have to figure out a way to afford it because if things didn't get done *now*, Rosalie would start trying to pay for things because her new husband was loaded.

Franny claimed it was pointless Wyoming stubbornness that kept Audra refusing Duncan's overtures, and maybe she was right, but Audra wanted to know that she… Well, that she was better than her parents.

And sure, that was probably worthy of some therapy in and of itself, but she couldn't afford that either.

Back home, she scraped off her muddy boots on the outside mat, then immediately toed them off in the entry. She carefully lined them up where they belonged before making her way into the kitchen, where she flipped through the mail, then retrieved scissors to open the package.

She studied it more carefully now. It was addressed to "the family of Audra Young." Which was…weird and definitely not from Rosalie. Weirder still was the bright orange sticker on the bottom corner that read Cremated Remains.

Audra paused. Her father had been cremated, but that was four years ago, and the remains had been given to his other family. Audra was quite fine with that.

Had they changed their minds? Divvied some up? Did Audra want to know?

Not wanting to dive into those questions, she dealt with the rest of the mail first. She threw away the junk, put the bill in the to-pay pile and then turned back to the counter, where she'd left…*the remains*.

She sighed. She had to do *something* about them. She couldn't just leave a box labeled Cremated Remains lying around. Unless Audra hid it away in her room, Franny was likely to come across it and neither of those options suited.

Gripping the scissors, Audra grimaced and cut through the tape keeping the box closed. Maybe if the ashes were in a smaller container she would be able to find somewhere to hide it away. Maybe Rosalie would…want this.

Though Audra doubted it. Rosalie used to worship their dad, but Audra had ruined that when she confessed last year that Audra had been the one to do or make Dad do all the things Rosalie had given him credit for over the years.

Audra still regretted coming clean, except Rosalie had needed to know that in order to get over her reservations about Duncan. And he was perfect for her. Now they were married and happy and…

Audra blew out a long breath. "Okay, Audra. Be a grown-up." She pulled the flaps of the box back to reveal a bunch of bubble wrap. Trying not to think, just act, she pulled out the contents, then slowly began to unwrap them.

Eventually, a fancy black urn came into view. It had to be Dad. It had to be.

There was a little engraved plaque on the side, so Audra turned it over and read…

Audra Gail Young.

For a long moment, she stood perfectly still, having absolutely no thoughts in her head as she stared at her name engraved on this container.

Cremains.

And her name.

But she was here, and alive, so there was some kind of *mistake*. She had to remind herself of that in order to take a breath.

A mistake. Similar to when the power had mistakenly gone out for three days right around Rosalie's wedding because someone had called the power company and told them she was dead.

Then there were the messages she kept getting from a cemetery one town over.

Audra put down the urn, then stepped back. She rubbed at the tight band of stress that tensed in her chest, frustrated to have such a visceral response over a *mistake*. It wasn't like her.

Even when different types of trouble cropped up around the county, sometimes affecting her loved ones, friends, or neighbors, Audra rarely worried. Anyone who knew her thought she was a soft, sweet thing. And she supposed, in some respects, she was.

But she was tougher than anyone gave her credit for and had the target-shooting awards to prove it.

The problem was...*shooting* wasn't going to get her out of her identity somehow getting mixed up with a dead woman's, and Audra didn't have the first clue how to solve that problem.

She couldn't go to Rosalie. What was her sister going to do from *Rome*, where she was having the most amazing and romantic honeymoon *ever*? Audra didn't want to go to Thomas, her cousin's husband—not with Vi so close to her due date.

But there was someone who would help, who wouldn't worry. Someone Audra couldn't pretend she *liked*, but... Well, he wasn't all bad.

She hoped.

COPELAND BECKETT SAT at the desk that he shared with another detective and sipped the horrible coffee he'd poured himself after arriving at the Bent County Sherriff's Department.

Laurel Delaney-Carson was already out on a case this morning, and Thomas Hart was coming in late in order to go to a doctor's appointment with his wife.

Things had quieted down lately, which was good for Bent County, but left Copeland feeling...edgy. Too much time where his brain wasn't actively engaged left it free to do its own thing.

No thanks.

So he was happy when someone walked into his office even if, had he placed a bet on who'd walk into his office on this cold, gray morning, she wouldn't have even been on the list.

He stood. There was something about Audra Young that

seemed to call for a chivalry he would have claimed he didn't possess. Cowboy-code nonsense.

He was definitely no cowboy, but he supposed she was, in a manner of speaking.

"Hart isn't in yet," Copeland said by way of greeting.

Her polite smile didn't change, but her blue eyes got a little frosty. She was the kind of woman that could be polite and frosty all in one look, and Copeland found on the seemingly soft and quiet Audra Young, he didn't know what the hell to do with it.

Or her.

He wouldn't say that she was prettier than her sister, exactly. Rosalie was a short, annoying firecracker. Audra was a slim, icy...he didn't know. Sometimes she reminded him of a statue of a goddess. All untouchable ivory. Her hair wasn't as red as Rosalie's, but it leaned that way. Her eyes weren't nearly as violet as her sister's. They were a dark, summer-sky-blue.

She was dressed in what he'd learned was the typical uniform for ranchers around these parts. Boots. Lots of denim and flannel. Hair in a long braid down her back. She didn't wear a hat, but he had no doubt there'd be a Stetson on the dash of her giant truck.

He knew she didn't like him. No matter that he'd helped find her cousin when the woman had been kidnapped. Never mind that he'd apologized to her sister when their concurrent investigations had led to Rosalie getting injured.

He knew when a woman didn't like him, because it was a rare thing indeed. Oh, he was an abrasive SOB, but women found him charming, or interesting, or a challenge.

Except the Young sisters. It was annoying from Rosalie because she was a private investigator, so she was always hounding him for information. But from Audra…well, Copeland wouldn't count it as *annoyed*.

So he smiled because he was a little perverse and wanted to see how far he could make that dislike go.

"I wasn't looking for Thomas this morning," she said carefully, shifting a box she carried in her arms. "I have a problem that I'd like your help with." She powered on before he could even register shock. She moved forward and put the box on the desk between them. "This was sent to me."

Copeland raised an eyebrow at the bright orange sticker that read Cremated Remains. He peered in the box. A shiny black urn sat in there. He might have thought nothing of it except the plaque on it read *Audra Gail Young*.

He looked up at her, already knowing the answer, but he was a detective. Had to ask. Read the reaction. "Some same-named relative of yours?"

"Not that I'm aware of." Her hands clasped together in front of her before she released them. She managed a strange gesture, almost like a shrug. "That's my name. And when I put that together with some of the other issues that have been going on, I… I know it might not be criminal, exactly." Her eyebrows drew together. "But I don't know what to do."

Always interested in a puzzle, Copeland didn't dismiss her out of hand. "What *other issues*?"

She went through them. Her power being turned off. Messages from a cemetery. He supposed it sounded like a mix-up, but it was definitely a strange one.

"I guess it's just some sort of mistake—they've mixed up my name with this poor person, but I don't know how to get to the bottom of it. I was hoping you could help, even if it isn't criminal…exactly."

Copeland considered. It was a bit of a strange gray area, and he didn't mind those. In fact, he rather preferred them to the Bent County obsession with black and white, right and wrong. If it had been anyone else, he would have jumped right in.

But this was Audra Young. He studied her. Stiff and polite. Pretty and untouchable. All Western tough girl with the strangest undercurrent of…soft princess.

And she absolutely did not like him—whether it was because of his abrasive personality, that Bent County distrust of outsiders, or something else, he didn't know. Didn't really matter. Except, he wanted to know.

"I do have a somewhat pressing question before I decide."

"Why am I bringing this to you and not…literally anyone else?" she asked, with just a *hint* of self-deprecation.

He tapped a finger to his nose. "You're smart."

She made a noncommittal sound. "Rosalie is enjoying her honeymoon, and I want it to stay that way. I don't want her coworkers at Fool's Gold to be put on the spot where they might have to lie to her. Vi's due any day now, and Thomas might not take his full paternity leave if he's handling this for me. With just about every other person I considered, this gets back to Rosalie or Vi. I know how they all worry about me out there by myself. I'd like to keep this…quiet."

"Being out there on a big ranch would be a cause of worry, I'd think."

Her chin lifted. Her eyes got frosty again. He couldn't help but smile at the attitude.

"Women have been out here on their own for centuries, Detective," she said in that clipped way he'd never heard her use with anyone else.

"It didn't end well for a lot of them."

"And that's on the male species, isn't it?"

"Or bears."

This time, the visitor wasn't Natalie—so no food, more's the pity. Though she did still have some of what she'd brought over last night that she could warm up for dinner. Plus, she'd pulled one of her homemade loaves of bread out of the freezer this morning, so it should be thawed enough to make sandwiches. And there was some cookie dough in the freezer she could bake.

Once she was close enough to make out the fact it was a Bent County Sheriff's Department cruiser with a man standing in front of it, she slowed to a stop.

Not just any man. Copeland stood there, leaning against his police car, the wind whipping through his jet-black hair. His gaze was on the mountains in the distance, where the setting sun made them look like golden sentries. The side of his face that she could see was hidden in shadow, but there was no denying the profile was impressive. Handsome. All sharp edges and strong lines.

He looked like a movie star. Playing an honorable but gruff police officer in the shadows of a beautiful landscape. If Franny had been here, she'd build a whole story about him. Tragic backstory for the gruffness. A shield to protect a hurting heart.

For a moment, just a fraction of a moment, really, she wondered if that was true. If all Copeland's sharp, abrasive edges were simply hiding a hurting heart. If that was why he'd left Denver and plopped himself down in the middle of nowhere, where he hadn't known a soul.

Ridiculous, of course, but the idea of the *story* of it, the *romance* of it, cheered her up some anyway, so she started walking again.

"I've been waiting," Copeland called out once he noticed her.

And right there, any romantic inklings were deflated in

an instant. *Thank you, Copeland, for your terrible attitude, clearly shielding nothing but typical* male *baloney*.

"You could have called me," she replied once she got close enough not to have to shout. "I left my cell number."

He shrugged. "I was already out and about." He turned, regarding her with those dark, direct eyes. "Figured you'd be done mucking out stalls or whatever you do by dark."

Out and about. Was he going to tell her she was worrying over nothing? Had he figured it all out so quickly that she would now feel like a total idiot? She braced herself for any and all conclusions, except…

"I'm still having trouble getting in contact with anyone at the cemetery. Through the number you gave me or anything online. But I did come across a reason they might have been trying to contact you."

He held out his phone. She had to scoot closer to him and lean forward to see the screen. Her heart did an uncomfortable jerk in her chest. There on a gravestone was her name. And…

"That's my birthday," she managed to say, though she knew her voice sounded affected. Because she *was* affected. Especially by having a death year, like some kind of threat.

"I figured," he said. He slid the phone back into his pocket, surveyed her again, but they were closer now. She could smell the faint hint of leather from his coat. "Older than you look."

She fixed him with a glare. She supposed it was a compliment, but somehow his delivery made it seem anything but. "I guess I look pretty good for a corpse too."

His mouth almost quirked into a smile, and something very unwelcome fluttered inside her in response to that handsome face showing some humor. Or in response, maybe, to just how close they were standing.

She took a step away. "There's something else. Maybe. When I got home last night, Mrs. Kirk told me that there'd been some damage to a fence."

Copeland had helped with the issues at the Kirk Ranch last year, so he knew who all the players were, and how their properties butted up to each other.

"Norman went ahead and fixed it up, because some of my cattle had gotten over onto his side. But… I don't know. It feels off. Not the normal fence wear and tear."

"I want to take a look."

"I've got a picture."

He shook his head. "Sure, I'll look at that, but I want to see it too." He gestured out at the ranch. "Show me."

She scowled at the order. Wanted to argue. God, she was cold and hungry. But he was taking this seriously, which was more than she'd hoped for. She needed to be cooperative. Not grumpy just because she'd had a long day.

But something about the idea of showing him the fence had her hesitating. Had her resenting his entire place in this. Left her with the very uncharacteristic need to needle him.

"You know how to ride?" she asked, smiling sweetly at him. "A horse, that is." She doubted it *very* much.

She watched his expression flicker ever so minutely, and only because she'd been looking for it. Irritation. But he didn't make any excuses.

"Yeah. Sure."

"Then let's saddle up."

COPELAND *DID* KNOW how to ride, no matter how dubious she looked about it.

Knowing *how* to do something and *liking* it were two different things though.

Hart had insisted he learn back when he'd first started

filling in during Laurel's maternity leave. Insisted that being a detective in a ranching community meant knowing how to get around in all different ways.

Copeland wasn't one for having someone insist that he do something, but he trusted Hart. Hart might be a native, but he hadn't grown up on a ranch, so Copeland didn't think he was biased by any cowboy nonsense. It was a necessary tool he'd need out here in the wannabe Wild West. And Copeland had been bound and determined to make this job work. To make his way up to detective again.

To leave Denver and that life behind.

So he'd learned. Hated every minute of giving up all his control to an animal, but he'd learned. He much preferred the snowmobile Hart had taught him to drive this winter.

Audra led him to a building that was obviously the stables. Everything was clean, but it all kind of…sagged. Like the years had worn on it no matter how well kept the whole place was. Everything about the Young Ranch felt that way, actually. Especially if he compared it to the Kirk Ranch, which had a newer, more modern feel to it.

But he wasn't a rancher. Didn't know a damn thing about ranching. Maybe she liked things kind of old and dilapidated. Maybe it suited whatever kind of operation she ran.

Somehow, he doubted it.

She had two horses inside the building, and she went to each little stall and got the animals saddled. Copeland didn't allow himself to watch her. He took in his surroundings instead.

Neat. Clean. But there were issues. A rotted gate here, a rusted lock there. "You handle all this on your own?"

She didn't stop what she was doing, but he saw the way her shoulders stiffened. "Rosalie helps when she can. So does Franny."

"So, yes, you handle all this on your own."

She scowled at him, then led one horse out of its stall and handed him the reins. She said nothing. Then she led the other horse out and gestured for him to follow.

He gave his horse a dubious look. "You better cooperate," he muttered, then pulled the horse out into the fading daylight behind Audra.

"You need any help getting up?" she asked, with that same fake sweet smile. For the first time in all their interactions, she actually reminded him of her annoyance of a sister.

He watched with some satisfaction as her face registered surprise with how easily he mounted the horse. He flashed a grin at her. "What did you expect?"

She made a scrunched-up face but didn't say anything, just got on her own horse. No doubt her moves were a little more fluid. A kind of gracefulness that spoke to a life around horses and riding them. An innate ease with every move.

Maybe it was kind of hot. Maybe she was hot, and it was hard not to notice. Maybe he had a lot of issues. Well, no maybes there.

She urged the horse into a trot, and he did the same, following her lead as best he could. He couldn't see himself, obviously, but he was sure the difference in ease and comfort would be clear to even the casual observer.

Her braid streamed behind her, the hat low on her head. The sun was almost completely hidden by the mountains in the distance now. Gold and pastel pinks and oranges streamed up from behind the craggy peaks.

Pretty. Breathtaking, really. He couldn't deny there was something about all this space that he *liked*, but mostly his gaze kept going back to Audra.

There was something about her. He couldn't put his finger on what it was. She just…didn't fit into any easy categorizations. He couldn't get a handle on just who she was. The quiet, demure woman who stood in the background while her sister raged around. The tough rancher lady handling all *this* on her own, basically. The frustrated woman who'd given him the cold shoulder when she thought he'd been responsible for her sister's injury.

None of it melded together to make sense to him. *That's* why he found her fascinating. Once he could peg her, this uncomfortable reaction to just how pretty she was would fade away.

After a cold if short ride, she came to a stop and swung off her horse, easy as you please. Copeland followed suit and dismounted without making a fool of himself. Audra pointed to the fence. He could see exactly where it had been fixed, so he handed her the reins of his horse and got to work.

Happy to have a purpose that wasn't *her*, he got out his flashlight and looked at the now fixed fence. He wished he could have examined it before they'd mended it, but between the cattle prints, boot prints and horse prints all in the melting, blowing, falling snow…he probably wouldn't have found much.

Still, he took a few of his own pictures just in case.

"Let me see the picture of what it looked like broken."

Audra held out her phone, and brought up a picture on the screen. "It's a little blurry. Norman isn't the best with technology, but you can make it out."

He could. One post had been completely pulled out of the ground and tossed down. "Someone did that."

"Norman thinks it was a cow."

He could hear it in her voice, the obvious thread of doubt. He glanced up at her, met her gaze. "You don't."

"No," she said, shaking her head. Her blue eyes looked desolate, even in the encroaching dark. "I don't."

He had the annoying reaction to want to soothe her. But she was tough and what did soothing do for anybody? Sure didn't solve the problem.

"I'm going to need a list of anyone who might have it out for you, Audra."

She laughed, though there was clearly no humor in it. "Out for me? No one has it out for me."

"Everything that's happening says different."

"It's all just a weird mix-up."

"Then why did you come to me? A police detective. Some extensive ruse to get my attention?"

When she laughed this time, it was with humor, though maybe a little *more* than he'd been going for. Even if it was good to see her laugh. And she looked a damn sight prettier when she did that instead of looking scared and beaten down.

Still. "It's not *that* funny," he muttered.

"Right. Right." She cleared her throat and fixed a very serious expression on her face. "Seriously though. I don't know anyone who'd... Why would anyone want to mess with me this way? I can't think of a soul."

"Think of it less as who *could* or *would* do this and just focus on anyone you might have made mad. Even something that seems superficial to you. Any person who might be a little ticked off at you."

She sighed, and in the sound he heard an exhaustion born of something deeper than whatever this was. "I'll see what I can come up with. Come on, let's head back before it's full-on dark."

It scraped at him as they rode back. The way she seemed so defeated. It just...wasn't right. Out of character. Not that he knew her character. Having a few run-ins with somebody didn't mean he knew them, even if he was usually pretty good at pegging people quickly and accurately.

They got back to the stables. This time he dismounted first. When she did the same, the dismount was as smooth as her mount, but then she...stumbled when her feet hit the ground. Not *over* something, just like her legs kind of gave out.

He was quick enough to grab her before she tumbled forward. For a minute, she seemed to struggle to get her feet under her, and her whole body trembled a little bit.

He wasn't stupid enough to think it was some reaction to him catching her, but the fact he *wanted* to believe that irritated him enough to be frustrated. "Jesus, what the hell is wrong with you?"

She jerked out of his grasp, and he thought she was more angry with herself than at him, but took it out on him just the same. "I'm exhausted and starving, that's what's wrong with me."

"Well, why don't you eat and sleep?"

"Gee. I hadn't thought of that." She took the horses into the stables. He knew enough about the whole process that she had to take the saddles off and he knew how to do all that, so he nudged her out of the way. "I can do it," he muttered.

He could *feel* her wanting to argue with him, but she didn't. She watched, and once she seemed satisfied that he wasn't completely ignorant, she filled something in each stall with water and handled other things he supposed were important.

He got the equipment off and put it all back where she'd had it before the ride. They worked in silence until done. Then she shut the stall doors. He followed her back out into the freezing cold night.

"Thanks," she muttered. "Listen, I've got some food, if you're hungry. We can discuss next steps." She started walking toward the house.

"You don't want me to eat with you."

She didn't respond for a moment. "No, I don't, but it's the polite thing to offer."

Something about that really amused the hell out of him. That she was honest enough to admit she didn't want him there, but had a belief that politeness should trump what she wanted. Ridiculous.

But kind of sweet.

He should get the hell out of here. What was he doing being intrigued by *sweet*? Not his MO.

But he couldn't deny he was curious to see what the inside of the house looked like. What Audra's dinner might look like. How exactly this woman, who claimed no one would be mad at her, lived.

"Then I guess it's the polite thing to do to take you up on it."

He didn't miss the way she sighed regretfully. In fact, it made him grin. But she didn't try to get out of it, just trudged toward the house in the dark, with him close behind.

Chapter Four

Audra didn't know why she let good manners put her in this situation. Copeland Beckett in her house. Eating her food at her table. And why? Because she couldn't keep her mouth shut. Because manners her parents had taught, but not employed themselves, still ruled her no matter how hard she might try to be more like Rosalie and not care about what people thought of her.

Oh, he'd only accepted the invitation to irritate her, no doubt. He was one of those people who lived to irritate.

She could recognize it when she saw it. She'd grown up with Rosalie. She even kind of respected it, because too often in her life she bent over backward for someone else, to her own detriment.

She'd promised herself she'd turn over a new leaf after Dad had died, after all his secrets came to light, and sometimes she managed. Telling Copeland they were going to ride horses had been a needling move.

But then he'd handled the horse just fine. And thinking about the horse had her thinking about the *dismount* from the horse.

She would have fallen. Even now, her hands were shaky and she didn't feel remotely steady. She knew she needed food. She'd pushed herself too hard too many days in a row,

and she *knew* better, but sometimes life just didn't let a person take care of themselves.

But he'd grabbed her. Just snatched her and kept her from falling over. He was strong. Stronger than he looked. And that was saying something because he didn't look like any kind of slouch.

She pushed into the front door, fighting between the instinct to say nothing and the desire to tell him to wipe his boots. Trying to shove down her ridiculously physical reaction to him helping her not face-plant because it had been a lot more than simple relief.

But he spoke first, after he wiped his boots on the mat and hung up his coat on the hook on the wall without her having to tell him.

"You don't lock your doors?" he demanded.

She sighed. She usually did. When Vi had lived with them, after running away from her abusive ex-husband, they'd gotten in the habit of locking up to make Vi feel safer. But Audra still sometimes forgot when she was stressed because it had never been a habit. "No one came out this way" was the old mantra.

But someone had done that to her fence, hadn't they?

"I do at night. During the day, I don't always remember."

"I'd start remembering."

She didn't bother to argue with him. Not when he was right. Even if there wasn't trouble, even if it was isolated out here, she had guns and cash and all sorts of things that could be easily swiped by some very intrepid thief wandering off the beaten path. She was alone out here, and lots of people knew it.

But they were good people, *her* people. And they weren't the ones playing these pranks now.

You hope. A horrible little thought, that voice in her head, the voice of doom.

She led Copeland straight from the front door into the kitchen and pointed to the kitchen table. "Go on and sit. It'll just take a few minutes to throw things together."

She moved to the sink to wash her hands, but Copeland just followed her, not taking instruction. *Go figure.*

But he held out his hands, like he was going to wash his too. "Put me to work. Or is that not the polite thing to do?" he asked with a grin she would *not* be fooled by. He was being irritating.

Not charming.

"Guests sit," she said primly.

"I'm not a guest. I'm a cop."

She didn't know why that made her laugh, but he washed his hands, and she figured she'd eat faster if he helped. Then she'd feel steadier. Then she could deal with this better, more clearly.

"I've got some roast beef. We're going to make sandwiches." She grabbed a bread knife and handed it to him, then pointed at the loaf of bread she'd set out to thaw that morning. "Cut some slices of bread."

"Sure."

She moved to the fridge, getting out the meat from Natalie and a block of cheese. The little tub of mayonnaise that had maybe enough for one sandwich. She didn't have much to offer in way of beverages. She hadn't gone to the store since Franny left, so she was out of milk, beer and soda. There was a bottle of wine in the pantry, but she wasn't about to suggest *that*.

Water would have to suffice. She sliced the cheese, then brought the sandwich fixings over to the counter, where

Copeland had sliced the bread, but she stopped short at the mess he made of her loaf.

The bread slices were all over the place. One so thin it wasn't even a full piece. One so thick it could have been three pieces.

"What on earth did you do?"

He scowled at her. "Normal bread comes pre-sliced."

She shook her head. "Better bread comes homemade." She put the plate of sandwich stuff next to the atrocity he'd made of the bread, then handed him a plate. "Assemble at will."

He slapped everything together in the most haphazard manner she'd ever seen. Even Rosalie had more kitchen sense than this man.

"Don't you live on your own?" she asked, appalled.

"Sure, but out in Fairmont. Where they have takeout."

She wrinkled her nose. "You can't look like that and eat takeout for every meal."

His eyebrows raised in unison with the corners of his mouth. "Look like what exactly?"

She felt her entire face heat. What an idiotic thing to say. "You know. Like…" She waved a hand at him, but she knew he wasn't going to let her off the hook. "Fit," she finished lamely.

"Fit?"

She huffed, went back to assembling her sandwich and decidedly *not* looking at him. "Yes, fit." Once she was done, she sailed to the table with her nose in the air. She would *not* be embarrassed in her own home.

At least while he was in it. She'd wait until after he left to curl up in a ball and curse her dumb mouth.

Copeland took the seat next to her, when he could have

taken the seat on the opposite side. She kept her gaze expressly on her plate.

"Kind of a big place for one person."

Audra shrugged. "It's rarely just one person. Franny travels some, and it's an adjustment not to have Rosalie underfoot, but they're right next door. We miss having Vi and Magnolia around, but we all get together plenty."

"But all those fields out there. Someone came in, damaged your fence, left, without you having any clue."

Audra tried not to shift in discomfort. She didn't like to think of it like that, though admittedly the past few years had brought home just how…vulnerable they were out here.

But that wasn't just because she was a woman alone. Natalie and Norman had dealt with a *murder* on their ranch that had taken a while to solve. It was more the realization that no one was really ever *safe*.

"Yes, it's impossible to secure a ranch this size. But there's not much I can do to change that. It is what it is." She sighed, frustrated with the entire situation. "I don't understand why anyone would want to mess with me. I run my ranch. I help with the agricultural society. If I'm not doing that, I'm helping the Kirks, or hanging out with my family. I don't date. I don't party. I don't stomp around town pissing people off."

He'd stopped with his sandwich halfway to his mouth. Slowly, he put it back down on the plate. Something in his gaze was a little too…intense for her to hold.

"You don't date? Ever?"

She would *not* read in to that perfectly reasonable question. She would simply answer it. While staring very hard at the mangled bread that made up the top of her sandwich. "I did. Before my father died and my mother moved away.

There was more time, more money, more…everything. I had a life back then. But not much of one since."

"And how long has that been?"

"Four years." She wouldn't feel embarrassed about it. She was too tired to feel embarrassed.

"So angry ex-lovers are likely out. Unless you think someone would have held a grudge?"

She laughed, maybe harder than she should have. "I did not leave a string of bitter, broken hearts in my wake, Copeland. I tended to be the dumpee over the dumper." Which sounded just *pathetic*, and so beside the point. She really needed to change the subject. "Maybe someone Rosalie did a case against is targeting me to get to her?"

"Then why is it your name on the urn and the gravestone?"

"I'm her sister. Hurting the people someone loves might hurt them?"

"If she was still living with you, I might look into it. But she's not even in the country. If someone wanted to get to her, they'd wait until she was around to do something about it." Copeland shook his head. "It doesn't add up, Audra. This is about you, and we're going to have to do some digging to figure out why."

COPELAND FINISHED OFF his sandwich, surprised at how much better it was with her fancy bread—even if he had botched slicing it. Growing up, his father had held pretty old-fashioned views about where a son belonged—and the kitchen wasn't one of them.

Copeland had grown up and rebelled in his own way, he supposed, by adopting a modern sensibility about gender roles and the like. Hilariously, it backfired, because his parents had only followed suit, and had evolved themselves, along with him.

Still, Copeland had never felt like learning his way around a kitchen more than to survive.

Tonight wasn't about *him* though.

He asked her more questions about people who might have something out for her. Ranching rivals. Someone in her agricultural group she'd slighted.

She was adamant she didn't make anyone mad.

And he just kept going back to her saying she hadn't dated or essentially had a life outside this ranch for *four years*. It should have sounded pathetic, but instead it stirred some long-buried sense of sympathy for her.

He knew all too well what it was like to feel so beaten down that life just became going through the motions to survive.

Once they were done eating, and he'd run out of questions, he helped her clear the table, then figured he'd overstayed what little welcome he had. She walked him to the front door.

"I've got some next steps," he told her, shrugging on his coat. "I'll be in touch."

She nodded and opened the door for him. He stepped out into the cold night.

"Thanks," she offered, leaning there against the doorframe. It was dark outside, but cozy light spilled around her from inside. Then she smiled, and he realized just how little she'd been doing that. Understandable, but it was a pretty smile and she should do it more. *Feel* it more.

"You're not so bad, Copeland," she said, with some humor.

But since she still looked a little sad behind it, he found

himself trying to poke that sad away. "Hell, Audra, stop trying to flirt with me."

She rolled her eyes and shook her head, but she didn't seem quite so desolate. Not that it was any of his business what she felt. Not that he *cared*.

He started to make a move for his car, but something ate at him. Mostly how damn secluded this little place was. He'd been out to plenty of ranches over the course of the two years he'd lived here, and they were all like this. Felt like tiny islands of complete and utter isolation. Nothing but mountains and sky and animals, and the potential for danger in every lurking shadow.

Which he supposed was fine and dandy when someone was used to it. She was used to it. She'd grown up here. Been taking care of herself for years, clearly. Even if Rosalie had lived with her before, her private-investigator life probably had necessitated leaving Audra alone here plenty of nights.

And Audra had plenty of people who cared, so why the hell did he need to? He didn't.

"You guys have security?" he demanded, irritated with himself. With her. With the whole damn situation.

She studied him from where she stood still leaning against the doorframe. He didn't know what she found in that study, but he didn't like it. Still, she responded. "Yeah."

"Lock the doors and use it." He barked it out like an order, when he probably should have softened his words. But he wasn't a soften-it kind of guy anymore, if he ever had been.

She hugged herself, but she nodded. "Yeah, I will."

He stomped off the porch to his car and got in. Drove down the lane. All the while he kept glancing into his rearview window. What was she doing living out here by herself? So far from any help. It was reckless, that's what it was.

He should turn back and tell her so. Insist she head into

town to stay with Thomas and Vi. Hell, get a hotel room if she didn't want to put her pregnant cousin out.

But she didn't want to worry the Harts, and he understood that in spite of himself. She probably couldn't stay in a hotel with running a ranch solely on her own. And what other alternatives were there? What was *he* going to do? *Stay?* That hardly solved her problem.

Solving the case was the only way to do that. So that was just what he was going to do. And he was damn well going to trust the adult woman who'd spent her whole life on that isolated ranch to handle herself.

Because it was none of his business.

No matter how it scraped at him.

Chapter Five

Audra woke up the next morning with sunlight streaming on her face. She flew into a sitting position, glanced at her clock and swore.

It was almost nine o'clock. How had she overslept? She went over last night as she hurried to throw on some clothes and put her hair back into a tie. She'd cleaned up after her... very odd dinner with Copeland, then taken a shower, and...

She'd been so worked up about all the embarrassing things she'd said, and that stupid stumble in the stables, that she'd forgotten to set her alarm.

"I so do not have time to be so careless," she muttered to herself, hurrying down the stairs. She didn't have time for breakfast. She didn't have time for anything.

It was bitterly, bitterly cold even with the sun shining, but Audra shoved out into the freezing bright and went through another day of relentless work, with few breaks, and definitely *not* treating her body like a temple. She knew something had to give, and yet she couldn't find it.

But she made it through the day without incident. Got all the absolute necessities done just before darkness fell completely, then trudged home in the cold again and warmed up canned soup for dinner.

"I'm going to have that damn wine," she announced to

the quiet kitchen. She puttered around, ate her soup and drank a glass of wine with it. She read an email from Rosalie, smiled at the adorable pictures attached. Rosalie and Duncan in front of the Colosseum. Rosalie with a giant plate of pasta. A selfie, in which Duncan pressed a kiss to Rosalie's scrunched-up cheek, some glittering Italian city in the background.

Audra brushed a tear off her cheek. She was so happy for her sister. Rosalie absolutely deserved a loving husband, a fancy honeymoon and to look just that happy. Ninety percent of the tears were happy ones. But about ten percent were the aching from missing having her sister in this house, as a partner.

Everything kept changing. Everyone kept leaving.

Except her.

She blew out a breath, set down her phone and went about doing the dishes. She wouldn't leave. This ranch was in her bones. It was her heart. Maybe some days it felt like a trudge, but the idea of leaving was too awful to bear.

So she'd weather the changes, be happy for her sister and take a long, hot bath with *one* more glass of wine. Because she deserved it.

Before she headed into the bathroom, she set her alarm for tomorrow. She couldn't afford any more mistakes. A bath. One glass of wine. Then bed.

She made it scalding. Dawdled in the water. Sipped the wine until it was gone. Closed her eyes and relaxed until the water had chilled too much to stay in any longer.

She almost felt human, she decided, as she got ready for bed. The extra hours of sleep that morning had been perhaps a *bit* of a blessing in disguise. Now she just needed to find some time to go to the grocery store tomorrow and she just might be back on track.

She *would* be back on track. Unless something else happened, like an urn with her name on it, or property damage or—

"We are *not* thinking about that tonight. We are getting a good night's sleep." She backtracked through the house and made sure all the doors were locked and the security system was engaged.

Finally in bed, she snuggled in and instantly fell asleep. So instantly, she had no idea how long she'd been asleep when she woke with a start in the pitch-black. Her heart was racing. Had it been a dream or—

Something crashed, in the distance but not distant enough.

Glass breaking, and she was too familiar with guns not to know that was the exact sound that had woken her up.

Gunshots.

And then the glass crashing wasn't so *distant.* It was somewhere in the house.

COPELAND WASN'T THRILLED by how little progress he'd made on Audra's case, but a burglary had come up and Laurel had been in court, so he and Hart had jumped on it. Because Copeland could hardly tell Hart he was busy with another case when he couldn't tell him what that case was.

Of course, technically, he could. He could rat out Audra to her extended family. It was no skin off his nose.

But he didn't.

After they'd taken care of the burglary and Copeland was back in their office, he scowled. There were no returned phone calls from the cemetery or the crematorium. No new leads to follow, and that ticked him off.

He grumbled out his goodbyes, went home to his apartment in what citizens of Bent County considered the bustling metropolis of Fairmont. Hilarious.

He heated up the frozen meal, thinking about Audra and her homemade bread. When did she have the time? He didn't know jack about making bread from scratch, but didn't it take longer than running to the grocery store?

Well, maybe not if you lived out in the middle of nowhere, he supposed.

He settled himself on the couch, turned on a random sporting event and paid absolutely no attention to it, because his mind was occupied with Audra's case. Not *Audra* herself. He had to understand the woman to understand who might want to hurt her, that was all.

He didn't taste his dinner—there wasn't much to taste anyway. He got out his laptop and did some more research into crematoriums, the systems in place to get someone declared dead, and made a mental note to call the vital-statistics department tomorrow.

It was late when his phone rang. He glanced at the screen and wasn't sure what to think of the unknown number, well past midnight, but it was the local area code. Too used to late-night calls for work, he answered.

"Beckett."

"Copeland. Hi."

He didn't want to think about how easily and quickly he recognized her voice. "Audra. What's—"

Before he could even finish, he heard a faint *pop*, followed by…crashing.

He jumped to his feet. "Was that a gunshot?"

"I… It appears someone's shooting out my windows."

"Did you call nine-one-one?" He was already strapping his own gun on and shoving his feet into his shoes on his way out the door.

She sighed heavily, and he was about to swear at her, but at least her answer was reasonable.

"Unfortunately, yes. They're on their way, but I need you to keep Thomas out of it, okay? I don't know how the police stuff works. When they call in detectives, and who or how, but—" Another *pop*. Another *crash*.

He was already in his car. "I'm on my way. Where are you?"

"Huddled in the bathroom upstairs. No windows. Lock on the door. I've got a gun. I could—"

"You'll stay right where you are, you hear me?"

She sighed again. "Yes, that's what the nine-one-one operator told me as well. Only she was nicer about it," Audra muttered.

She sounded okay. Not hurt, not terrified. And still he flipped on his lights and ran code. Someone was *shooting* at her house.

Played that one right, leaving her out there all alone, didn't you?

"I'll be there in…" Too long. Why did she live all the way out in the middle of nowhere? "A while. Stay on the line with me until the police get there. Were they sending county or Sunrise?"

"I'm not sure. She… The dispatcher wanted me to stay on the line, but I wanted to call you so you could stop Thomas from getting involved."

"Has anyone ever told you you're a damn martyr?"

He took her silence to mean yes. He floored it down the mostly empty highway, knowing it would take too many long miles to get there. Hart wouldn't have been much closer. Hopefully the 911 dispatcher sent someone from Sunrise. If that tiny department even had someone working night shift.

"Just…stay on the line with me. Go through the whole thing. Start to now."

"I woke up…something *woke* me up. I assume it was a gunshot, because I heard a crash, but it was outside." She sounded clear, careful. Not scared. He'd take that as a good sign. "But then…the second one. It was definitely a window in the house. Everything's locked up. I set the security system before I went to bed."

Copeland screeched a turn onto the highway that would lead him out to her place, gripping the phone between his shoulder and his ear. *His* heart pounded like a maniac, a fear he didn't want to untangle clutching his chest. But she kept giving him a calm, clear rundown.

"I knew it was a gunshot the second time, so I grabbed my phone, and got a gun out of my bedroom safe. I didn't think I should look out the window if they were shooting at them, which is the only thing I could figure would sound like crashing, so I went into the closest room without windows. The upstairs bathroom. I called nine-one-one first, then I called you. I should call the Kirks. I don't *think* they'd hear anything all the way over there, but if they did…"

"You'll stay on the line with me, Audra," he said firmly. What if someone got in? What if someone *shot* her?

He didn't like all the what-ifs jangling around. That wasn't what being a cop or detective was about. She'd given him the facts, and he was worried about the maybes.

Unacceptable.

"They're here. The police, that is."

"Are you sure?"

"Yeah, something about the pounding and people yelling 'Bent County Sheriff's Department' tipped me off. No one's made a shot for a while now. I'm getting off and going to talk to them."

"Audra…" He didn't know what to say, and she was quiet, waiting for him to say *something*. "I'll be there in a few," he muttered, then hit End, tossed his phone in the passenger seat and gunned the engine again.

It took what felt like forever, and he knew he should take a minute to take a breath, calm down. Adrenaline was pumping and he was likely to lash out at the wrong people, but when he realized that only two deputies were standing outside Audra's house, any fear of lashing out disappeared.

Two lousy deputies for a full-on shooting? He got out of his car, slammed the door shut and marched over to the deputies. Deputy Stanley was a bad cop with a bad attitude and Copeland couldn't stand him, so it figured he'd be one of the responding officers. But the other was Morris. She was a decent deputy, and she was the one who walked over to talk to him.

She clearly knew the players, because she blocked him from having a conversation with Stanley.

"Whoever the shooter was, they were gone before we got here. We've collected some evidence, but nothing that's probably going to lead us to a perp. Too many guns around this area. Victim has doorbell cam and a security system, so I imagine you'll want to start there. The shooter shot out the windows in the truck parked right there." She gestured to Audra's truck. "And the two front windows on the lower floor."

Copeland cursed. "You need to keep looking for the shooter. Plenty of places to hide. How can you be sure you looked through all of them?"

"Detective…" There was a heavy sigh. "Whoever it was is long gone. We searched the outbuildings, but Ms. Young said the last gunshot was a good ten minutes before we got here. We didn't pass anyone on the highway, so they must have headed south, or out into the pastures or mountains. There's no finding them now."

"Some emergency services," he muttered.

"We do the best we can."

It was said flatly, but Copeland knew he'd ruffled feathers he'd have to unruffle tomorrow. But that was tomorrow's problem.

"Yeah, yeah. I'll talk to her about getting the video from that doorbell camera." But what would it have caught in the dark? It wasn't like she had the kind of high-tech security that might help out. "You take her statement?"

"Yes. It'll be on your desk in the morning, along with our report."

"Alright. I can handle it from here."

Deputy Morris looked back at the house. The lights were on inside, and he could see the cracked glass of all the front-facing windows. "She shouldn't stay here. Going to get cold real quick in there."

"I'll handle it," Copeland repeated, already striding for the front door. His boot crunched on the first stair. Glass. It littered the entire porch. If he had to guess, there'd been at least two bullets, if not three, shot into each front window on either side of the door. There was almost no glass left in the panes.

He didn't bother to knock. Just shoved the front door open. Audra was right there in the living room, broom and dustpan in hand. She was wearing flannel pajamas and heavy work boots.

She looked up, exhaustion written into every down-turned line on her face. "I suppose you didn't have to come all this way." She dumped a pile of glass in the dustpan into a paper bag.

"I'll be investigating the case," he replied. "I'll need access to your doorbell cam."

"I already looked. You can't see anything."

"I'll still need it."

She shrugged, then swept another pile of glass into the dustpan. She wasn't crying or shaking or reacting in any of the ways he might have expected. She was just methodically cleaning up the mess.

It left him...unsettled. Unsure how to proceed. If he didn't have to comfort or bully, what the hell was he supposed to do?

Your job. "I'm going to look into it, obviously, in connection with everything else that's been going on."

She nodded. Another dustpan full of glass going into the bag.

"I'll read over the deputies' report and the statement you gave to them, but if you think of anything else besides what you told them or me, you let me know."

She nodded again. Swept methodically.

He didn't know what to say. What to do. And that pissed him off. He jammed his hands in his pockets, trying not to let his irritation leak out.

"I'll talk to neighbors tomorrow. Anyone who might have noticed something off. An out-of-state vehicle. Someone lurking around."

"That's a waste of your time."

"Nothing is a waste of time in an investigation."

She shrugged, as if she didn't agree with him. When *he* was the expert. Temper licked against old, softer instincts he'd thought had long since withered away and died. Which didn't help with his increasing frustration.

"You won't want to stay here tonight."

"I'm afraid I have to. By the time I get this mess cleaned up, the windows boarded, it'll be time for me to get my morning chores done. Don't worry, I'll carry my gun and keep an eye out."

"Audra, you can't stay here."

"I can't *not* stay here," she returned with a snap in her tone. "I don't have that luxury." She dumped another dustpan full of glass, and he realized just how slow going her cleaning process was going to be.

But she was being unreasonable. She couldn't *stay* in a house that had just been shot up when they didn't even have one lead on a suspect. Telling her what to do wasn't going to get through to her. He should have known that even before he started.

Audra Young required a softer approach because she was a softer kind of woman. So Copeland tried to find that kind of approach inside him.

"You have every right to be scared," he said, pleased with how calm and comforting he sounded. "Every right to be upset, but you have to think about this rationally."

"Scared? *Upset?* I'm furious!" As if to prove it, she tossed the broom onto the floor with a loud clatter. "Do you know how much this is going to cost me? Do you know how much time and effort and *money* it's going to take to replace these windows and—"

"Someone shot at you and you're worried about the *cost*?" It was the most ridiculous thing he'd ever heard.

"They shot my windows out, Copeland. If they wanted to shoot *me*, I'd be dead."

He saw it then. The first flicker of it fully hitting her what had happened, what kind of danger she'd been in. She'd used anger to deflect it, but now her hand shook before she balled it into a fist.

And she looked so damn desolate again he just…couldn't stand there. He crossed to her, took her by the elbow. The urge to soothe was painful, and reminded him of his much younger self, so he shoved it away and nudged her not ex-actly gently onto her couch.

"Do you know how much a new window costs?" she demanded, but her eyes were starting to get suspiciously shiny. "Hell, the lumber to even nail it up against the cold. I might have enough in the barn, but that's a might. And my truck..." She shook her head, then dropped it to her hands. "What the hell is happening?"

He knew how to respond to this, even if knowing her meant he felt more sympathy than he should. "We're going to figure it out. They were bound to have left some evidence behind." He said it because he believed it. Had to. "We'll find it. Tie it all together. We'll figure it out."

"How much more am I going to lose before you do?"

It scraped at him, the vulnerability and sheer unfair-ness in this question. "Isn't your brother-in-law loaded?" he asked, not kindly. Because he didn't want to be kind or worried about *vulnerability*.

She shook her head. "I'm not taking Duncan's money."

It was none of his business. None of this was any of his business, except getting to the bottom of whoever was doing this to her. "I'll help you clean and board up."

"You don't have to—"

"Maybe your family loves the martyr bullshit, but I don't. I'm going to help. And then you're going to have three choices until we find out who did this," he said, hold-ing a finger up for each of them. "Go over to the Kirks and stay with them. Go into Bent and stay with Hart and Vi. Or I'm bunking here." He knew she wouldn't take the last one, but hopefully it'd spur her in the right direction faster.

She laughed. "Copeland, I am not putting anyone I care about in danger. I'm not even going to worry them. I can't leave. I have cattle and work to see to morning, noon and night. And you are most definitely not going to stay here. That's absolutely ludicrous."

He shrugged, not about to let her call his bluff. He'd call hers first. "Watch me."

She stared at him, her mouth a pretty little *O* of shock. Which quickly sharpened into anger. "Fine." She hopped back into a standing position, anger overtaking the fear and the sadness. "I'd *love* it if you stayed, because anything is better than putting everyone I care about in danger." She lifted up that surprisingly stubborn chin. "I'll make you up a room. We'll have to pull out all the blankets. It's going to be a cold one even once we get that boarded up." She gestured at the broken windows where the frigid wind swept in.

But he wasn't about to retreat now. She'd relent before he did. "Great."

"Fantastic." She whirled away from him and stormed upstairs.

And he took the broom and attacked sweeping up more glass.

She'd change her mind by the time it was cleaned up.

He was almost sure of it.

Chapter Six

Audra gathered all the blankets upstairs when she should be downstairs cleaning up. When she should be doing anything but proving a stupid, *stupid* point.

Still, she was upstairs making up Rosalie's old room so Copeland could allegedly stay there—she wouldn't bet on it—because she needed to have a bit of a cry, and she'd be damned if she'd do it in front of Copeland Beckett.

Well, she didn't like to cry in front of anyone, but there was something about Copeland that made that *extra* important.

Once the room was made up, and she'd let out a sufficient amount of tears, she moved into the bathroom where she'd holed up in terror at someone shooting up her house. She didn't want to think about that. She'd rather focus on anger and pride, and never think about the sounds of gunshots and crashing glass again.

She washed her face with cool water even though the house was already getting cold. She blotted away the water and tried to blot the redness from crying along with it. Once she was satisfied there was no trace of tears on her face, she went back downstairs.

He'd made a dent in the amount of glass that had shattered on the inside. A little prick of guilt settled in her gut.

It wasn't his mess to clean up, and no matter how irritated she was at him, that didn't mean she should have left him to clean up *her* mess.

Deep down, she knew there was something a little twisted about considering this *her* mess, since she didn't ask anyone to shoot her windows out. But she didn't have time for *deep downs* right now.

"If you sweep up the rest of this mess, I can get started on boarding up the windows," he said to her.

He was telling her what to do as just a matter of course without thinking it through at *all*. Guilt turned over into frustration. "You don't know where the boards, hammer, or nails are."

"Alright, then I guess I'll keep cleaning and you can go get the stuff." He said this with an easy shrug, dumping another dustpan full of glass into a new paper bag.

"Thank you for taking charge," she replied dryly. "How would I know what to do without you?"

He stopped what he was doing, glanced over at her. His expression was one of frustration, and she figured that was fair because it matched her own.

"I never said you had to clean up," she said, before she could help herself.

"What am I supposed to do? Just stand around in the middle of a bunch of shattered glass not doing anything like a jerk?"

She wanted to say something nasty, like: *if the shoe fits*. But it wasn't fair. He wasn't being a jerk at all. Just…bossy. Which was probably natural for him, considering he was a detective. And he'd been a detective at a much bigger and busier police department before he'd landed in Bent County.

She had to stop snapping at him. It wasn't like her, and

it wasn't nice. She prided herself on being nice. On being the calm, even-keel that Rosalie wasn't.

But Rosalie wasn't here, so maybe she was just off balance. When Rosalie came back…

Well, she'd be building her new life as a wife. So Audra had to start getting used to life without trying to be Rosalie's balance.

She didn't care for that thought at *all*, so she turned her attention back to the mess and what needed to be done. Copeland didn't know where anything was, but she would need help if they were going to get this done before daylight. And she'd have chores to do once the next day broke.

She really, really hated needing help. Not that she *needed* it exactly. She could get this all done herself. It'd just leave her behind schedule with her daily chores, and then…when would she make up the difference?

"Leave that for now," she told him. "I'm going to need your help carrying everything in from the stables. Especially since my truck is a mess." She surveyed him and came to a startling realization. "You're not wearing a coat." It was absolutely freezing in here now, and he was just in a sweatshirt and some athletic pants that didn't look to be thick or warm at all.

He looked down at himself, as if he hadn't even considered that it was *freezing* outside. "Guess I didn't think of it."

Because he'd rushed over here to help. And as mad as she wanted to be at him, what she'd said when he'd left the other night held true. Even when he was making her angry.

He was a good guy. He'd dropped everything in the middle of the night to come out here, to investigate this case, and now he was helping her when he didn't expressly have to.

And she was most definitely the one being a jerk.

He shrugged. "No big deal. I'm fine. Where's the stuff we need? Where the horses are or—"

"Hold on," she muttered, feeling small and guilty. And dreading what she knew she had to do. "I'll find you something to put on."

"I really doubt your wardrobe is going to fit me, Audra."

"Just wait here."

She trudged back upstairs, no righteous anger to propel her. She could not begin to express how much she didn't want to go digging through the tub of her dad's old clothes, but the man needed a coat.

She'd gotten rid of most of her father's things. He was dead and he was an asshole. Rosalie had kept some more sentimental items, but she hadn't cared about the clothes. Audra hadn't wanted to either, but...

She'd loved Tim Young in spite of it all and hadn't been able to get rid of a few of his ranch things. No matter how selfish he'd been, no matter how much of a liar he'd been, he hadn't *always* been a terrible father. He'd taught her how to ranch with a patience and reverence that stuck with her still.

She went into her room, opened the closet, pulled out her little step stool and got on it, so she could reach the back of the top shelf. She pulled down the tub and opened it up. The smells of tobacco and soap and horses hit her like another blow.

For a moment, she squeezed her eyes shut and willed the tears away. She'd already cried. No time for another one. She jerked the work coat out of the bin, some gloves, a stocking cap. She didn't have anything for Copeland to put on over the pants, not that pants would fit. Dad had been a lanky beanpole. Copeland was probably just as tall if not taller, but he was sturdy.

So she went to her drawers, and did not let herself think

about how *sturdy* Copeland's body was. She'd kept a bunch of Dad's wool socks to wear herself on winter mornings, even though they were too big. She pulled out a pair and then headed back downstairs, doing everything she could not to let the old smells transport her back to a time when everything hadn't fallen on her shoulders.

Except, even then, she'd taken on more than her fair share for a kid. She'd wanted to give Rosalie the image of a perfect family. Find a way to make Rosalie feel loved by their parents, when Audra had never been sure they even knew how to love. Not their kids, and certainly not each other.

Hadn't stopped Dad from starting a secret second family, of course. She'd tried reaching out to her half siblings when she'd discovered they existed after he died. She'd wondered, did they feel the same? Or…was she just that hard to love?

And with *that* awful and not at all helpful thought, she arrived back downstairs and shoved the pile of clothes at Copeland. "You'll still be cold, but this'll help."

He lifted an eyebrow. "Keep a lot of menswear around?"

She could say yes and leave it at that, but she didn't want him making any more comments about it. "They were my father's. He's dead, so he's not using them."

Copeland opened his mouth, but nothing came out. It was a little bit of a win for the day, to make Copeland Beckett speechless even if it was over something she wanted to stop thinking about.

"Put it on, Copeland. We've got work to do."

It took all night. The sun was creeping up over the horizon by the time the glass was cleaned up, inside and out, and the broken windows boarded up.

Copeland had insisted on cleaning out her truck while she swept the porch. He was just about done, just needed to tape up some plastic over the windows so no precipitation got in before she had a chance to get the windows fixed.

He was tired if he stopped to think about it, and very hungry, but it wasn't like he'd have gotten any sleep if he'd gone home. Plus, she'd still be working on this.

He'd have thought the porch sweeping could wait, but she was worried about wild animals, of all damn things. Once she'd finished bagging up the glass from the porch, she came over to help him.

But he figured she'd done enough. "Don't worry about this, I'll finish. Why don't you go on up to bed? I've got my computer in my car. I'm going to grab it and see if Morris sent me the report. I can work from out here for a bit."

"You don't have to do that."

Even though the automatic dismissal grated, he saw it for what it was. Knee-jerk. Not about *him* most of the time. Maybe it was incomprehensible to him that she lived out here all on her own—or with her sister or cousins, though he saw no evidence they were big parts of the *ranch* life Audra had going on. But it was her life, and she was simply used to handling things on her own.

"How about this? We make an agreement. You stop telling me I don't *have* to do things, and I won't have to waste my breath telling you not to waste yours. I'm not going anywhere if you're not. Not until we find the shooter."

She didn't say anything for a few humming moments. He knew she waged some kind of war with temper, and he didn't think temper was a usual part of her life, but what did he know?

Not a damn thing about her, and that was just fine.

You know she can bake bread, hasn't dated in four years, holds too much on her shoulders, smells like lilacs at the

*strangest times. Dead dad, annoying sister. Expressive blue
eyes a shade you can't quite match to anything.*

"I'll make some breakfast," she finally said, saving him
from the ridiculous turn of his thoughts.

"You need to get some rest."

She shook her head. "I'm starving. I've got some stuff
already prepared. Just need to warm it up and get the coffee on."

"Alright. I'll finish this."

He watched her hesitate. No doubt she wanted to do it
all on her own. Hell, he should let her. It was none of his
business if she wanted to work herself into an early grave.

But after that moment of hesitation, she walked away and
went inside. Copeland finished taping up the plastic cover.
He collected the tools, figuring he might as well get some
breakfast before he grabbed his laptop and got to work, but
as he turned, he stopped.

In the east, the sun rose. He was frozen to the bone, and
yet he couldn't quite force himself to go inside. The sky was
a riot of colors as the light reached up its bright fingers and
shimmered, changing the sky from night to day in an awe-
inspiring display of pure beauty.

He'd seen his share of natural beauty since moving to
Wyoming, even back home in Denver. The mountains. Sun-
rises and sunsets. The West was full of pretty landscapes
he'd spent his entire life seeing.

But this was something else. Less a landscape and more
a vibrancy that seemed to pull at something deep inside of
him. It was strangely poignant, a feeling he couldn't quite
ever remember settling over him, and he was afraid if he
inspected that feeling too deeply, it'd be something too close
to *belonging*. When he hadn't moved to Bent County—the
middle of nowhere—to *belong*. In fact, quite the opposite.

So he turned away from the pretty sunrise that was *just* a sunrise. Same as the sun rising anywhere else. There were mountains in plenty of places. Nothing special about these.

He headed inside, following the smells of coffee and cinnamon into the kitchen.

It was very nearly warm in here. Maybe he could imagine taking off the coat she'd loaned him. Oh, in an hour or so.

It was some kind of strange homey picture, even with her bundled up against the cold. She moved around the kitchen with the same efficient certainty she did everything. Her braid swung with each movement. She moved a pan of some kind of frosted roll onto the table.

"Sit. Eat," she instructed. Two plates and two forks were already set out, and she moved back into the kitchen, pouring coffee into two mugs.

The *two* of it all was really messing with his equilibrium. Because he'd been here before. Not *here* here, but he had a whole other life of being a *two*, and he'd moved here to leave it the hell behind.

Since he was feeling unmoored, he didn't know what else to do but follow instructions. Besides, he was frozen and starving. Why not sit and eat? Audra wasn't his ex-wife or anything else. They were no couple. So he should stop being an idiot.

He took a sip of coffee first, nearly closed his eyes and groaned in appreciation. Warmth. Caffeine. Then he helped himself to two giant, gooey cinnamon rolls.

After the first bite, he pointed his fork at her in accusation. "These did not come from a can."

Her mouth curved, ever so slightly. "No, I make big batches from scratch, then freeze them. Then you just have to cook them and thaw the frosting."

"There shouldn't be a *just* in that sentence. That's got to be a ton of work. Far more work than separating a log of dough and tossing it on a pan."

"Maybe, but the reward is worth the work. Besides, baking is fun. A hobby, I guess."

"You would have a hobby that was probably more for other people than yourself."

He could tell she didn't like that observation by the way she scowled briefly before smoothing it out into that haughty, chin-in-the-air expression of hers.

"My other hobby is shooting things," she said coolly.

He tried to picture her shooting *anything*. Couldn't. "I know word on the street is you can handle your own, but I cannot even begin to visualize it."

"I'll give you a demonstration."

He grinned in spite of himself. "Sounds hot."

She snorted, clearly in spite of *herself*. Then shook her head. She ate a few bites, sipped her coffee and kept her eyes on the unbroken window on the other side of the table that looked out over her ranch.

He didn't *know* her, but it didn't take a psychic to watch her gaze and know she was making a mental list of everything she had to do today. When she *needed* sleep. He didn't exactly know his way around a cattle ranch, and it was certainly none of his business if she got rest or not, but… It was just the sensible thing to do to offer a hand.

In fact, it *was* sensible. Someone was targeting her, and if he stuck close, maybe he'd catch whoever was trying to scare her. She wouldn't accept *that*, so he'd offer to help. Not that she'd accept that, either, but he'd push until she did.

"Since I'm going to be staying here, you should put me to work."

Her gaze whipped to his, sharp and irritated. "You are *not* staying here."

"Good. You've come to your senses. I'll help you pack so you can go stay with Hart."

"I'm—" But her furious retort was cut off by a loud knock on the door. She pushed back from the table, muttering as she went to answer it.

He doubted the shooter was *knocking on the door*, but he followed her anyway, casually resting his hand on the butt of his weapon.

She opened the door to an older woman he recognized because he'd worked on the murder at the Kirk Ranch last year.

"Natalie," Audra greeted, surprise tinging her tone. And maybe embarrassment. "Uh. Good morning."

"I came as soon as I heard. Why didn't you call?" She engulfed Audra in a tight hug. "Oh. I see," the woman said, her eyes meeting his across the room.

Copeland stood in the doorway between kitchen and living room, pinned by the older woman's steady gaze.

It was obvious what Mrs. Kirk was thinking—which was *hilarious* considering why he was here. Considering what Audra thought of him.

And what you think of her, right?

"Morning, Mrs. Kirk," he offered, as Audra turned to look at him. Embarrassment was etched into her gaze.

"Morning, Detective."

"Copeland is investigating everything," Audra said. And he didn't miss the way she used his first name, the way she imbued it with a kind of familiarity they didn't *really* have. Because she didn't sound irritated and like she wanted to prove she could shoot things with him as a target.

Quite the opposite.

"He's sticking around during the investigation. You don't need to worry about me, Natalie."

Mrs. Kirk's gaze moved from Audra to Copeland. "I'm

glad you're here watching over our Audra." She gave Audra another squeeze. "You can ask us for anything. And if Copeland can't be around, you know we've got room and all those safety measures Duncan put in place last year. You can depend on us."

"I know. I do. But it'll be easier if I stay put, and Copeland will…be here."

"Good," Mrs. Kirk said firmly. She glanced at the boarded-up windows, her expression one of concern.

Why Audra couldn't suck it up and take her friend's concern *baffled* him.

"Natalie… If Duncan and Rosalie call, please don't mention this. Let them enjoy their honeymoon. They deserve it."

Mrs. Kirk's mouth firmed. She clearly didn't *like* the request, but eventually she nodded. "As long as it's cleared up in a few days. If it's not, no promises. Your family deserves to know when you're in danger, when you need help."

Audra nodded along, but he knew she didn't agree. It was written all over her stiff posture. "Sure, but I've got Copeland," she said.

He wanted to laugh. What a *liar* she was. She'd just tried to kick him out a few minutes ago. He wondered what made this woman so determined to reject help. He understood from *him*. But her own friends? Family? What the hell was that about?

"Be safe, Audra," Mrs. Kirk said, hugging Audra close to her, and giving Copeland a look like "you better take care of her."

And, because he didn't know what the hell else to do, he nodded like he would.

Mrs. Kirk stepped back, gave Audra a wave and left. Audra closed the door, but didn't move. Didn't turn to face him. She just stood there, back to him.

He could have let it go. He *should* have let it go. But he couldn't deny he was shocked that she'd let Mrs. Kirk think anything was happening between them. He'd have thought her pride would be too big to handle the weight of such an outright lie.

"You let her think we're sleeping together."

Her shoulders slumped a bit as she turned and leaned back against the door. He watched with more fascination than he should have as her cheeks turned a deep shade of pink. "She won't worry so much if she thinks you're hanging around for…personal reasons," Audra muttered.

"And heaven forbid anyone worry about you?"

Her chin came up. "I've been taking care of myself for a long time."

Yeah, he didn't doubt it. And it was certainly none of his concern, not his responsibility to swoop in and take some of those weights.

But he was *here*. "Put me to work, Audra."

Chapter Seven

Audra didn't want Copeland underfoot. She was convinced he'd be more hindrance than help.

She should have known better. Everything she told him to do—mostly grunt work that required little more than muscle and following directions—he did. Easily. Efficiently. Without complaint. Quite the improvement on Rosalie, who helped when she had time, but didn't *enjoy* ranch work and liked to be verbal about that.

Except when she was feeling guilty about how much Audra did. Then she'd try to keep her mouth shut, and that was always worse. Because Rosalie's guilt made Audra feel guilty, and like she had to prove just how much more she could handle it all on her own.

She was too exhausted today to even convince herself this wasn't easier. If she didn't have Copeland helping, she would have spent *weeks* recovering from how far behind she'd be. She likely would have *had* to ask Norman for some help.

And then Duncan and Rosalie would have tried to convince her *they* should hire some help, because *they* had the money to spare, and it was a *family* ranch.

Except she was the only one who cared about the ranch. So why should she accept their pity money? She could do this on her own. She *was* doing this on her own. This was just a blip because…

Someone…wanted to scare her for some reason.

She just wished she had any inclination about *who* would want to scare her and make her life harder. The fact that she couldn't think of anyone left her feeling…stupid. Was she that naive? Thinking most people she dealt with liked her or didn't think of her at all?

She glanced at Copeland as they walked back to the house. It was early yet, but the sun was setting and he'd made some complaints about her wandering around after dark. Complaints she couldn't quite argue with.

Especially since he hadn't complained about working through lunch. Hadn't asked for a break or said he had to go do his own work. He'd actually been…the perfect help today.

How annoying. "I guess you're a natural," she told him. "For a city boy."

He grinned at her, and that wasn't fair. The way that grin crinkled his eyes and softened the harshness of the sharp angles of his face. The way it seemed to dance inside of her, far too close to attraction for her to accept.

"Actually, I grew up in the suburbs," he said. "Moved to Denver when I got a job with the PD."

"You know, to us folks out here, city and suburbs is essentially all the same."

He looked around, and she didn't know what he felt when he took in the mountains, the pastures, the vast, never-ending landscape. "Guess that's fair, all in all."

He stopped abruptly, and when he did, she heard the faint putter of an engine coming up the drive. Copeland put an arm in front of her to stop her forward movement, and she noted his other hand went to the weapon she hadn't fully realized he'd kept on his hip, because it was hidden under her father's coat.

When the car came into view though, Audra recognized

it. "It's just Thomas and Vi." But Audra didn't move forward as a terrible thought took hold. "You told them," she accused.

He shook his head, expression grim. "No, I didn't. But there was no keeping it on the down-low at Bent County, Audra. It might be a growing department, but everyone knows everyone. And people love to gossip. If Hart was in the office today, he heard about it."

He started moving forward, and Audra followed. Should she feel guilty for accusing him? She didn't have time to fret over it, because the minute Thomas put Magnolia down on the ground, she was squealing in delight.

"Aud-da!" Magnolia yelled and came running toward her. The enthusiastic greeting had Audra smiling, and she kneeled down so she could accept and return Magnolia's happy, sticky hug.

For a moment, she closed her eyes, inhaled the scent of the toddler and let herself relax. She missed having this little bundle of enthusiastic energy under her roof, even if she was happy for the new life Vi and Magnolia were building.

She stood, hefting Magnolia with her. Vi and Thomas were both frowning at the boarded-up window as they approached Audra and Copeland in front of the porch. Audra didn't dare look at Copeland.

Vi was smiling as she waddled up, hand on her belly. Thomas carried a couple boxes of what was clearly pizza.

"We brought some dinner. Thought we could all eat together."

"Pizza pah-ty!" Magnolia shouted, wriggling happily in Audra's arms.

"Well, you're speaking my very hungry language. Come on inside."

"We'll be right in," Thomas said, handing the pizzas off

to Vi. He smiled at Audra, but she saw the tension in his expression. It made her nervous that he wanted to talk to Copeland alone, but Vi and Mags shouldn't be out here in this cold.

So she led them inside. Settled Magnolia on a chair and then set about getting plates and cups together.

"I'm sorry we didn't give you advanced warning, but... Audra." Vi stopped Audra's forward movement by stepping in front of her. "Why didn't you tell us?"

Audra sighed. "Vi." She placed a gentle hand on Vi's giant belly. "You take care of you and yours. I'm just fine."

"You are part of that *yours*," Vi said fiercely, putting her hand over Audra's. "Someone shot at you."

"No, they shot at the house." Audra took her hand back and gestured for Vi to sit down. "Broke some windows, which is all they were trying to do. They didn't try to break in. They didn't try to shoot me."

"Oh, well, I feel *so* much better," Vi muttered, taking a seat as Audra put a piece of pizza on a plate for Magnolia and began to cut it into toddler-size pieces.

"Who would want to scare you like that?" Vi demanded.

Audra thought of the urn, the gravestone, all the other issues. "I really don't know."

"Come stay with us, Audra. I know you've got chores, but it's so much easier to keep someone safe in town, in a smaller house."

Audra didn't point out that Vi had been kidnapped from the very house she now lived in, even though she wanted to. But she didn't want to remind anyone of how scared they'd all been.

"Vi, you're going to be induced tomorrow if you don't pop today." She filled a sippy cup—something she kept on hand just for Mags—with some of the chocolate milk Vi had brought, then went to fix Vi a plate. "So what are you going to do from a hospital bed?"

"Thomas will—"

"Be by your side and take his paternity leave. Copeland is handling this. You're always telling me he's a good detective and not as unfriendly as he seems."

Vi sighed and looked into the living room, where Copeland and Thomas were coming in the door, talking in very low tones. "He *is* a good detective, and a good guy, under all that gruff. But… Come stay in town. I don't like you out here so isolated."

"I have too much to do on the ranch." She put Vi's plate in front of her, plus a glass of milk. "Besides, Copeland has got it in his head to play personal bodyguard until they have a suspect." She filled her own plate, then sat next to Magnolia.

Vi leaned forward, something sparkling in her eyes that left Audra feeling…uneasy. "How *personal*?" she asked, with *some* excitement.

Audra felt her cheeks heat and she wrinkled her nose. "It's not like that."

Vi leaned back and sighed. "Too bad."

"Too bad?" Audra looked out at where Thomas and Copeland were talking in front of the boarded-up window. No doubt about the shooting. "He is so not my type."

"You're too busy to have a type. Besides, what's not to like?"

"He's bossy, overbearing, never compromises?"

"Sounds like literally everyone in your life that you love."

Since she desperately wanted to change the subject, and it brought up a new one, it was Audra's turn to lean forward. "Don't tell Rosalie if you talk to her."

"Audra."

"She shouldn't cut her honeymoon short for this, and she

would. And for what? So she can storm around shooting right back and making things more complicated?"

Vi pulled a face, rubbed the side of her belly. "I'll think about it, but I'm not making any promises."

THEY ATE DINNER and didn't discuss the shooting or the threats. Hart didn't come out and say it, but Copeland got the impression that he hadn't shared *all* the details with his wife.

So they talked about baby names and paternity leave and so much family stuff Copeland wanted to jump out of his own skin.

He didn't do family stuff. He could go for a beer with Hart and hear about the kid, or even listen to Laurel and Hart yammer on about family life at work, but doing it at a family kitchen table just made everything…awful.

There'd been a time he thought this would be his future. The wife. The kid. The dinners at a kitchen table, just like he'd grown up with. It was long ago enough that it shouldn't still cut like a rusty blade, but it damn well did.

When Magnolia gleefully knocked over her cup of milk, Copeland faked a phone call and stepped out of the room. Into the cold night. Until he could breathe.

But before he could go back in, the front porch light flicked on and the whole crew spilled out of the front door in noisy, cheerful exuberance.

Audra was carrying Magnolia, and Vi was laughing about something she'd said. But Hart jerked his chin toward Copeland's cruiser, and started walking that way, so Copeland followed him.

"You're sure you're good with staying? At least until Vi's out of the hospital. Our parents are coming, so I've got help. I can take a turn or two out here. I can—"

"Take care of your family, Hart," Copeland said, irritated

at how sharp his voice sounded. "I've got this handled." He glanced at the two women standing in the dim glow of the porch light.

They made quite the pair. Vi's hair was reddish brown, just like Audra's. Even with the big baby bump, she had a…fragile air about her. Copeland knew Vi's story—abusive ex she'd escaped, twice—so he knew she was tough, but she didn't have the *look* of toughness about her. Not like Audra did.

Audra had little Magnolia on her hip while she spoke to Vi, who looked huge and uncomfortable and reminded Copeland of too many things he'd left behind.

So Copeland forced his gaze onto Hart. And, in spite of himself, tried to soothe his worry. "This stuff, it's all connected. But it's all…weird, petty stuff. You guys don't need to worry. I'll figure it out."

Hart only frowned. "A gravestone feels more threatening than petty."

"I'd agree, but they shot to destroy. Not to hurt."

"It hurts."

"You know what I mean." He glanced back at Audra. Couldn't seem to stop himself. "She can't think of anyone, not *anyone*, who'd want to mess with her. Who doesn't at least have one enemy?"

"Audra Young."

Copeland grunted. "She suggested someone after Rosalie. It makes more sense on paper, but in reality…"

"This is all really personal."

"Yeah."

Hart sighed. "Maybe this goes without saying, but since I'm going to be focused on my wife tomorrow, I have to say it. Audra's my family, even if it's only by marriage. If anything happens to her…"

"I've got it handled. She doesn't want me here, but I'm not leaving. Blood on my hands isn't my MO."

"Yeah, that all it's about?"

Copeland didn't stiffen, though he wanted to. "What else would it be about?"

"You're not exactly a monk."

"Yeah. Exactly. I'm not looking for serious. Audra Young's got serious written all over her. This is just a job, and a favor to a few friends who consider her family."

"It's not so bad," Hart said, in that gentle way of his that always made Copeland feel itchy. "Serious. Family."

Copeland only grunted. Hart clapped him on the back.

"I'm counting on you, Copeland."

Copeland didn't consider himself part of any community. He didn't make friends anymore. Didn't get involved in people's lives. He'd left that behind in Denver.

Or so he'd thought. Because it struck him as a surprise, just how much that *counting on* weighed.

Because Hart was his friend, and Copeland didn't want to let him down. He watched as Hart moved over to the group, took Magnolia out of Audra's arms, smiled, chatted. Then wrapped his free arm around his wife and moved her to the car.

They got in with waves and goodbyes, leaving Copeland in the yard and Audra on the porch. Alone, essentially, together in the dark.

"Moved to this damn place so I wouldn't have any ties, and here I am all tied up," he muttered to himself, turning to walk over to the porch.

But apparently she wasn't on the porch. She was right there.

"Why didn't you want any ties?" she asked, tilting her head and studying him even though dark hung around them.

Irritated with himself, he shrugged, tried to be casual. "Long story."

"Seems like we've got a lot of time for a long story since you insist on being underfoot."

"Seems like," he agreed, moving for the house. "But not tonight. You haven't slept a wink."

Instead of admitting that was true, she got all stubborn about it. "Neither have you," she said, following after him.

"Used to it. Life of a cop."

She moved in front of him, stopped his forward movement by planting herself in front of the porch, fisting her hands on her hips. "Well, *I'm* used to it. Life of running a ranch on my own."

"Are you always this stubborn or is it just on my account?"

She huffed. But he was a cop. He knew how to deescalate a situation and knew that was absolutely not what he was doing right now.

But he didn't seem to care. Neither did she.

"I grew up with Rosalie," she retorted. "*I* am not stubborn. *I* make compromises. You're inexplicably here, aren't you? Doing chores and cleaning up messes that aren't yours. If I was stubborn, or more stubborn than you, I'd be the one doing all that."

"They aren't your messes either. In fact, as the investigating detective, it's more mine than yours."

She threw her arms up in the air. "That's ridiculous."

"*You're* ridiculous." And he was tired, no doubt, which was the only reason he snapped. Why else would he be so easily irritated? "You've got person after person coming here, worried about you, wanting to help you, and you just shove them all away."

"Oh, because a normal person would want their family and friends in the line of fire?"

"A sensible person takes help. A *sensible* person knows when they're out of their depth."

"Out of my *depth*?" She all but screeched it. He was actually kind of fascinated, watching her temper fracture. She even reached out, as if to give him a little shove, but instinctually, he gripped her hands to stop her from landing it.

They stood there, too close. Her hands on his chest, his hands curled over her wrists. Connected with moonlight settling over them like a blanket. Both looking at each other, both breathing a little too hard.

He wasn't thinking about how mad he was anymore. He didn't think she was either.

Which was...dangerous.

He dropped her hands. Sidestepped her block of the porch. "Well, *I'm* going to use my sense and go get some sleep. Don't forget to lock up." Then he marched his frozen ass inside, determined that he wasn't doing any chores tomorrow.

He was finding a shooter.

Chapter Eight

Audra considered it lucky that she slept. Exhaustion won out over anger.

And all the other things storming around inside of her.

The problem was, when she woke up to her trilling alarm the next morning, they were all still right there. Anger less than before, but the other things…

She shut off the alarm, then lay back in bed and stared at the ceiling and scowled. It grated that she found him attractive, that she had a *physical* reaction to him. She didn't want that.

But it had shimmered through her, twining with frustration, last night on the porch. She didn't know what had come over her. She'd just…needed to act out. Give him a little shove. Not to *hurt*. She wasn't a violent person. She just wanted to prove a point.

Instead, he'd stopped her, put his big, rough hands around hers, and then held them there. In the frigid night with starlight dancing around them.

And her body had felt too many things at once—a warmth that shouldn't have existed on a cold winter night, a shudder deep inside that seemed to awaken old desires she'd pushed way, way, *way* down under responsibility, and the thrill of something she didn't want at all.

Unpredictability. Surprise. Uneven footing.

No matter what her body thought of that, her brain knew better. *That* was a recipe for heartbreak and disaster.

She'd love to live in denial, but that didn't get her anywhere. She was attracted to Copeland, and that was annoying with him underfoot. Because she wasn't about to do anything about that attraction. She didn't want anything to do with the man, even if he was hot.

Her perfect guy was kind and quiet. The stoic rancher type with a squishy heart of gold. They'd take care of the ranch together. He'd know how to cook. She'd bake. They'd have kids and a dog and a nice, quiet, happy, *predictable* life. She hadn't met him yet, and maybe she never would, but she definitely didn't want a grumpy, arrogant *detective* from the city who'd probably never been predictable a day in his life.

So why did she find herself reliving that moment like it was some kind of romantic overture from one of the romance books or movies she loved?

He'd stopped her from pushing him. The end.

She rolled onto her stomach, groaned into her pillow. It was five seconds of indulgence, and now she had to get up and get moving. She still needed to do something about her truck…at some point.

She didn't know where the money was going to come from. She might actually have to accept some help from Rosalie, which left her feeling grumpier than being attracted to Copeland did.

She got dressed and trudged downstairs, but she stopped short halfway across the living room. She smelled…coffee. Even when Rosalie and Franny were here, she was always the one to get up and make coffee. Except on the rare occasions Franny pulled an all-nighter to meet a deadline, but even then, the coffee was usually old and bitter.

She gave a fleeting thought to retreating, but that was cowardly, and more than that, she couldn't skip breakfast. Not when she had so many chores to do *and* figure out how she was going to get up to the hospital once Vi had the baby.

Maybe her truck was drivable. Sure, it didn't have windows, but she could bundle up. Maybe.

That was a problem for later. First, she needed coffee and breakfast. So she powered forward, into the kitchen, where Copeland already was.

He stood at her sink, his back to her. He was looking out the window. Beyond his silhouette, the sun was starting to make the mountains glow gold, even as the immediate world around the house remained dark.

For a moment, she had the strangest sensation of déjà vu. Like she'd seen this exact moment before, maybe in a dream.

But that was ridiculous. It was just weird because a man hadn't stood in this kitchen first thing in the morning in well over four years. Thomas and Duncan came over for dinner sometimes, but they never spent the night. So it was just weird because the last guy who did this was her dad, and she kind of hated him, even if it was wrong to hate dead parents.

She didn't think she made any noise, but Copeland looked over his shoulder at her. He hadn't shaved, and the dark stubble gave him an even more dangerous look. Not that he *was* dangerous, in the sense that someone shooting out her windows was dangerous.

But she felt…a strange kind of threatened when he looked at her like that. A fluttery kind of threatened, torn between running away and…

Well, she didn't want to consider the *and*.

He gestured at the coffeepot. "I can assure you, it's cop coffee, so it's not any good, but it'll get the job done."

She nodded, still feeling weird and shaken. So wordlessly

she went over to the cabinet and got out her favorite mug and poured herself a very...thick semblance of coffee. She choked down the first sip on a grimace.

His mouth twitched. "You can always make your own."

She crossed to the fridge, rummaged around until she found cream. She checked the date. Only two days past expiration. Better than making her own pot of coffee. She dumped some in. It wasn't going to be enough, so she moved to the pantry, grabbed the bag of sugar and dumped some in.

"When are you going to go to the hospital?" he asked.

She could *feel* his eyes on her, but she was not about to look at him, even if she was surprised he was thinking about Vi. She'd choke down the sludge disguised as coffee and pretend like it was oh so normal to have this man in her kitchen. "It depends. You may be unaware, but babies don't let you know when they'll arrive. Even when you're induced."

The silence to that was incredibly uncomfortable, and she wasn't sure why.

"I'll drive you in when you're ready," he said, after the silence had stretched out. "Head into the station and handle some things. Then I'll drive you back. In the meantime, I'll help with the chores again."

It was the high-handed way he said all that, without *asking*. Without even *suggesting*. Just swept into her life and told her how things were going to be.

"I don't recall hiring a bodyguard."

"You'd do well to think about it."

With what money? she wanted to retort. But she didn't, because she had pride. Maybe too much, but better too much than too little. "Don't you have a job?"

"Guess what? Finding out who committed property damage and is making threats against a Bent County citizen *is* my job. Lucky you."

God, he was so grating. "But your job is not *my* chores. You don't—"

He interrupted her, gaze steely. "Don't say it, Audra."

"—have to."

He huffed out his own irritated breath. "Damn, you have a complex."

"Well, it's my complex to have. Maybe *you* have a *helping* complex."

He snorted. "Yeah, tell that to my ex-wife." Then he stiffened, his expression tensing. Clearly, he had not meant to let out that little tidbit.

Ex-wife.

So none of her business, but she stood still, tense herself, just…absorbing this new piece of personal information about him. She would never have claimed to know him. Literally the only thing she knew about his life before Bent was that he'd been a detective in Denver.

The end.

Ex-wife. He had an *ex*-wife. He'd been *married* when he seemed like such a loner. Maybe that was why he had an ex. *Ex*-wife.

But she wasn't Rosalie. Or Franny, for that matter. She didn't ask uncomfortable questions. She didn't poke into other people's private business. Even if she desperately wanted to know more.

Had to know more. "You were married," she said, instead of keeping her mouth shut like she *should*, like she normally would.

The stoic expression and tension in his shoulders didn't change. "Yeah."

"And divorced."

"That's usually what the *ex* means."

"I… Is that why you moved here?"

He lifted a shoulder. "Yes. No. Complicated."

She wanted a real answer, and knew she didn't have a right to one. "Right. Sorry. None of my business."

"You got any ex-husbands rolling around?"

She laughed in spite of herself. "No." She didn't know what possessed her. She knew she shouldn't say it. It had nothing to do with him, and it was ancient history, but it felt…fair, somehow, to let him into a piece of her not-so-great past. "I did date Xavier Stanley."

"That asshole? Damn, Audra." He shook his head, but he didn't seem so uncomfortable. He seemed almost faintly amused. "Have better standards."

"I do. Now. But in high school I was just thrilled someone asked me out. He wasn't as big of a jerk then, but he was working on it. Anyway, we all make mistakes."

He looked down at his mug, pushed off the counter he'd been leaning against. "Yeah, we do. We better get to work. I've got some calls to make later, when it's an appropriate time to be awake."

She nodded, agreeing with him, except…

What kind of mistakes had he made? What kind of mistakes led to an *ex*-wife and a downgrade in job status? It wasn't her *business*, but…she couldn't let it go.

She didn't know what divorce was like, because her father had preferred to keep two wives rather than let one go. Was Copeland the kind of man who would have done the same? She didn't want to think it of him, but…she had to know. Even if it was absolutely *none* of her business.

She had to know.

SHE DIDN'T FOLLOW him at first. Which was fine and dandy because Copeland didn't want those big blue eyes on him looking all…he didn't know. Certainly not sympathetic. Not that she should be.

Sure, he hadn't meant to mention Danielle. He usually didn't think about her or the life he'd left behind, but the past few days had…dredged stuff up, he could admit.

When Audra did finally follow him, she had a strange look about her. He couldn't quite read her expression or the way she was wringing her hands together.

"Copeland. You… With your wife. Ex-wife. You didn't… It wasn't…"

He stared at her, wondering what the hell she was getting at. Wondering why the hell she was harping on this. Wondering why the hell he was letting her.

"Spit it out, Audra."

"It's just…" She shook her head. "You won't get it. I know you won't. But my dad had this whole secret family. For years, he built a life with two different women, raised two different sets of children, and we never knew about each other until he died. And then it was such a mess. All because he didn't think about anyone but himself."

She was getting all worked up. He couldn't imagine going through that. His dad was just…one of the best men he'd ever known. His parents, their stability and goodness, were the foundation of his life, and the only reason everything back in Denver hadn't totally ended him.

But why was she bringing it up? She'd already done a tit for tat when she'd admitted to dating that prick Stanley. "What exactly are you asking me, Audra?"

"I don't know. I have to trust you, don't I? To stay here and allegedly protect me and all that. And I didn't really think about that on a personal level, because you're a police officer and Thomas trusts you and likes you and…"

"I didn't cheat on my wife," he ground out. Disgusted

with himself and the situation and *her* for drawing this very private and none-of-her-business information out of him. He didn't *owe* it to her, any more than he needed her to trust him.

But he found he wanted her to know, whether he liked that want or not. "Quite the opposite." But that wasn't the whole story, was it? "Doesn't mean I wasn't a bad husband."

"I…"

"It also doesn't mean I'm a bad cop. In fact, probably the opposite. I'm not going to go start a second family, or even a first. So I don't see what it's going to do with anything."

"That isn't what I was getting at."

"Yeah, I know." God, he hated apologizing, but he was being a jerk, and he didn't have any reason to be. Maybe she was poking into his personal life, but…

He didn't know.

"Look, I'm sorry." He scowled at her. "Sore subject. Obviously."

"I…shouldn't have poked."

"No, you shouldn't have."

She huffed out a breath. "I just… I *know* it's none of my business. But I guess the idea of cheating and hurting people in a marriage is *my* sore spot, and I just want to be able to think of you as a good guy."

"Never said I was that."

"But you are."

She was so earnest sometimes. He didn't know what to do with it. "Then stop telling me not to help out, huh? Let me be Mr. Good Guy."

Her mouth curved, ever so slightly. "The good men I know aren't so grumpy."

"Even when you poke into their personal life?"

She pulled a face. "Not my usual MO. I leave that to Rosalie. But she's not here. So everything's out of whack."

He chuckled a little, imagining Audra being the yin to Rosalie's obnoxious yang. Maybe they did balance each other out, but Rosalie wasn't here and someone was harassing Audra and…

"Wait a second." He whirled around and she nearly stumbled back because she'd been moving with him toward the door. But with everything she'd said, it finally clicked.

"Second family. Death. Estates. Did your dad leave stuff to them? To you guys? A will? Contested? Ugly?"

"I…" She blinked. "Not ugly, I don't think. Mom was happy to sort of wash her hands of anything. Dad had transferred the ranch over to me before he died because he'd taken a job in agricultural sales. Well, that's what he'd claimed anyway. He didn't leave a will for the rest, so it was messy, but not ugly because we didn't fight for anything."

But death did funny things to people. Thinking they deserved things made once rational people act really irrationally.

"These other kids were okay with you getting all this?"

"I don't know what there's not to be okay about. I grew up here. This is my family's land. I…run this place and did before my dad died. I tried to reach out to them after I found out about them. I tried…to bridge a gap, but none of them wanted anything to do with me."

"I want names. And any legal documents about estates, possessions. Any legal document about the end of your father's life."

"Copeland, I really doubt some half siblings I've never met have some vendetta against me having the ranch. He's been dead for *four* years."

"I want names, Audra. It's the closest we've come to a lead, and I'm following the lead."

She had that stubborn look on her face. "It's a waste of time."

"My time to waste, sweetheart."

But he didn't think it was a waste at all.

Chapter Nine

Audra ended up having to put off doing her chores so she could list her half siblings who refused to talk to her for Copeland, and then give him the folder full of paperwork on her father's death. At least the paperwork that had been given to her. She suspected his other wife and kids might have some of their own that Audra had never seen.

She'd been fine with that. Maybe she loved her father, but she'd been happy for whatever he'd given to his other family to stay with them. Happy to wash her hands of whatever he hadn't given *them*.

Could one of her half siblings really be behind these strange, petty pranks? For what? And why after all this time? It just didn't make sense, and it frustrated her that Copeland wanted to go down this avenue because she couldn't see the *point*. Except digging into old, ugly wounds she didn't want dug up.

And she couldn't even be snippy about it, because she'd been poking into his divorce wounds, and she didn't even have a good reason.

Quite the opposite. That meant his wife had cheated on him, right? And that was probably why he was so grumpy and irritating. Or that was just who he'd always been. He said he hadn't been a good husband, but Audra refused to accept any kind of *excuse* for cheating. It was the most unnecessary way to hurt someone.

And none of this had anything to do with *her*. Once Copeland had everything he wanted, she went out to start her chores. She was behind now, and had to rush through or skip some things she'd have to come back to tomorrow, but if there was one thing she could use to justify rushing through or skipping, it was the prospect of meeting her new...

Well, Audra didn't know the exact specifics. Vi was her second cousin, but they always just called Magnolia her niece, and the new baby would be her nephew. And she'd be Aunt Audra to the both of them and whoever else came along.

If it made her a little wistful that marriage and her own kids seemed like such an improbability when she never got off the ranch and had *no* interest in anyone in the agricultural club, that was just life. She could throw herself into being an aunt.

She would.

But right now, she threw herself into ranch work. She checked fences, water, feed. It was a sunny day with a hint of spring warmth and that, along with an impending baby, put her in a good mood.

Until she stumbled, twisting her ankle and landing on her side. Surprised, shocked, she looked down at the ground and noted...something had been dug up behind the stables. And considering *she* hadn't been digging anything up...

She frowned at the overturned earth in a perfect rectangle. It was shallow, but it was long. Almost like a...

Grave.

Her heart gave a jerk and she looked around. The sky was blue, the scenery vast. She saw some cows out in the east pasture. The fence that separated her land from the Kirk Ranch.

But she was utterly alone out here. Her, the sky, the mountains. And only the vague hints that anyone would hear her if she screamed.

Everything that had once been a comfort now felt vaguely threatening.

You're being ridiculous. She got up off the cold ground, winced at the pain in her ankle. She didn't have time for a sprained ankle. Not that it was that bad. Just…she should probably stay off it for a bit and that wasn't happening.

She looked around again. No sign of anyone. Just this… shallow, rectangular hole. Maybe she was overreacting. Maybe Norman or someone from the Kirks had dug this for—for…something.

She shook her head. As much denial as she'd like to be in, with the ashes, the gravestone and the *shooting*…this was too much.

She pulled her phone out of her pocket. Instead of calling him, she just sent off a text.

I know you're busy, but I need you to come out to the stables.

In a few seconds, his response popped up. Asking for help? Are you dying?

She didn't reply to that as it felt a little too close to the overall vibe of the situation. She reminded herself that no one had tried to hurt her. That this was all silly scare tactics.

But *why*?

She waited, leaning her weight on her left leg over her right, until Copeland finally appeared over the rise, huddled into her father's coat. Still weird.

When he finally reached her, his expression was the usual stoic, not-quite frown, definitely not a smile. Until he saw the hole. His eyes narrowed, his mouth firmed. Anger danced there.

"What the hell is that?"

"I don't know. It wasn't there yesterday, and it looks like…"

"Yeah, I know what it looks like." He pulled out his phone and began to take pictures. "Let me guess. You don't have any cameras out here?"

"On the entrance, but not here in the back." She would have gotten her back up about the way he was talking to her, but she was getting used to it. Starting to understand all that irritation was how he dealt with the situation, not really anything to do with her.

He swore under his breath, took a few more pictures. Then looked around, all while Audra stood still. She didn't want to move. Didn't want him seeing her limp. She had a feeling that would make his bad mood worse.

She wasn't foolish enough to think he cared about her, but she did think under all that bluster he *cared*. A sort of generic care that had driven him to be a cop, to solve crimes for a living. Whatever Thomas saw in him, under all the prickle, that made him consider him a friend.

"What should I do?"

"Leave it for now. I don't know that there's really much we can do with it, but I want to think it over before we mess with potential evidence. That doesn't mess anything up for you, does it?"

She shook her head. "No, it's fine as is." She'd need to stick a flag or something to mark it so she didn't trip and turn her *other* ankle, but she wasn't going to tell him that.

Especially with the way he was looking out at the horizon. There was an intensity in his gaze. Like he could just *look* and see whatever threats were out there.

She really hated thinking threats were out there.

"What else do you have to do? You shouldn't be out here alone."

"I've got a gun on me."

"You still shouldn't be out here alone. What else is there to do?"

She opened her mouth to tell him she could handle it, but then he'd get mad at her for saying he didn't need to help. Which was ironic, because it wasn't even about that now. She just didn't want him to see that she'd hurt herself.

Maybe she could walk on it without limping. Maybe she could...

"Why are you being weird?" he demanded. "What aren't you telling me?"

"Nothing. I was just thinking. I think that's about it for the day."

He looked up at the sky, then back at her. "You've worked yourself to the bone until dark every day I've been here."

"I planned a light day so I can go see the baby," she lied. Then she smiled at him. "You go on ahead. I'll catch up in a minute. I just have to lock up the stables."

He narrowed his eyes at her. She was usually a pretty good liar, but something about the man unnerved her. Always made her feel like he was going to see right through it.

"You've got dirt all over the side of your pants."

She looked down at them. "Oh. Well, you know. Ranching. Dirty work."

"You didn't have dirt all over your pants yesterday."

"Every day is different. The joys of ranching."

He shook his head. "It's a no-go, Audra. Spill. What happened?"

She blew out a frustrated breath. "I just stumbled on the hole. I'm fine." She took a step to prove it. She had to prove it. And winced and couldn't quite put her full weight on it. Cursed herself and the hole and whoever the hell was harassing her in the most obnoxious ways.

"You're limping."

"Just twisted my ankle a bit."

He bit off an oath. Just as she suspected. So irritated. So put out. "*Sorry* that someone is out to get me, and I can't seem to make that go away. You don't have to—"

He stepped toward her, and she stepped back instinctively, then let out a yelp when she put weight on the twisted ankle.

"Stand still," he ordered.

"What are you going to do?"

"What any sensible human being would do with someone who twisted their ankle. You could just lean on me and hop and hobble all the way back to the house, but that's dumb. I can carry you, so I'm going to carry you."

"You can't carry me."

"Is that a commentary on my strength or your stubbornness?"

"Neither. Copeland. It's—" But she didn't finish the sentence. He grabbed her, swept her legs out from under her, and then she was just…in his arms. And he began marching across the long expanse of yard.

It wasn't comfortable. It certainly wasn't *romantic*. But it did do something unfair and foreign to her insides. Scrambled them up. Because he *was* strong. She wasn't exactly a lightweight. Maybe she leaned toward skinny when she wasn't taking care of herself, but she was tall and sturdy.

He carried her like she was nothing. In her dad's coat that didn't smell like Dad anymore. He grumbled about her stubbornness the whole way, but he didn't put her down until he got her inside, where he dumped her on the couch. Except it wasn't exactly a *dumping*. He did it in a way that protected the injured ankle.

She couldn't find her voice, because that had been a whole…*situation* her heart and breathing hadn't recovered from.

He'd *carried* her. And now… Now, he was kneeling in front of her, unlacing her boot and tugging it off.

Gently.

Then he pulled off her sock. Her *sock*. His bare hands were on her ankle, and that was hardly sexual. It was hardly *anything*. Her ankle hurt when he pressed his fingers to it, but the rest didn't hurt. It skittered little sparks of something she would not name while he was doing it all the way up her leg, to tangle at the center of her like something very, *very* dangerous.

"It's swollen," he muttered. "You need to ice it, tape it up and stay off it."

The order cut through all the things happening inside of her body. She sat up a little straighter. "I can't stay off it."

"You can. You will. I know where the ice is. Got anything to wrap it with?"

"Yes, but—"

"Tell me where."

COPELAND PUT ICE in the baggie he found, tossed it at her, demanded she elevate her ankle and put the ice on it. He didn't listen to her reply, just stomped to the upstairs hall closet she'd said the wrap was in.

He grumbled to himself as he pawed through the closet. She hadn't known exactly where it was, just that there was some in there. Figured.

It was a nightmare of packed shelves. Huge, and everything was in neat little rows, but the rows were of such disparate items it felt like a disorganized mess. He found all sorts of things. Old curling irons and other hair paraphernalia. Piles and piles of colorful towels of all sizes. Stacks of linens. A tub with the image of a cowboy on a horse full of loose pennies. A box of bullets. A medal of some kind. Two trophies that depicted a woman holding a gun.

He thought he was getting close when he found an old shoebox full of medicines with labels so faded they looked like they'd been here since the 90s. He pushed aside the box, paused when he came face-to-face with another box. This time of condoms.

Hell. He really did not need to think about that. He was about to give up, let her stomp around on her twisted ankle and her own stubbornness and call it a day, but as he was moving the medicine shoebox back into place, he noted a spool of wrap and grabbed it, muttering to himself.

Because now he was going to have to touch her again.

And he knew there were condoms in her closet.

No. She had two perfectly good hands. She could wrap her own ankle. She would be the first to tell him she could handle everything her damn self.

He marched down the stairs, propelled by that righteous certainty, until he made it to the couch. She held out her hand, that prim look on her face. Like a queen ordering a servant about. "I can do it."

He rolled his eyes, even though letting her do it had been his plan. It was an *ankle*. It wasn't the 1800s. He wasn't a man who got hot and bothered about an *ankle*.

He was damn well going to wrap her ankle. "Sit up."

"Copeland."

"Sit. Up."

She sighed heavily but sat up, moved her feet from their elevated position on the arm of the couch to the floor. He kneeled down. The pant leg of her jeans was still cuffed from when he'd checked out the status of her ankle.

He'd been in sports all through high school, so he knew how to handle an elastic bandage.

He kept telling himself that as he unwound the piece of fabric, then had to touch her again.

It's an ankle. Get a grip.

But no amount of self-flagellation seemed to make a difference. Touching her was like touching silk. This tough, do-it-all-herself ranch woman who had *shooting trophies* in her hall closet was soft and warm, and it really twisted something in him he'd long since refused to let be twisted.

Damn her.

As he wrapped her ankle, anger and frustration and something that felt far too close to fear not to put him in a bad mood, swirled inside of him until he'd certainly worked himself up into a lather.

He knew he should keep his mouth shut. He knew a lot of things. But temper won.

"Now, you're going to listen to me. I don't care how I-can-do-it and stubborn you want to be, you have to stay off this ankle. It's not a terrible sprain, but it's not going to heal if you're hobbling around."

"That's all well and good, but—"

"There are no *buts*. If you need help, you call in some help. I can handle a few things, but the Kirks *want* to help, so you're only being a stubborn idiot by refusing it. Well, sorry, pal. That's done."

He was still crouched in front of her, but he'd leaned forward, and now she did too, poking a finger into his chest.

"I didn't ask for you to be here. I didn't ask for your help or your opinion. I can handle myself."

"You're doing a piss poor job of it."

She dug the finger in deeper. "Screw you."

He put his hand over her wrist, pulled her finger out from drilling into his chest. "Yeah, right back at you."

He was too close, he realized in the silence that settled over them, fraught and angry. He held her wrist and they were eye-to-eye, practically nose-to-nose, in this odd little position.

Her cheeks were flushed with temper, and those blue eyes flashed with it. Her temper might have stoked his, but it wasn't just that. This close, just like last night, when they'd argued, it became something else.

Because neither leaned back. He didn't drop her arm and she didn't try to pull it away. They stayed right where they were. Too close and too annoyed by each other.

And too…something else. That incessant pull. A magnetic force all its own. A throb, an ache. He knew he shouldn't drop his gaze to her mouth, all twisted up into a scowl. And he knew *that* shouldn't make that ache deeper.

But it did.

She was just so damn pretty. Stubborn and obnoxious, and he was perverse enough to like exactly that. She didn't fall apart at…*anything*. And why that made him want to handle it all, he didn't have a clue.

But it was more than handling things because he wanted his hands on her and that was a line he absolutely had no business crossing.

Damn, he wanted to.

It would be an absolutely colossal mistake. There would be no defense, no crawling out from under it. If he touched his mouth to hers, everything imploded no matter how carefully he handled it.

And still, he was just a whisper away from doing it. Because no amount of rational thought seemed to break through this ridiculously tight magnetic pull that seemed to exist.

Then her phone rang, and they both jolted apart. Like caught, guilty teenagers.

For a moment, maybe just a second, they stared at each other, maybe in mutual shock. What *had* they been thinking?

But then she looked down and pulled the phone out of her pocket. He didn't miss the way her hand shook. The way she cleared her throat and licked her lips. And that was the problem.

He could deal with a little one-sided and inappropriate lust. It was a harder thing to do when the feeling was clearly mutual. *That* was going to lead to a very dangerous mistake.

"I-it's Thomas," she said, looking at the screen of her phone very, *very* intently. "Vi must have had the baby."

He gave a sharp nod, moved into a standing position, and tried to be very grateful about the perfect timing of the baby's arrival as Audra answered the phone.

Instead, he just felt edgy and irritable.

And it was all her fault.

Chapter Ten

Audra felt like she'd touched an electric fence. Her skin vibrated. And it wasn't a pleasant sensation.

Mostly because there was no *cure*. Except something very, very, very stupid.

And that wouldn't solve anything. Copeland Beckett was no knight in shining armor, even if he could look at her like that and turn all that frustration and anger into something else entirely.

She swiped the screen of her phone to answer the call before it went to voice mail, trying to pretend Copeland wasn't still closer than she wanted him to be.

And somehow not close enough at all.

"Hi, Thomas," she greeted, wincing at how shaky she sounded.

But Thomas must not have noticed, thank goodness.

"Baby's here. Fox Frederick Hart. Twenty-one inches. Eight pounds even. Pictures incoming. They're both doing great, and Vi said she's up for visitors whenever you want to come out."

It was the best distraction she could have hoped for. She could stop thinking about that low throb in the pit of her stomach, and the way Copeland's dark eyes hooked right into her and focus on new babies and family.

"Fox, oh, isn't that a perfect name? Magnolia and Fox. I love it. I'm going to head out right now. Can I pick anything up on the way?"

"No. Between my parents and Vi's, we're drowning in just about anything we could need. We aren't going anywhere. I think she's going to video-call Franny. Too late in Italy to call Rosalie just yet, but we'll get there eventually. Vi just wants to see you, but no rush. Whenever you get here is just fine."

"I'm on my way. I can't wait. See you in a few." She clicked End. She didn't want to acknowledge Copeland, but she had to. Even if she didn't *want* a ride into town, she didn't want to fight with him over it. And worse, she didn't think she could drive very well with her ankle feeling the way it did.

He'd stood, taken a few steps back, but he regarded her with those intense dark eyes, and that stern expression made all the more *stern* by the stubble of the equally dark beard.

Just looking at him made her stomach do leaps and left her completely speechless.

"You need to stay off that foot," he said, which reminded her that words existed and so did her own will.

"I need to meet my honorary nephew."

"He'll still be around in a few days."

"I'm going to the hospital, Copeland. You can drive me, or I can drive myself. But I'm going." She even pushed off the couch to prove it. She put all her weight on her left foot and speared him with a stern look to rival his own.

He rolled his eyes. "Fine. Enjoy a bum ankle for weeks. What do I care? I'll drop you off like I said. I imagine you'll want to spend a few hours."

"Yes."

He nodded. "That'll give me time to head over to the station. Sit down and get your shoes on."

"I've got a present. It's upstairs." She gestured at the stairs.

"And I suppose you'd like me to get it?"

"I can—"

"Hell, Audra, just ask."

She didn't want to. She really, really hated asking for things, but hobbling up the stairs would be embarrassing and no doubt bad for the ankle. But she could leave it, give it to Vi later...

And that was too stubborn even for her. "Would you please get the present that's up on my dresser in my bedroom? It's wrapped with a bow, just sitting on the top."

"Did it kill you?"

"Not immediately, but maybe it will. A slow, silent death."

He chuckled, his eyes crinkling at the corners as he smiled and shook his head. It wasn't fair, that rare smile, that rare humor. Not at all fair that it had her insides getting all mushy. She much preferred the buzzing anger/attraction from fighting over anything that made her feel *soft* toward him.

He disappeared upstairs and she worked to get her boot on. She tested putting some weight on it. She could get by with a little limp, and not too, *too* much pain.

When he returned it was with the present, and a bottle of something in his hand. He tossed the present on the couch next to her, then disappeared into the kitchen. He returned with a glass of water, and two little pills she figured were ibuprofen in the other.

"Take those."

"Has anyone ever ordered you around?"

"Sure. I went through the police academy."

"And how much did you like it?"

He shrugged. "Part and parcel."

She scowled at him but took the pills because it was the sensible thing to do, even if she wouldn't mind being *asked*.

He didn't carry her to the car, which she was glad about. Certainly not disappointed. But he helped her hobble over to it, carrying the present under his other arm.

The drive to the hospital was mostly silent. He turned the radio on at just enough volume to discourage speaking. Audra figured that was best. They'd probably just argue.

But in the silence, she found herself wondering about things she shouldn't. Like his ex-wife. Like what kind of husband he'd been. Like the fact he had been *very* uncomfortable the other night around Magnolia.

He pulled into a parking spot in the front of the hospital. "What lie are you going to hand out for why you're limping?" he asked as he shoved his car into Park.

"I'm not going to lie. I'm going to say I tripped and fell, which I did."

"Over a damn grave hole," he muttered.

"It wasn't deep enough to be a grave hole."

"Do you ever just let things go?"

"I let *everything* go. You're the one who doesn't let things go."

He just shook his head. "You got it from here?"

"Aren't you coming in?"

"Nah, going to head into the station. I've got too much to do. Just text when you're ready to head back."

She hesitated then, knowing that she'd do best to stop thinking about him, wondering about him, poking into his personal life. She'd do best to treat him like what he was. A detective on a case she was involved in. Beginning and end.

She couldn't manage it, because too many things added

up, and now that she knew he had an ex-wife… She just had to know. "You don't…have a child, do you?"

He didn't look at her, stared straight ahead, his hands still on the steering wheel, but there was a tension in him. Still, his answer relieved some of hers. "No."

"It's just… You get a little…fidgety around Magnolia. When the topic of kids comes up, and now, you won't even come in and see the baby and… I just didn't know if it's something I should avoid. If—"

"I don't have a kid," he repeated. Stiffly this time, and with something in his eyes that she might have called *haunted* if she thought someone like Copeland had feelings.

Still, it was *something*. "But there's a sore spot there?" she pressed, not fully recognizing herself. She wasn't a presser. Though she did hate to accidentally tread on soft spots.

He sighed. It was the only sign he wasn't fully made of stone. "Sure. Sore spot. Yeah."

She couldn't imagine what it meant, but it made her heart hurt for him. "Okay. I'll be gentle around it."

He glared at her. "I'm a tough guy, Audra. You don't need to be gentle."

But that was just silly. "Everyone needs a little gentle, no matter how tough they are." She gave him a small smile. "I'll see you in a bit."

First, Copeland drove home and packed a bag of his things so he could stop borrowing Audra's dead dad's stuff. Then he drove to the police station. Grumbled some greetings before he made it to the detectives' office.

Where he would dive into work and forget about *gentle*.

Laurel was there but was clearly in the process of getting all her stuff together to leave. She glanced up at him.

"You been to the hospital yet?" she asked.

Copeland considered his answer. *Yes* wouldn't be a lie, but if she went in and talked to Hart, he'd be found out as a liar, and then they'd both demand to know why. "Not yet. I needed to get a few things done first."

She nodded, slipping a cross-body bag over her shoulder. "You still going to be MIA here tomorrow?"

"Unless another more pressing case comes up. I've got some leads on the Young shooting. Another little...weird happenstance. In fact, I'd like your take if you've got a few."

"Shoot."

He went over it with Laurel, wanting someone else's opinion on the matter. Because on the surface, this was all weird, petty scare tactics. But underneath it was all about *death*, and that was threatening. Not to mention the sheer amount of time and effort that was going into all these things.

"The father's second family is definitely something to look into," Laurel agreed. She'd taken a seat on the edge of the desk she shared with him. "But the way they're doing these things without leaving any clues, any evidence, it speaks to more local. Someone who knows the ins and outs of that ranch, of the system."

"She's got security, but it never seems to be where she needs it." He chewed over that. Someone who knew the ranch well. Could it connect to the Kirks? All the trouble they'd had last year? It didn't sit right, but he'd have to look in to it. "It just doesn't add up."

"My advice? Don't try to make things add up. People's motives don't have to. Keep following the evidence. Anything from the crematorium yet?"

"No, still wading through the red tape. Whoever runs the cemetery lives in California, and the maintenance guy I talked to didn't have any information. I've tried to figure out who made the stone, or engraved it, but I'm going to need records from the cemetery."

"I'll follow up on some of the phone calls tomorrow for you, see if it needs a woman's touch." She said that to irritate him like she always did, but he couldn't be ungrateful for the help. "Put Vicky on the records stuff. She's good at cutting through the red tape, and it's hard for you to do cozied up on the Young Ranch."

He snorted at the word *cozied*. "Yeah, it's a laugh a minute."

Laurel studied him, and he didn't like it. Especially when she changed the subject to something that made no sense.

"Did I ever tell you how I met my husband?"

"No, and you'll be shocked to hear this—I don't care." Not that he wasn't a *little* curious how the buttoned-up, professional, pain-in-his-ass Laurel had ended up with her bearded, tattooed, *wild*-looking husband.

She'd tell him anyway, but he kept up the image of not caring and went to his desk and pulled out his laptop. Booted it up and pretended like Laurel wasn't still standing there.

"It was a case. I was a newly minted detective, and Grady's half brother was suspected of murder. Clint's a mess, but he's no murderer."

He kept his gaze on the laptop. "Super."

"Grady was the opposite of me in every single way. Rival family even."

This time he did look at her. "Only in these backward places do you have rival families."

She grinned. "Bad news, Copeland, and I think you might already know this, though you'll pretend not to. You *love* this 'backward' place."

He scowled back down at his computer. Maybe Bent County wasn't so bad, but he wasn't about to admit it out loud.

"So Grady and I worked together to get to the bottom of it," she said, because Laurel never took a hint or even a direct no for an answer. "What do they call it? Forced proximity. One thing led to another, and here I am, all these years later. A husband and four kids under my belt."

"Good for you."

"It is. Really good. Because this job can be a black cloud, and it's good to have a reminder—whether it's family or friends—that there *is* good in the world."

He looked up at her again. "Do I look like I need some kind of weird pep talk?"

She met his gaze, both serious, instead of their usual ragging on each other. "Yeah, you do." She tapped her hand against the desk. "Email what you need done to Vicky. I'll talk to her if she has any questions. And visit Hart at the hospital. You're part of this community, whether you like it or not."

He didn't like it, he told himself, pulling up his inbox so he could write an email to Vicky. In fact, he hated it. Maybe he'd put in his two weeks. Head down south to sunshine and absolutely no ties. Yeah. That sounded good.

And even while he pretended, he knew he never would.

Chapter Eleven

The overjoyed parents were too besotted with their perfect, wonderful bundle to notice Audra limping. She got to sit and hold Fox in his perfect preciousness. She read an impatient and grumpy Magnolia a book for a little while to keep her occupied. She chatted with Thomas's parents, and Vi's dad, who carefully tiptoed around the subject of Audra's father, his cousin.

All in all, it was nice. It was refreshing to be in a happy environment, with family and friends and love and hope and excitement. For a little while, she relaxed and didn't think about being behind on chores or all the things happening to her that *seemed* harmless but had a whole lot of *death* in common.

She got sucked into *life*, and it felt wonderful.

Just when she was starting to consider texting Copeland because it was clear Vi was getting tired, even if she said she wanted everyone to stay, he appeared.

He brought flowers with a little balloon that said It's A Boy tucked into it. No doubt from the hospital gift shop, but it was still a sweet gesture. One that made Audra's heart mushy again.

"Do you want to hold him?" Thomas asked, angling the bundle toward Copeland.

Copeland stepped back as if Thomas was offering a grenade. "Nah, I like 'em a little sturdier. Congrats and all, though. I'm going to take Audra back, if that's alright."

Audra got to her feet, didn't wince. The ibuprofen *had* helped, and even if she hadn't elevated her ankle, she'd stayed mostly off it. She bent over the baby bundle, gave Fox's forehead a gentle kiss. She gave Thomas a hug, Vi a hug, and Mags a big squeeze. Exchanged goodbyes with all the happy grandparents, then followed Copeland out of the hospital room, high on family and love.

"Here," Copeland muttered, taking her arm so she could lean on him a little bit while she limped.

And that was nice too. She couldn't depend on it. She probably shouldn't even enjoy it. There was no one to lean on in this life except herself.

Which was the depressing pinprick to her bubble of happiness. Once in Copeland's car, it was another silent ride back. So silent, Audra actually dozed off in the passenger seat. She woke up, groggy and out of sorts, realizing only after a few blinks that the car wasn't moving.

They were parked. In front of her house. The world was dark around it, but lights shone on the porch and upstairs. He must have left them on since she knew she hadn't. He must have done it on purpose, with forethought to when they'd return.

Her heart ached. She wanted someone to do that sort of thing, someone to lean on, and yet she never let herself lean, so where did that get her?

Alone with no one to lean on.

But not disappointed. Not hurt. Just…drowning, apparently.

She shook her head. It was just this weird threat thing. It was messing with her equilibrium. Once it was solved, and Copeland was back where he belonged, she'd be back to normal again.

He was getting something out of the back of the car, so she pushed out of her seat. She limped toward the house, but Copeland quickly caught up. He had a duffel on his shoulder but grabbed her arm. "What part of staying off your feet is difficult for you to comprehend?"

She decided to ignore him. "It was nice of you to bring flowers."

He shrugged. "That's what people do, I guess."

"But you were going to avoid it." They stepped into the cozy living room. She turned to look at him. "What changed your mind?"

"I wasn't going to avoid it. I just had some work to do first."

She opened her mouth to delve into that, then remembered she'd promised not to poke at his sore spots, so she just nodded.

"Hungry?" She moved for the fridge, realized she should have asked him to stop at the grocery store. The only thing she had to offer was eggs.

She pulled out the egg carton, glanced at him to ask him if he had any preference for how she prepared the eggs, but he was standing there, scowling, something angry and volatile pumping off him.

That sore spot, vibrating with pain. She desperately wanted to know what had caused it, how to soothe it. She wanted to know so much, but she'd promised...

"Fine. If it'll get you to stop looking at me like that, *fine*."

A little stung, she tried to argue with him, because she was *trying* to let it go. "I'm not looking—"

"It's nothing, but you're not going to let it go."

Completely offended now, she set down the eggs a little too hard. "I—"

"My ex-wife was pregnant when we got divorced."

That shut her up right quick, with a sharp ache of pain for him. No wonder kids and family were a sore spot. Because however this story turned out, he'd said he didn't have a child. And she could see the pain in his eyes even if he didn't want it there.

"The kid wasn't mine. She let me think it was though, for a while anyway. So, yeah, the whole my-friend-is-a-new-dad thing is a little weird and reminiscent of a terrible thing that happened a long time ago. The end."

She didn't breathe. It was...terrible. She knew he didn't want sympathy or thought he didn't. But she also knew, whether he realized it or not, he was saying this because *he* needed to. Because it was weighing on *him*, eating at *him*.

He'd stepped into a hospital room where he once thought he'd be in Thomas's spot, but instead he was just this...solitary outsider.

Even though she wasn't sure he'd welcome it, she moved over to him. Put her hand on his shoulder, rubbed her palm up and down in a hopefully comforting move. "Copeland, that's awful."

He didn't jerk away like she expected him to. He stood there, glaring at some point on the wall behind her. His breathing wasn't quite steady, and the anger and grief pumped off him. He'd no doubt bottled it up all evening, and now it needed to come out.

But when he spoke again, most of his anger had fizzled into a sad kind of bitterness. "You know what the worst part is? I would have stayed. I offered to stay. Be a dad, because the father was dead, and I'd loved him too. And after all that—cheating on me with my best friend, mourning him with me when he was killed, telling me she was pregnant with *my* kid—she still said no."

"That's…"

"It was a long time ago." He stepped away from her hand. "I don't know why I…" He shook his head. "We need to eat something, get some sleep."

"We'll do scrambled eggs and toast. Not exactly gourmet, but it's all I got." She limped over to the counter, tears burning in her eyes. He would *not* appreciate them, so she blinked them back as best she could as she scrambled the eggs, sliced some bread and tossed it in the toaster.

He got out plates. She was out of juice, and it was too late for coffee, so he filled glasses with ice water. They worked in easy silence as they got the meal ready and then sat at the table and ate it.

She managed two bites before she couldn't take it anymore. "Tell me the whole story, Copeland. I think you'll feel better."

He shook his head, merely pushing the eggs around on his plate. "There's no feeling better."

"Maybe. But bottling it up… Believe it or not, I get it. I'd rather never talk about a lot of things, but Rosalie always makes me. And it's usually better. It's like…you know, getting the toxins out. Have you ever talked to anyone about it?"

"My parents know everything."

"But have you ever…laid it all out? Told the whole story. Got it out of your system? The grief doesn't just disappear— how could it? But everything's magnified when you just hold it in. Until one day, it explodes." She mimed the explosion with her hands.

"You mean like dumping that all out on a near stranger."

"I think cohabitating has moved us up from stranger to

at least some form of acquaintance. Maybe even friend. The kind of friend that lends an ear when someone needs it." She refused to look away, instead held his hurting gaze. "Like it or not, admit it or not, you need it."

THERE WAS JUST something about her. Against all his normal excuses and certainties, Audra dug under something. She weakened that wall he'd built between himself and the past. He didn't *want* to go back there, but she made it sound like he had to.

Like he might actually survive if he did.

Copeland wanted to resist that pull. Resist this…connection. But she was just sitting there, looking at him, pretending like she knew how to make all this pain go away, and he was desperate enough to listen to her.

"We grew up together, Ethan and I. Became cops together. I went into the detective bureau. He went into SWAT. He liked the immediate danger. I liked the puzzle. I met Danielle while we were out one night, started dating her, got married. He gave me a hard time about tying myself down, but when we bought a house, he bought the one next door. I figured someday he'd settle down too, we'd raise our families next to each other. Our wives could be friends. It's hard being a cop's wife. Good to have community."

It still hurt, a deep, pounding pain that he thought he'd never escape. Those dreams he'd had for a future, and just how almost everyone he'd loved and trusted had made it impossible.

But he wasn't one of those guys who blamed everyone else. He'd had to look at himself clearly and honestly to make the decisions he had. And one of the honest truths he'd uncovered was that he maybe kind of deserved it.

"I loved being a detective once I made my way up the

chain. I threw myself into cases. I wasn't home. The job became my life, and Danielle became someone…at home to handle everything. Ethan worked different hours than I did, so he helped her out. I can't be shocked she cheated. I can't begrudge her that." He'd worked very hard to believe it.

But Audra's words were hard, surprisingly hard from such a soft woman. "You can. You should. You got married. You made vows. The least she could have done if she wanted to break them was tell you that. Up front. And what about him? Your *friend*? He owed you more. Better."

Copeland shook his head. Maybe that wasn't altogether untrue, but… "It's complicated."

"I don't doubt it, Copeland. And no one's a mustache-twirling villain here, but the truth is pretty simple. Hard, but simple. They wanted the easy way out, and you don't get to blame that on yourself."

He let out a long breath. Wondering if he'd ever feel more like a stab-wound victim, always just barely surviving bleeding out.

It was easier to blame himself, because then he could live with it. If it was his fault, his mistakes, then he deserved it. And he handled that a lot better than thinking he didn't.

"So your wife and your best friend betrayed you. And they were *wrong*," Audra said, so firmly, like she knew, even though she'd never met Ethan or Danielle. Never known him as he'd been back then.

It was disorienting.

"She was pregnant. Was it his?" She asked it so matter-of-factly, but it didn't make him feel matter-of-fact. Nothing could.

"Before I knew she was pregnant, maybe even before she knew, Ethan was shot and killed in a hostage situation. It was rough. I thought it was odd how hard Danielle took it, but then I decided it was about…me. She was worried it could happen to me. It changed my perspective. I realized all the ways I'd been failing at being everything outside of a detective. Then she told me she was pregnant and I… I wanted that. A shot at that. The kind of family I'd had growing up. My parents are great. My childhood was great. I just thought, hey, I can make that happen. I could learn something from losing Ethan. It wouldn't have been in vain."

Sometimes, he wondered if that had been the worst part. That he'd wanted to make something good out of the bad and just gotten more and more bad in return.

"It lasted a few months. I went to appointments. We started planning a nursery. I thought…things were going to be okay. I was going to make up everything I'd screwed up. Then one night we got in a fight. I don't even remember about what. Something small, I'm sure, and she said she wished it was me that had died instead, at least then the baby's real father would be around."

Audra touched him then. Her hand over his fist. He hadn't realized he'd curled it on the table, but he could still see it in clear, perfect color. The anger, the bitterness, the *hate* on Danielle's face.

And then, the ensuing miserable guilt.

She'd apologized, but it had broken something. For both of them. And even when he'd offered to stay out of some kind of misplaced duty, she'd refused.

"She apologized, and after we'd calmed down, I offered to stay. Start over. But… She just wanted me out of her life. A fresh start. Her and her baby. The end."

And that had been that. She'd walked away, and there'd been no way to make her stay. No way to repair what she'd broken. Except to pretend like they'd broken it together. Pretend like the kid he never met didn't mean anything to him. Just…pretend, and pretend his way into being someone else.

"I tried to… I don't know. Keep working. Keep living. But I was someone else. I'd lost everything, even that…core of who I was. I couldn't stay there. I wasn't me anymore. So that's why I came here. To be someone else."

It sounded ridiculous when he said it out loud. So why had he? Why had he let Audra drag this out of him? It was so…

"I know how that feels," she said very quietly. So quietly, he had to lift his head, to make sure he wasn't dreaming she'd said those words.

She wasn't looking at him. She was frowning at the kitchen sink, but her hand was still over his. "To feel like two different people. Before and after, even if I didn't leave. Everything in my life is before my dad died, and after my dad died. And not in that sort of…grief way. In an angry way. That loss of something that wasn't right, wasn't fair. It's…sharp, so it just sits there. Bitterness. I don't like to be bitter. I don't like the way it…infects everything, and the people I love. So I liked it like that. Before. After. I could be someone else after."

Why should she understand? Why should she be the one to hold them accountable? Why should this unplanned forced proximity have led him *here*, talking about things he'd wanted to bury and leave behind?

Except he hadn't left anything behind. The past always clung to him. A layer of something he'd never been able to wash off. Weights that had stayed right there, his whole time here.

Until now. Somehow, she'd been right. Laying it all out— from start to finish—was a weird kind of exorcism. He'd always hate it. That betrayal would always be a part of him. The loss of a child that wasn't even his.

But…there was something about laying it all out to someone who hadn't been there, didn't know anyone, so stoutly saying what he'd always felt deep down, always tried to talk himself out of.

No matter what *he'd* done wrong, they had been wrong to hide it from him. Danielle had been wrong to let him think he was going to be a father. They had been cowards, and he wasn't perfect, God knew, but he'd always been honest.

"You know, I kept this secret from Rosalie for years. I mean, *years*. And I finally told her last year. I didn't want to tell her. I hated telling her, but I had to. And then, I felt better. To not have it anymore. To be able to tell her everything I felt. You just have to be able to let it go sometimes."

"What was the secret?"

She pulled her hand away from his, looked down at her plate, poked at what was left of her eggs. "Oh, I'd just sort of… Our parents sucked. Always. I was pretty aware of it, but Rosalie was younger. So I just…did a lot while we were growing up so she didn't know how little they cared about us. I made sure my parents paid attention to her, wished her happy birthday, got her presents—that kind of thing. I did things for her and gave credit to my parents. So, in a weird way, when we found out about my dad's second family, it hit her harder. Because she'd idolized him, but what she really idolized was the version of him that I'd created."

He could only stare at her. It was completely and utterly selfless. She hadn't done it for herself. Just for her sister, and even if it had backfired a little, she'd had the best of intentions. She even felt *guilt* over those best of intentions, like it was somehow her fault.

He had never met someone so bound and determined to hoard every responsibility for themselves, and he imagined she'd just been soldiering that weight her whole life. The weight of this ranch and her sister.

She wrinkled her nose. "I guess that doesn't do anything to deny the martyr claims." She got up, took their plates and crossed to the sink.

He grabbed the glasses and followed. He could say something nice. He actually found that he *wanted* to, but it was dangerous ground here. He recognized that enough to agree with her. "No, it sure doesn't."

She started rinsing off the plates. "I guess I am." She shrugged. "It is what it is. And now we've gone down those little memory-lane trips, gotten to know each other a bit, we can call each other friends now," she said, forcing some cheer into her voice. Then she looked at him and smiled.

Copeland didn't get involved. He didn't get wrapped up. He didn't vomit out his past at the drop of the hat. Whatever she turned him into, it wasn't *him*.

This wasn't exorcising anything. It was dragging it all up and tying her to it.

And he wanted her more than he could ever remember wanting anything. Especially when she laughed. Especially when she looked at him like she was just as irritated she wanted him as he was that he wanted her.

When she looked at him and *smiled* and said they were *friends*. When she'd done something he'd stopped everyone else in his life from doing.

She stood up for him. Pointed out the flawed thinking that he'd had a role in what two people he'd loved and trusted had done fully behind his back.

Oh, he knew his parents blamed Danielle, and even poor dead Ethan, for what they'd done. But he hadn't let them act on that, or say it to him. It had been easy to brush off any of their commentary as a parents' blind eye to their only child's flaws.

But Audra wasn't blind. He hadn't been exactly *nice* to her, even if he'd helped her. He didn't think she had any pie-in-the-sky ideas about who he was. And still, she'd seen everything he'd laid out for what it was.

Wrong.

He'd never had that. Hadn't *let* himself have it, and he wouldn't have even all these years later, but it had just… happened. *She* had just happened. And he didn't know anyone like her. Never had. She was damn confusing, was what she was. One minute all soft and self-sacrificing, the next hard and demanding and always…*always* carrying too many weights on her shoulders like she was the only one who could.

Her smile faded. She probably saw what was in his expression, but she stood her ground. He could walk away. He could—

But she stepped forward. She didn't shy away from meeting his gaze. She had to see the conflict there, between the things he shouldn't want and the things he did. And maybe he thought he saw the same things in her gaze. That was what gave him the permission.

Because if anyone deserved the things she wanted—even if she shouldn't—it was this woman right here.

So he kissed her. Just swooped down and pressed his mouth to hers, settled his hands on her hips and drew her in.

He kissed her until he forgot there was anything else in this world except the feel of her mouth against his.

She kissed him back. That impossible mix of sturdy and soft. Demanding and giving. And when she leaned against him, of her own volition, he felt like he'd won a war.

It wasn't wild so much as rooted. Tangled. It felt like

being pulled under and into something he didn't understand, or maybe was afraid to. But the honeyed pleasure of the taste of her in his mouth coated any fear.

She wrapped her arms around his neck, leaned into him fully. He would have leaned right back, but something flickered in his peripheral vision. For a second, he thought maybe he was seeing stars, but it penetrated. How wrong it was. The flicker against the dark. He managed to get his mouth off hers, turned his head and...

"Audra. Out the window. Fire."

Chapter Twelve

Audra didn't understand the words at first. Her body was a riot of sensations and…fire.

Fire. Actual fire. All that heat, sizzle, fascinating intensity, drained out of her into a cold, icy fear as her eyes finally accepted what she was looking at.

Copeland had already started moving for the back door. His phone was to his ear and he was barking out orders to whomever he'd called.

She took a stumbling step forward, her twisted ankle forgotten until pain shot up her leg. She swore at herself, then limped another step toward the back door.

Copeland wrenched it open, but he turned to face her. His expression was all sharp lines, his words stern. The kind of order meant to be obeyed without question.

"Stay put."

She looked beyond him, to where the tool shed was engulfed in flames, shooting light and smoke up into the dark sky above. The shed was the closest outbuilding to the house. Luckily, it housed no animals, but it contained a lot of her yard tools and very little that could have just… spontaneously combusted.

He nudged her back. "Fire department is on their way. I need you to stay inside. I'm just going to look around the perimeter. You stay inside and lock the door."

She wasn't trying to be a pain. She wasn't trying to cause a problem. She was trying to understand, and she couldn't do it if she stayed inside. She couldn't comprehend… "Copeland. It's my place."

"I know it."

The conviction in his tone was strong enough, out-of-character enough, she moved her gaze from the fire to him. His dark eyes were intense, but it wasn't that impatience she was so used to. There was something more understanding there.

"You can't go limping around when someone was out there starting a fire on your property. You are the center of this Audra, like it or not. You have to protect yourself."

"What about you?"

He patted his hip, where he still had his gun from earlier. "It's my job, Audra. I'm damn good at it. I need you to let me do it, okay?"

She supposed it was that he was *almost* asking this time around that allowed her to nod.

He looked around the flames, the backyard. Cursed. "Look, stay off the foot if you can, but if you're looking for something to do, get yourself a gun. The front door is locked but I need you to lock this one behind me."

But locking him out sounded…bad and dangerous. For him. Her purse was right there on the counter, so she pulled her keychain out of it, then jerked open the junk drawer and retrieved a flashlight. She handed both to him, but he hesitated.

No time for that, she understood. She grabbed his hands and forced everything into them.

"Fine," he muttered. Then he was out the door, but she noted he waited.

Against her own instincts, she went ahead and flicked

the lock. Her brain was scrambled. Everything was…too much. Everything was…

Burning. She blew out a breath. No. Just the shed. Unlikely to spread anywhere else. But it was a threat or *something*, so Copeland was right to tell her to get a gun. She limped out of the kitchen and over to the closet in the living room. She kept most of her competition rifles in the basement, but she kept a handgun on the main floor and one up in her bedroom. Both locked away in safes, and not loaded, but it always made her feel safer.

She shoved the tubs of winter hats and a few board games to the side of the top shelf of the closet, typed in the code for the safe, then drew the gun out. Cursing her painful ankle, she went back to the kitchen, opened the junk draw and pulled out the box of bullets shoved to the back. She loaded the gun and then just stood there, looking out the window at the flames.

It couldn't be a coincidence. It had to be another thing being done *to* her. Why? Just *why*? These strange, dangerous but petty things. Escalating in frequency. In danger. Nothing overt. No evidence left behind. Just constant attacks on her.

No, not even her. The house, the truck, the shack.

It's my place.

Her place. Her ranch, and…everything that had happened so far connected to *that*, didn't it? Not her, the *ranch*.

The power going out, the windows and her truck being shot up, the shed on fire. These were attacks on the property—but not on anything that she needed to maintain the cattle. Not on her actual person. These were petty things, things meant to make her feel fear.

But they weren't hurting the *ranch*.

And if she wasn't here. If she was dead like whoever it

was had tried to make it look like with the cremains and the gravestone, the ranch wouldn't be hers.

But still, no one had tried to *kill* her. She could not make sense of it, but it felt like some kind of revelation. Not *her*. The land.

Someone wanted her afraid? Maybe someone thought she'd run away? It didn't fully make sense, but she thought there was the seed of something there.

The flames still shot up into the sky. If Copeland was anywhere around it, she couldn't see him. She didn't know if she should feel relief about that or fear. Could something have happened to him?

She swallowed down the fear. This was his job. He knew what he was doing. She had to trust that. Even as her heart hammered against her chest and she imagined about fifty million different terrible things befalling him out there in the dark.

But then she heard a siren in the distance, and eventually began to see flashing red lights, even though the fire truck hadn't appeared yet. She limped her way through the house to the front, only to remember there were boards there instead of windows now.

After a moment, the door jiggled, the knob turned. Terror clawed up her throat, but she reminded herself she'd given Copeland a *key*. Bad guys didn't have *keys*.

Copeland stepped into the dim entryway bringing cold air and the smell of burning in with him.

"Fire truck is here. They'll take care of it." He locked the door behind him before moving over to her. She watched as his eyes went to the gun, just a quick flick of his gaze. She didn't know what he thought of it, but there was *something* there in his expression she really couldn't read.

Didn't matter. What mattered was— "Copeland. I don't think this is about me. Not really."

"Hell, Audra." He stalked toward the kitchen.

She followed, trying not to wince at the pain. "No, listen to me. It's about the ranch. It's about…getting me off the ranch. So that's about me, I guess, but if someone wanted me dead, they could have done it quicker and easier before all this. All these scare tactics that haven't caused me any actual physical danger. They don't want *me*—dead or alive. They want the ranch. Or *something* about the ranch. If I'm dead, I don't own it, but they've only tried to make it look like I'm dead."

He didn't brush her off this time, though she wasn't sure he was actually listening to her either. He studied her, and there was no glimpse of the man who'd let her into the secrets of his painful past, no signs of the man who'd kissed her until her knees were jelly. This was *Detective Beckett*, and she was just a victim with information he wasn't sure he believed.

"Who would want your ranch?" he asked, in that same detached manner.

"I don't know." She really didn't. She didn't have the biggest or best spread. There was nothing particular or special about the Young Ranch. It was just an old family ranch like all the rest of them in Bent County.

But she knew she was on to something, because he didn't say anything. Didn't argue with her. He was considering, pulling at that thread. Or she thought he was.

Then he pulled a chair out from under the kitchen table and grabbed her arm. He nudged her into it, holding her weight so she didn't have to put any on her injured side.

"Stay off that damn ankle," he muttered. "And start thinking about who'd want to scare you off this place so they could have it for themselves."

THE FIRE WAS OUT, the firefighters and police that came were mostly dispersed now, but there was still one fire truck and one vehicle parked in Audra's front yard, and two men standing there talking too quietly for Copeland to hear from his place on the porch.

He was bundled up in his own coat *and* Audra's dad's coat because, hell, it was freezing out here. His only consolation was that he'd convinced Audra to stay inside. He'd suggested she make some coffee to offer, which wasn't exactly keeping off her ankle, but it was better than her standing out here.

One of the men was a firefighter Copeland thought was named Kline, if he remembered right, and the other man was Hawk Steele. Hawk was the fire inspector for Bent County. Lucky for Audra, he didn't live too far away. His place on the Hudson property with his wife and kids was just outside of Sunrise, so he'd appeared on the scene before the firefighters had gotten the blaze under control.

Copeland had worked with Hawk a handful of times, didn't have any negative impressions about the guy. He had a reputation for good work.

Which was a positive, because Copeland didn't need to know anything about fires to know that this one had been set on purpose.

Hawk probably wouldn't want to divulge much before he could do a more thorough examination in the daylight. Run tests on whatever he found, but Copeland hoped he'd be able to at least get confirmation of some things he was reasonably sure were true.

Both men approached the porch.

"The fire is fully out," Kline said. "No danger of it spreading. Steele here will go over with you what needs to be done to keep the scene from being contaminated for his investigation. Any questions or concerns, you've got my number."

"I'll want a copy of the report."

The firefighter nodded. "You'll both get it." He turned and headed for his truck, but Hawk took the stairs.

"I'm going to need to speak with Audra."

Copeland nodded, opened the door and gestured Hawk inside. "She's in the kitchen. You know Audra? One of those Bent-County my-cousin's-wife's-sister's-aunt's-stepmom-changed-my-diaper things?"

Hawk smiled. "I didn't grow up here, Beckett. But my wife works at Fool's Gold with Rosalie. I don't know Audra that well, but our paths have crossed."

"How much have you heard about what's been going on here?"

"Bits and pieces," Hawk confirmed. "Property damage. Death threats?"

"Sort of. I'll send you my reports on it, if it'll help your case."

"Can't hurt."

When they stepped into the kitchen, Audra had a full pot of coffee and some mugs out on the table, along with a small carton of cream and a little bowl of sugar.

"Hawk," she greeted and gestured at the table. "Coffee to warm you up? I made decaf, but I can put together a pot of—"

"Decaf would be fine," he replied easily. "Why don't we all sit down and talk?"

Audra nodded and moved for the table. She didn't limp, and Copeland knew it cost her. Just like he knew she *looked* calm and collected, but there were nerves in her eyes, if you knew where to look.

It was a little concerning that he knew exactly where that was. But that was a concern for a much different time.

She poured coffee for all of them, let everyone doctor

their own mugs. Hawk took a sip. His nose and cheeks were red. No doubt the warmth was welcome, but he didn't waste any time. He got right to it.

"I'm going to want to take a look again once I've got more light, maybe collect a few more samples, but I got the overall gist. It wasn't hidden or sneaky. Someone deliberately set that fire to your shed."

Audra swallowed as she nodded. "Yeah, that's about the only way I could have seen this going."

"I'm not fully familiar with the other trouble you've been having here, but Detective Beckett is going to share the case information with me, and I'll take it into consideration as I run some tests and see if we can figure out who did this."

Audra blew out a breath. "It'll be whoever is doing all the other things. And they haven't been too great at leaving us evidence to go on."

Hawk nodded. "It might be difficult, but fire's a bit more volatile. Harder to keep a distance from. We'll see what we can find, and I'll work closely with Detective Beckett since it seems likely it's related. That being said, and I hope you'll agree, Detective, Audra, you shouldn't stay here overnight. It'd be reckless to be alone out here at all, any time of day, until we know who's targeting you."

Audra opened her mouth, no doubt to argue because she was still the same infuriating woman, but before Copeland could tell her to knock it off, Hawk continued in his calm, even way.

"I know enough ranchers to understand it's a tall order to ask you to leave. You've got animals and a business to take care of, and I get that. But this is not a safe space until we know who's doing this. Fire is dangerous. Maybe they only meant to burn down that shed, but it was the closest structure to the house. Had the weather been dry, things could have ended up much worse. Just because no one's specifically tried to hurt *you*, doesn't mean you won't find yourself in the crosswind."

When Audra looked at Copeland, the pleading in her eyes about took him out, but he wouldn't relent. Couldn't when her safety was on the line. "He's right. You know he's right. You've been lucky so far."

"Lucky," she said disgustedly, pushing away from the table, coffee mostly untouched.

Hawk rose as well. "I'm going to head into the office, handle a few things, then I'll stop by once it's light. I'll keep you both updated."

Copeland watched as Audra turned to Hawk, plastered on that fake smile. "Thank you," she said, sounding like she meant it.

Copeland knew she didn't.

"Stay safe, Audra. Beckett? I'll be in touch." With that, Hawk nodded at both of them and let himself out.

For a moment, the kitchen was fully silent. Audra stood by the sink, brooding out the window. Copeland sat at the table watching her.

He could probably read her mind. She was trying to figure out how to convince him she should stay. Which was *stupid*, but worse than her stupidity was his. Because he was trying to rationalize it to himself.

If he stayed with her, she'd be safe. He'd protect her. He'd been here since the shooting, and nothing had touched her, even if it had touched the outside.

But someone had started that fire while he'd been *right* here. "If you're right, and this ties to the land and not *you*, then removing yourself from the land makes you *safe*."

"And leaves my home, my life, my *livelihood* unprotected."

"But you'll be *alive*, Audra."

Her shoulders slumped at that. "This place has been mine—my responsibility—since... God, I don't even know. It feels like always, and you're asking me to abandon it."

"I'm real sorry about that, but nothing is yours if you wind up dead. And Hawk is right. Maybe no one is after hurting you, but these things they're doing aren't benign. Shooting and fires. It's dangerous to be around, even if you're not meant to be the main target." He wasn't getting through to her, so he had to be strategic. "Franny will be back eventually. Are you going to let her stay here with all this going on?"

She glared at him. "You know just what buttons to push, don't you?"

"You said it yourself, right? We're friends. Friends know stuff."

Her glare didn't change. "*Friends* don't kiss like that," she muttered.

He could handle that reintroduction a lot of ways, but he wanted to see some of that horrible tension in her expression dissipate. So he went for light. "How do they kiss then?"

"They *don't.*"

"Oh. Bummer."

The sound she made was *almost* a laugh, and that eased the pain in his chest a lot more than it should. But it didn't last. The weights, the worry, the hurt all came back. Settled in her shoulders, her expression.

She inhaled, and it shook. The vulnerability in the sound unnerved him, but also prompted him to move toward her, with some ridiculous urge to comfort, to fix.

He got a hold of himself before he touched her. He had to get a better grip on his reaction to her. The kiss hadn't helped, but he had to be stronger than some little kiss.

Little. Ha.

She turned to look at him then, tears swimming in her eyes making them an unearthly shade of blue. "I can't leave. Maybe you can't understand. But I can't leave this place. It'd be like leaving my soul behind. I'm not trying to be reckless or foolish. I wouldn't know how to be reckless if I tried. I've never had the time to be foolish. Leaving isn't an option for me, Copeland. I have to be here. I have to face this. I *have* to."

He studied her. Yeah, it was the martyr complex talking, but there was something deeper at the root of it. Something deeper than her desperate need not to put anything on anyone else's shoulders. She'd clearly been doing that since she was a kid. He didn't understand what kind of awful parents could instill that on their child, but what impressed him was that Audra hadn't let it make her bitter. Oh, she was a mess of issues, but she wasn't angry or bitter. Her kindness seemed inexhaustible. Her concern for others admirable… and contemptible when she let it supersede reason.

She needed someone to take care of her. To take some of those weights. No one could change her into someone who didn't take on too much, but she needed someone to share the load. Whether she liked it or not.

Not that it was going to be *him*. Not that it was any of his business how many weights she carried. That was her business. Her deal.

But he wasn't about to let her wind up dead in the process. Just because she loved this place like some people loved their children. Just because he couldn't bring himself to demand she leave when she had tears in her eyes and pleas in her voice.

"Fine."

Her entire posture relaxed. She even reached out to touch

him, just a gentle brush of her hand against his arm. "Thank you, Copeland, for understanding. It means—"

"Don't thank me just yet. There's a stipulation."

Wariness crept into her expression, but she nodded, chin high. "Alright."

"You don't leave my sight. Twenty-four seven. You're somewhere? So am I."

Chapter Thirteen

Audra didn't respond at first. Mostly because far too many reactions to that *stipulation* rattled through her. Anger. Frustration. A bone-deep weariness that made her just want to sink to the ground and give up. Luckily, she was used to that feeling. She'd been fighting it for years now.

What she didn't know how to fight was the other emotions battling for space inside her.

Relief. Pleasure. Copeland would be by her side and that meant—

Nothing. It means nothing.

"Isn't that what we've been doing?" she asked, trying to sound casual. Trying to fight away all the *reactions* and just deal.

"No, I left you alone yesterday. That's when you tripped and hurt yourself. I left you alone at the hospital. I'm not being metaphorical. I'm being literal. Twenty-four seven or the deal's off."

That did nothing to ease the mix of emotions. He couldn't possibly do that, and she shouldn't want him to, but she kind of did.

She'd been denying her wants her whole life, so why stop now? She turned to face him, taking a deep breath meant to center, calm. She was used to dealing with Rosalie's ridiculous stubbornness. She could deal with his. She fixed him with the same older-and-more-with-it-sister glare she used on Rosalie.

"Copeland. You cannot be by my side twenty-four seven. You have a job, for starters. Not to mention all the *private* parts of a person's day."

He shrugged. "I'll figure it out. Now, let's get some sleep. It's been a long day. *Days.*"

He was starting to poke at her temper. *I'll* figure it out, like she didn't have a say, when all she had were says. "You're not in charge of me."

"The hell with that," he retorted, without much heat, but a lot of conviction. "Someone ought to be. So while we're at it, you're going to have to tell Rosalie. Maybe you've got a few days, because she's so far away, but this is going to get back to her. Too many people know. Too many things have happened. You really want her catching wind of this from someone else?"

It was awful. Both prospects. Really awful because he was right. Hawk would no doubt mention something to his wife, and while Anna wasn't going to call up Rosalie on her honeymoon, there was just too much of a chance that it all got back to Rosalie sooner rather than later.

"Are you trying to make me cry?" she demanded, because she'd just gotten a handle on it, and now he was making it worse.

"No, and I'd really prefer it if you didn't."

She managed a watery laugh at that, blinked back the tears. "Yeah, I'd prefer that too."

"Come on," he muttered. He moved to her side, wrapped an arm around her so she'd lean on him more than put weight on her ankle. They walked like that in silence to the stairs. She tried to reach for the railing, but Copeland stopped her.

"You've got to give that ankle a break."

"You're not going to carry me again."

"You keep being so very wrong." And then, just like last time, he picked her up before she even had a chance to talk him out of it. Just an arm under her shoulders, another under her knees, and easy as you please, just up the stairs. Like she didn't weigh a thing when she most decidedly did.

He didn't stop there. He walked her all the way to her room. Then he very carefully set her on her feet and crossed over to flip on the lights. He surveyed it with those cool, detached cop eyes.

"Decent-sized bed," he commented. "Going to share it or am I sleeping on the floor?"

She gaped at him. Her mouth hanging open like a fish. "What?"

"Twenty. Four. Seven. I'm sleeping in this room with you." He patted his side. "Armed."

"I have a gun up here."

"Great. Two's better than one."

"Copeland." She knew there should be a reasonable spate of refusals to bring up, to get through to him, but all her brain seemed to come up with was: *what*?

"You're going to have to save us both time and energy and stop trying to argue. This is the deal struck."

His deal. *His* decision. As if her life was his to determine, when she'd been determining *everything* for her entire adult life, if not more.

It was his *job*, sure, and at the end of the day, as ridiculous as he was being, she knew she needed help. She knew whatever was going on was beyond what she knew how to handle or stop.

But she hardly thought that extended to sharing a room, to losing all her privacy and agency. She could tell him all that, but it wouldn't change anything. If there was anything the past few days had taught her, it was that there was no getting through to him, no winning this. He'd find a way. He had every single time, no matter her objections.

It infuriated her. She usually got around *everyone* with a sweet smile and doing what she wanted anyway. She usually convinced everyone she was so fine, so with it, so...*good* that she didn't need overbearing determinations.

Why was he different?

She went into the closet, pulled out the spare pillow, some clean sheets, perhaps a little unreasonably angry at him for being that different. She tossed everything on the ground, spurred on by fury and, if she was being honest with herself, maybe a little panic that someone had finally gotten through. "There. Enjoy."

She went back to the closet, grabbed some pajamas. Then tried to stride out the bedroom door, but he was right there. Right behind her the short walk across the hall.

She turned to scowl at him in front of the bathroom door. She gestured at it. "Just the bathroom, warden. I need a shower."

"I said you're not out of my sight. I'll amend that to give you private bathroom privileges, but that's it."

Bathroom privileges? How was he possibly serious? She fisted her hands on her hips. "Oh, well since I'm your prisoner did you want to handcuff me while you're at it? Maybe shower together so I'm never out of sight?"

He studied her, something about the way his eyes changed reminding her of when he'd kissed her. Her cheeks reddened. Because that was *not* what she'd meant, but the image...

Jeez, she needed to get a grip. So she turned on a heel

and jerked the bathroom door open. She closed it behind her, not with a *slam*, but with a firm *snap*.

She flicked back the shower curtain, wrenched the water on hot, then paused because…it was so *weird* that he was right outside the door, and she was going to take off all her clothes.

And if she called it weird, she wouldn't have to acknowledge that there was something else fluttering through her as she got undressed and stepped into the hot spray. Like the idea of *sharing* a shower. Or that kiss they'd shared. Or mixing it all up into one very inappropriate fantasy.

Yes, it is totally normal to fantasize about sex with a bossy, overbearing detective who is only here because your life is falling apart.

She wanted to groan, maybe beat her head against the wall a few times. Instead she washed up, got out of the shower, dried off and dressed, and then decided she'd handle the rest of the night by not speaking, not thinking, not worrying.

He could sleep on the floor. She'd sleep on her bed. And that was that.

Determined, recalibrated, she gathered up her dirty clothes and opened the door to move out into the hallway.

Copeland was leaning against the wall, looking at his phone. He lifted his gaze when she came out. His eyes moved over her. Not exactly a detached-cop look. No, there was the flicker of *something* in their dark depths.

She could convince herself the kiss was a mistake for a lot of reasons, but it was hard to remember those reasons when she was faced with the fact that whatever she felt about him, whatever reactions she had to him, she wasn't alone. He wasn't immune to her.

"I'm going to run through myself," he said. "You can

head into your bedroom, but you stay there. We're leaving both doors open."

She wanted to have a snarky retort, but she just limped into her room, dropped the dirty clothes in her hamper, turned off the light. She crawled into bed. Her body was fully and wholly exhausted. Her ankle throbbed, so she took the bottle of ibuprofen out of her nightstand and took two with the water from the water bottle she kept next to her bed.

Then she flopped back on her pillow knowing that no matter how exhausted she was, everything plaguing her would keep her awake. And not just because Copeland was currently in her shower. Naked, no doubt. With the door open. She could hear it running. She could hear the occasional creak of his weight shifting the old house.

She squeezed her eyes shut and tried to fight off that potential image. Didn't she have bigger problems than an unfortunate and untimely attraction to a man who…

That was the trouble. She wanted him to be like he seemed. Cold and abrupt and cocky. And he was all those things when he wanted to be, but it was clearly an armor put on after a really awful time in his life.

He was here because he wanted to help. No doubt that was why he was in law enforcement. But she also knew, somewhere along the line, whether either of them admitted it to themselves, it had become at least a *little* more. And she didn't just mean the kissing.

He returned, but didn't flip on the light. She heard him move, the sheets rustle as he settled himself into his makeshift bed.

On the cold, hard floor. After everything he'd done to help her. She didn't *want* to feel guilty. It made her really mad that she felt guilty, because he didn't *have* to sleep on her floor, he didn't *have* to take on this responsibility.

She knew that was rich coming from her.

"I can't sleep with you lying on the floor," she muttered, staring at the ceiling in irritation.

"So trade with me."

"I'm not *that* big of a martyr," she replied, though she was beginning to wonder.

"Sure about that?"

Frustrated with him as much as herself, she sat up, leaned over the end of the bed to peer down at him. It was shadowy dark, but she could make out the lump of him lying on the hard, cold floor. She'd never be able to sleep knowing it.

"This isn't an invitation."

She couldn't see his eyes in the dark, but somehow she could feel his gaze all the same. "What isn't?"

"It's a big enough bed to share. If you can stay on your side."

Maybe she expected him to put up a *little* bit of a fight, but he *wasn't* a martyr. He immediately moved. He tossed the pillow onto the side of the bed she wasn't on, then she felt the weight of the mattress dip.

Why had she thought this would make it easier to sleep? Sure, guilt wasn't eating at her now, but everything else was. How close he was. How odd it was to feel the weight of someone else in her bed. The smell of her shampoo that he must have used mixed with whatever made Copeland... Copeland.

How had she gotten here, and how was she ever going to explain it all to her family when they returned?

Natalie thought she was sleeping with Copeland, and now she was in the most literal way possible. Rosalie would be furious she'd kept so much to herself. Franny would be hurt, because she could visit her parents anytime, so Audra really should have told her, let her come home.

And now she probably had to tell them both before she wanted to, just so they didn't hear some small-town-gossip version of everything.

Just the thought had the tears returning. She didn't know how to make it okay. How to make Rosalie not worry. How to keep Rosalie from ending her honeymoon early, or Franny rushing home. They wouldn't want her to handle it alone and they *should*.

The guilt of it was too much. This was *her* ranch, *her* problem. She wiped one of her now wet cheeks against the pillowcase. She breathed carefully through her mouth as the tears streamed down her face. She wouldn't let him know she was crying, this man who was stubbornly and platonically sharing her bed. She wouldn't…

"This isn't an invitation either," he muttered, drawing her close, then rolling her over so that she was tucked into his warm, hard chest. He ran a palm down her hair, brushed tears off her cheeks, and held her while she cried.

And because he did, she let it out. Sobbed out the whole awful ordeal. Just like what she'd said to him about telling her the whole story about his ex-wife. It was releasing toxins or *something*. She hated it, but at least it served a purpose.

She didn't like to cry on Rosalie's shoulder, or Franny's, or Vi's. Or Natalie's or *anyone's*. It made her feel weak and like she'd failed.

But this wasn't so bad.

COPELAND WOKE UP to sunlight streaming on his face, and a warm body moving next to his. For a moment, he instinctually held on. It was nice. It was…

His eyes popped open. He would have shoved into a sitting position, but he was met by blue eyes fixed on his face.

God, she was pretty. He didn't know how she could give

off the aura of slim, delicate spring flowers knowing how strong, sturdy and determined she was. He knew she could handle anything and had, but he wanted to erect full fortresses to keep her safe.

He went from half-asleep to alert in a second, realizing he had one arm under her shoulder, and she was resting her hand at his inner elbow. Like maybe they'd fallen asleep, wrapped up together, after she'd cried herself empty.

He should get up. Leave this warm cocoon of...*something*. He'd comforted her while she cried, and that was it. Friendly. Helpful. He was hardly going to use an emotional breakdown as a kind of catalyst for...whatever this moment seemed to demand.

But *she* didn't get up. She didn't scoot away. They were so close their noses were almost touching. And neither jumped up to move. Neither looked away.

He knew he should do something to stop this, but she was just so soft and warm. So damn beautiful it *hurt*. Something was beating through him. Heavy, important, mixing with desire and the hazy notion that this wasn't at all wrong.

It was, instead, exactly right.

She moved closer, close enough her body brushed his. Her mouth was just a whisper away. Her blue gaze never left his face.

He could close that little distance between them. He could kiss her, touch her. He could calm this thudding, needy conflict inside of him.

He could extricate himself. Slip out of bed. Pretend this wasn't happening.

But he waited, watching her.

Until she pressed her mouth to his. Sweetly and gently. Her hand coming up to trace his jaw, then raking through his hair. She was a descent into soft, honeyed perfection.

"Just so we're clear," she said against his mouth. "This *is* an invitation."

"Good, because I'm taking it." He rolled her under him, gratified when she made a little sigh of pleasure beneath him. When she met every kiss, every touch, every whisper with one of her own. And it released all that had tied so tight, because he'd wanted this for days now. Just this. Just her.

Sex had been a game since his divorce. Fun. Spontaneous. And very, *very* superficial. Something to do, something to prove to himself that even if he kind of sucked in the whole being-a-human department, he still *was* one.

There was nothing superficial about the way her skin felt, the way she moved under him, the way she kissed him. That was all a heavy, complicated braid of emotion, responsibility, want and something deeper than he had the words for.

It wasn't just sex, certainly wasn't a game. And he could try to convince himself of either of those things, but she already had too much weight in his heart for him to manage.

Being tangled up in her was a privilege and a hope. A tangled, changing dance. As pleasure throbbed, flowed and released in shuddering tandem that took both of them under in the early morning light.

He tucked her close and closed his eyes, and for a moment just breathed. There was so much to do, to handle. This was a distraction that wasn't right when danger lurked.

But, damn, it felt right.

"I guess you've got chores you're late for now," he said when he trusted his voice not to sound heavy with all the emotions waging war inside of him.

She made a contented noise, low in her throat. "I might have finally found something worth being late to chores for."

He should be distancing himself, but instead he pulled her in tighter, settled his face between her jaw and shoulder. Inhaled the faint, flowery scent of her skin that came from the soap she used in the shower last night, and it settled through him. Calm. Warm. Right. "I can make you even later."

"No, you can't and that's *not* a challenge."

He made a considering sound, pressed his mouth to the underside of her jaw. She shoved at him, but with a laugh and with a lightness in her whole body he hadn't seen this whole time.

It was a heady feeling to be the one that got to take some of the weight off Audra Young's shoulders. Dangerously heady, and maybe he would have given himself a stern talking-to about that, but he heard the chime of a doorbell ring through the house, and they both stilled.

"Expecting someone?" he asked casually, trying to remind himself that people who shot out windows and set fires didn't *ring the bell*, so he wouldn't go tearing downstairs, gun in hand.

"No." She hopped out of bed, and he got one tantalizing glimpse of everything before she tugged on a hideous, fluffy robe. "It's probably Natalie." She sighed, weight seeming to pile back on her shoulders. "She probably heard about the fire. I'll be right back."

"Audra, wait—"

But she was already out the door. He cursed under his breath as he got out of the bed. It probably *was* Natalie, but she didn't know that for sure, and with everything that was going on, she had to be more careful.

He couldn't find his shirt, but he wasn't about to let her go downstairs on her own, even if was just Natalie. Twenty-four seven meant twenty-four seven whether she liked it or not, and sex certainly didn't change that. He pulled on his pants as he walked, then jogged down the stairs.

She had the door open, and he could hear her even though he couldn't see who was on the other side yet.

"Oh. Hello. Are you looking for Copeland?"

"Yes." Laurel's voice. "And you. We've gotten a few small breaks in tracking the cremains. I was on my way out to Sunrise for a different case and thought I'd stop by and catch you two up."

"Oh. Okay. Well, come on in." Audra moved out of the way and Laurel stepped in. She glanced around the room in a quick, cop sweep. She spotted Copeland at the bottom of the stairs in nothing but his unbuttoned jeans. Her eyebrows immediately raised.

"I—I'll make some coffee," Audra offered, a little too brightly. "We'll talk in the kitchen." Her cheeks were bright red, but she moved with just the hint of a limp, toward the kitchen, in her bathrobe.

Laurel followed Audra, but her gaze stayed on Copeland. He couldn't quite read it. Not contempt. Definitely not approval. Something more appraising.

"Nice tattoo," Laurel said under her breath as she passed him.

Cursing, Copeland went upstairs to find his shirt.

Chapter Fourteen

Audra wasn't sure how her life had spiraled so far out of control. Sleeping with Copeland was one thing. The kiss before the fire had sort of made *more* feel like an inevitability, and even now she couldn't regret it.

She'd been in long-term relationships before and nothing had ever felt like that. It wasn't just the physical part, though—*wow*. It wasn't that she'd felt like she'd uncovered something, discovering the coin-size tattoo on the front of his shoulder, in the shape of a police badge. It was that it had been *more* than all of that.

More than her usual trying to make a relationship last, work, be the *end*. It wasn't about relationships at all. It had just been about waking up to him holding on to her, knowing that he was…a good man. And she'd wanted some piece of that.

The weight of it had been important, somehow. And it was one thing to try to work through all *that*, but for his *coworker* to show up… To see it. That was something else entirely, even if Detective Delaney-Carson was being very nice and pretending like she didn't know what was going on.

Audra stood at the coffee maker, discarding the remnants of last night's decaf and getting it set up to brew. Copeland reappeared with his shirt on before she finished.

He gruffly ordered her to sit down. Audra didn't miss the

considering gaze the detective gave Copeland, but she pretended she did. She sat, not bothering to tell Copeland her ankle was feeling better. He'd just argue with her.

"Sorry to interrupt your morning," Laurel said, giving Copeland a pointed look when he put a mug of coffee in front of her. She moved her gaze to Audra, and it was kind. "But all the ranchers I know are up at the crack of dawn and I have a meeting in Sunrise in an hour. I figured I'd stop by instead of having you two come out to the station, because we've got something of a lead."

"You could have called," Copeland muttered. He put a full mug, with a dash of cream, like she always took it, right in front of Audra.

"I did," Laurel replied. "Left you a message. I guess *you* could have checked your phone."

Copeland's gaze flicked to Audra, and she couldn't stop the heat from creeping into her cheeks, because obviously they had been *busy* when that call came in.

"What kind of lead?" Copeland said, his attention back on Laurel. He grabbed his own mug of black coffee and sat down in the chair between them.

"We still don't have any suspects, but we've managed to trace the payment to the funeral home that made the arrangements for the cremains. Unfortunately, the payment was made from a fake identity, but the money still had to come from somewhere. We don't have an answer to that just yet, but we do know the payment came from Florida, and we're working on the theory that the person, regardless of fake identity, is somewhere in Florida. Or was. Florida feels like where a lot of this is originating from, even if someone is here now doing these things."

Florida. Audra heard a strange buzzing in her ears, like she'd been transported somewhere else. Florida.

A coincidence. It had to be a coincidence. Florida was a big state. It wasn't... Why *would* it be?

But when she came back into herself, certain it was a weird coincidence, Copeland was frowning at her.

"Do you have any connections to Florida, Audra?" Laurel asked.

But Audra couldn't look away from Copeland.

"You know someone in Florida who might be out to get you?" he asked grimly.

She shook her head. "No, I don't know anyone who's out to get me." Not here. Not anywhere. Why *would* she?

He narrowed his eyes. "Audra, who do you know in Florida?"

She managed to find her voice, though it was a hard-won thing. She couldn't look at Copeland as she spoke, so she looked at some vague point on the wall. "Only one person. My mother." She tried to smile. "Obviously my *mother* doesn't have anything to do with this."

But Laurel and Copeland exchanged a look that said "not so obviously."

"My mother doesn't want the ranch," she continued quickly. "Or to hurt me. She'd have to care about either. She left the minute she could. She wanted *nothing* to do with this place once she found out about Dad's other family. She wanted nothing to do with..." Me. Us.

"And before that?"

She looked at Copeland helplessly, because this wasn't a lead. It couldn't be. "Before what?"

"Before she found out about the other family. Before his death. What did she feel about the ranch before that? Because you guys were here, so she had to have some feelings. Why did she leave?"

Audra couldn't find any words. Maybe because as impossible as it *seemed*, she… She knew how angry her mother had been. Understandably. *Rightfully*. But it had turned against everyone, and for so many reasons, the experience with her father was easier to deal with. He'd lied, cheated, betrayed. Died. It was easy for Audra to hate him and be done with it.

Everything she felt about her mother was a jumble. She couldn't blame Mom's bitterness on anyone but Dad. Couldn't blame Mom for leaving her and Rosalie to clean up the mess. He was their father, their blood. Not hers. To her, Dad was just a mistake she'd made for too many years.

Maybe Audra had thought…a good mother stayed for her kids, supported her kids, regardless of the father, but she also couldn't pretend to know the level of betrayal from the man you were married to having a whole other family he left things to.

So she tried not to blame Mom too much. She tried not to expect anything out of her either. She tried to be neutral. Maybe she'd been leaning closer to anger when Mom had refused to come to Rosalie's wedding, but Audra didn't think Mom knew that. Or cared.

And none of this was…right. "She left because she hated this place," Audra told Copeland. "She wouldn't come back just to…mess with me. She doesn't care about anything here. Florida is a coincidence. It has to be."

Laurel and Copeland shared a look. Not disbelieving exactly, but the kind of look that said they were going to look in to it one way or another.

Audra knew she was just going to have to deal with it.

COPELAND WALKED LAUREL out to her car. They paused at the hood, and he glanced back at the house. Audra would know they were talking about her, about her case, but he didn't want her hearing it even if she knew the topic.

"Can you look in to her mother? I imagine you've got enough background to go off of."

Laurel nodded. "Yeah. What I don't know I can dig up. And we'll keep digging on the fake identity. Vicky got the name of the gravestone supplier, so she's chasing down the payment information there today. If it's the same name, we'll keep picking at it until we hit something."

"I'm getting reports from the fire department about last night. Hopefully there's some more evidence than we've come across. Audra isn't wrong about people too often, and I don't think she has rose-colored glasses where her mother's concerned."

"But it's too big of a coincidence not to look in to," Laurel said, finishing for him.

"Yeah."

"She probably shouldn't be staying here."

He knew it, and it frustrated him, because he also understood why she was being stubborn about it. "She won't go."

Laurel studied the house, then him. "So I suppose you won't either."

"It's the job."

Laurel laughed. "Uh-huh. The *job*." She shook her head. "I give it six months."

"You give what six months?"

She opened her car door. "You know, I was pregnant by my first wedding anniversary."

He gaped at her before he found his voice. "What the hell is that supposed to have to do with anything?"

She shrugged. Held up a finger. "Worked a case." She held up another finger as she took a step back toward the car. "Fell in love." With every step, she held up another finger and gave another ridiculous point. "Got married. Kids one, two, three, four." Then she slid into her driver's seat. "You'll beat me, I bet. On a spread like this? I'm guessing five or six."

"What in the ever-loving hell are you talking about?"

Laurel only laughed and closed the car door, waved as she backed out of the drive. Copeland watched her go, figuring that she was just... Well, obviously she was just messing with him. What did he care about her life? Her kids?

Five or six. She was messing with him. And regardless of *any* of that, he had things to do. Like stick to Audra so she was safe. Like stop whoever was trying to scare her, hurt her, even if it *was* her mother.

Five or six. Laurel was out of her mind. And just *messing* with him. He stomped back into the house. Audra was in the kitchen, where he'd left her with instructions to stay put, surprised that she'd done it.

But she was putting together some kind of breakfast. "I really need to go to the grocery store, but I found some waffles hidden in the back of the freezer," she said with fake, forced cheer. "I've got some chores that need handled first, but I suppose you'll want to come with me for both."

He wanted to tell her he didn't *want* to, but he was going to. But that would be a lie. He wanted to be where she was, and it was a problem that it wasn't only about safety.

"I don't like the idea of us leaving this place alone. It gives whoever is doing this time and access. Can't you have groceries delivered?"

She spared him a disapproving glance as she plated up the frozen waffles she must have toasted in the oven. "No one delivers groceries all the way out here, Copeland."

"We'll figure something out." If he had to he'd ask a

favor of someone, since God knew she wouldn't. He'd figure it out.

She tried to take the plates to the table, but he grabbed them from her. She didn't look like she was limping quite so badly, but she could be putting on an act. He didn't know how it could possibly heal when she wasn't giving it rest.

He put the plates on the table, then looked back at her. She was just standing there, looking at the table. Misery and sadness were etched all over her face. She met his gaze with shiny blue eyes. She wasn't going to cry. He could tell from the way she held herself. But she wanted to.

"She's going to look in to my mother."

He could lie. Reassure. But it would be pointless and wouldn't help her any. "Yeah."

She put a palm to her chest, rubbed, like she was having pain. He couldn't stand that, so he crossed over to her, wrapped an arm around her like he had last night. Just comfort.

Maybe for the both of them, because her hurt did *something* to him. He wanted to fix it.

And that didn't mean there was *marriage* in anyone's future, or five or six *anything*. It was just…the moment.

She leaned against him. "I feel like someone took a whisk to my brain. It's all scrambled eggs up there."

"Great sex will do that to you."

She snorted out a laugh as he'd hoped. But then she sighed. "I know you're going to get mad at me, but I'm sorry. Sorry your coworker showed up here and saw…everything."

"Why are you sorry?"

"It must be embarrassing."

"Why would it be embarrassing?" He didn't think about Laurel and her sudden insistence on telling him about how she'd met her husband or how many kids they had. "There's nothing embarrassing about being with you, Audra." Maybe that was a little too naked, all in all, but she relaxed into him even more.

They stood there a few minutes in a pleasant kind of silence, the smell of waffles and syrup filling the kitchen. It was homey and nice and...just, *right*.

"Apparently I've got a soft spot for martyrs," he said, more to himself than to her, but she made a noise in response—half amusement, half despair.

"Well, that's something I guess." Then she moved up and brushed a kiss across his mouth. "Let's eat before the sad freezer waffles get soggy."

Yeah, it was a hell of a soft spot.

Chapter Fifteen

Copeland was true to his word in that he didn't let her leave his sight. Sometimes it was nice—an extra hand with the feeding and a repair she had to do on the north fence line, especially with her ankle still a little tender. Sometimes it was frustrating—when he told her she needed to stay off her ankle as if she wasn't the one dealing with the pain.

She didn't know how he did it, but he wrangled someone from Fairmont to bring out a full load of groceries. She winced a little at the sheer number of bags he carried in. How was she going to afford all this food at one time?

But she forced herself to smile at him. "Impressive. How much do I owe you?"

"Nothing."

Her smile faded. "Groceries cost money, Copeland."

"They do, and since I'm here, eating your groceries, that you cook, by the way, I buy."

He said it in that way it was clear there was no arguing with him, which had anxiety creeping into her chest. She wasn't going to owe him, rely on him. She'd find a way to repay him. Maybe she didn't know the total, but she'd estimate. And somehow, some way, she'd find a way to give him that money back.

"But before we get started on lunch or cooking, you've got something you have to do." He steered her into the living room, nudged her onto the couch, then set her laptop on the coffee table in front of her.

"What?" she asked, even though she knew. She knew and she didn't want to. Why did she have any affection for this man who was constantly pushing her to do the things she didn't want to?

"Call your sister, Audra. You don't think I know what time it is in Italy? You wait any longer, you'll be claiming you don't want to wake her up. Call her now. Tell her what's going on before she hears it from someone else."

Another order, in that same steely voice that was impossible to argue with. But she didn't need to argue to get her way. She'd learned how to get around the always-up-for-an-argument Rosalie. She did need to tell Rosalie *something*, but it didn't need to be everything. Just pertinent pieces, so if something *did* get to her, she didn't overreact.

Audra smiled placidly at Copeland. "I will call her—right now, in fact—if I can get some privacy."

"Nope."

Her smile withered into a scowl. "Copeland."

He stood there, handsome and obnoxious, arms crossed over his chest. "I'll stay out of the shot. You don't have to tell her I'm here, unless you want to. But you have to tell her everything else. And if you recall the deal—"

"Twenty-four seven. Yeah, yeah, yeah." How was she going to get around this now? She'd figure out something. She was quick on her feet, and surely Copeland understood the concept of leaving out a few details.

She pulled up the video-conferencing app and clicked Rosalie's name. Rosalie answered after only a few rings, her face popping up on the screen. She was framed by a pretty window with a bunch of buildings in the background. On the other side of the world.

It was so weird. Their whole lives since Rosalie had been born, they'd lived in the same house, been in each other's pockets, and then Rosalie had moved out last year and now she did things like jet off to Europe.

Audra knew some people probably thought she was jealous, but she wasn't. She didn't want to leave or go anywhere. But she was *so glad* Rosalie, with all her restless energy, was doing it. Especially with a husband who appreciated her just the way she was.

If there *was* jealousy, it was maybe there, in the doting partner, but Audra wasn't about to think about that with Copeland staring at her from across the room.

"Well, look at you, Ms. Italy," she greeted, forcing herself to smile.

Rosalie grinned. "It's probably sacrilege to say while I'm here, but I think you'd hate it."

Audra laughed in spite of herself. For all the different regrets she might have had about her life up to this point, staying put was never one of them. Even with danger swirling, this was the only place she wanted to be.

But Rosalie's smile faded. "What's wrong, Aud?" Rosalie asked, concern in her tone. "That's your fake smile. Stiff and weird. Which is concerning since Natalie and Norman had very similar smiles when we talked to them the other day. Everything's okay, right? With Vi and—"

"Vi's perfect and so is Fox. This isn't about them. Or Franny. Or anyone really. There's just some…issues with the ranch. I asked Natalie and Norman not to worry you about it. I'm handling it."

"You always do." But Rosalie was frowning. "What kind of problems?"

"You don't need to worry."

"I didn't ask if I needed to worry. And if you tell me what

kind of problems, I won't. Because I know you can handle it. If you won't tell me, that makes me think it's more than just the ranch."

"It's not. It's just…a few odd things. The power went out. We had some fence damage. A little fire in the shed."

Rosalie's forehead scrunched up. "That's a lot of odd things. How did a fire start in the shed?"

"Well, they're still trying to figure that out," Audra hedged.

"Who's they? Did they put the fire inspector on it? That means someone set it. Did someone set a fire in the shed? Who would do that? What's going on?" Rapid-fire demands. Exactly what Audra had wanted to avoid.

But she didn't scowl. She didn't let her frustration shine through. She smiled placidly and spoke calmly in return.

"Rosalie. It's fine. I'm sure they'll come back with some reasonable explanation." She was so deep in her lie she forgot Copeland was there. Until he said her name.

She glared at Copeland, but he looked wholly unrepentant.

"Who's that?" Rosalie demanded, bringing Audra's focus back to the screen.

"Uh." Audra looked to Copeland, feeling helpless and stupid. If Rosalie knew Copeland was staying here…

"Tell her or I do," he said with absolutely no softness or give.

"Alright. I'm getting freaked out, Audra. Who the hell is that *guy* and—"

"It's Copeland," Audra said flatly, trying to keep her sheer fury at him out of her tone. "The fire was set by someone. Hawk Steele is looking into it. All the other problems we've had here are *small* and *petty*, but someone is doing them, and Copeland is investigating."

Rosalie's expression was *all* worry now. "You've got a detective and a fire inspector investigating these so-called odd things. That's not *odd*, Audra. It's threatening and dangerous. How long has this been going on?"

She was going to lie. It would have been so easy to lie, but Copeland was glaring at her and he was going to undercut the lie if she told it, which would make things worse. Damn him.

"Just…a few weeks."

"So the *whole* time we've been gone? Oh my God. We're coming home."

"Rosalie, no."

"I'm ready to come home. I miss everybody, and I want a whiff of Fox before he doesn't smell like newborn anymore. This is a better reason than me just being whiny and homesick. We're coming home."

Audra blinked back tears. What a failure this was. "I wish you wouldn't."

Rosalie fixed her with a stern expression through the computer. "I've had a three-week tour of Europe with my exceptionally hot husband. Who can certainly afford to change our plans. Feeling guilty I didn't get the last week is stupid and insulting. Where's Franny? I want to talk to her too."

"I… She's in Washington."

Rosalie's expression went to furious. "Damn it, Audra. Tell Franny about this. You shouldn't be alone when someone is… I don't know what this is. Petty pranks? Except it's causing damages. You cannot be alone. Go stay with Norman and Natalie."

"No."

"Audra."

"Rosalie, I'm not here alone. I have everything handled, like I always do. I have involved any authority who needs to be involved, and nothing bad has happened to me. I'm not in any *danger*. It's just…something. The right people are looking in to it, and I am fine."

"If you're not alone, who's staying with you?"

When Audra didn't answer right away, Rosalie's eyebrows went up and she leaned forward. "This is serious enough that you've got the police staked out at the ranch?"

She couldn't let Rosalie think that, not that she wanted Rosalie to think other things. She just… Oh, she hated Copeland for putting her in this situation. "That's not exactly it."

"What exactly could it…" Rosalie trailed off, her eyebrows still drawn together in a confused kind of expression. Then she leaned even closer to the screen, lowered her voice to a whisper.

"You and Copeland?"

Audra flicked a glance at him over the screen. He was in the same exact position. And she felt…a million conflicting things.

"No. Yes. Sort of." She shook her head, irritated she was so mixed-up. "I can't have this conversation with you while he's glaring at me from across the room."

"Copeland Beckett, if you hurt my sister, I'll gut you like a fish," Rosalie shouted, as if he couldn't hear everything that was going on anyway.

Copeland sighed, walked over and took a seat next to Audra so he was in the frame. "Don't worry, she's bound and determined to hurt herself before anyone else gets a chance."

Rosalie scowled. "Sounds about right. We're on our way home. You both better be in one piece when we get back."

"It's a promise," Copeland said, all cop seriousness. But the hand he put over hers on the couch wasn't *cop* at all.

Audra didn't know how she could be so bone-deep angry

at him…and still want to lean into that touch and him and believe his promise held weight.

When she knew exactly what believing did.

COPELAND SAT ON the couch, waiting for Audra to yell at him once she'd carefully closed the laptop after saying goodbye to Rosalie.

But she only sighed. "Well, I hope you're happy," she muttered, pushing to her feet.

Copeland's gaze followed her, but he didn't get off the couch. He didn't know what part of the conversation she was referring to, but it didn't matter. "I am."

She didn't say anything. Didn't lay into him. She just got that very prim, cool look about her. "I suppose we should eat some lunch."

It reminded him of last year, when Rosalie had been in the hospital getting stitched up and he'd gone in to give her an apology. Audra had watched him like he was the gum she'd scraped off her shoe.

It didn't bother him if she looked down at him in this moment. He'd done what was right, and if she wanted to get all prissy about it, that was her choice.

But he saw the anger flashing in her eyes that she was trying to hide. So he leaned back on the couch, crossed his arms behind his head, adopted his best dispassionate tone.

"You can tell me how you feel about it. It won't change anything, but a good yell or tantrum might make you feel better."

She blinked once, a flicker of her anger deep in her eyes before she iced it away. "Tantrum," she echoed.

"You can call it a lecture if it'd make you feel better."

"Nothing is going to make me feel better, Copeland," she said, every word bitten off with that ice, but underneath it was all flickering flame. "My sister is canceling her honeymoon over a few silly pranks."

"No, your sister is ending her month-long honeymoon a *little* early, because you, or this ranch that you won't leave, is under a credible and dangerous threat. If you want to turn that into some grand sacrifice on her part, that doesn't make it what's really happening."

She shook her head. "You don't understand, and you don't care that you don't. It's just 'I'm Copeland Beckett and I know everything.'"

If he knew everything, she'd be out of this mess. If he knew everything, he wouldn't be jumbled up in her life. If he knew *everything*, things here would be a lot different. But he didn't say that.

She whirled away from him. "I'm so angry with you right now. Screw your twenty-four seven. You've crossed every line. Pushed every boundary."

Some of his detachment was starting to fade. He tried to fight back the anger because it wouldn't get through to her. It would just end up with them fighting, but damn, she pushed at all his buttons. So he stood, in an effort to channel his frustration into his body rather than lash out.

"Someone has to." Okay, maybe he was going to lash out, anyway. "Your lines and your boundaries suck." He wasn't handling this right. It didn't take a rocket scientist to know that, but he was pissed too. And she wasn't walking away from him while she was in danger, whether either of them liked it or not.

She whirled back around, hands curled into fists, eyes flashing with fury. "I beg your—"

"You built those boundaries to keep everyone out, so you couldn't be disappointed? So you could control everything? Spoiler alert. Both are part of life."

She fisted those hands on her hips. "Thank you for those wise words and a lesson I wouldn't have been able to fathom on my own. I've certainly never been disappointed or had all my control stripped from me."

"Get snarky all you want. You know I'm right. Rosalie knows I'm right. Franny and Vi and everyone else would side with *me*, if they knew, but they're too indebted to you to raise a stink about it. Me? I don't owe you a damn thing. You could have kept putting it off, but you know as well as I do, it wouldn't have gone away. You'd have to have told her all about it anyway, and you'd feel the same."

"Not if it was handled and over."

"Okay, how about this? Rosalie would have felt the same sense of betrayal, if not a little worse, if she came home to you having handled all this on your own without telling her. That what you're going for?"

"No. You're being a jerk."

"Kinda my MO."

Her shoulders slumped, her eyes closed, as if she was in pain. She shook her head. "No, it isn't. You only wish it was."

Ouch. Still, she could get her licks in and it didn't change anything.

She opened her eyes, fixed him with one of those lost gazes that just about scraped his insides raw.

"This is how I get through it, Copeland. All my life. This is how I function. You cannot just sweep in and try to change it. This is who I am."

She must not have realized how absolutely beat-down she sounded. She must not have realized that her *get through* was sad, and it was making *her* sad. "Maybe it's gotten you through, Audra, but that's about it. It *isn't* who you are. Take it from someone who has spent the past few years just *functioning*. It's not the same as living."

She turned to face him. "Is that what we're doing?"

"You think a what-are-we conversation is going to send me running?"

She wrinkled her nose, some of her anger and sadness fading into something else. "At least temporarily."

"Tough. Yeah, we're living. I'd say we're both discovering something we haven't had in a while, or maybe at all."

She blinked at him once, straightened in that way she had that reminded him of a bird ruffling its feathers. She opened her mouth, but no words came out, so she closed it.

There was something about all this—the ways she thought she could send him running, the ways she clearly didn't expect *anyone* to stick around, stick it out, had him going further than he probably needed to.

"I care about you, Audra. Do I know what to do about it? Hell no. Am I going to run away like some kind of coward because of it while you're in *danger*? Double hell no. I'm going to protect you, from whatever's happening and your own stubborn pride. Deal with it."

This time when she blinked, he saw the telltale sign of tears in her eyes. But they didn't stay there, some fell over onto her cheeks. Like little daggers to his heart.

"And stop crying, damn it." He crossed to her. Brought her into his arms. "I can't take it," he muttered into her hair. "It just kills me."

"I never cry in front of anyone, so it's all your fault." She sniffled as she leaned into him. He felt the tension in her shoulders ease a little.

He ran a hand down her spine. His heart just *ached* when it came to her. And he didn't particularly care to think of the state of his heart, how he was twisting it up in someone that was part of a case he was working. He knew he was just *asking* for trouble that would come once this whole thing was settled.

But he couldn't stop himself. Maybe he didn't want to.

When his phone rang in his pocket, he muttered a curse, eased Audra away so he could answer it. "Beckett."

"Hey," Laurel said. He could hear the sound of her driving, so she must have him on Bluetooth. "Vicky's going to send you the details, but I just got another bit of a something. Not a lead exactly, not Florida, but it's interesting. One of the names of Audra's half siblings just popped up. He's been listed as a missing person out of Idaho. I don't know how it'd connect exactly, but I want us to look in to it."

Chapter Sixteen

Audra felt like she'd been through some kind of very strange gauntlet. She knew about gauntlets that were all bad. Gauntlets that were mostly good—like when Vi and Thomas had gotten married, or Rosalie and Duncan had. Gauntlets that were terrible—when Dad had died, when Vi had been kidnapped.

But this was a mix of everything. Failure and depression over drawing Rosalie into this. Dread over having to tell Franny. Anxiety that they had no answers. And twin feelings of joy and terror that Copeland had stood across the room and said: *I care about you.*

How? Why? Was he lying just to keep her safe, just to do his job?

No. That wasn't him. As hard as it was to understand why he would care about her, she knew he wouldn't say it without meaning it. Not Copeland.

He was still talking into his phone. She got the impression it was to someone from work, probably Laurel. When he hit End, then slid the phone into his pocket, he took a minute before he turned and looked at her.

"Interesting development. Do you know anything about Austin Young?"

Audra tried not to frown. "I know Austin is the name of

one of my half siblings." She thought back to what they'd learned after Dad had died, who she'd reached out to. "Not the youngest. The middle? I think he was in college when Dad died, but it wasn't a college I knew, so I don't remember the name. But he'd be out now, I'd think."

"He's been reported missing. He's been living in Idaho, but his sister, Karly, reported it from where she's living in Colorado. His mother and other siblings corroborated they hadn't heard from him, so the police did a welfare check. Boss hadn't seen him, friends hadn't seen him."

Audra tried to center herself with this new strange information. This Austin she shared half her DNA with but had never met had gone missing. "Karly. She's the oldest." Audra had reached out to Karly specifically, because they were almost exactly the same age.

There had been no response.

It didn't make sense that it might be connected. Idaho. Florida. "Do you think he…?"

"I'm not sure what to think yet, but there's something I want to cross off the possibility list." He studied her in a way that had her feeling wary. It was a *cop* study, like she was simply a piece of evidence to be slotted into place.

She didn't care for it, but a lot of it softened as he reached out, put those big hands on her shoulders. "Audra, I've got a big ask."

"Oh, an *ask*. How novel to not be *told*."

He didn't smirk or laugh or do anything else, which had dread curling in Audra's stomach. This was serious.

He held her gaze, and there was something warm and empathetic in his eyes, which made the dread dig deeper.

"I want you to call your mom."

Audra didn't allow herself to immediately react. She

stayed very still, kept her expression frozen, until she could work through all the reactions inside of her.

"For the case," she said, very carefully.

"Yes. I want you to have a mostly normal conversation, but then I want you to ask if she knows someone."

"You think Austin missing connects…to my mother?"

"It could. She could. It more likely doesn't, but I don't want to leave that stone unturned. Something is coming out of Florida, where your mother is. Someone I was looking into went missing around the time all this started. I want to make sure those are two separate things."

Audra swallowed. "She wouldn't have anything to do with my father's other kids. She won't even…"

"Have anything to do with her own?" he asked, finishing gently for her.

She couldn't hold his gaze, and even she knew the little shrug she'd meant to be casual was nothing but jerky under his hands. "Yeah."

"Categorically her loss, Audra. But you know that."

Did she? She wanted to know it, but sometimes… Sometimes it all just felt like she'd been rejected over and over and over again by everyone.

Not Rosalie. Not Franny. Not Vi or Magnolia. Not… Copeland.

Not yet, anyway.

She shook away that thought. "I could call her. I will, if that's what you need for the case, but we don't usually talk. There'd be no reason for me to call her up, unless I tell her I think she's the one terrorizing the ranch and I don't think that's going to go over well."

Copeland shrugged. "Tell her you want her to come up. Meet your new boyfriend."

She wrinkled her nose. "*Boyfriend*. That makes us sound

like teenagers." Not that he'd said *he* was the boyfriend. It was just a conceit.

"You got a better word?" he asked, like…

"No." *Boyfriend.* But Copeland wasn't that. He was…

He wasn't saying they were though. He was saying to tell her mother they were as an excuse.

"She wouldn't even come for Rosalie's wedding. Why would I think she'd come to meet a boyfriend?"

"Just pretend you live in eternal hope she'll change her mind."

Audra knew her mother never would, but…"What if she says yes?"

"What if she does? I can meet your crappy mom, Audra. I'd even be on my best behavior. Mostly."

Audra didn't have the slightest clue what to say to that. To making it feel like a real thing when it wasn't. It was all too muddled and confused. Pointless to think about. Mom wouldn't come. She didn't have any connection to Austin.

But Copeland's hands were still on her shoulders. He gave them a squeeze. "The word *boyfriend* doesn't bother me. I don't shake easy, Audra. Not once I'm dug in. And I'm getting pretty damn dug in."

She wanted to cry again, but it was getting ridiculous. The whole thing was ridiculous and… *Dug in.* She didn't know how. Couldn't understand *how.* But she supposed, as much as it terrified her, he deserved a little of the same certainty.

"Me too."

"Good." He squeezed her shoulders one last time. "Let's call your mom."

HE DIDN'T LIKE this version of her. The hurt version. The woman who'd been failed by too many people who should have loved her unconditionally. Watching a woman as caring and sweet as Audra dread calling her own mother twisted his guts into knots.

But this had to be done. He had her put the phone on speaker before she dialed her mother.

"She might not answer," Audra said as it began to ring. She kept her gaze on the phone sitting on the table, clearly hoping for that eventuality.

"Then leave her a message to call you back."

"She might not—"

The ringing stopped and a woman's voice scratched out from the phone receiver. "Audra."

"Mom. Hi."

"Is everything alright?"

"Yeah, of course. I just… It's been a while. I wanted to check up on you."

There was a beat of silence. Copeland could almost *hear* the suspicion in it. "Well, I suppose it's about time."

Audra linked her hands together. Her head was bowed, no doubt to hide the misery on her face, but he didn't need to see her expression to know this was a misery to her.

"Rosalie's wedding was beautiful. Did you get the pictures I sent?"

There was a kind of sniffing noise. "Easy to be beautiful when your husband is loaded," she said bitterly. "But you know, I'm seeing someone myself."

It was petty and superficial. Childish, really. Copeland couldn't believe the woman on the other line was a mother, let alone the mother of adult children. Once this case was over, he was going to send his mother flowers as a thank-you.

"I suppose Rosalie thinks she wins with a baseball player

and his boatload of money, but my Isaac? He's a burgeon-ing artist. He's going to make such a splash."

"Oh, that's…great, Mom."

"It is," the woman said firmly, but Copeland's mind was whirling.

He'd been looking in to all of Audra's half siblings, so he knew bits and pieces about them. Like that Austin worked at an art gallery in Boise and was attempting to become an artist himself.

A coincidence. It *could* be, but what kind of insane co-incidence was that?

"Is there anything else, Audra? I am very busy."

"Oh. No, I guess not. I just…heard recently that one of my half siblings has gone missing. Austin. He's the middle one I think and—"

"I can't believe you'd even utter that name to me."

"I'm sorry," Audra said, in what was clearly an automatic, knee-jerk apology. "It's just…upsetting and made me think of you. Worry about you."

"And you think I'd care about *that*? After all the *upset-ting* your father put me through? With that *other family*? Honestly, Audra, what *are* you thinking?"

"I suppose I wasn't. I'm sorry." She pushed a finger into the corner of her eye, like a headache was drumming there, and Copeland had the acute stab of guilt that he was put-ting her through this.

But *art* and Florida suddenly had a connection, and they wouldn't have stumbled upon it without this little foray into the heart of Audra's pain.

"I have to go. This has been *very* upsetting. Next time you call, I don't want any topic that even remotely connects to your father. Do you understand me?"

"Yes, ma'am."

"After what he did. After... Oh, I'm so worked up now. That's what I get for taking a call from you. There is no reason to call me again unless it's *actually* important, Audra. And you can tell that to your sister too. Goodbye."

"'Bye, Mom." But it was clear the connection had ended before she'd even gotten the goodbye out.

Copeland fought the urge to bundle her up and just hold on until this all went away. But it wasn't going away, and they had to get to the bottom of this more than deal with her completely understandable issues.

He'd send his mother two bouquets of flowers.

"Well, no need to use the boyfriend excuse," Audra said. She sounded very much herself, but he could see the way she chose each word carefully. The way she held herself just so, as if she was still enough the pain couldn't get through. "She was too busy bragging about hers." Audra sighed deeply, closing her eyes and leaning her head on the back of the couch. "She doesn't know Austin, Copeland. You heard how she reacted. She's not connected. She can't be."

"Do you know what your half brother does for a living?"

"Huh?" She opened her eyes, looked at him in confusion. "No. I don't..."

"He works at an art gallery in Boise. And does some of his own painting on the side with a clear desire to make it to the big time."

"That's..."

"A pretty big coincidence."

Chapter Seventeen

Even though he had leads to follow, Copeland didn't insist she stay put, like Audra expected. After they ate lunch, he insisted on doing her chores with her. Well, after she'd ripped off the Band-Aid and called Franny too.

No doubt by tomorrow she'd have a full house again. Would Copeland stay? Did she want him to?

Questions she didn't want to ponder right now. They had stalls to muck, and she really wanted to tell him he didn't need to help. She *really* wanted to tell him she could handle this. She just had to find a way to explain it to him in a way that didn't sound like martyring herself.

"If something comes up that you need to handle—"

"Relax, Audra. Laurel will handle it," he told her as they shrugged their jackets on. She'd scrounged up some very old work boots of her dad's in the stables and he was using those when they were out on the ranch.

"She's got Austin's information, the name Isaac and your mother's whereabouts to go off of," he continued, stepping outside with her. "I'll look in to what I can later, once we're done with this, but if we're going through all the work of staying put, you might as well get your work done."

Audra didn't know what to say to that, because it made her feel guilty, but she also realized Copeland wasn't *try-*

ing to. Which meant the guilt was her own doing, and she didn't love that realization.

They walked over to the stables in quiet. If she kept taking the ibuprofen at the correct intervals, her ankle mostly didn't bother her, which was a relief. Copeland barely even bugged her about it now.

Audra knew Copeland wore a gun, knew the way he walked, looked around, was all in that *cop* manner. Looking for threats. Looking for clues. But when they came to a stop at the stables, and she unlocked the padlock that kept the doors shut, she turned back to see him gazing out at the horizon. It wasn't the first time she'd seen him look out at it like that.

Not coplike. Not detached. Not seeking out a threat. But just…a soft kind of appreciation of the beauty all around them. Like he enjoyed it here. Could find some kind of belonging here.

Which was ridiculous, of course, and her fairy-tale heart complicating things just like it always did. Best to nip that in the bud.

She opened the doors, gestured him inside and went to gather the tools. She handed him his shovel, met his gaze with clear, determined eyes of her own.

"I'm sure Rosalie and Duncan will insist on staying here once they're back, even though they shouldn't. Add Franny and it's a full house. You won't have to stay here. I'll have help and constant babysitting."

He didn't say anything at first, just took the tool and turned to the first stall. After a few stretched-out moments, all he said was "We'll see."

Audra didn't know what the hell to do with that. So they worked in silence, cleaning up the stalls, brushing down the horses.

With her truck still out of commission—something she wished she'd taken care of or could get taken care of before Rosalie got back, but too late now—she'd need to take the horses to go back on a windbreak on the far corner of the property. It looked a little weak the last time she'd been up that way. She also needed to check on a few of the cows and make sure they weren't getting too thin with all this bitter cold. She'd need to do some separating soon if there wasn't a change there.

Lots to do, always, but the stall cleaning went quickly with Copeland's help. Once they were done, Audra surveyed his work. "You're not so bad at mucking stalls."

He grinned at her. "It's not such a bad chore. Kinda nice to do something physical outside of a gym. The horses might even be growing on me."

"Well, good, because we're going for a little ride to check on some things."

He agreed easily, helped her with saddling them up. He seemed interested to learn, not just help, which Audra didn't know what to do with. Rosalie helped with the ranch a lot, didn't require any teaching, but there was no love there. No *interest*. It was a duty and duty only for her.

Franny offered to help, but her head was in the clouds and it was usually easier for Audra to handle it herself and let Franny tackle any household tasks she felt necessary.

Sometimes Norman or a hand from the Kirk Ranch came over and helped, but Audra always made sure she returned the favor. She wouldn't let herself grow debts that made people resentful, like her parents had.

So she didn't know what to do with Copeland's interest, pleasant attitude, or aptitude for the chores and the riding. Except take things one step at a time.

They rode out to the windbreak, and as Audra suspected,

part of it had fallen over. She'd need to nail some boards back into place. She gave Copeland a few instructions, hauled her tools out of her saddlebag and then got to work.

It would have been nearly impossible to do on her own. She probably would have been forced to call Norman. Then she'd have felt she owed him a favor, and that would have sat like an uncomfortable debt there in her brain.

Almost like you're your own problem, Audra.

But what if she couldn't handle it all? Everything would fall apart. She'd been holding everything together for as long as she could remember. She was the glue, the foundation. Without her...

She rubbed at her chest. It was getting tight, and while she wasn't *prone* to them, sometimes when things were especially stressful, she suffered a panic attack or two. But she handled it. She always handled it. And no one knew, because she handled it.

But Copeland was right there, and she knew he sensed something was wrong when his arm came around her shoulders.

She breathed carefully, kept her expression as neutral as possible. When she trusted her voice, she gestured at the windbreak. "We do good work."

"Yeah. And this really helps the cows stay warm?"

She nodded, some of the tightness in her chest easing. "Yep. Next up, we've got to check on a few of them. If they get too thin, they'll have to be separated so I can ensure they're eating and can give them some winter supplements."

"And if this was some random winter, with no threats, you'd just be handling all of this on your own."

"I have help."

"When and if you take it. Big *whens*. Big *ifs*."

She wanted to get away from him, but his arm was holding her in place. She squinted at the mountains in the distance. She couldn't put into words the *need* to do all that. It came from a place too deep to fully verbalize.

And if she tried to tell him, it felt like it would uproot the strength of purpose that kept her going.

"I have no doubt a lot of people around you know this, that maybe even tell you this, and you probably don't listen to them, and you probably won't listen to me, but it's impressive what you do, what you handle. All on your own."

It was just the kind of compliment that should have touched her. Instead, it made her want to shrug away the words. Pushing every boundary, just like she'd accused him of earlier.

"Would it kill you to take a compliment, Audra?"

God, sometimes it felt like it might.

"I know they did a number on you, but it doesn't have to keep doing the same number."

"He says, from experience," she grumbled, only half-irritated. Because it was true. Both what he said, and where he'd come up with it. They weren't trite words. It was his own experience.

Someone had done a number on him, and he'd changed his whole life rather than live in the bowels of that.

"I'm getting there, I think." His arm stayed around her, that comforting warmth, this unknown glow of being able to let go, let someone else handle something when none of her usual get-arounds worked.

Because Rosalie was tenacious and demanding and sometimes managed to wheedle Audra into accepting some help, some credit, but mostly—because she'd grown up with Rosalie and knew all her tender points—she knew how to move around her sister.

She didn't know how to move around Copeland. Not

when he was poking into things that were about *her*, not the case. *Life*, not threats.

"You could get there with me, Audra," he said, very carefully. "All it takes is a little leaning."

She laughed, knew it was bitter-sounding. "Is that all? Because every time I've let myself lean, I've fallen flat on my face."

"You won't with me."

The worst part was she believed him, even when she knew she shouldn't.

THEY FINISHED HER CHORES, and while Copeland was eager to get back to the case, to find some answers for her, he'd also enjoyed himself in a weird way. There was something different about doing a lot of physical labor and seeing your efforts have physical manifestations. So much of his own work was nebulous. Sure, he solved mysteries, helped people out of danger, but then it was left up to the mess of the judicial system.

The only thing that could undo the windbreak was Mother Nature.

He glanced at Audra as they walked from the stables to the house. Speaking of things that needed an act of nature to move.

She needed a push, and it wasn't coming from the people she'd learned to fool with her walls and boundaries.

So it was going to have to be him.

Something he'd think about later, when there wasn't a strange car in Audra's drive.

He stopped her progress, situated himself in front of her. Rested his hand on his weapon. "You recognize that car?"

"No."

A woman got out of the driver's seat. Copeland gestured

for Audra to stay put, and he did the same, watching as the woman crossed the yard with purposeful strides.

"Hello. I'm looking for Detective Beckett."

"You found him."

The woman smiled, and there was something about the eyes, almost the same shade as Rosalie's, that had him more wary than the sudden appearance of a stranger. She held out a hand as she approached, offered a firm handshake. Cop or military, he was almost certain.

"My name is Karly Young. It was brought to my attention that you've been looking in to my brother."

Definitely the same blue eyes. He glanced back at Audra. She looked a little pale. But she stood there, strong as ever, ready to face something she shouldn't have to face.

"Bent County is a bit of a hoof from Schriever." He'd looked into all the half siblings, so he knew Karly *was* military, currently working at a Space Force base in Colorado. He wanted her to know that he'd looked in to her as well as her brother. Maybe this was innocent, but he wanted her to know he wasn't caught unaware.

"I suppose it is, but I'm desperate to find my brother. You were looking in to him before he was reported missing."

Copeland studied her. "Where'd you hear that?"

She smiled, maybe a little ruefully. "I know people. I want to know your connection."

Copeland gestured at the house behind him. "You really going to pretend like you don't know the connection?"

Karly's expression hardened. Copeland noted she had expressly not looked in Audra's direction.

But Audra clearly couldn't resist. "It's cold," she said from behind him. "You should both come inside and have this discussion."

The woman—*Karly*—looked at the house. She did not look at Audra. "No. Thank you." The words were clipped. Icy.

Hurt crossed over Audra's face, and it made him want to be difficult with Karly for the sake of it, but that wouldn't get them answers.

He weighed his questions, his next moves. Decided being forthright without explanation was the best course of action. "What connection does Austin have to Florida?"

Karly frowned. "None."

He could have played along, but he was tired of Audra living in a world of nonanswers, so he didn't even play that game. "That isn't true, and I know it. So you can either give me the truth, or you can leave."

He watched the woman's face. Hints of Audra, but something harder and sharper. Angrier. There was a deep-seated bitterness there that even when Audra found some bitterness within her, didn't twist like this.

Copeland found his hand creeping back up to his gun. There was something about this woman he didn't trust.

But some of that softened. Not into anything *soft*, but something far more resigned. Karly looked back at her rental car, shook her head.

"Some internet girlfriend. He'd talked about visiting her in Fort Myers. Honestly, the first day he was missing, I figured that's what he'd done. But I can't find any evidence he went to Florida." Everything in her expression went hard again. "I want to know where my brother is."

"So do I," Copeland returned. "Would your brother have any reason to want to harm this place?"

"Of course not." But Karly's gaze looked at the boarded-up house windows. The plastic-wrapped truck windows. "You've had trouble."

Copeland could have corrected her. Pointed out it was

Audra's trouble, not his. But it felt a little too tenuous. So he kept talking to Karly like Audra wasn't there, even though he knew it hurt all of them. "Lots of it. Coming from someone who has connections to Florida." Something occurred to Copeland then. Maybe Karly didn't know what her brother was up to, but she had the background.

"When your dad was alive, did he give your brother any reason to think this ranch was his?"

She snapped right back up—all bristle and offense instead of any hint of exhaustion or defeat. "I don't have to answer these questions. I came looking for my brother, and I want to know why you were looking in to him before he disappeared."

"You're looking at it," he said, pointing at the boarded-up windows.

"Then you're a really bad detective," Karly snapped, then turned on a heel and headed back toward her car.

Chapter Eighteen

Audra didn't think. She just acted. Because she'd never been this physically close to anyone from her dad's other family. Every overture she'd made since he died had been met with refusals or silence.

But Karly was here now. *Here*. And Audra wasn't about to let that go. She followed her, pulling away from Copeland's attempt to stop her. She moved between Karly and the car so Karly couldn't get in and speed away without some kind of altercation.

"We're sisters," Audra said firmly.

But Karly appeared wholly unmoved by the word. "All you are to me is a reminder my dad wasn't who he was supposed to be. I don't need that in my life. Sorry."

She didn't sound sorry, and maybe that's what had Audra's temper straining. Or maybe she was emboldened by the fact that Copeland stood back, didn't try and interfere or step in now.

"He wasn't who he was supposed to be to us, either. You aren't special or unique. We're all in the same Tim Young shipwreck."

"Maybe. We want to use that metaphor? My brother is lost at sea, so I've got more pressing concerns than someone else's wreck." Karly looked her up and down, like Audra was the center and cause of everything their father had done. It sent a cold chill through Audra.

"I'm sorry," Audra said, and she meant it. As frustrating as this was, she understood more than anyone what it was like to be her—*their*—father's victim. "I'd like to help."

Karly shook her head. "I didn't come here for help."

"Then what *did* you come here for?"

Karly's eyes darted to the house behind them. The broken windows. Audra couldn't read the expression, but it wasn't *neutral*.

"You knew this existed," Audra said, striving to keep her voice even. "I invited you all here. I wanted… I wanted us to see if we could be a family."

Karly snorted bitterly. "Benevolent of you."

Audra shook her head. "No. I was trying to find some way to mitigate the grief of losing him twice. The finality of *death*, and the death of the man I thought he was. Which wasn't all that great. I wasn't under any illusion he was great. He was selfish. He was careless. He was so many crappy things, and caused me a lot of pain and strife, even before I knew he had a whole other family." The next words stuck in her throat. She didn't want to admit them, but she saw Karly's stonewall expression and knew the only way through was to find some common ground. "And I still loved him."

Maybe Audra was taking it too far, but in the grand scheme of things, couldn't Karly see that the man between them was the enemy? The man who'd put them both in this position and got to die rather than deal with any of the fallout.

Karly swallowed. Hard. The anger, the bitterness, the sharp edges didn't dull, but something in her…slumped.

"Okay, yeah. Maybe Dad talked about his ancestral home." Karly scowled at the house, encompassed it in one dismissive gesture. "Weaved big, tall tales about the Wyoming ranching life. How someday, it'd all be ours." Her hard blue gaze turned to Audra. "I didn't buy it then."

Audra inhaled sharply, because the implication was clear. "But Austin did."

There was a war playing out on Karly's face. A face that had little hints of Dad in it—the sharp chin, the blue of her eyes Audra often saw in her own reflection. Little things that reminded Audra of Rosalie—the way her mouth turned down in anger, the arch of an eyebrow.

Audra didn't know how the word *sisters* couldn't mean anything to her.

"If Austin did this," Karly said in almost a whisper, "I'm sorry. Dad's death hit him hard. He's…" She blew out a breath. "He's spoiled. Only boy."

Audra supposed she should have some sympathy since Dad's death—or the secrets that had uncovered—had hit them *all* hard, but…maybe that was why she couldn't work up any. "Only boy on both sides."

Karly's eyes fixed on hers, hard and cold. "I don't want there to be sides. I don't want you to exist."

"I guess that's too bad, because I do."

"Not to me." And with that, Karly sidestepped her and opened her car door. Audra didn't know what else to do but let her.

It wasn't a confession exactly, but it certainly added to the idea that Austin might be behind this. Ancestral homes. Ties to Florida…and yes, Mom lived in Fort Myers because of course she did. Spoiled men ruining the lives of the women around them.

Audra refused to let her life be ruined, even if it felt

a bit like her heart was breaking all over again as Karly drove away.

Copeland came up behind her, put his hand over her shoulder and gave it a comforting squeeze. He didn't say anything. Didn't offer any trite words. Didn't try to make it okay. He just stood there behind her, like some kind of… pillar.

She didn't let herself have any pillars that weren't her own two feet anymore. He was making that hard. He was making it seem like for once, for *once*, she really could depend on someone without losing her own sense of self.

Which was scarier than everything going on with Karly and Austin, so she focused on her half siblings rather than everything she was feeling for Copeland.

"I'm glad, in a way," she said to him, even as she still watched where Karly's car had disappeared. "To meet her finally. I never could understand their point of view when it was just a refusal to talk to us. I still don't fully grasp it. Ignoring something doesn't change it. But at least I see that's what they're doing. If they pretend Rosalie and I don't exist, they can pretend he wasn't what he was."

"They're not doing that great of a job of pretending though, are they?"

Audra shook her head. This visit hadn't made much sense, but she tried to put herself in Karly's shoes. What if Rosalie wanted to do something stupid? What if she wanted to hurt the other siblings in some way? Would Audra have been able to stop her?

No.

Would she have excused her?

Audra didn't *love* the fact she would have. She would have done anything to protect Rosalie from mistakes born of her own grief. Which told Audra everything she needed to know about Karly and this visit.

She turned to face Copeland, met his gaze with her certainty.

"She came all the way here, this place she doesn't want to exist, not for me. Not even *about* me. She came because she thought *you'd* be a lead to him since you'd tried to investigate him."

Copeland's response was measured. "Maybe."

"But I don't think she's worried about his safety, or the fact he's missing," Audra continued. "She's worried about what he's going to *do*."

"Or what he's already done," Copeland said darkly. His expression was as hard as his words and Audra hugged herself against all the *cold* she felt.

"Why… It still doesn't make any sense. I reached out. I tried to… I would have invited them in. I would have… shared just about anything." Emotion hitched in her chest, but she'd be damned if she was going to cry again. "And why is my *mother* involved, however unwittingly?"

He reached out again, pulled her into him. He was always doing that. Offering a hand, a squeeze, a hug. She had never considered herself a particularly physical person—it wasn't how she or Rosalie were raised, and while they might hug on occasion, while they were *easy* together, it wasn't like this.

Because you never let yourself lean, Audra.

And she knew she shouldn't. There was a deep-seated knowledge this was wrong, but there was something new undermining it. She hadn't meant to let him in, hadn't meant to trust him, fall for him. She knew it was a bad, *bad* idea, but she couldn't seem to help it.

Because he held her close, smoothed a hand down her spine. And she knew she was safe here, even if she tried to convince herself she couldn't lean on anyone outside her tiny little circle.

"We're going to get to the bottom of it," he said firmly. He pulled her back, but only enough so he could look into her eyes. "Whether she's covering for him or something else, she made a tactical error. She came here. She gave us something to go on. And we're going to go on it."

He was so certain. So determined to press that certainty upon her. So good at being there, no matter how she tried to convince him he didn't need to be.

She knew she shouldn't. She knew she would regret this. Leaning. Trusting.

Loving.

But it was already there. So she moved forward, onto her toes, pressed her mouth gently to his. "Thanks," she murmured, against his mouth.

He held her close, kissed her again before tucking her head under his chin. "Anytime."

THEY WENT IN and ate dinner. Copeland sent an email to Laurel, updating her on everything and requesting more background information on Karly Young.

It felt clear Austin was the threat, but there was something about the woman and her visit here that just didn't settle right. He needed to know about her, just as much as he needed to track down Austin Young.

It was a gut feeling, and Copeland always trusted his gut. Occasionally, it led him astray, but no investigation was so straightforward a detective didn't take some wrong turns along the way. It wasn't about doing everything *right*. It was about knowing how to recalibrate if you went a little wrong.

After dinner, Copeland decided Audra needed a little bit

of a breather from *everything*. Maybe it was a selfish decision, but he'd never claimed to be anything else.

He talked her into the shower, together, and loved that he was able to make her laugh—and tremble—as the specter of everything haunting them was pushed away for a little while. They curled into her lumpy bed together—she really needed to take better care of herself—and slept.

Copeland woke with a start to the sound of someone in the house. In less than a second, he had his gun in his hand and was out of the bed. Audra had barely stirred when someone shouted from out in the hallway.

"Audra!" It was Rosalie's voice, immediately followed by the bedroom door slamming open. Copeland breathed through the moment of panic and the thought that if Rosalie hadn't *yelled* before she'd opened the door, he might have shot her.

Rosalie made a distressed sort of noise, threw her hand over her eyes. "Oh my *God*. Gross."

Fighting his own embarrassment, the mix of relief and terror coursing through him at being awakened so suddenly, Copeland surreptitiously slid the gun back onto the nightstand shelf, where Rosalie wouldn't be able to see it and worry even more.

Maybe Audra *had* rubbed off on him.

He picked up his pants and pulled them up. Audra was scurrying out of bed now while he collected his shirt and pulled it on.

"Rosalie… How… You weren't supposed to be here until this afternoon."

"Yeah, well Duncan greased some wheels. We picked Franny up on our way too." She dropped her arm with some trepidation, and aimed a wrinkled-nose expression in Copeland's direction.

But Audra had already gone into full big-sister mode. Had he thought she wouldn't? She was moving toward Rosalie, arm outstretched. "Let's go downstairs. I'll put something together for breakfast. You and Duncan must be exhausted. You should head on home and rest."

Rosalie didn't budge. She stared at him over Audra's shoulder, like she could "gut him like a fish" with her mind.

He didn't wither. Did *she* think *he* would?

"Rosalie."

Rosalie finally looked from Copeland to Audra. "We're going to all go downstairs and talk this through," Rosalie said firmly. "And regardless of the outcome, just know Duncan and I are staying here until things are settled."

"Rosalie."

"Try to stop me," she replied firmly. Then hooked her arm with Audra's and sailed out of the room, dragging her sister along behind her.

Audra looked back at him a little helplessly, but he only shrugged. He didn't mind more bodies here. More help. Anything and everything that upped the odds of keeping Audra safe worked for him. Even if it was bound to be… awkward.

He could handle awkward.

Copeland followed them down at a safe distance. When he reached the bottom of the stairs, Franny had already engulfed Rosalie and Audra in a hug so that the three women held on to each other and swayed gently. They spoke in low, private tones. He didn't have to hear the words to know Rosalie was chastising Audra, and Audra was assuring Rosalie and Franny that everything was fine.

Copeland found himself…relieved. Maybe she was only giving them half truths, but here were two women who cared about her, who would *try* to take care of her. She wasn't as solitary and alone as she'd seemed this past week.

Had it only been a week? How had she upended everything inside of him in a few days? It didn't make any sense. He hadn't been looking to be upended.

But here he was.

He glanced at the man who came to stand next to him. Duncan Kirk surveyed him. Copeland had once watched this man play baseball on national TV. He'd always been a fan, though he'd never let Duncan know it. Especially when he'd been investigating the murder over at his parents' place last year.

So Copeland figured he deserved the clear lack of friendliness on Duncan's face.

"Beckett," he greeted, but coolly.

Copeland matched his tone. "Kirk."

"We've got everything under control," Audra said above Rosalie and Franny's demands. "The police are looking in to a few leads, and nothing violent or dangerous has really happened. It's all small, petty things."

Rosalie turned to face Copeland with a glare. "Is she telling the truth?"

Audra looked up at him helplessly, and no doubt his loyalty was to Audra, but he also knew what she wanted from him wasn't right.

"There's a lot of truth to what she's saying," he agreed. But he couldn't help the *full* truth. "She's also downplaying it."

Audra stiffened, aimed a glare at him. But he could only shrug. "You are. There haven't been any physical threats made to her, that's true, but they *are* threats all the same. And you never know when threats will go too far."

Rosalie looked angry. Franny looked distressed. And Audra got that detached queen-of-the-manor look about her.

"There's no need to worry—"

"There *is* need to worry," Copeland interrupted her, even though it earned him an icy glare. "But there's no need to panic. We've got leads. We've got strings to pull. Which is an improvement. That doesn't mean we can be careless…" He moved his gaze from Rosalie and Franny to Audra. "Or martyrs," he added firmly.

That chin came up, shoulders back. She was pissed, but there was no way to get through this without making her angry. He already bent as far as he could by not making her leave. Everyone here needed to know how serious the threat was.

"I'm going to make some breakfast," Audra said, turning on a heel and marching into the kitchen, Rosalie and Franny trailing after her with another round of questions.

Copeland made a move to follow, but Duncan stepped in his way.

"You know, it seems to me, Audra is surrounded by family now," Duncan said, his tone polite, but very, *very* firm. "I'm not sure she needs you hanging around here unless it's official police business."

Copeland thought about that. How it would be easiest, maybe even best, if he took a few steps back. He could put everything he had, everything he was, into getting to the bottom of Austin and Karly Young. He could give her the space she likely needed, deserved.

But he'd never be able to focus if she wasn't in his sight. He'd be worried, every second of every day, that something had happened. Someone had gotten through. Something had snapped.

And more, he understood that she knew how to manipulate all these players. Maybe it wasn't a fair word, but she'd *maneuver* Rosalie and Franny, convince them everything was alright when it wasn't. She couldn't do that to him. Maybe someday she'd be able to, but not yet.

So he shook his head, even though he appreciated that there was *someone* in this world who was protective of Audra. Besides him.

"She might not need me," Copeland agreed easily. He didn't look away or let any of his own personal discomfort over his feelings show. Because maybe he was making every kind of mistake, the kinds of mistakes he'd made before, but for Audra it just wasn't possible to step away. "But she's got me."

Chapter Nineteen

Audra's temper fizzled through breakfast. Because Copeland was very clearly not welcome, but he settled himself at the table and filled in everyone on what had happened in a very matter-of-fact police way that didn't leave much room for Rosalie or Franny to overreact too, *too* much.

And she knew that was by design, not accident. He was trying to *help*, even when he was doing what she expressly wished he wouldn't.

She didn't know how to fight him. He was too...reasonable. Too fair. And she didn't know how to stay angry with him when he did things like sit at the breakfast table with just about everyone she loved and weather their hostility like it didn't matter to him in the slightest.

Which was something he probably dealt with at work plenty. Not everyone liked the law poking around, and not everyone liked what a detective might find. She could sit here and try to convince herself that was all it was—work.

But it wasn't.

"Whether she wanted to or not, Karly made it pretty clear Austin is our culprit. Or could be. We're working on tracking him down, seeing if we can prove it," Copeland explained in patient cop tones. "There's a lot of anger and bitterness there, so it tracks."

"Wow, they're so unique," Rosalie muttered, stabbing at her eggs. "Bitterness. Anger. Over our SOB of a dad. Weird how I didn't think to take it out on the random kids we didn't know he had."

Those words settled into Audra differently, because hadn't she essentially said the same to Karly? They were the same. They were all victims of their father.

But the anger and bitterness she'd felt from Karly was geared toward *her*, toward the ranch. Not the situation. Not Tim Young.

With Rosalie back home, something about the entire interaction with Karly suddenly had a far more discordant note. Pretending someone didn't exist didn't mesh with anger. Anger was born of time and offense and hurt.

Then again, there'd been time—all these years—to nurture that hurt, so maybe it made sense, even if Audra didn't feel the same. Not everyone was going to react to betrayal in the same way.

But something was chewing at her, deep in the pit of her stomach. She'd make sense of it, but she needed...work. Cold air, animals, physical labor. Some alone time.

"I'd better get started on chores," Audra said, pushing back from the table. She wanted to clear the table, clean up after breakfast, but chores were more pressing and—

Duncan and Copeland stood, like they were some kind of partnered unit. Without even discussing it, they blocked her path.

"Duncan and I can handle it," Copeland said, like he spoke for *her* newly minted brother-in-law. And he must, because Duncan stood next to Copeland looking like just the same kind of brick wall.

"But—"

"Catch up with your family," Copeland said. *Ordered.* "And lock the door behind us."

She would have argued. She would have told him where to shove it, but he simply stepped forward, pressed a hard kiss to her mouth, then walked away, like that was that and he just got to…tell her what to do.

And kiss her in front of everyone.

She stood there, frozen with irritation and embarrassment and…something a lot warmer and nicer than those two things. But the darker emotions felt easier. Safer.

So why were the warmer, nicer ones winning?

"See?" Franny said, gesturing at Rosalie once the men were out of earshot.

Rosalie only scowled as she moved forward and locked the door.

"See what?" Audra demanded.

"You need someone bossy," Franny said with complete sincerity. "And hot. Copeland fits the bill."

"Bossy is obnoxious," Rosalie muttered before Audra could think of something to say.

They were moving around her. Everyone was taking over, and Audra simply didn't know what to do. It was like she was stuck in some vortex, some alternate reality, where she wasn't the one holding everything together.

"You say that because you're the bossy one in your relationship," Franny retorted as she began to clear the table.

Rosalie scoffed.

"Duncan's a marshmallow for you," Audra addeed with just a hint of wistfulness, unable to stop herself. Then she grabbed the rest of the dirty dishes and walked over to the sink. She wasn't going to be…helpless, frozen, *vortexed.* This was her life, her family, her ranch. She'd always been in charge of all those things.

Always.

"Oh, Duncan's plenty bossy." Rosalie wiggled her eyebrows until Franny and Audra were laughing, and it felt good. For her sister and cousin to be home. To be laughing.

But… She wasn't in control, and she didn't know what to do with that feeling. Except wrestling some of it back. She bumped Franny away from the sink. "You must be exhausted, rushing home. Why don't you go unpack and rest?"

"It was hardly a rush or a sacrifice. I can go back and visit my parents anytime, Audra." Franny bumped her right back out of the way. And then Rosalie slid in between them, like she was going to fight Audra off.

So Audra started in on her campaign to get Rosalie out of here. "I hope you know you don't have to stay here, and Duncan certainly doesn't need to help with my chores. Your house is just a stone's throw away. Franny's home and—"

"And you've got a detective cozied up in your bed?" Rosalie interrupted, arms crossed over her chest, expression somewhere between disapproving and assessing.

Audra wasn't sure what was going to happen now that everyone was back. She'd try to get Copeland to leave too. She'd have to convince him that she was well taken care of now, and he didn't need to be here twenty-four seven.

She didn't want to.

Which made saying the rest hard, but she'd swallow her pride if it got her sister living her very nice life over worrying about Audra's. "If it'll get you to go home and stop putting yourself out for me, he can stay here."

Rosalie rolled her eyes. "*He can stay here*, my butt. You couldn't get him out of here at gunpoint. Or you would have by now."

Audra opened her mouth to argue with Rosalie, but she couldn't find the words. Because she was a little too scared that she was letting her personal feelings for Copeland undermine all the strength she'd built up these past few years, which had been scary enough on its own, but with her family back it felt…dangerous.

Everything was flying out of control, and Audra needed to find a way to center it all, anchor it all, before…

Before *something*.

Maybe if she convinced everyone to leave her alone, she could accomplish something and feel more in control.

"I'm so glad you're both back," Audra said, forcing some cheer into her voice. "I wish you hadn't closed out your trips early, but it's good to have you home. And since you are, I just… I haven't had a moment to myself in days. I… I just need some alone time. To think things through. Copeland's been all up on this twenty-four-seven nonsense, and I haven't had a moment to myself."

She smiled hopefully at Franny, who kept her head bent and focused on washing the dishes. So she turned to Rosalie, who was scowling.

"How about this, just this once, for the slightest change, you try to *talk it through*, instead of isolating yourself and thinking through a problem without any help. I'm a private investigator, Audra. This is my *job*. I'm your sister. This is my family."

Maybe it was Karly firmly rejecting those terms—*sister, family*—that had Audra relenting. Because she liked to think she could maneuver Rosalie when she wanted to, but not when Rosalie sounded hurt. Not when there was someone who wanted to be her sister.

She let out a long breath. Maybe it was only fair to give Rosalie this, even if Audra wanted to handle it herself. Even if she wanted…

What the hell do you want, Audra? She felt like Cope-

land Beckett had swept into her life—on her own invitation—and jumbled it all up.

But Rosalie tugged on her arm, nudged her into a seat
at the table. "I want to hear the whole story. The real story.
From *your* point of view." Rosalie went to a drawer, pulled
out a little notebook and a pen. "This might be Copeland's
case, but it's mine now too."

"And once we're done with that," Franny said, settling
herself on Audra's other side, "you can share the details on
just what twenty-four seven with Copeland Beckett entails."

"It entails Copeland Beckett in his underwear in her bed
this morning," Rosalie grumbled, clearly disgusted.

"Ooh," Franny said, clearly *not* disgusted.

The juxtaposition almost made Audra smile.

"First things first. Start at the beginning. No leaving
things out to keep me from worrying. I'm worried. There's
no more or less."

Audra really didn't want to, but it was clear Copeland
wasn't going to let her minimize this to Rosalie, and Rosalie would get the details out of *someone*, one way or another. So Audra had no choice but to relent.

Which left her feeling…exhausted and like a failure.
Something she was so tired of. So…over.

What if you stopped blaming yourself for everything?

She wanted to laugh, because the voice in her head
sounded far too much like Copeland blaming her for being
a martyr. Because she was. Because… Because by handling
everything these past four years, she'd built her life on the
crumbling foundation of her father's lies, and it wasn't earning her any awards.

What if she could…use this as a new starting point? What
if she could…think about change, about *leaning* instead of
all the holding tight that hadn't really served her?

It was *terrifying*, but she started with the very small step of telling Rosalie and Franny everything from the beginning, without glossing over things. Without downplaying or insisting it was fine.

Franny was gripping her arm by the time she got to the fire, and Rosalie looked like she was going to start throwing punches, but Audra forced herself to keep going. All the way to Karly's arrival and her interaction with their half sister.

Audra thought about the conversation as she relayed it. Those earlier thoughts about how odd it had been came circling back. "Karly said that Dad always talked about his *ancestral home*."

Rosalie snorted in disgust. "Yeah, fat lot he cared about that."

"He did though. Maybe not the way we wanted him to, but he did. And he signed it over to me a while before he died. Before his son would have been old enough to have any part of it."

"Not to protect you, Audra."

"No, I don't have any illusions about that. Because he told his son about it. His son who, according to Karly, bought in to the whole thing. So why did Dad tell his son about something he'd given me? Acted like he'd get it one day."

"Because he was a dick?"

Audra sighed. "Yes, but it's *more*, isn't it? If you set aside the hurt daughter and think like a PI. Copeland's trying to track Austin down, but he's missing, so we can't go to the source. If Karly knows why he told them, she won't say. So I have to try and think about this from Dad's point of view. If you're living two lives, how do you make sure they never connect?"

Rosalie shrugged. "Be a lying bastard?" She wrinkled her nose when Audra frowned at her. "Okay, okay. Think like a PI. You'd just have to make sure those lives never connect, right? They were in Idaho. We were here, and pretty isolated here at that. We had no reason to suspect anything, so…isn't it that easy when you're a lying bastard?"

"Maybe, but I'm starting to wonder… She was so angry. Karly. So bitter. About me, about us. She only came here because she thought Copeland would be a lead to Austin. And if Austin is the one doing this, that's even more than anger and bitterness. It's like…"

"Revenge," Franny said thoughtfully. "Blame and revenge."

"Yes. I guess," Audra said, nodding at Franny before turning her attention back to Rosalie. "Which means they both have so much anger and bitterness. No curiosity about us, about creating a relationship. And I know you weren't as gung-ho about reaching out as I was, but you weren't… angry at *them*, you know? Even at breakfast, you weren't… mad at *them*. You were mad at Dad."

"And still am."

"Sure, but don't you see what I'm saying? They've nursed these bad feelings. It's not ambivalence. It's…ire. And maybe they used that for these years since Dad died. Maybe they leaned on anger over grief and that's all there is to it."

"What other *maybes* are there?" Rosalie asked, but not like she didn't know, like she wanted Audra to say it. While her expression sharpened into that private-investigator look.

Audra shook her head. This was the thought she didn't like, but it kept poking at her. The *hate* in Karly's gaze. The rejection right after the funeral and every moment since. Where did that kind of rejection and vitriol come from? *Maybe* just grief. But maybe…

Audra really thought it had to be deeper than a secret brought to life. "Rosalie, what if they *knew*?"

"Knew…about us?"

"Yes. Before Dad died."

"You think Dad told them about us in an effort to keep us…divided? Apart?"

"I think it might make more sense than them being as blindsided as we were and as…closed off as they've always been."

Rosalie's expression softened into a hurt frown, not that her sister would ever admit it was hurt.

"That's worse," Rosalie said flatly. "I never thought a secret could be worse, but telling one side is *worse*."

"It is, and I'm sorry—"

"Don't apologize for him, Audra. You've done that enough."

She had. She really had. She didn't like to admit that taking on all the blame made her feel…safer. Safer than trusting and believing in anyone again. Safe to know you handled *everything*.

Safe, maybe, but not happy, not fulfilled. Hadn't Copeland said that? Surviving not living. Not…actually all that strong. Just safe in the most basic of ways.

But she hadn't felt *safe* since Copeland had swept in, broken down all her usual walls and boundaries.

Because, like he'd said yesterday, her boundaries sucked.

Audra let out a careful breath. "I'm going to change the subject for a minute. Because you guys are here, and Copeland isn't, and… I just…" She looked from her sister to her cousin, her best friends in the world. Rosalie's words about *talking it out* instead of figuring it out on her own rattling around in her brain. "I think I'm in love with him. I don't know how it happened."

Franny made a squealing sound and grabbed her hand, but Rosalie just regarded her with a detached cool gaze.

Audra swallowed at the lump in her throat. Tried to settle the terrified trip of her heart. "I've been trying really hard not to be," she whispered. "But he just…won't shake."

Rosalie inhaled, exhaled, slowly. Her gaze went to the door that Copeland and Duncan had exited out of this morning.

"Yeah, I guess I know the feeling," Rosalie muttered.

Audra's heart fluttered. Rosalie had been a little reticent about starting something with Duncan, and Audra had certainly given her a push in that direction, but that was different. That was…them.

"I don't think…all that is in our future, but—"

Rosalie turned on her in a quick sharp turn. "Why wouldn't it be in your future, Audra?"

Audra blinked, surprised at Rosalie's tone. "I don't know. Copeland and I are just…too different, probably." Admitting she'd fallen for him was one thing, thinking that meant a future was something entirely different.

"Yeah, and Duncan and I are two peas in a pod." She rolled her eyes. "Look, maybe I have my reservations about Copeland, but…if you care about him, and he cares about you, and he won't be shaken by the expert shaker, why are you already ruling out a future?"

"Aren't you the one who always told me I should stop believing in fairy tales?"

"And then I lived one, more or less. You were right, Audra, and you should be right for more than just me."

Audra wanted to believe that, but the bone-deep fear she couldn't was still lurking there. Still, arguing about it wouldn't get them anywhere. "Maybe," she said, managing to scratch out the word. "But, first… First, we have to figure this threat out. Whatever it is."

"It all centers around your father," Franny said gently. "And who knew him better than you, Audra?"

Which…actually gave Audra an idea.

COPELAND FOUND DUNCAN to be an easy enough chore partner. They didn't have to talk to get the work done, and it kept Audra safe and inside. He had a feeling Duncan had things he wanted to say, but he took his sweet time about saying them.

So Copeland maintained the easy silence, focusing on the work, and trying not to laugh at how…coming out and dealing with horses and cows and fences and the bitter cold had become *normal*.

And very nearly enjoyable.

They worked until it got close to lunchtime, but before Copeland could suggest going in for food, or checking in on Audra because the fact she hadn't come poking her nose into the chores despite his orders was downright *strange*, and had to be chalked up to Rosalie and Franny maybe tying her to a chair, Duncan spoke.

"It's too big of a place to keep secure. I know that from experience."

There'd been trouble at his parents' ranch next door last year, and since Copeland had worked part of the case, he knew Duncan had tried to install a lot of security measures, but still, things had slipped through the cracks.

"I agree," Copeland said, surveying the vast stretches of land around them. "There was a time I tried to convince her to leave, stay in town with Hart, or *something*, but now… I think staying is the right choice. As long as she's never alone. She's right that the threat isn't to her. I really do believe that. Someone wanted to scare her off. They didn't know her, and thought she'd scare easily."

"Not those Young girls," Duncan said with the ghost of a smile. Because even though Duncan had spent over a decade off in California being a professional baseball player, he'd grown up right here. Next door to the Youngs.

Which gave Copeland an idea. "What do you know about Tim Young?"

Duncan gave him a once-over, then shrugged. "Not much. Rosalie's version of him is a mustache-twirling villain, and he was a worthless SOB, don't get me wrong, but I don't have any insight into him that isn't that."

Copeland could press Audra on the details, but he kept... pulling back there. Maybe he needed to—

"My parents might," Duncan said.

"Would they talk to me?"

"If I told them to." Duncan squinted off into the distance, toward his parents' place to the east. "But they might be more forthcoming with me." He glanced at Copeland. "If you tell me what you want to know, I could go over there right now, probably get some answers."

Copeland considered. He'd rather do the questioning himself, but... Well, it made sense. Duncan was an insider. His parents would trust him to use the information wisely without second-guessing if they should be handing it out. Copeland was still an outsider, so they'd be more...careful.

"I want to know their impressions of him. Anything *they* know about the second family. I think it's pretty clear what kind of man he was, but I want to know...an outsider's point of view. What, if anything, they might have known or suspected about his second family."

Duncan nodded. "I can get that, if you think it'll help."

"Can't hurt." No, it couldn't hurt. "Maybe ask if there's anyone in town he was friendly with. Someone who might know more about that second family that I could question."

Duncan nodded. "Sure. I can go right now."

"Yeah. I'll finish up out here. And listen…"

"If you're going to tell me not to tell my wife about this, it's a no-go. And if you think she won't tell Audra…well, I think you know Rosalie better than that."

"He's a sore spot for Audra. She's got enough of those."

Duncan studied him with that same scrutiny he had since he'd arrived on the scene. "Some advice you didn't ask for. You can't protect them from their sore spots, but you can be there when they hurt."

Copeland didn't have the first clue what to say to that. He supposed it was fair advice all in all. But right now, he had more important things to worry about than if Audra'd…let him be around for any hurts.

"I'll finish up here. You let me know what your parents say."

Duncan nodded. He put away his tools, gave Copeland a little salute, then headed off toward the Kirk Ranch on foot.

Copeland watched him go for a few minutes, trying to figure out his next steps. Rosalie and Franny were with Audra, and he had no doubt Rosalie wasn't letting her out of her sight. It gave him the chance to do a full perimeter check. Someone had to be coming in from somewhere to shoot the house, dig the holes, set fires, et cetera.

It wasn't coming from the front road. And he'd wanted to poke around the back of the property, but without her. Now was his chance.

Audra wouldn't appreciate him doing it alone, but he had his gun, and he was a *detective*. This was his job. He eyed the horse he'd been riding during his time here.

"Well, Bo, let's see what we can do on our own." He got the horse saddled and out of the stables, then mounted easily enough. "See? I'm a pro," he muttered to himself before urging the horse into a trot.

He rode out to the west fence, then trotted along the property line. He scanned the area around him for entrance and exit points. He studied the ground for misplaced footprints or tire tracks. He rode through a warming afternoon and felt the strangest sense of peace being on the back of a horse, in this gorgeous landscape. Almost like he belonged.

Something to think about, and maybe worry over, later. He was coming up on the far back area of the ranch where he'd never been before. The land kind of changed, became overgrown with lots of stumps forming some kind of line. Was it a property boundary? He'd expected a fence, but—

The sudden explosion of a gunshot had the horse rearing, and since Copeland was reaching for his own gun in response to the shot, he didn't have a tight enough grip on the reins. He tumbled onto the ground with a hard, painful crash while the horse whinnied and galloped away.

Copeland swore, but he didn't have time to be hurt when he knew that had been a gunshot. Maybe it hadn't hit him, but it had been meant to he was pretty sure. He struggled to roll over to get his arm free to reach his gun. Pain shot down the arm, stars danced in his vision. Broken, no doubt.

He swore some more, then clamped his teeth together and got the gun in his left hand. He wouldn't be able to aim worth a darn with his left hand, but maybe it would be enough of a scare tactic to…

"Drop it."

The female voice was sharp. He heard footsteps approach, looked behind him at the overgrowth where a figure was emerging. Maybe he should have been surprised, but it just made too much sense.

"I wasn't going to hurt anyone." Karly Young looked

down at him with those cold, flat eyes he'd *known* were trouble. "You shouldn't have looked in to me." She cocked the gun. "Now you've only got yourself to blame."

Chapter Twenty

Audra's head ached from the effort not to cry. They'd all gone up to her room, dragged out the tub of Dad's things, and the box of files Audra had kept for the ranch—just in case—then sat down on the floor to go through it together with an eye toward...

Well, she wasn't quite sure. Franny was right, though, it centered around Dad. So they had to dig in to what they had from the man and see if it sparked *some* idea of what was going on with his other family.

But it was mostly like digging in to an old wound she thought she'd healed, but instead had just festered under the scar of it all. Maybe she *was* bitter, she thought to herself as she shuffled through the paperwork of Dad signing the ranch over to her.

"He should have shared it," she grumbled.

"Why? We grew up here," Rosalie said. She was flipping through papers in another file. Taxes, maybe. When they were done, they handed things off to Franny, who organized them back where they belonged.

"You did *everything*," Rosalie continued. "Kept this place going when no one else would or could. Why should he have shared it with them?"

"Because they were his kids too. Like it or not."

Rosalie stopped her flipping, glanced at Audra. "Yeah,

I don't like it. But I guess you're right. Maybe they think we're the ones who kept it from them? Maybe that's why Austin is doing this."

"But then why not take my offer after the funeral?" Audra looked back down at the documents in her hand. Especially then, she would have… If they had even been remotely receptive to a relationship, no doubt she would have martyred herself then and there and given them all pieces of the ranch.

For good or for ill.

Would she now? She didn't know. Certainly not if Austin Young was the one behind these threats, and if Karly Young was the one trying to protect him… At the same time, she couldn't change the fact her father had other kids, that the Young Ranch was part of their family legacy.

And yet, how could she give up pieces of everything she'd shed blood, sweat, and tears over? Everything she loved?

It didn't matter because she didn't have the opportunity, and that above all else settled in Audra like a grudge. But maybe that was the core of all this—grudges, even if she didn't understand them.

"Wait. Did we know this?" Rosalie asked, scooting over to sit next to Audra. She held out a piece of paper. "He sold this back strip of land to the lumber company just a few months before he died." Rosalie held out the map, the bill of sale.

Audra studied the papers. "Oh, right. I do remember that. I was mad because he didn't run it by me first, but he said he needed the money. They cleared the land years ago, and it's mostly been empty ever since. Can't remember the last time I saw or heard anyone back there cutting trees or otherwise."

Which had a cold chill slithering through her. She thought back to the strange goings-on over the past few weeks, and wondered…

"When the windows were shot out, I didn't hear anyone drive up or leave. Usually I can hear cars come and go on the drive. The gravel. The engines. The house just isn't that soundproof. I didn't hear anything. I chalked it up to being half-asleep, but what if they didn't come up from that way?"

It would make sense. The hole, the fire. Things that seemed impossible to do sneaking in from the road, or the boundary with the Kirks. But if the lumber company wasn't doing anything on the land in the back, couldn't someone set up a little home base there?

Rosalie was already on her feet and at the bedroom door before Audra could fully formulate a plan. But she knew her sister, and so did Franny, because they both jumped up at the same time and trailed Rosalie down the stairs.

"You can't just go running out there," Audra said authoritatively.

"Why not?" Rosalie replied. She went straight for the coat closet, where one of the gun safes was.

Audra's heart beat erratically, but she forced herself to breathe. To think. She knew the answer, even though it was…asking someone else for help. "We have to tell Copeland. He should have uniformed officers do it."

Both Franny and Rosalie slowly turned to face her, expressions registering shock. Audra tilted up her chin. "What?"

Franny wrapped her arms around Audra. "It *is* love," she said dreamily, earning her a bit of a shove from Audra.

"He's the detective on the case. This could be dangerous. It makes sense."

"Yeah, but when have you ever worried about being sensible? Come on, let's go see where—"

But Rosalie was cut off by the sound of the back door opening, so they filed into the kitchen.

It was only Duncan who entered. Alone. *Hours* after he and Copeland had left. Audra felt one quick lurch of panic before she set it aside. She managed a smile.

"Where's Copeland? We've got something we want him to look in to."

Duncan stilled in the middle of moving toward Rosalie. He looked at Audra, blinked, and that feeling of dread in the pit of Audra's stomach dug deeper.

"He didn't come back?" Duncan replied, clearly confused.

Audra refused to panic. She absolutely could not let herself panic. She kept the placid smile on her face. Maybe he'd just been tired of chores, of having too many people in the house. Maybe he'd simply gone into Bent to *work*.

She didn't want to believe those things, but worse, she couldn't. He wouldn't have left without telling her, no matter the circumstances.

"I haven't seen him since you two left this morning," Audra said, choosing her words very carefully.

Duncan looked behind him at the door they'd left through. "He was just supposed to finish up some things while I went over to my parents'. He was going to come in for lunch."

"Lunch." That was at least two hours ago.

All eyes turned to her.

"Call Laurel," she said, very calmly, because she felt like there were two versions of herself right now. One that had flown off into the terror stratosphere, and one right here, who needed to handle the reality of whatever this was. "Tell her what we found, Franny. Tell her Copeland is missing. The cops will take it from there."

Franny scrambled for the phone on the wall, but Audra didn't stick around to listen to what she'd relay to the police.

"What are you going to do, Audra?" Rosalie asked, following at her heels as she moved to the back of the house, where her rifle safe was. Calmly and quickly, she turned the dial to unlock the safe.

"You can't go searching for him if you actually think he's in danger," Rosalie said sternly. "What happened to letting the cops handle it?"

Audra said nothing. She calmly pulled her favorite gun from the safe, then a box of bullets.

"You can't go out there, Audra. Do you hear me?"

Only once she had calmly loaded the chamber did she look at her sister. "I can. I will. I am. You can either bring your gun and join me, or you can stay here."

COPELAND HAD TO blink against the roiling sense of nausea. He was glad he hadn't passed out when he sat up, but he didn't really know the medical risks of a broken bone that wasn't seen to right away.

Of course, he had more pressing concerns. Karly Young pointing a gun at him chief among them.

"Put the gun down," she said, very calmly.

It was the calm that worried him. Calm meant...in control. It meant...planned. It meant, she knew what she was doing, and it'd be harder to talk her out of whatever she was trying to accomplish.

And it made it very hard to relinquish his one chance at stopping whatever this would be. Not that he could use his right hand to *shoot* the gun, but still.

"Stand up and move away from the gun. If you don't, the next bullet will hit its target."

"Aren't you going to kill me anyway?" Copeland asked, unwilling to let the grip on his lifeline go just yet. "Since I know you're behind everything now. And you're holding a gun on me."

Karly seemed to give this some thought, eyebrows beetled together as she surveyed him. "I didn't want to hurt anyone," she said, still far too calm for comfort. "I just wanted what was mine. I am just taking back what *is* mine." She started to move closer, the aim of her gun squarely on his chest the entire time. "She could have just left," Karly mumbled, maybe more to herself than him. "She should have just left. It's on her now. Her fault. All her fault."

"Audra?" He almost couldn't believe what she was saying. "She... She reached out to you. She thinks of you as a sister. I watched her try to talk to you, be *kind* to you."

Karly scoffed. "You believe that? You're a sucker."

For several seconds, Copeland could only stare. He'd dealt with people who refused to engage in reality plenty, but this... It didn't make any sense. But he was starting to realize, it wouldn't. Because Karly... She wasn't dealing in reality, and she wasn't calm or collected any longer.

"I know what they are. I know what *she* is." Karly stood next to him now. He could see her chest rise and fall in exaggerated puffs. He could feel the anxious, vibrating anger coming off her. He could see the *intent*, and the wild desperation behind it, now that she was close.

Copeland didn't want to relinquish his grip on the gun, but with the broken arm, he wouldn't get a shot off aimed properly or in time anyway.

"You don't think my father told me exactly what she is?" Karly demanded. She kicked out, her heavy boot meeting both Copeland's hand and the gun. The gun went flying. New pain shot up Copeland's uninjured arm and he fell back, unable to brace his fall with his broken arm.

He laid there in the grass, feeling like a chump. He was a cop, damn it, and this unstable woman, who was trying to paint *Audra*, of all people, as some kind of villain, was winning.

He couldn't let that happen. Unable to bite back a groan of pain, he managed to sit up again. He was sweating despite the freezing temperatures, his teeth chattering now as the pain seemed to come in strange waves that were both numb and excruciating. But he met Karly's wild gaze with a calm one.

"I think you've got a lot of facts mistaken, Karly. But I think we can clear it up. If you put the gun down, if you stop trying to scare Audra…"

"You're right. I need to stop scaring." Karly was nodding now, swallowing as her eyes filled with tears. "I need to start *hurting*. The way she hurt my father."

Copeland had been in dangerous situations before, and he knew how to keep his calm. He held her gaze, and spoke low and firm. "Audra didn't do anything to your father."

"He was trapped by them!" Karly yelled. "Trapped. She was always keeping him here. It was *her*. It's all their fault. Everything he did. Every promise that didn't come true. It was *their fault*."

She'd known. Before Tim Young's death, she'd known about Audra and Rosalie and she…blamed them. And if Copeland wasn't mistaken, Tim Young had leaned into that blame. Let it fester there in his child.

Copeland didn't know how to work around that. Clearly, Karly believed it wholeheartedly, so trying to convince her otherwise wasn't going to get him anywhere.

"What about your brother?"

Karly's scowl dug deeper, but Copeland's gaze was on her other hand coming up to steady the dominant one pointing a gun at him. "Austin was *supposed* to stay put. He was *supposed* to take the fall. A little connection to *her*, and you would have picked him up in Idaho. You think *he* was smart enough to create a persona and fool that woman?"

Karly shook her head. For a second, the gun came down a little and Copeland thought if she took one more step toward him, he could use his own legs to kick out, to catch her off guard.

"What woman?"

Karly looked at him like he was somehow completely brain-dead. "You're supposed to be a detective? That *woman*. I won't speak her name. But her connection to Austin's fake identity was supposed to lead you to *him*. She fell for it. Hook, line and sinker. Of course she did. But Austin didn't stay put. He wouldn't *listen* to what needed to be done. He didn't care about our legacy. Spoiled, spoiled, *spoiled*."

She was all but shrieking now, and she sucked in a breath. Clearly trying to center herself. The gun came back up steadily, and was aimed at his chest. "I didn't want to hurt anyone, but you all are making me."

"I'm not making you do anything, Karly," Copeland replied, keeping his voice calm as he tried to inch closer to her without her reading anything into it. As he tried to make sense of what she'd just told him. Karly was behind making Austin the internet boyfriend of Audra's mother? This wasn't just…scaring or grudges. It was full-on insanity.

So he had to keep his cool, his calm. He held Karly's wild gaze. "I just went on a horseback ride, Karly."

"You looked in to me. Not him. You kept *poking* in to *me*, not him!"

"I investigated both of you."

She curled her finger around the trigger, and Copeland stilled his movement forward. Close range, that bullet was going to end him in less than a second.

He couldn't let that happen.

"She'll come looking for you," Karly said to herself. "I bet she will. And then… I'll just have to kill all of you. I'll just have to. I don't want to, but I have to. It's mine, and it'll never really be mine if I don't kill you."

The poor woman was crying now. Copeland had been in a lot of messed-up situations, but he'd certainly never felt a modicum of pity for the person holding a gun on him.

But he did now, and it made it difficult to go after her the way he knew would save his life. "Karly, the wires got crossed somewhere." He got onto his knees, carefully, watching for any indication she might shoot. "But if we take this step by step, we can uncross them." He managed to get to his feet, even though the pain threw off his balance. He held his hands in the air, a sign of surrender, even though he wasn't surrendering. "And no one has to get hurt. I promise you. No one has to get hurt."

Karly stared at him, tears streaming down her cheeks. "You believe that," she said, almost like it was a revelation. But then she shook her head. "What a shame you believe that."

Chapter Twenty-One

Audra didn't bother to wait and see if Rosalie was keeping up. She had one mission. Get to the back side of the property.

She was certain that was where Copeland was. He was either digging into things alone, in which case she might shoot him herself. Or he was…

She threw that *or* away. Let the terrified version of her deal with it. Right now, there was only getting to him and figuring out what was what.

The answer came before she reached the back of the property. She heard the pounding of hooves, looked over to one of the pastures, where Bo was running in a kind of endless circle.

Bo. The horse Copeland took when he rode with her. Audra swallowed. She wanted to run, but that would only scare Bo even more. She approached, in careful steady strides, speaking in low, calming tones.

"Whoa. Whoa." She managed to approach Bo, grab her reins even as she reared back up. Audra stayed out of the way as the horse came back onto all fours. "It's all right, sweetheart. I've got you now." But she didn't have time…

Rosalie caught up, and so did Duncan and Franny, who Audra hadn't realized had followed them out.

Franny moved forward, took the reins from Audra. "I've got her," Franny said firmly. "I've got her. I'll be okay. You guys go."

Audra took off, but Rosalie was right behind, talking to Duncan. "You two go back to the house. Get Bo put away. Then you can lead the cops to us once they get here."

"Rosalie." Duncan's voice was little more than a growl, but Rosalie kept pace with Audra and just spoke louder.

"We can handle it, Duncan. We have to handle it. Go with Franny. Please."

Audra didn't pay any attention to see if Duncan argued or not. She kept resolutely walking to the back of the property. She could have grabbed a horse—Bo, even—but she wasn't sure Bo was okay, and any other horse would take too long to saddle. Her truck could have made it back here, but she would have had to backtrack. The UTV was out of gas, so on foot it was.

"Audra…" But Rosalie never finished whatever she was going to say. She just kept up with Audra's relentless, determined pace. Over hills and dips, along the fence line and to the back of the property.

Maybe Audra was breathing heavily from exertion as they began to approach the end of her property line, but she hardly noticed. Out there in the distance, she saw a figure.

No, two figures.

Only when she saw the sun glint off the metal of what was likely a gun did she begin to slow. But she didn't stop.

Because she could see clearly one figure was standing with his hands in the air—that was Copeland. And one figure held a gun toward him—that was Karly.

If it meant something, if she felt something, it didn't penetrate the icy shell inside of her. The only thing she really concentrated on was a renewed sense of determination. She lifted her rifle as she walked closer.

"Audra, we should try to sneak up on her. We should—"

"There's nowhere to hide," Audra replied. Because all around them was just the rolling grassy land of Young Ranch and the spot they'd sold off to the lumber company with years-old stumps lining the ground.

Whether it was their voices or something else, Audra didn't know, but Karly looked toward them, the gun still pointed at Copeland. Audra thought she'd turn it toward her and Rosalie, considering they were armed, but Karly didn't do that.

She stepped closer to Copeland, behind him almost, but not fully. Because she pressed the metal to his temple.

Audra stopped on a dime, but she didn't lower her gun. She didn't feel panic or terror or worry. She was so calm, everything around her felt like some...unreal dream. She could feel Rosalie behind her, but all she saw, all she felt, was the calm dark gaze of Copeland from across the grassy expanse between them.

"Audra." Rosalie sounded scared, but Audra didn't feel it. She was numb. She was calm. She knew what had to be done.

She kept Karly in her gunsight. "I'm going to shoot her," Audra murmured.

"She's using Copeland as a shield."

"I can see that. I can also see exactly where I need to aim to hit her and not Copeland."

"But... Audra, what if you hit him?" Rosalie asked on a concerned whisper.

Audra's hand wanted to tremble, but she wouldn't let it. For years, she'd won shooting awards. Hell, she'd helped save the ranch with the money she won a few years in a row. Now she'd help save the man she loved.

"I won't hit him." Not when everything depended on this. On her.

She'd been preparing for this moment, whether she knew it or not, all her life.

THE GUN WAS pressed to his temple. Copeland had no doubt Karly would pull the trigger if pushed even a little bit. She was holding on to everything by a thread. He could *feel* her desperation. Her loss of control, and maybe loss of hope that she could turn this whole messed-up endeavor into what she'd envisioned.

Audra didn't look the least bit scared. She held the impressive-looking rifle against her shoulder, aimed at...well, he knew it wasn't aimed at *him*, but it sure felt like it with Karly using him as a human shield.

If Audra had any feelings about that, she didn't show it. The sun blazed behind her in a riot of deep reds and oranges. Her expression was calm, her eyes direct.

"Drop the gun," Karly called out over the distance between them. "You've got ten seconds, or he's gone."

Audra's gaze didn't move. The gun didn't drop. Her finger was curled around the trigger. Karly was on his right side, so his arm couldn't do much. He could maybe land a kick before *she* shot him, but he didn't know what the hell Audra's plans were.

Karly started counting, but Copeland couldn't pay attention. He was focused on Audra. Her blue eyes were on her target, and they didn't waver.

She was going to shoot...and whatever happened, well, he'd have to deal with it.

When the gunshot went off, Copeland didn't even flinch.

The gun fell from his temple, exploded loudly near his ear, but he didn't feel any impact. He turned to Karly.

She'd fallen backward, and she was screaming...though it was muffled to his ears. Her hand was bloody, but even as she shouted and cried, she was trying to reach out for her dropped gun with her left hand.

Copeland scooped it up easily before she did with *his* left hand. Karly was screaming at him, but he couldn't make out the words. The gunshot had exploded too close to his ear.

Then he felt arms come around him. He couldn't hold back the groan of pain or stop himself from swaying. Audra held him firm though, and he wrapped his good arm around her.

She was saying something to him, though he couldn't make it out. But he got the drift when she started searching him for signs of injury or blood maybe.

"I'm okay. I'm not shot. I just took a tumble off Bo. Hurt my arm a bit." His own words sounded weird and muffled. Audra's blue eyes were bright with tears, but they didn't fall. Rosalie appeared, holding a gun pointed at Karly.

Both Rosalie and Audra were saying things, but he couldn't make out the words, so he just squeezed Audra tighter, trying to ignore the pain. "Gun went off a little close to my ear, so it's all a bit muffled right now." Easier to admit that when she looked so worried than that his arm was broken.

"Audra." He looked at Karly, still writhing on the ground with Rosalie holding her at gunpoint, then at Audra, who only seemed to have eyes for him. He had to tell her. "It was Karly all along. She knew about you guys, this place, and I think... I think your father convinced her it was all your fault you had this and she didn't." He spoke in low tones, keeping his good arm tight around her. "She was just trying to frame Austin for it. Down to the fake identity cat-fishing your mother."

Audra watched him as he spoke. *Dazed* wasn't the right word. She just seemed detached. Or partially detached, because he thought the emotion was starting to break through.

The muffled sound and pain in his ear were starting to ease a little, he thought, when he heard the faint sound of sirens.

It was when the police cruiser and the ambulance crested the rise that Audra began to shake. Then a tear slid onto her cheek.

He squeezed her tight. "Baby, you held that gun steady and shot somebody with about a centimeter of wiggle room. I don't think you get to fall apart now."

She pressed her forehead into his shoulder. She was still shaking, but he didn't know if she was actively crying since she'd hidden her face. "Sure," she said, her voice squeaky, even to his muffled hearing. "I'll just keep it together then."

"You kept it together when it counted." He pressed a kiss to her temple. "Hell, Audra. I don't know anyone who could have made that shot. Not a soul. Except you."

Chapter Twenty-Two

Audra gave her statement to Laurel while they loaded Copeland into the ambulance. She allowed herself to be fussed over by Rosalie and Franny, all while Copeland was taken to the hospital.

And she cursed the man when Laurel informed her he was going into surgery for a broken arm. "He knew it was broken," she told Rosalie darkly back at their kitchen table with cops prowling the property. "He knew it the whole time and didn't tell me."

"Well, we'll go down to the hospital and you can yell at him about it."

Audra frowned, because she wasn't going to yell at him. The minute she saw him, she'd probably fall completely apart. His words kept echoing in her head.

I don't know anyone who could have made that shot. Not a soul. Except you.

Like somehow, it was all meant to be. Like somehow, she shouldn't feel guilty about asking Copeland for help, about his broken arm he'd got because of *her*.

She did, of course, feel guilty and blamed herself, but there was a little inkling deep down that maybe she *shouldn't*.

Still, once the police presence moved out, she let Rosalie drive her to the hospital because she needed to see Copeland. She wouldn't take a full breath until she did.

It was late by the time they got to the hospital and made their way toward Copeland's recovery room. Before they reached it though, they saw Laurel talking to a uniformed police officer outside a hospital room at the front of the hall.

The two stopped talking as Rosalie and Audra walked by.

Rosalie studied them, then the door. "Is it Karly?" she demanded.

Laurel gave them a kind of cop smile. Sympathetic but guarded. "She's doing just fine. She'll likely have some permanent damage, since the wrist is a hell of a place to get shot, but she'll make a full recovery. And then we'll see about justice."

"Can we see her?" Audra asked, without fully thinking the question through. Everything just felt...so unsettled, even with what Copeland had told her.

Laurel looked from Rosalie to Audra, then back to the uniformed officer outside the hospital-room door.

"It'll be up to her. I'll go see if she's okay with it, and I'll have to stay in the room with you."

Audra nodded, and Laurel slipped into the room.

Rosalie turned to Audra, concern etched across her features. "Why?"

"I don't know. It just seems... Dad convinced her of all this stuff that wasn't true, and she was acting on it in good faith."

Rosalie scowled. "She would have killed Copeland. And possibly you. Even if she believed every lie Dad ever told, that's not an excuse for *murder*."

"She had chances to do both and didn't."

Rosalie shook her head. "I don't know how you can have any sympathy for her, Aud. She's a damn criminal."

"She's troubled. She needs help. She's our sister."

Maybe, just maybe, that softened Rosalie a little. When

Laurel reappeared and ushered them into the room, Rosalie linked arms with Audra. They stopped at the end of Karly's hospital bed.

She was hooked up to an IV and some other kind of machine. Her gaze slowly landed on them, settled on their linked arms while a scowl sank into her face.

"Well. What do you two want?" she said it with a sneer. "If you're expecting an apology, you can jump off a cliff. *You* shot me."

Audra supposed it should make her mad, but all she could seem to work up to was sympathy. To be this…angry at all the wrong people. It was just sad.

"I'm sorry it was the only option," Audra said, and meant it. "But I think we both know you were ready to kill someone, and that's just…not okay."

Karly's belligerent gaze moved out to the window, even though it was dark outside, and her jaw worked, like she was trying to hold back tears. Like she *knew*, deep down, what she'd done was wrong.

Maybe it was wishful thinking, but Audra, who'd given up on wishful thinking since her father had died, decided she wanted some of that hope, some of that belief back.

"I would have given you a piece of the ranch," Audra said very calmly and clearly. "I would have given you so much. I offered. You didn't even consider my offer."

Karly stared at her. There was hate deep in the eyes the same shade as Audra's, but Audra thought she saw something else. Maybe she was fooling herself, but she hoped she saw some doubt.

So she pressed. "*He* tricked you. He tricked all of us. He's the enemy. And if you can ever accept that, believe it, I'll be here."

"We'll be here," Rosalie corrected, surprising Audra.

Because her sister wasn't exactly known for her forgiving nature.

Karly still said nothing. She would do some time. Hopefully she'd get some help, and maybe someday in the future they could put this behind them.

But if they didn't, at least Audra tried.

"Whatever," Karly muttered. "Go away."

Audra exchanged a glance with Rosalie, who nodded. They'd done what they needed to do for some closure, and left the door cracked open if Karly ever decided to step through it.

COPELAND SWAM OUT of the dark in a weird fuzzy kind of confusion. He didn't feel much of anything, least of all his body, but when his eyes opened to a bright, white hospital room he was met by a familiar dark gaze.

He stared for a full minute before it made sense. "Mom?"

His mother was frowning disapprovingly at him from a seat next to his hospital bed. "Well, who else would be here?"

Copeland shifted uncomfortably, not sure if it was the anesthesia from surgery wearing off or what. "You didn't have to come all the way here."

"My son was in surgery and I didn't have to come all the way here." She scoffed. "Leave it to you, Copeland."

He might have laughed, but his brain didn't feel like it was firing on all cylinders yet. "I…" He wanted—needed—to see Audra. They'd wheeled him into surgery before he'd had a chance to talk to her, they'd both been so busy giving statements and ensuring the loose ends of Karly Young had been tied up.

Now he wanted… God, he just wanted to see her. But

his mother was here. She'd come all the way from Denver and… "Mom, it's just a broken arm."

She made a considering noise. "We were overdue for a visit. For seeing your life here. I know you've come home, but why shouldn't we come here for a bit? Good for your father to get away from his precious lawn for a week or so."

See your life here. No, he'd kept them away from it. Hell, he'd tried to keep himself away from life, but he'd built one all the same. No matter what he'd tried to do. It hadn't started with Audra, but it all seemed to center on her now and… His parents were *here*. So…

"I'd like you to meet someone."

"It wouldn't happen to be a pretty woman named Audra who introduced herself to me as the reason you got hurt?"

He sighed heavily. Martyr until the end. "That'd be her. It wasn't her fault."

"You don't think I know that? Sometimes it's easier for people to take the blame and feel in control of everything that's hurting their heart, than it is to accept bad things just happen."

Maybe he'd realized that a bit on his own, but his mother articulating it clarified all that martyr in her. And maybe even a little in himself.

"She's helping your dad hunt down some decent coffee," Mom continued, her gaze shrewd. "She's a sweet girl. First impression? I liked her."

"Good." Maybe it was the drugs. The exhaustion. Maybe it was just seeing his mother here in Wyoming. But the truth came tumbling out. "Because I think I'm in love with her."

Mom didn't react outwardly, but he saw her gaze study him, like she could see through him and determined it was true. "My suggestion would be not to use the word *think* when you tell her. Your father made that mistake. I nearly ended things then and there."

He laughed in spite of himself. "Noted."

But he saw, or felt, his mother's...concern. Trepidation maybe. Because he'd run away from one problem, and maybe she was worried he was just repeating old mistakes. So he felt like he had to tell her, had to explain...

"It's not just her, you know. It's this place. It's a community. I have friends. No matter how hard I tried, everything, everyone...became more than just a job. More than just an escape from Denver. I left to...hide, I guess. Numb myself. But..."

She reached out, brushed his hair off his forehead, just like she'd done when he'd been a kid home sick from school. "But it sounds like you found your home instead."

"Yeah, I think I did."

"That's all I ever wanted for you," she said, and though her expression was calm, her eyes filled a little. But she didn't cry. She wouldn't—that wasn't his mother's way.

She cleared her throat. They both turned to look as the door to the room opened. Dad stepped in first, but he was followed by Audra. She had shadows under her eyes. She needed rest and home and...

She was here, and that was exactly where he wanted her to be.

"We're going to stay a few days," Mom said briskly. "Until you're out of the hospital at least. No arguing. We're going to go check into the hotel now. We'll be back in the morning." She reached out, took Audra's hand. "It was good to meet you, Audra. I'm sure we'll see more of you before we leave."

Audra smiled in return. "I hope so."

For a second, Copeland watched his parents and Audra

and wondered if this was all a very elaborate dream. But then Audra sat in the chair next to his bed. She reached out, touched his face, and that touch was real.

He felt himself relax into the pillows beneath his head. Real. All this was real, and once he was out of here, it'd be time to figure out just what that meant.

"Your parents are very nice," she said, a bit primly, but he knew she was trying to keep herself from apologizing about his arm.

"Yeah, they are."

"How are you feeling?"

"Weird. Groggy. But okay. Guess I've got desk duty for a bit."

She glanced at his cast, pain and no doubt a bit of self-flagellation there in her gaze, but she didn't speak it. That was progress, he thought.

"I'm not going to tell you I'm sorry," she said, very clearly struggling with that. "But only because your mother told me not to."

He laughed at that, for so many reasons. He shook his head. "Audra, you are something else. I'm just glad you're safe, and we got to the bottom of it, no matter how accidentally. I wish I could have done more, sooner, but we're okay. And... Hopefully Karly can get the help she needs."

Audra's mouth turned down. "But...she tried to kill you. She was going to. You don't have some sort of...revenge feeling about that?"

"Normally I would, but... I don't know. She just seemed so damn sad. It was impossible not to feel sorry for her."

Audra swallowed, her eyes swimming again. She got up out of the chair just enough to brush a light kiss across his mouth. "I thought so too." She offered him a trembling smile.

And he just…said it, because it was there, and it should be said. She should hear it. Know it. Always. He didn't even use the word *think*.

"I'm in love with you, Audra, and believe me, that was *not* the plan."

She kind of plunked back into her seat, shock etched across her face. She opened her mouth, but nothing came out. So he figured he'd just press and press and press while he could.

She was stubborn. He'd have to get through to her.

"Guess I'll be laid up for a few weeks, but I make a pretty good ranch hand."

She swallowed. "You do. Cheap too."

"Audra."

She sighed, gaze lifting from his cast to his face. Her blue eyes were tired, soft. "I always wanted… I wanted to fall in love. To find someone who felt like a partner. I chased that feeling, and it only ever broke my heart. So I wasn't looking for you either. I was done chasing. Done…believing." She took a long, careful inhale. "But you're worth believing in, Copeland. And I love you."

For a few moments they just stared at each other, like the moment was nebulous, fragile, breakable.

Then Audra laughed, got up again, and pressed a firmer kiss to his mouth.

He held her there with his good arm before she could sit back down. "You're going to have a hell of a hard time getting rid of me, I hope you know that."

She smiled, pretty and bright, just like she was, all the way through. "Good."

* * * * *

PROTECTIVE LAWMAN

JANIE CROUCH

This book is dedicated to the little girl who came up to me at a restaurant and told me I was 'so pretty'… Kid, you have no idea how your sweet words made my heart sing. May we all remember to be so kind.

Prologue

Officer Aaron Ward sighed in frustration as he closed another case file. He rubbed his eyes, which were gritty with exhaustion, and decided he was going to need another cup of coffee—or seven.

For a few months he had suspected that something not quite aboveboard was going on in North Carolina's Kings Mountain Police Department, where he worked. He had started poking around as inconspicuously as he could. Paying attention to what certain officers were—or weren't—doing, and taking a closer look at the ones he thought might be involved in suspicious activities.

Of course, he couldn't do this during normal work hours because he had his actual job to do, plus he didn't want anyone to know what he was doing yet. So, he'd been putting in extra hours, staying at the station long into the night when he should have been home sleeping. Hence the need for more coffee.

He knew he would need to take this up the chain of command eventually, but he wanted to gather more concrete evidence first. He couldn't request a meeting with his captain or the chief of police and only present his own opinions and suspicions. He had sworn an oath to serve and protect the community of Kings Mountain, and he intended to do that, even from other officers who didn't take that oath as seriously as he did.

He was getting close to gathering enough evidence. There was a group of officers that he suspected were corrupt—taking bribes, withholding important investigative information, and bullying witnesses, among a laundry list of other shady things. He needed to make sure that he knew which officers were involved and in what capacity.

He saved the most recent case file he'd looked at to a folder on his computer and decided to call it a night. He'd have to be back at the station in just a few hours, and he was going to need some rest if he was going to be able to work a full day and then put in more hours afterward again. Plus, he got to work with Bailey tomorrow. She was new to the force but she was a good officer and he enjoyed working with her. There were other feelings there too that he refused to acknowledge, especially while he was her superior.

He powered down his computer, turned off the lamp on his desk, and walked toward the parking lot, his mind still running through the information he'd found. He was about halfway across the lot when he heard the sound of another car door shutting. He didn't think much of it; it was a police station, after all, and people were around at all hours of the day and night. But when he looked in the direction of the sound, he saw that there were several men approaching him quickly.

Warning bells went off in his mind. This wasn't normal. He continued walking to his car, hoping that if he didn't engage them, they would continue on without bothering him.

No such luck.

He squinted as the men got closer, trying to make out who they were.

"Hello, Ward," one of them sneered.

Ziegler.

"Hey, guys. What brings you here at this hour?" Aaron asked.

Ziegler laughed humorlessly. "We could ask you the same thing."

Aaron shrugged. "Just finishing up some work."

Ziegler moved closer, getting in Aaron's face and pinning him against his car. His cronies—Moore, Benning, and Lee—flanked him. "Yeah, that's why we're here, snitch."

Aaron's stomach dropped. So he'd been right. These guys were crooked.

"We know you've been keeping tabs on us and doing your own little investigation." Ziegler poked a finger hard into Aaron's chest. "You're not as sneaky as you think you are."

Ziegler pulled his arm back and slammed it into Aaron's gut. He doubled over in pain, gasping for air. "And just so you know," Ziegler spat, "we have eyes on your precious Bailey right now. She's at home, reading a book. And we could take her out in a second if you don't get out of town, and pretend none of this ever happened. You understand?"

Before he could reply, Moore jerked Aaron back upright and Ziegler hit him again, this time in the jaw, knocking him to the ground. All bets were off as soon as he went down. Before Aaron could attempt to regain his footing, Benning started kicking him in the chest while Moore jammed his boot repeatedly in his back.

Aaron tried to fight back, but once the other men joined in, he knew there was no way he could win. Ziegler, not to be left out of their fun, focused on his face and head. The more they beat him, the more he wondered if he'd even survive. Pain was radiating throughout his entire body and he was pretty sure they broke some ribs, among other things. His last thought before everything went black was that he had to get Bailey away from these men, before she got hurt too.

Chapter One

Six Years Later

Bailey Masters smiled to herself as she rounded the corner, and the small town of Kings Mountain came into view. Finally. After all this time, she was back home again.

It felt like a lifetime since she had left Kings Mountain and, in some ways, it had been. Her life here had been so different from the one she'd led before, sometimes it was hard to remember that she had lived here, worked here, and made a name for herself here when she had been a rookie cop.

She could still remember the first day she stepped into the station, that flood of pride and excitement that hit her like a ton of bricks. She had wanted to be a cop for as long as she could remember, arresting her toys and reading them their rights before she put them in a little makeshift prison made from her toy box when she was a kid. It had always been in her blood, and she had been determined to make it as soon as she found out it was a career option for her.

But that had been before—before she'd been kicked out and moved across the country, before she had faced up to the fact that the man she had idolized—and almost loved, too—had turned his back on her and made it clear what he really thought of her.

Sometimes, she struggled even thinking about him. She grimaced as she drove down into the town, through the familiar streets she had called home for so long. How long had it been? Six years? Just over that now. There had been a time when she was sure she would never get back, but the relief of finally having returned to her hometown wasn't going to be ruined by the memories of the man who had thrown her out of it in the first place.

Aaron.

She tried not to think about him. The two of them had been assigned to work together when she had first been starting out, and she had been so excited. Working with someone like him, someone with his reputation and impressive backlist of cases, she knew she was going to learn so much.

And she did. Because the two of them worked together really well. Or, at least, that was what she'd thought, before reality had slapped her in the face. They would spend most of every day together, driving around and helping out with whatever small cases the people around the town needed them to look at. They got to know each other really well, because how could you not in those circumstances? They understood each other better than anyone else in the world. Even now, knowing what he had done, she still missed him.

She had developed a crush on him, of course. All the time they spent together, combined with his charming personality, made it impossible not to fall for him. At least a little bit. She told herself it would fade with time, but if anything, it had just grown more insistent. She couldn't deny how she felt about him, and she didn't want to. No, she wanted to spend even more time with him, get to know him even more deeply than she had. She could tell from the way he looked at her sometimes that the thought had at least crossed his mind, too.

And then he'd betrayed her. Written a scornful report that had landed her being stuck at a desk job across the country for years now. She still didn't know exactly what he'd put in there, but it had been enough to get her blackballed from her old position and moved into a new one she would never in a million years have asked for. Almost in the blink of an eye, too.

The added kicker of it was, he hadn't even had the guts to face her and do it himself. He'd just turned in the report and called out of work—faking sick—and had someone else do his dirty work. She'd even had a weak moment after the shock of it wore off and tried to contact him, with no response. Not that she had been surprised by then.

Sometimes, she still had a hard time believing it. She had turned it over a thousand times in her head, trying to figure out what had caused him to turn on her the way he had, but she had never been able to figure it out. Either way, that wasn't the problem now. He was out of her life, and she wanted it to stay that way. Anyone who would stab her in the back the way he had wasn't the kind of person she wanted in her life.

She focused her gaze on the road ahead, and took the turn at the end of Main Street to take her to the police station. It was going to be so weird, being around all the people she had started out with when she was a rookie cop. She had been so young when she'd first begun her tenure here, just out of training and ready to take on the world. She could still remember the excitement she had felt, how much she had looked forward to every day at work. Her other friends from high school were in college or had started to settle down and raise families, but her career was the only thing she gave a damn about.

She pulled the truck to a halt outside the station, and paused for a moment before she turned off the engine and got out. How would she be greeted? Would they be friendly or skeptical of her being back after all these years? What were they going to say when they saw her again? Of course, they knew she was coming, but seeing her in person was going to be different.

What if they thought she had gone soft from being behind a desk for so long? She hoped they knew that she'd been struggling the whole time, wishing she could get back out in the field as she filed endless stacks of paperwork. She had fantasized all day long about getting back out there, about actually making a difference and helping people in the real world again. There might have been cops who were happy behind a desk doing paperwork, and that was fine for them, but that was not her. She wanted more.

She always had.

She climbed out of her truck, strode toward the door, and mustered up all her courage. She wasn't actually starting work until the next day, but she wanted to check in and see what was happening right now and say hello to whoever was inside. She was looking forward to seeing the people she used to work with again.

She had been invited back to a couple of events around the holidays the first year after she left, but honestly, she couldn't stand the thought of facing them after the embarrassment of being ousted and forced to ride a desk instead of being out in the field doing real cop work. She knew she was better than that, and she hated even the idea of being seen as some pencil pusher locked away in an office all day long instead of on the streets, working cases and helping others. Living her dream.

But now? It was different. She was back on the beat again. Back out and ready to take on the world. She could hardly wait to see what it had to offer. Pushing open the door, she stepped inside, and was greeted by a round of hellos from the cops she had worked with as a younger woman.

"Wow, Bailey, I can't believe you actually made it," Philip Benning exclaimed, jumping up from his desk and hurrying over to her. "Thought you would have been safer behind that desk in Pallas Bay."

"Safer, but way more bored," Bailey replied with a chuckle, and she reached to give him a hug. She normally wasn't a hugger, but seeing these guys again after so long had her feeling sentimental.

Brian Lee, one of the older cops who served as the muscle for the station, emerged from his office and grinned when he saw Bailey standing there.

"You made it back," he said.

She nodded. "Took me long enough."

A moment later, Stanley Moore and Jay Ziegler appeared from their offices and came over to greet her, too.

"Good to have you back," Ziegler told her.

She grinned widely. She couldn't keep the smile off her face. She was back—she was really, truly, finally back.

"Yeah, good to be here," she replied. "So, what needs to be done? What cases are you working right now?"

Ziegler laughed. "You've only just arrived," he reminded her. "Take a minute to catch your breath before you dive back into work."

"I've been stuck at a desk for years," she shot back. "I've waited long enough."

"We're actually just finishing up for the day," Lee said.

"We were going to head down to the bar. You want to come with? Catch up before you're back on tomorrow."

"That sounds great," she agreed.

She had been on the road all day, and the thought of a cold beer was tempting.

The guys packed up and headed out to their cars and down the street to the bar. Bailey followed in her truck, glancing around as she took in the familiar sights around her. It was going to be a while before she really felt settled here again, but just being back was everything she had been dreaming of these last few years.

Well, almost everything. Maybe it wouldn't be the same without Aaron. Working with him had been one of the things she loved most about the job. She knew things were going to be different than when she'd worked in Kings Mountain before.

But it was better this way.

She never wanted to see him again as long as she lived. He must hate her. Nobody could betray someone like he'd betrayed her and not hate their guts. She didn't need that kind of negativity in her life. She was back in Kings Mountain and nothing—and no one—was going to mess it up for her this time. She'd worked too hard to get to where she was to let someone from her past affect her present or future.

When she got to the bar, she noticed the guys were already inside. She must have been a little more lost in her head than she thought, so she quickly jumped out of her truck and hurried to join them. They were just walking up to the bar, so Bailey rushed forward to buy the first round of drinks. She was determined to make a good impression so they'd see her as a team player from the start and want to keep her around. They retreated to a table at the back of the room, and she noticed a few people glancing in their direction. Some of them were familiar faces—cops she hadn't seen in years—and some were regular patrons winding down after work or meeting up with friends.

"To Bailey's return!" Ziegler led a toast, and everyone clinked their beers together. Bailey sipped on hers, not wanting to get carried away, and her eyes darted around the table. She had been out with these guys before, but there had always been someone else there, too. Someone she couldn't help but miss, despite all of her better judgment.

"So, what have you guys been up to these days?" Bailey inquired, hoping to get a little background of what'd been happening lately.

"Ah, same old, same old. Not much has changed. We're still kicking ass and taking names," Ziegler replied with a dark chuckle. Her eyes darted to him, and she started to feel a little uneasy at his tone.

"Still the biggest and baddest," Moore added with a smirk.

"Here, here!" they all called out, and clinked their bottles together again.

"Where's Aaron these days?" she asked, doing her best to keep her voice casual. She figured it was better to just ask upfront. No point in pretending she didn't notice his absence.

"Oh, I heard he's fixing fences for some lodge for wimps, even if they call it Warrior Peak," Lee replied, waving his hand. "Haven't heard from him since…well, since you left, actually."

"Good riddance," Benning muttered, shaking his head. Her ears perked up at once.

"What do you mean?"

"We're better off without him," Lee cut in, trying to shut down Benning before he said too much.

"Yeah, we don't need his whistleblowing ass," Benning snapped.

Bailey froze for a moment, not sure how to respond.

"Whistleblowing?" she asked, the hairs on the back of her neck standing on end.

"Yeah, we don't need someone who doesn't stand by his fellow cops," Ziegler added. Suddenly, the atmosphere at the table changed and she felt the tension rise. Something was off, and she didn't like it at all.

"But that's not a problem we're going to have with you, is it?" he asked, leaning toward Bailey.

She drew her beer closer to her, as though it might provide some degree of protection.

What were they talking about? Aaron was a whistleblower? When had this happened? Or...or was that why she had been sent away? Her mind raced, but she could tell one thing for sure—this wasn't the welcoming outing she had thought it was.

Ziegler lowered his voice, making sure only Bailey could hear him.

"Exactly how far are you willing to go to keep this job, Bailey?" he asked her.

She shifted in her seat. *Crap.* She had no idea what to say.

Instead of answering him, she pasted on a smile and stood up. "Well, guys, it was great to hang out like old times but I better be going. I still have a lot of unpacking to do at my new place, and I want to be rested for my first day back on the beat tomorrow."

She tossed a few bills on the table to cover her half-finished beer and turned to leave, trying to look casual as she walked away and not like she was rushing toward the exit. Her heart was pounding in her chest as she headed to the door and she could feel their eyes on her. It took all her willpower not to glance over her shoulder.

She waved to a few people she recognized on her way out but once she was outside, she started walking faster. The bar was crowded so her truck was parked pretty far back in the lot. She was about halfway across the lot when the loud music from inside the bar filtered out like someone had opened the door.

Deep down she knew it was them and real panic was setting in fast, but she still didn't look back. She kept herself moving as quickly as she dared toward the safety of her truck. She allowed herself to feel a little bit of relief as the truck finally came into view.

Had she blown that conversation in the bar out of proportion? It had made her uncomfortable, but the guys hadn't said or done anything explicitly damning. Maybe she had overreacted.

She would have to apologize for her quick and awkward exit tomorrow at work. But just as that thought entered her mind, she heard a noise close behind her. She spun around to see Ziegler and the others closing in.

"Where are you going in such a hurry, Bailey?" Benning said in a taunting voice.

"Like I said, I need to unpack and get some rest," she said, trying to keep her voice steady.

Just another few steps and she'd be at her truck. She kept the men in view but continued backing toward the driver's door. They were in a dark corner in the back of the parking lot where no one would hear her call for help. And even if she'd parked closer to the bar, the music was so loud that it was unlikely that anyone would hear her. She was going to have to do this alone.

"Stop right there, Bailey. We just want to talk," Ziegler said.

Her back hit the side of her truck. She realized too late

that she had made a tactical error by effectively trapping herself between the truck at her back and the men in front. Now there was no way she'd be able to get herself into the safety of her truck without turning her back on her enemy. A rookie mistake. She'd spent too many years behind a desk, after all.

She was out of time. She needed to do something.

Fast.

With one final deep breath she swiveled her upper body as quickly as she could to reach for the door handle. But it wasn't enough. She heard someone move and in the next moment she was slammed into the side of her truck with the men crowding her on all sides. She felt hands groping her, someone yanking her head back, hot breath on her neck, and then someone smashed her head into the side of the truck. The hit was hard enough to stun her, and caused her to groan in pain.

She could hear the men murmuring at her back and everything started to spin as she was quickly whipped around to face them. Spots danced before her eyes and a flash of something shiny—a knife? —was coming toward her. It was the last thing she saw before everything went black.

BAILEY SLOWLY REGAINED CONSCIOUSNESS, moaning at the pain racking her entire body. Her head was pounding and she could tell her leg was bleeding, but beyond that, she had no clue what the damage was. Just that everything hurt.

One thing she did know—she needed to get off the ground and get out of that parking lot immediately.

She got herself into a sitting position, trying to clear the cobwebs from her head. She looked around, taking in her surroundings as best she could. Cars were still in the parking lot and music was still blaring from the bar. She must not have been out for too long. She didn't sense anyone nearby, but she still felt an urgency pushing her into action.

Leaning heavily on her truck, she pulled herself up to standing and gripped the side panel when everything started to sway. Concussion? Probably. Blood loss…definitely. She untucked her shirt and ripped the hem so she could make a tourniquet for her leg. She'd figure out the rest of her injuries later but she needed to stop the bleeding now.

Once she had her leg wrapped, she worked her way to the driver's door and slid into the seat. She had no idea what had just happened, or why. But she knew one person who would be able to shed a little light on this whole situation. The one person she had sworn she would avoid as long as possible.

Aaron.

Chapter Two

Aaron hissed with pain as he felt a sliver slide into his palm. He really should have been used to it by now, but the splinters always got him. That's what he got for not wearing gloves. Leaning down, he drew his hand into his mouth and sucked until he felt the splinter dislodge, and spat it to the ground before he stood back to admire his handiwork.

See, now *this* had been worth a few splinters. For the last few months, he had been working on rebuilding the outbuildings for the horses here at the Warrior Peak Sanctuary. He was fixing them up so they could keep the hay dry during the spring, and so the horses would have somewhere to shelter out of the heat of the sun. It would be summer soon and he didn't want to leave them with nowhere to rest on a hot day.

And he had done a pretty good job of it, if he said so himself. It had been almost relaxing for him, being able to come out here every day and enjoy the peace and quiet as he set to work with his hands. As the end of spring approached, it seemed like the whole landscape was blooming to life around them, green punctuated by purples and reds as flowers began to blossom. Against the clear blue sky above, it was downright gorgeous. Another reminder as to why he had come here—and why he had been so willing to leave his old life behind to do so.

He was about to get back to work when he heard a whistle from behind him, and he turned to see Lawson Davies, one of the owners of the lodge, striding toward him through the long grass.

"Hey," Aaron called to him.

Something shifted as Lawson got closer to him, a tingling in his palms—it was something he'd learned back in the day that meant he should be worried. He tried to push that aside, reminding himself he was safe here. At least, that was what he hoped.

"Hi," Lawson replied as he glanced over to the work Aaron had been doing. "It's looking pretty good out here."

"Just 'pretty good'?" Aaron shot back.

Lawson grinned. "Hey, I actually came here for a reason," he remarked. "There's someone up at the main lodge asking for you."

A ripple of uneasiness pulsed through Aaron's body. "Who is it?"

"I don't know," Lawson replied with a shrug. "But they came asking for you specifically. Seemed pretty important."

Who the hell could have found Aaron out here? The whole point of coming to this place was that it was in the middle of nowhere. Nobody should have been able to find him out here. His eyes darted back and forth, looking around as though the answer to his question might have been somewhere in the forest surrounding the field.

"Should I be concerned that there are strangers asking for my handyman?" Lawson asked, clocking Aaron's body language.

Aaron tried to relax and shook his head quickly. The last thing he wanted was for any of them to second-guess his presence here. This place was the best thing that could have happened to him in the aftermath of his life imploding, and he wasn't going to let anything get in the way of it.

"It's a woman, if that changes anything," Lawson offered. "Pretty, red hair, green eyes. She didn't give a name and it looks like she's been through it."

"'Been through it'? What does that mean?" Aaron asked.

"She drove up in a beat-up truck and looks a little rough herself," Lawson replied. "But you should come see for yourself. She seemed pretty insistent. Said she'd only talk to you."

"Yeah. Sure," Aaron replied, tossing down his tools to follow Lawson back to the main building. His mind raced as he tried to put the pieces together.

Who could possibly be looking for him here? He had come here to get away from everything that had happened before, and he wasn't sure what he would do if his past came back to haunt him after all this time. There was a nudge in the back of his mind but he refused to let it surface. He'd known a beautiful redhead with bright green eyes and a sassy attitude years ago. But there was no way she would be there looking for him.

As he walked, his mind rushed through other potential people it might be. He didn't have family, no sisters, aunts, or cousins who might have come looking for him. So who the hell was this? And how did she find him?

"There, that's her truck," Lawson told him, pointing to a beat-up blue truck sitting in the main parking area. Aaron stared at it for a moment, willing it to bring back some memories that would help him make sense of all of this, but he was coming up blank.

"Ring any bells?" Lawson asked curiously.

He shook his head. "Guess I need to see her," Aaron replied, trying to keep his voice steady.

He could count on one hand the number of times people had come to Warrior Peak looking for him over the last six years. He tried to convince himself that it was nothing to worry about, even if his mind was running so fast he was having a hard time getting his thoughts under control. He didn't want his fear to show on his face.

Lawson had been kind enough not to demand too much in the way of explanation when it came to his presence here. Neither he nor the others pushed him to share his past and what brought him to the lodge all those years ago. They knew there was something Aaron was running from. Hell, he'd arrived broken and bruised and paranoid of almost everything. So it wasn't a huge leap to think he'd suffered some sort of trauma. But they never pushed. Just offered support and assistance for him to get back on his feet and then offered him a job, if he wanted to stay. So, he did. He'd given up everything from his old life and made a new start here at Warrior Peak. He'd burned the only connection he'd ever cared about and didn't have anything to go back to, anyway.

Inside, the main building was quiet except for a few people chatting in the corridor as Lawson led Aaron down to the meeting rooms. Who was there for him? His mind drifted back to the truck. Something about it had twinged something in his gut, and he wasn't sure what it was.

Maybe he should just turn around and tell Lawson that he had changed his mind. He'd rather head back out to continue his work, anyway. He couldn't think of any good reasons why a random woman would be here looking for him. It could only mean trouble.

But when he saw Xavier Michaels, Lawson's business

partner, pacing in the small space outside the meeting rooms, he knew he wasn't going to be let off that easily.

Xavier raised his eyebrows at him. "What's going on here, Ward?" When he used his last name, Aaron knew Xavier was not happy with him. He wasn't sure exactly why he was mad at him, but he'd do whatever was necessary to make it right. This place had been a sanctuary for Aaron since he had left his old life, and he would do anything it took to make sure that didn't change.

"What has she said to you?" Aaron asked, trying to keep his voice even. He didn't want Xavier to think he was worried. Xavier was protective of Warrior Peak, of everything they had managed to do here, and he wasn't going to let anything get in the way of it.

"Nothing," came Xavier's frustrated reply. "She's said she's only willing to talk to you. Wouldn't even give us a name."

Aaron sighed.

"And she won't let anyone treat her injuries. At least until she sees you," he added.

Aaron froze. Injuries? Why was an injured woman here looking for him? This was bad news. Really, really bad. The nudge in the back of his mind was getting more insistent.

"I'll talk to her," Aaron replied, rolling back his shoulders. Whatever he had to handle here, he could take it on.

"She's got an attitude on her," Xavier warned him. "I don't know what she just walked out of, but her fuse is basically nonexistent."

"I can handle that," Aaron replied. He'd been a cop, after all. He knew how to handle people in high-pressure situations, and he wasn't going to let his fear get the better of him.

Xavier jerked his head toward the door, and Lawson

stepped over to it. The glass was frosted, blocking out his view of whoever was inside, but he could make out the dark shape of someone sitting there. Someone waiting for him.

Someone who might just know who he really was.

Xavier pushed the door open. "Miss. Aaron is here to see you."

"He is?"

Aaron's body tensed when he heard that voice. He had never imagined in a million years that he would ever get a chance to hear it again. His heart leaped into his throat as he pushed by Xavier and stepped inside the room.

There, wincing as she propped herself up on the chair opposite him, was the green-eyed, redheaded ghost from his past.

Bailey.

Chapter Three

Bailey gripped her stomach as she tried to stand up to greet him, but the throbbing in her thigh and various aches and pains overloading her body caused her to rethink that idea so she settled back in the chair. He pushed the door shut behind him, giving them some privacy.

Bailey stared up at him. Aaron. Aaron Ward. She couldn't believe it. He turned back to face her, and looked down at her for a moment. His eyes roamed her form, stopping on each injury, causing her to shift in her seat under his intense gaze.

Her heart twisted in her chest. It was him. It was really, truly him.

"Bailey?" he murmured. God, it had been so long since she'd heard him say her name, and something in her softened at once. All of the memories of them were flooding back to her, all the safety and comfort she'd felt in his presence. It was exactly why she'd come here. She knew there was nobody she could trust like him, even after what he'd done to her.

And, after what had happened last night, she knew she needed him more than ever.

He moved through the room, pulling the curtains shut, and she followed him with her eyes. He looked just the same as ever—the same purposeful gait, the same piercing green eyes, the same broad shoulders. She was even sure he was wearing the same aftershave, the scent drifting through the air as he walked by her. Mixed with something else, too— wood, the smell of grass.

But there were a few differences that she noticed as she kept watching him. Out of his police uniform, in a pair of jeans and a casual shirt, he looked more...relaxed. His light brown hair was a little grown out, and there was a smatter- ing of stubble on his chin.

The same man who had betrayed her all those years ago. But the only person she could think of to run to when things had gone bad. Her mind ran in a million different directions. There was so much she wanted to say to him and ask him, but she also wanted to chew him the hell out for what he had done to her. She had sworn to herself she would never see him again, but here she was, sitting in front of him, and praying he was going to be able to help her.

"Are you okay?" Aaron asked as he noticed her winc- ing again.

She pressed her hand into her lower rib cage, trying to stem the bolt of pain that was rushing up her side. "I'm fine."

"You don't look fine," Aaron replied skeptically.

She shook her head. "It's not as bad as it looks."

"You've had someone take a look at you?"

"Not yet," she admitted. She hadn't had time to stop by a hospital to get checked out, and she could feel the wet- ness of the blood starting to seep from her leg again. She thought she had stopped the bleeding, but clearly, that wasn't the case.

"You need to let someone here take a look," he told her.

She shook her head. She didn't want to be seen by any- one else if she could help it. What if some of the people here were working with *them*? What was going to happen to her? If they found her, they might not let her walk away this time.

"I'm fine," she attempted to say again, but her voice wavered dangerously as the blood began to leak through her jeans once more.

"You're bleeding," Aaron replied bluntly.

"Nothing I can't handle," she replied.

"Then why are you here?"

Bailey felt her cheeks heat. He had called her bluff, and he was right. She wouldn't have come here, to him of all people, if she thought there was any chance in hell that she could handle the situation herself. He stepped back, giving her the space she needed, but she could see the concern written all over his face.

"Because I got into some trouble and I need a place to lie low until I can get back on my feet," she replied.

Did he buy it? She scanned his expression, trying to read what was going on in his mind. She used to know him so well, she could tell what he was thinking just from a look— but it had been so long now she wasn't sure what the furrow in his brow meant.

That was all she was going to give him, for now. She needed to rest and clear her head before she got into details. She couldn't risk spilling the truth of what had happened to drive her out here before she was ready. She had no idea how she had even managed to find this place, but when she had staggered in to the reception and told them she was here for Aaron, she knew at once that she had come to the right place. The shock on the face of the woman behind the desk as she'd darted off to find someone else was burned into her brain. Did she really look that rough?

"So, why did you ask specifically for me? If you were

just coming here to lie low, there was no reason for me to even know you were here."

Damn. He had a point. He would be the last person she would want to see, so what made her ask for him? What would he believe?

"I heard you might be here, so I asked. I really wasn't expecting you to show up after—" She snapped her lips closed. She didn't want to open that can of worms right now. She had enough on her plate to deal with. "It doesn't matter. Call it curiosity, that's all."

He narrowed his eyes at her, weighing her words. She knew he didn't believe her, but hopefully he wouldn't call her on it now.

"Fine," Aaron replied, shaking his head. "What can we do to help?"

He hadn't changed. Always focusing on the practical solutions to any problem and what he could do to make the situation better. That was Aaron in a nutshell. She wasn't sure she needed anything practical right now, though. She wasn't even sure how to feel about all of this.

She was scared and worried they were going to find her and finish what they started last night. She was still sad and angry about Aaron's betrayal, but she also felt unexpected joy and another feeling she couldn't quite name now that he was standing in front of her. It was all just too much right now to process.

Bailey slowly released the breath she didn't realize she was holding, then winced at the movement. She really needed to get someone to look at her injuries. She was starting to feel a little woozy.

"It's fine, I'll figure it out. Sorry to pull you away from whatever you were doing. You can go," she replied, though she hoped he wouldn't take her up on that. Even though she was still mad and confused, she wanted him here with her. She was scared. Really, really scared. She had never been hurt this badly. Her whole body was in pain. She'd been running on pure adrenaline until she had gotten here, but now that she could actually rest, she felt like she might pass out.

"You can't dismiss me. I'm not going to leave you to figure things out alone, Bailey," he replied firmly. He crouched down in front of her. Even as her vision started to get a little hazy, she could make out the piercing green of his eyes.

His eyes swept up and down her body again. She knew she looked horrible, and that she was going to need medical attention if she was going to avoid any long-term issues. But the thought of doing anything except sitting—or lying—down was too exhausting, she couldn't force herself to care.

"Who did this to you?" he asked, his voice low and angry. Like he wanted to take them on himself, make them pay for what they had done to her. She didn't know what to say. Part of her wanted to blurt it all out to him, tell him the truth and beg him to protect her against what was coming her way. Another part of her wanted to run and tell him to forget he had ever seen her again.

Suddenly, it was all too much, emotions and pain both battling for dominance. Emotions seemed to be winning as anger sparked in her chest. She managed to sit herself fully upright, and looked him in the eye.

"You don't get to know that," she growled at him. She knew she was being irrational, but once the anger started rising, she couldn't stop it. He was the one who had turned his back on her and gotten her blacklisted and put on desk duty with whatever he had written in that report. Now he was acting like he cared and wanted to help? She knew she must seem crazy since she was the one who had come to him, but she couldn't stop herself.

"Bailey, I'm trying to help you," he told her, his voice as patient as it could be, given the circumstances. "We have people here who can check you out and make sure you don't need any further treatment. There's a hospital—"

"I don't want to go to hospital," she snarled. She was desperate for him to help her, but seeing him again like this was like a blade through her heart. Her pride was holding her back. She didn't want to have to rely on him, not after what he had done to her.

Planting her hand on the chair for leverage, she dragged herself to her feet. Her knees shook wildly, and her head spun when she was upright. Her body screamed at her to sit back down, but she ignored it. She glared at him, unable to believe she had been foolish enough to come here. Why did she think he, of all people, would be able to help her when he had been the one to wreck her life in the first place? She was such an idiot. A scared and desperate idiot.

She started toward the door as fast as her injured legs would allow. "I shouldn't have come here."

"Bailey, sit down," he ordered her, a hint of the old cop in him coming through again. He tried to catch her around the waist as she wobbled dangerously, but she pushed him off before he could get hold of her. She didn't want his help.

"This was a mistake," she said, as she continued to inch her way to the door with her hand on the wall to steady herself. She just had to make it back to her truck, then she could rest for a while before getting back on the road to God knows where.

"You're still the same bastard you were when you ruined my life six years ago!" she exclaimed. She whipped her head around to face him when she dropped that bomb. She had no idea if he knew that she was aware he had been the reason she'd ended up in the Bay for so long. Stuck out there behind a desk in the middle of nowhere, wasting her training and potential, when she could be making a difference out on the street.

"What are you talking about—Bailey!" he exclaimed, as she buckled and fell against the door. She managed to catch herself just before her head went crashing into it, and she righted herself too quickly. Dark spots appeared all over her vision, and she knew she was going down.

This time, as she slipped to the ground, Aaron didn't wait. He reached an arm out and caught her, wrapping it around her waist before she could hit the ground. She felt almost weightless as he lifted her into his arms before laying her down on the couch. Her eyes felt so heavy she couldn't keep them open any longer. She could hear voices, though they sounded distant.

"Someone come help!" Aaron called out the door. Her head slumped to the side as the pain and exhaustion pulled her under. All of her fight and anger that was keeping her upright melted away. She couldn't remember why it mattered in the first place.

Her mind sank into the blackness of unconsciousness. The only thing left was the aching pain tearing through every inch of her body.

Chapter Four

Aaron paced back and forth outside the door as he tried to listen in to what was going on inside. He knew he should give River the space to work, but he wasn't going to be able to rest until he knew Bailey was okay.

His mind was racing. He had no idea what she was doing here, and judging by the way she had blown up at him when he had tried to find out, she wasn't going to be forthcoming with the answers. Who had hurt her like that? It killed him to see her so beaten-up, and she wouldn't even tell him who had done it.

But he had an idea. How could he not? It was the same thing that had been hanging over his head for all these years, even though he had tried to leave it behind. Getting her out of there had been the only way he could think of to protect her. He had accepted that she would hate him for what he'd done, but he figured that would make it easier for her to move on. She wouldn't come looking for him, because she wouldn't want anything to do with him.

For the last six years, that seemed to have been true. He hadn't heard from her. And he had accepted that he was never going to see her again, even though the thought of being without her stung. The two of them had worked so well together, but it was more than that. Her sweetness, her sense of humor, her laugh—all of it had led to him developing feelings that were totally not appropriate for someone in his position.

He had tried to ignore it for so long, but even six years later he still dreamed of her sometimes. He missed her so much, he couldn't think about anything else some nights, but he had accepted it was over between them. As if someone like her would ever have been seriously interested in a man like him, anyway. She probably had a million guys who would love to take her on a date. Guys who she didn't have a past with. Hell, she could be involved with someone now. He didn't think that was the case, though. If she was with someone else, why not go to him? Why seek Aaron out instead?

But she had come to him. And he couldn't for the life of him figure out how she knew where he was, or that he would even have been able to help her when she arrived. Some part of her, even if that part was buried so deep down under her anger that she couldn't feel it, knew he would do whatever it took to make sure she stayed safe.

River, Cade's fiancée, was working on her right now. River wasn't a doctor but she had extensive medical training from growing up in a wilderness compound. He prayed she would be able to handle Bailey's injuries. If not, he'd need to drive Bailey in to town to the doctor, or maybe even the hospital, depending on what kind of injuries River found. He didn't know exactly what had happened to her, but from what he could see, she looked bad and he could tell she was in a lot of pain. He had gone so far, done things he could never have imagined, to try and protect her, but what if it hadn't been enough? What if she was still in danger?

Warrior Peak Sanctuary was a place for military and law enforcement members to come and heal when they needed it—physically or mentally. But he'd never dreamed Bailey would be one of those people.

Xavier rounded the corner, followed by Lawson, and Aaron could tell from the looks on their faces that they had some serious questions for him. And he couldn't blame them. This woman had just turned up out of nowhere, after all. This place was important to them, and they weren't going to let anyone in who they didn't totally trust.

"Are you going to tell us what's going on with her?" Lawson demanded, nodding toward the door.

Aaron sighed. He didn't even know where to start. Their relationship had been so damn complicated, and it didn't look like it was about to get easier anytime soon.

"I used to work with her," he explained, trying to keep it vague. "We…she started out as a rookie when I was a cop. I was training her."

"How long ago?"

"A little over six years now," Aaron told Lawson, sinking down into one of the seats outside the room. He could hear River talking to Bailey inside, her tone soothing, though he couldn't make out what she was saying.

Xavier and Lawson exchanged curious looks. "Why would she come and find you after all this time? And what happened between the two of you?" Xavier finally asked.

Aaron stared off into space for a moment as he tried to figure out how best to answer that question. He knew they deserved an answer. They had been kind enough not to press for information about his past when he had first arrived. Told him he could share what he was comfortable with when he was ready. He'd told them a little after a while, but never shared much. Thought it was better all around to just let the past go. He definitely never intended on sharing this part of his past. But with Bailey turning up out of nowhere, looking like she did, he didn't have much of a choice now.

"I...like I said, we were working together," he admitted. "She was just getting her start, and I took her under my wing. I was a sergeant in the Kings Mountain Police Department at the time, and I could see something in her, even though we were just working in a small town. The other guys on the force, none of them had anything on her. She had good instincts, always knew how to handle herself, even when things got hard. That's why I..."

He trailed off again. Crap. He didn't know if it was safe to talk to them about this, even after all this time. He had done such a good job of putting it all behind him, it almost felt wrong to dredge it all up like this. But now that Bailey had appeared in his life again, he needed to find out what was going on with her. He had to get to the bottom of what brought her to Warrior Peak looking for him.

"I thought I knew the guys we were working with," he explained as best he could. "Usual small-town cop stuff, you know. That was, until I found out there was way more going on in that department than I had realized."

"Like?" Lawson prompted.

"Like...they were covering stuff up," he continued. "Hiding things, making sure certain information about certain investigations was lost so they could keep their contacts out of prison...bribery, threats. I had started looking into closed cases, some things that seemed suspicious, coincidences that just didn't add up. I was getting close, but didn't have time to get to the bottom of it all before they started to figure out that I was on to them. I guess they had their own suspicions and had someone watching me...and Bailey."

His gut clenched at the thought. Even now, he could still remember the night when they had confronted him about what he knew. When they had cornered him at his car, he thought they might be fishing for information, maybe toss out a threat, throw a punch or two.

When Ziegler had pinned him against his car and the others closed in, he knew they were out for blood.

They beat the hell out of him. Busted ribs, a concussion, and a slew of cuts and bruises. He could empathize with Bailey's condition right now. And that alone would have been bad enough to make Aaron rethink what he was doing, just for his own safety. But he would have still stayed if it wasn't for the threat they made to Bailey.

We could take her out in a second if you don't get out of town, and pretend none of this ever happened. You understand?

Even the thought of it had been enough to scare him. He hadn't realized how deeply he cared for her until he was faced with the thought of losing her. He knew he couldn't let it happen. He cared for her way too deeply, and he needed to know she was safe.

And while she could handle herself, she couldn't take an attack at the level he had just suffered. She was so vulnerable, and she didn't even know it. He hadn't told her a thing about his investigation, not wanting to involve her until he had something solid to go on.

And so, he'd fled town. But first, he had written a scathing report about Bailey and left it on his captain's desk. Something that he knew would get her sent to another department and stuck behind a desk instead of out in the field and in harm's way. He'd felt horrible writing those disparaging words about her performance, but at least he knew she'd be safe from the corruption and threats. That mattered more to him than her feelings. He filled Lawson and Xavier in on the story as quickly as he could. When he was done, Lawson let out a long whistle between his teeth.

"No wonder she was chewing you out earlier." He shook his head. "She thinks you just turned on her out of nowhere. I would be mad, too."

"Yeah," Aaron muttered, hoping her anger would fade. Surely, it had to, if she was here to get help, right? He knew she wasn't safe, and he had a sneaking suspicion that the same guys who had caused so much chaos in his own life were the ones behind her problems now.

"So what do you think she's doing here?" Xavier asked, frowning. "Must have been something serious if she was willing to put aside what you did to her to come here."

"Yeah, it must have been," Aaron agreed. He could still see in his mind's eye the way she had looked at him when he had asked her who'd done this to her—the split second of vulnerability, covered up by how much she hated him and what he had done to her. Did she have any idea why? It was all part of the process of protecting her from those men. Without him, she would've been easy pickings for them. Either she would have been forced to join their corrupt circle, or they'd have disposed of her in any way they saw fit. Neither option sounded like a good one to Aaron at the time.

"So, from what happened to you, you think the same guys are after her now?" Xavier continued, crossing his arms over his chest. "You know how important it is that we keep this place secure. Especially after what happened when Cade brought River here—"

"I know, I know," Aaron replied, nodding. It had been a safe space for him when he had needed it most, and he was going to do his best to ensure it stayed that way. He just needed to get Bailey to talk to him, to confirm what he already thought to be true.

He wasn't the only one either. Aaron knew exactly what Xavier was referring to—when Cade had stopped to help a woman on the side of the road. He'd given her a ride to War-rior Peak and they had ended up falling in love, and then her past had caught up with her. She'd had her own dark stuff to face, but with the help of Cade and the others there at the lodge, she'd done it. Now, River, the woman treating Bailey right now, was an essential part of Warrior Peak Sanctuary.

AARON HADN'T BEEN aware of all the details regarding Cade and River because he had kept to himself in the background. He had been busy trying to escape his own past rather than getting involved with others. He would never forgive him-self, though, if his presence at the sanctuary compromised the safety of others again.

"So you need to find out who did this to her," Lawson added, with a scowl. "I don't care what happened between the two of you in the past. What matters now is the present, and we need to have all the information we can upfront so we know what we might be dealing with."

"I'll do my best once she's patched up," Aaron promised, hoping they believed him. He had been working here for the better part of six years, and it had earned him a little grace—they hadn't turned Bailey away when she had come asking for him, after all. But that was only going to last so long. If he couldn't get some information out of her soon, there was going to be trouble.

"You want a coffee while you wait?" Xavier asked, jerk-ing his head toward the cafeteria.

"No, I'm going to wait here," he replied.

Xavier paused for a moment, clearly about to add some-thing, but then thought better of it. "Okay, fill us in on what you find out as soon as she's settled," he said instead. Then he and Lawson walked away, leaving Aaron alone with his thoughts once more.

He shot a look toward the door, wondering if Bailey would let him come in right now. He just wanted to see her. Being so close to her again after all this time was almost surreal, like something out of a dream. She had been such a big part of his life for so long, but he'd had to sever the ties between them bluntly and brutally with no explanation. Even if she did end up with a better understanding of what had happened, would it be enough to convince her to forgive him?

And what if this had something to do with the corruption he'd discovered before? What if she had walked back into the middle of it and found herself faced with a harsh reality she wasn't ready for? She was a principled woman, always had been, and she wouldn't have stood for that kind of behavior in any of her colleagues. But her principles wouldn't have been enough to keep her safe if they turned on her, and he hated the thought of something happening to her. Maybe if he had told her the truth back then...

He tried to push the thought to the back of his mind. He couldn't obsess over what had happened before—that was in the past now. All he could do was focus on the present, and how he was going to get her to tell him who had hurt her and why. She might have been more willing to speak with one of the other women there, but he needed something to report back to Lawson and Xavier. They wouldn't want her here if she refused to tell them the truth. He understood why.

He and Bailey had shared a real trust back in the day, and he just needed to find some way to tap into that again. He had missed her every single day since he had walked away from his old life. Seeing her again brought up a million of the old emotions he had done his best to forget.

But things were different now. He just had to find some way to handle whatever came next, and make sure she didn't end up with any more dangerous injuries in the process.

He looked once more at the door, then began to pace again while he waited. He had a feeling it was going to be a long day.

Chapter Five

When Bailey's eyes opened again, it took her a minute to remember where she was. She sat upright as quickly as her sore body would allow, and looked around.

"Hey, you're awake. Take it easy, you don't want to move around too fast," a soothing voice said on her left.

She looked over to see the woman who had been tending to her. She was sipping on coffee and sitting in a chair against the wall.

"What's going on?" Bailey mumbled, a little disorientated. The pain was better, but she was feeling a bit sick from the blood loss and lack of food. She actually didn't remember when she ate last, but she needed to get something in her soon. Plus, she had no idea who this woman who had been watching her sleep was. She seemed friendly enough, but she was a stranger. She kind of assumed Aaron would be there with her, waiting for answers.

"You passed out," the woman replied gently. "I was looking after you while you were resting. I've patched you up and gave you some painkillers, too."

Bailey tried to sit up straighter while keeping the woman in sight. She noticed the pain in her ribs was not as intense, and her leg wasn't throbbing as much. So that was something, at least.

"I'm River." The woman introduced herself. "I work here at Warrior Peak Sanctuary."

"Are you a doctor?" Bailey couldn't see a reason why this woman would be here looking after her otherwise.

"No, but I do have some medical experience. When someone's hurt, the guys usually get me first to see if it's something easily treatable before they call the town doctor or discuss going to the hospital."

That made sense. And Bailey was grateful for the assistance. There was no way she wanted to go into town, and definitely not to a hospital. That would lead them right to her.

"Well, thank you, River. I appreciate you helping me," Bailey replied, and she meant it. Even though she was exhausted and sore, her gut told her that she was in a safe place. That she didn't have to worry about those men finding her while she was here.

"You know much about Warrior Peak Sanctuary?" River asked.

Bailey shook her head slowly, noting that it didn't feel as bad as before, either. She hadn't known anything about this place, apart from the fact that Aaron worked here. That was the only reason she had come. On the run, she had only been able to think of one person she could trust, even if he was also the last person on earth she wanted to see.

"It used to be for law enforcement and military people who'd suffered through traumatic events and were recovering, but it's expanding now," she explained with a soft smile. "It's also for people getting out of dangerous situations who need a place to stay while they get back on their feet. So you're safe here. I promise. These are good guys and they just want to help."

Bailey nodded. There was a note of sincerity in River's voice, and she wondered if she had been through something similar—something crazy that had brought her here in the first place.

"And speaking of traumatic situations," she added, nodding toward Bailey. "You really got yourself beat up. In case you're unaware, you have a few cracked ribs and a stab wound on your thigh. I'd like to check you for a concussion, too, considering that goose egg you've got on your head."

"Sounds about right." Bailey sighed. The attack was still something of a blur to her, but she remembered hands on her, the flash of metal, the terror she felt in that instant, certain this was the end for her.

"You mind?" River indicated toward Bailey's head.

Bailey nodded slowly. "Sure. Go ahead. I don't think I have one, though."

"Let's just double-check to be certain," she replied, then asked Bailey to follow her directions as she examined her head further. Once she was satisfied there was no concussion, she sat back in her chair, giving Bailey space. "You want to tell me what happened?" she asked.

Bailey flattened her lips and shook her head at once. River might have seemed nice, but she didn't know a damn thing about her, and she wasn't about to go handing over her biggest secrets without getting to know her a little better. If these last couple of days had taught her anything, it was that she couldn't exactly trust everyone she thought she could. She needed to be way more careful about how she handled herself.

"No problem. I get it," River murmured, and she rose to her feet. "You stay put. I'm going to see if dinner is ready. You must be starving, and getting some nourishment and fluids in you will help you feel a bit better. We usually eat together in the cafeteria, but I don't think you're in any state to be getting up right now."

Bailey thanked her again, and let out a sigh of relief as soon as River closed the door behind her. She squeezed her eyes shut and tried to remind herself that she was here for one person and one person only—Aaron. She had to get the truth out of him. She was sure he must have known something about the nightmare that had driven her out here. Maybe it even had something to do with his sudden departure.

She was regretting how she had handled seeing him again. She shouldn't have blown up at him like she did. It wasn't her best move, going on the attack, when he was who she was here to see. Telling him to leave her alone and she'd handle it wasn't exactly her brightest moment. He must think she'd lost her mind. She needed to get herself under control before she saw him again.

River returned with another woman in tow, carrying three plates of food between them. River handed one to Bailey, who took it gratefully. It was just meat and veggies, nothing special, but to her hungry stomach, it looked like a damn cornucopia.

"This is Hannah." River introduced the other woman, who smiled kindly in greeting. Bailey vaguely remembered seeing her when she had rushed in the building asking for Aaron.

"Hi there. If you need anything while you're here, let me know. I tend to have the most interactions with the guests with their day-to-day needs. The guys are more involved with keeping the place running and the bigger problems."

"Thanks, I'll keep that in mind." Though Bailey had no idea how long she'd be here.

"I also heard your meeting with Aaron earlier didn't go too well," Hannah remarked. "So, I figured you would probably want some space to yourself to regroup and rest instead of going to sit with everyone else for dinner."

"Yeah, thanks," Bailey replied. These women were being so kind to her, but all she could think about right now was Aaron.

"So how many people usually stay here?" she asked, keeping her voice as casual as possible. She didn't want these women thinking she was trying to scope the place out, though that was exactly her intention. She needed to know how many people she was looking at, and then she could figure out where to go from there.

"Anywhere from ten to twenty on average," Hannah replied through a mouthful of food. "It's pretty busy in the cafeteria in the evenings, as everyone eats together."

"Well, thanks for giving me an out from that," she replied. She appreciated it. The thought of being around so many people she didn't know was discomforting right now, to say the least, especially after what had happened to her. Her instincts radar seemed to be malfunctioning.

"Hey, I get it," Hannah replied. "Most people who come here need a little time to themselves at first. It's not unusual."

She paused for a moment, staring at Bailey, and then exchanged a glance with River.

"So," she said, "how long are you planning on staying, exactly?"

Bailey didn't know. These women were being so nice to her and they hadn't asked her to leave, but she wasn't sure how to respond. She knew they were curious as to why she was here in the first place, broken and beaten no less. She wasn't sure what she could tell them that wouldn't guarantee more questions she couldn't answer. Not yet, anyway.

"Until I get what I came here for," she replied firmly. That was something, right? Enough for them to go on for now.

"And what did you come here for?" Hannah inquired.

"To get information from Aaron," she muttered, more to herself than to the other women. And with that, she turned her attention back to her food, shutting off the conversation before it could go any further.

Once they had finished dinner, River and Hannah cleared out and left Bailey to get some rest, much to her relief. She was exhausted, and her body still ached, despite the pain meds. She tried to remind herself that this wouldn't last forever—she would get better soon.

Right now, she just needed to rest and work on rebuilding her strength. Hopefully, they'd let her do that here. She could feel her eyelids getting heavy as she snuggled down under the covers.

She drifted off with thoughts of Aaron and the last time they were together before her life went to shambles.

Answers first, then she'd maybe see if there was anything left of them to salvage.

SHE STARTLED AWAKE and it took her a minute to realize where she was. Looking around the room, she felt everything come rushing back. Kings Mountain, her attack, finding Aaron, Warrior Peak Sanctuary. She suddenly felt like the walls were beginning to close in on her.

It was dark outside, and she didn't hear any activity or voices inside, but she needed to get out of this room. She slowly rose to her feet, even as her body screamed in protest, and silently opened the bedroom door. The painkillers were starting to wear off, but she didn't care. She needed some fresh air. Hopefully, it was late enough that she wasn't going to run into anyone.

She made her way through the quiet corridors of the lodge, half expecting to bump into someone, but found the place empty. She took a couple of wrong turns, but eventually managed to find the lobby. She stepped outside the main entrance and inhaled a big lungful of fresh air. Her ribs protested, but the stretch still felt good. She wasn't used to lying in a prone position for so long. It was colder up here on the mountain, she realized. The air felt crisper, cleaner.

In the distance, she saw the trees swaying in the breeze, the sound of the leaves rustling the only noise around her. Her back still ached like crazy, and she knew she wasn't going to be able to take a walk or anything like that, but at least she could get out of that room and try to clear her head.

She had no idea what she was going to do, now that she was here. Get the truth from Aaron, sure, but what then? She didn't have a clue. She was in no condition to go back to work, and even if she did, those corrupt cops in the department wouldn't allow it. If she ever showed her face around there again, she wasn't sure she would walk away with her life this time. She wasn't sure why she had now. The thought sent a shiver down her spine.

She spotted a small porch seat around the side of the building, and she slowly made her way to it, glad to take the weight off her injured leg. She hated feeling this weak. She might be small, but she had always prided herself on being strong and fit. To be enfeebled and injured was an awful feeling. She wanted to heal so she could take on the men who had done this to her. She wanted to expose them for everything they had done, not just to her but to the community. But right now, she couldn't have won a fight against a kitten.

She heard footsteps behind her, and without even having to turn around, she knew at once who it was. A weight landed on the seat next to her, and she smelled his cologne, the familiar scent of him that she had grown to love so much when they had been working together.

"What are you doing out here?" Aaron asked her. "You should be resting."

She didn't reply. She wasn't going to take orders from him, and she didn't feel like arguing. He wasn't her boss or even her friend, anymore. Nobody who really cared about her could ever have done something like he did, no matter the reasons.

But, as she felt the warmth radiating from his body, she knew she didn't have it in her to ask to be left alone. He was the reason she had come to this place. As much as she didn't want to admit it, she needed him. It would have been a whole lot easier if she could just forget about him, but that was never going to work.

"You mind if I sit with you?" he asked, and she shook her head.

"No." She sighed. She missed this, his closeness. There had been a time when they had known everything about each other—or so she'd thought.

"How are you doing?" he asked.

Her shoulders slumped slightly. "About as well as I can be, given that I was just beaten up by a bunch of dirty cops."

She felt the air shift between them at once. Was he expecting her to say that? Hoping she wouldn't? She didn't have a clue. She stole a look at him out of the corner of her eye, wishing she could just ask him what was going on in his head, but she had to be more careful than that. She had let this man close to her once before, and it had ended with her getting burned. She wasn't going to hand him the chance to do that to her again.

"What happened?" he asked her.

Rubbing her hand over her face, and trying to ignore the sharp twinge in her ribs, she reasoned with herself. She came to this place to find him, ask for his help. She had to tell him at some point so she could get answers. So, why not here? Why not now?

Chapter Six

Aaron's mind was reeling as he took in what she had just said. Dirty cops? The same ones he had dealt with? They had to be, right? There was no way she could have encountered anyone else. His skin crawled when he thought about what they might have done to her, but the best he could do right now was listen.

"I... I finally got out from under the curse you put on me," she snapped back. She was still defensive, but at least she was talking. It was a start.

"What do you mean?"

"When you got me sent out to the middle of nowhere to be stuck behind a desk all day?" she reminded him sarcastically, as though he might have forgotten. "I just spent the last six years there. Trust me, I've been counting every day."

The bitterness in her voice was obvious, and he hated hearing her so angry at him. But she had a right to be. He needed to give her the time to come to terms with it, because six years still hadn't been enough.

"I finally worked hard enough to convince them to put me back out in the field," she explained. "And there was only one place I wanted to do it. Kings Mountain."

His heart sank. So she had walked right back into all of that? With no warning? And he was sure Ziegler and the others would have gotten bolder with what they were doing, willing to push the boundaries even further than they had when he was there.

"I got a warm welcome, let's just say that," she remarked. "From Ziegler in particular."

Aaron felt a flare of rage in his system, as he thought about how vulnerable she must have been, and how quick they had been to make a move on her.

"How long were you back before it started?"

"It was the first night," she replied. "I wasn't set to work until the next day, but I was excited to be back. Dropped by the station to check in and say hi to everyone. They were the first ones who greeted me and asked me out for a drink to celebrate my return." She paused, and shivered like she was reliving it in her mind.

He clenched his fists at his sides to keep from reaching for her. "What happened?" he asked again.

"Everything was fine, at first. Then they started talking smack about you. It caught me off guard and when they turned the questions to me…how far I was willing to go to keep my job, stuff like that… I panicked and rushed out. They didn't hold back. I thought they were going to kill me," she whispered.

She paused again and wrapped her arms around herself, her gaze distant. Aaron slid closer to her, offering his warmth and silent support.

"I barely remember the attack," she murmured. "They had followed me out of the bar and ganged up on me in the parking lot when I was trying to leave. I had just made it to my truck when they shoved my head into the side of it. I vaguely remember hands tugging on me, someone yanked my head back, I think. The glint of a knife…" She trailed off and shuddered. "I woke up in a lot of pain and bleeding on the ground."

Aaron winced but didn't say anything, allowing her to continue.

"When I regained consciousness, I jumped in my truck and took off. I didn't even really know where I was going. I just wanted to put as much distance as possible between myself and those guys." She took a shaky breath and shrugged. "I drove home, threw some things in a bag, then I ended up here looking for you...and you know the rest."

"I'm so sorry this happened to you, Bailey," he said softly.

She looked at him out of the corner of her eye. "You knew about it, right?" she asked.

He nodded. No point in trying to hide it now. The truth was out, and she was in danger. No matter how much he wished he could undo what had happened to her, there was no walking away from this.

"Yeah, I did," he replied apologetically. "I was looking into them, trying to collect evidence to take to the captain. Apparently, they had their own suspicions about me and confronted me. Anyway, I'm glad you found me, but how did you know where I was?"

"Because *they* knew where you were. Lee specifically mentioned this place. That's how I knew where to come. They must have searched for you after you left."

Those words hung in the air for a moment as he processed them. They knew? For how long? Why hadn't they come to find him yet?

"Right," he murmured. He had no idea what to say to that. Whether she knew it or not, she was admitting that he was in danger—that both of them were. This wasn't a safe place for him anymore. The thought of Warrior Peak being compromised, of bringing more danger to the door of the people who had offered him sanctuary when he had needed it most made him feel sick.

"I'm going to stay here as long it takes me to get back on my feet," she told him, stretching her arms above her head and wincing. Her shirt rode up, revealing the bruising on her sides, and he clenched his fists when he thought about who must have done that to her. All of them ganging up on this woman? Four big men against one small woman. It was totally disgusting. She was lucky to have made it out alive, though he was sure he didn't need to remind her of that.

"And then I'm going back, and I'm going to bring them to justice," she added, narrowing her eyes. "Just because you could ignore it for six years, doesn't mean I can."

The jab stung. He had only left that place without doing more to stop them because he had known how much danger it would put her in, but he didn't know if she was ready to hear it. Or if she would even believe him if he told her. He wished he could just get her to trust him somehow, but he had broken that trust before and he wasn't sure what it would take for them to put the pieces back together again.

She rose to her feet, or at least tried to. She needed to lean heavily on the porch railing to get herself back upright, and he stood up and offered her a hand.

"You need some help?" he asked her, and she fired him a look and snorted.

"You really think I need help from you?" she demanded, raising her eyebrows. "All you've ever done is cause me trouble."

"All I've ever done?" he echoed.

Something in her face shifted as she looked away. "Not… not all you've ever done," she admitted, lowering her gaze to the ground. "When we were working together, Aaron, that was the happiest I'd ever been. I know I was young, but I…the connection we had, it was real. And then for you to turn and do that to me, without any warning, without giving me any chance to stand up for myself…" She trailed off, her eyes shining with tears for a moment. "I just didn't get it."

She shrugged, her eyes becoming guarded again. He wanted to reach out and take her hand, tell her that he had felt the same way about her, but he'd had to make a hard choice to try to protect her. And that he would have done anything he could to not hurt her, but the situation was so complicated.

"I looked up to you so much," she admitted. "And I wanted you to notice me as more than just a rookie, you know?"

Aaron knew exactly what she meant, and he wished he could tell her that he did—he had seen her as so much more than just her job. He had gotten to know her deeply, and the bond they had shared—beyond just a professional connection—was something he had never found since. She paused for a moment before she kept talking, her mind clearly racing.

"I would have believed you, you know," she told him, shaking her head. "I would have believed you if you'd come to me and told me what was going on in the department. I don't know what you were trying to protect me from, but you didn't need to do all of that to look out for me."

A million words were on the tip of his tongue, but he couldn't find a way to get any of them out that would actually make a difference. He knew she was mad at him. She probably would be for the rest of her life. They had worked so closely together, and now she was being faced with the reality of what had driven them apart. She didn't know every detail yet, but he was sure she would insist on getting to the bottom of it.

She hobbled toward the door and went inside. Aaron thought about going after her, but he knew it wouldn't have led to anything good. She still wasn't in a place where she could talk to him, but it looked as though she was going to be sticking around for a while as she got back on her feet. Maybe they would get a chance to talk while she was recovering.

Even though he was tired, he sank back down on to the porch seat and stared out into the forest beyond. The news she had given him, that they knew where he was, changed everything. He was going to have to find some way to protect himself, and this place.

Soon enough, he'd have to tell Xavier and Lawson about it, even though he wished he could find any way out of that damn conversation. He knew they were going to all but put this place on lockdown, and the thought of bringing that kind of stress to their door just didn't sit right with him.

But he didn't have a choice. Even if it would change this place that had been his safe haven. It had been so long, he had gotten comfortable—stopped looking over his shoulder and started to actually feel like he belonged here. He never expected his past to put the lodge—and the people who lived here—in danger. And he definitely never expected to see Bailey again after what had happened.

When he thought of what Bailey must have been through, he couldn't help but feel guilty. He had left her to that, whether he had meant to or not. He should have known that she would work her way back on to the streets again—she was too good to sit behind a desk. One negative report from him wasn't going to be enough to get the people around her to ignore the work she did. She had never been the kind of person to leave something unfinished, so he should have known she'd want to go back to Kings Mountain. He'd completely left her unprepared for what she'd face if she did.

But back then, he had hardly been able to think past getting her out of there. Thinking about her at all had been too painful for him, so imagining what would have come next for her was something he couldn't even let himself do. He had hoped she was safe, that she was happy, that she didn't hate him. But since she had walked back into his life, it was clear that none of that applied.

She'd admitted that she had feelings for him when they were first working together, and his head was still spinning as he tried to wrap his mind around it. He had never imagined she would have looked at him that way. Would he have acted on it then, if he'd known? He wanted to believe he was better than that, but his attraction to her had been intense.

It still was, if he was honest with himself. Even when she was as beaten down as she was, she was still fiercely captivating. She was still the woman he remembered from all those years ago, but this time, more sure of herself, with more life experience behind her.

And, when she was faced with danger, she still came looking for him. After all this time, she still sought him out. Obviously, even if she didn't seem willing to admit it right now, some part of her still felt safe with him.

He hoped he could do that part of her proud.

He had made peace with the fact that she was going to hate him after he wrote that report. But now that she was back in his life, he didn't know if he could live with it. He didn't want her walking around here, loathing him for his betrayal, when it was so much more complicated than that. Look at the state she was in now—it would have been even worse if they had launched this attack on her when she had been a rookie, without him there to cover for her.

The moon was high in the sky, bathing everything around Aaron in a bright glow. It was peaceful out here for now, but that was all going to change soon enough. Now that they knew where he was, his days of peace and quiet were over.

And he had to be ready for whatever came next.

Chapter Seven

Bailey eased herself out of bed, not wanting to move too quickly. She knew she had to give herself time to rest, no matter how tempting it might have been to just force herself to get back out there and pick up where she had left off.

After nearly a week here, she finally felt like she was getting her feet back under her again. Though she had mostly kept out of the way of the people milling around, she had been getting to know the horses that lived out behind the main lodge in the paddock. Hannah had told her that they were a relatively new arrival. They helped some of the people who had a hard time dealing with other humans. Bailey could see exactly what the appeal was—she didn't have to hide herself or worry about what she said around them, she could just relax.

She had formed a particular bond with Wheatie, an old palomino mare who had been taken in by them when her old owners had gotten too frail to care for her. She was incredibly gentle, and had started rushing up to the fence whenever she saw Bailey getting close, clearly not willing to let her get away without seeing if she had an apple tucked in her pocket for her first.

In fact, that was exactly where Bailey was headed right after breakfast. She tried to arrive at the cafeteria a little after everyone else, so she didn't have to worry about too many questions, and it was nearly empty by the time she got there today. Good. She hadn't seen Aaron in a few days, and she wasn't ready to talk to him again, not after their last conversation. She just needed a little more time to shore up her defenses before facing him again. That's why she'd been avoiding him.

She knew she had laid too much on the line, right there on her first night. She should have been more careful, held a little more back, but she couldn't stand the thought of him not knowing how much she had cared for him back then. He hadn't trusted her with the truth, but she would have listened to him—she wouldn't have shut him down or told him he was crazy. And she would have worked to bring those corrupt cops down right alongside him.

Confessing her once deeply held feelings for him felt like a risk she wasn't sure she should have taken. What was he going to think of her now? Had he felt the same way? Even if he'd had feelings for her back then, he had still betrayed her. Her heart still hurt when she thought of what he had done to her, and the fact he was capable of it. She didn't know if she could trust him again, but she knew she'd have to try.

Once she'd had breakfast, she headed out to the paddock, carrying her weight on her uninjured leg. The pain was still there, but it had improved a whole lot. River had tried to convince her to get checked out at a local hospital, but she had turned her down, not wanting to leave a paper trail so she could be tracked. She was sure the cops who had done this to her would be searching for her already, and she didn't need to make it any easier for them than she already had.

She had been convinced by Hannah to see Carter, one of the physical therapists. Carter's brother, Cade, had made sure to give him a glowing recommendation and passed it along to Hannah and the guys saying how much Carter had helped him when he first came to the lodge.

She reached the field and saw Wheatie trotting over to greet her, her mane bouncing with every step. Bailey couldn't help but grin, but the smile soon faded from her face when she spotted Aaron working on a fence at the edge of the paddock.

He glanced up and saw her coming before she could turn to leave, and he waved her over. Wheatie diverted her attention to him, nuzzling her head into his shoulder, and he reached over to stroke her nose.

"How are you doing?" he asked Bailey.

"I'm fine," Bailey answered, even as a bolt of pain traveled up the length of her leg. Ugh, she hated this. She wished she didn't have to deal with him right now. Being around him was so damn confusing, her head going in a million different directions at once. And she was embarrassed that she had been so vulnerable with him on her first night there.

"You sure about that?" he asked, watching as she leaned on the fence to take the weight off her leg.

She nodded. "Sure. You know, I never asked what you do around here."

He smirked slightly at her sudden change of subject. He paused for a moment, debating whether to let her off the hook before replying. "I got hired as Warrior Peak's handyman. Kind of a jack-of-all-trades, help wherever's needed."

"Ah, so how long you been up here?" she asked, directing her attention back to the horse.

"Been here around six years. A friend in the department had used this place to recover after he suffered injuries in an undercover sting operation. Said it was a good place to contemplate and re-evaluate life choices. Figured it wouldn't hurt to give it a try." He paused for a moment before he continued. Let her read into that what she will. He still didn't think she was ready to hear everything yet. "So...what do you know about Ziegler and the rest of the guys?"

She shrugged. "Not much. Definitely never would have thought they were dirty cops."

"How did it all happen?" he pressed, leaning forward with interest. "Did they try to get you on board, or—"

"No, no, nothing like that," she replied. "Like I said before, they invited me out for a drink to celebrate, and everything seemed normal, at first. They all seemed happy to have me back. And then I asked about you. You were the elephant in the room, after all, so I thought I'd just rip off the Band-Aid and move on. But one of them said something and the atmosphere of the place shifted. Something about you being a rat, then their friendly tones changed to more menacing and made me uncomfortable. So I threw out an excuse and left, and they followed me out."

His shoulders slumped as he took in what she was saying, as though he was blaming himself for it. Maybe he was. He was the one who had hidden it from her, after all. If she had known what she was walking into, she would have been better prepared to handle it.

"I'm sorry you had to go through that," he replied.

She frowned. "I think they could tell there was no chance I was ever going to go along with their corruption, so they had to get rid of me or scare me into silence. Now that I know what I'm dealing with, it's going to be a lot easier," she remarked. She could already feel herself shifting back into cop mode.

"What's going to be easier?"

"They were so impulsive...so reckless," she continued on, as if he hadn't spoken. "They've gotten away with their operation for so long that they're cocky, Aaron. There's no way they haven't made mistakes. We just have to find one and expose them. I know there's something—we just need to find it."

"We?" he replied, cocking an eyebrow.

She shrugged. "I can tell you're still a cop, under all of this," she replied, gesturing to his clothes. "The sergeant who trained me is still in there."

"I left the force for a reason," he muttered.

She shot him a look. "Yeah, I know you did," she replied. "Because you didn't think you could take those guys on by yourself. But you're not going to have to. We can do this together. I know we can."

Wheatie snorted, as though agreeing with her. She reached out to pet the horse, running her fingers through her silken mane.

"You should just let me handle this," he replied. "Like I should have done six years ago."

She shook her head at once. "I'm not letting you deal with this all alone again. That was the problem the first time around," she pointed out. "But we can't just let them get away with this. Think about how many people they must have hurt over the years, how many victims have gone without justice. I can't just walk away from this. Even if you could."

He winced. It was a low blow, and she knew it. But she wouldn't apologize. He should have stood up and fought all those years ago, even if it meant putting himself in danger. She had always seen him as a principled, passionate cop, but to know he had left without trying to do more made her doubt all of that.

He seemed to be able to tell that he wasn't going to change her mind, and he checked one of the nails in the fence before he replied.

"At least stay here while we work out a plan," he suggested. "That way, I know you're safe."

"You're sure you don't want to send me away again?" she fired back. "Maybe Florida this time?"

He glared at her, a flash of anger in his eyes. "You know I did the best I could at the time."

"Your best wasn't good enough," she spat back, even though she knew she was being unfair. She couldn't make herself care. Everything in her life seemed unfair right now, and she needed to take it out on someone. Since he was partly to blame, he was her target. If he'd only confided in her, let her help…

He took a step toward her, his eyes blazing. "You don't get to decide that," he told her. "If you had any idea of what I'd been up against—"

"I would have helped you!" she protested, shaking her head. "I would have done everything I could have to work with you and bring those guys down, you know that. You didn't give me the choice. You got me shipped off to the middle of nowhere because you thought you knew what was best for me."

"I wasn't going to let them target you!" he exclaimed. It was the most emotion she had seen from him since she'd shown up at the sanctuary. Even though it was more anger than anything else, it was a relief to see him as emotional about this as she was. Her whole life had been torn apart— the man she had admired, maybe even loved, had betrayed her. He couldn't expect her to just forget about it and move on, even all these years later.

"I cared about you too much to put you in the line of fire," he said.

"And I cared about you too much to believe you could do something like that to me," she snapped back. "You threw me aside like I was nothing. Like I was a bad cop. How was I supposed to feel?"

He opened his mouth like he was going to answer, but clamped it shut again with a sigh. He looked away like he would rather be doing anything else except having this conversation. But they would have to talk about it sooner or later. Better to get it over with now.

He scrubbed a hand down his face. "I wanted to keep you safe, and that was the only way I could think of to do it. I didn't have a lot of time to think through options," he told her. "It wasn't what I wanted. I never wanted you to hate me."

"What did you want?" she demanded.

For a split second, she could feel it between them again—that heat, the chemistry she had tried to deny for so long. It was like they were back in his cruiser, the two of them bantering over some case, just like they had back in the old days.

He took a deep breath and looked at the sky. "You."

Chapter Eight

Bailey just stared at him for a moment. Disbelief crossed her face. She drew in a sharp breath, just like she used to do when he took a corner a little too fast in the cruiser when they were on the move. He could still remember the way she shifted in her seat, how her hand would reach for the dashboard to balance herself. She was normally so composed, but those flashes of what was underneath always intrigued him.

And the times she had reached over to grab his arm to steady herself. He could still remember that feeling, her fingertips digging into his skin, how it made him feel like he belonged there. How he never wanted to be anywhere but by her side.

"You can't say that," she replied finally, her voice a little shaky. "It's not fair—"

"It's the truth," he replied. "What else do you want me to say? I wanted you, Bailey. And I wanted you to be safe above all else. I could never have forgiven myself if something had happened to you. That's why I did what I did."

He spoke fervently, meaning every word—every word he wished he could have said to her all those years ago, before he'd had to turn his back on her the way he had. He had lost so much because of Ziegler and his cronies, but worse, so had Bailey, and she hadn't had a choice in the matter.

"I know it feels like I betrayed you. I don't blame you for feeling that way," he continued. "But I... I couldn't have lived with myself if something had happened, and I knew I could have stopped it. Coming here, sending you away, they were last-minute decisions and the only things I could think of right then. I didn't exactly have a lot of space to put together a plan."

Bailey pushed her fingers through Wheatie's mane again, not looking at him, but clearly listening. She grimaced and began massaging her thigh around her wound, clearly still in quite a bit of pain.

"Here, let me help," he said, stepping forward and holding out an arm to lean on.

"I don't need your help," she muttered.

"I would do the same for anyone," he replied, and she reluctantly put a hand on his shoulder to steady herself as she waited for the pain to subside again. Her proximity was bringing up more feelings than he knew what to do with, so he swiftly shifted the conversation to something a little less loaded.

"How have the last few years been for you, anyway?" he asked. "I mean, besides hating my guts."

She sighed, like she didn't want to talk about it. He half expected her to just turn around and leave, and maybe she would have if her leg wasn't hurting her so badly. But instead, she answered him.

"Life wasn't all bad out there," she replied. "I loved being next to the ocean. And I got to know some cool people in the Bay, too—they were sad when I left, actually. I thought about sticking around there, but I had to go back to Kings

Mountain. That was where it all started for me. Felt like a full circle moment."

She shook her head.

"Maybe I should have just accepted that my career in North Carolina was over," she added. "None of this would have happened if I had just stayed put."

"Yeah, but you were always stubborn," he added, as she shifted her hand back to the fence.

"I wasn't that bad," she protested.

He laughed. "Bailey, remember I worked with you," he reminded her. "I saw all the sides of you. And how hard it was for you to let go of anything, even when it would have been a better idea."

Kind of like she was doing now, actually. If she had been smart, she would have seen that there was no reason to keep pushing to get to the bottom of this corruption scandal. They were small-time, and it would likely just cause her more suffering in the long term. But she had made her mind up, and when she made her mind up, there was no stopping her.

"Maybe I've changed," she remarked. "I had to learn a lot of patience working behind a desk all that time."

"Maybe you have," he agreed, though he wasn't sure he believed it.

He could tell by the way she carried herself she was the same Bailey he had known from all those years ago—the same woman filled with ambition and a sense of justice that ran deep down inside of her. These guys didn't know what they were up against. Getting Bailey involved in all of this might have been the biggest mistake they had ever made.

But, judging by the state of her now, it might cost her more.

"What about you?" she asked, turning the question around on him.

"What about me?"

She gestured around the paddock. "You always seemed like such a cop to me. You must have been going crazy up here, bored all this time."

"It's not as bad as all that," he replied. "Not anymore, at least."

He had struggled when he'd first arrived, trying to adapt to this new reality and this version of himself that wasn't a cop. The version of himself that wasn't out on the beat doing everything he could to make the world a safer place.

"It's been a good change of pace," he continued. "I get to help people here. I still feel like I'm doing some good. And the people who run this place, they're damn good guys. I'm grateful they gave me a purpose after I…"

He trailed off. No point in finishing that sentence. After he had given up his old purpose? That was what he really felt like saying. He had walked away from everything he had known, and getting settled here had been tough. He could still remember those first few restless months, feeling like he had made a mistake and wondering how long he could stick this out. Wondering if he could turn back time and undo what he had done, though he knew it was far too late for that.

"Never thought I would see you settle down, especially not in a place like this," she added. "It's just a plot of land in the middle of nowhere."

"That's what it looks like from the outside," he agreed. "But there's way more to it than that. Way more to everyone here, too. Everyone has their stories. Either they're running away from something, or they're searching for their own purpose. I guess I was a little of both."

"Guess so," she agreed, and he saw the flicker of a smile pass over her lips. He missed that smile, more than he would have cared to admit to himself. Seeing it again made his chest tighten. He shifted his gaze from her, not wanting to stare for too long. Their history was too long and messy now to let anything romantic get in the way. Even if he wished things were different.

"It's like it settles into you as you settle into it," he explained. "I didn't think I would like it here as much as I do, but the longer I stayed, the more I liked it. Maybe you'll find the same thing, too."

"Maybe," she replied with a shrug, as though she didn't really believe him. "You think you'll ever leave?"

He looked around at the paddock, Wheatie, and the other horses gallivanting around happily. This place was so far removed from his old life, it was hard to even imagine what being a cop had been like. Yes, there were times when he missed it, but this place had become his new home, and he didn't want to change that.

He shook his head. "I don't think so."

He was surprised by his answer, but it felt right. There was a time when he would have jumped at the chance to get out of here and return to what he had known before, but with Bailey standing in front of him, it didn't seem as pressing as it once had. Maybe it was her he had been missing, not the life he'd lived when they were working together.

"Well then, I'm happy for you" she replied. "If it works, it works."

It was about the first nice thing she had said to him without any qualification, and he appreciated it. It felt as though they were finally starting to come to a place of understanding. Maybe they could even work together in taking out the men who had done this to her—to them. When he thought of how they had turned on her, his blood boiled, and he knew he needed to pull himself together before he made any kind of move. If he went after them now, he wouldn't have been able to contain his emotions. Bringing them down would need the kind of cool, levelheaded planning he wasn't capable of when he thought of her being hurt.

She brushed a hand over Wheatie's nose again, and the horse snorted happily before she turned and trotted back into the field to graze. Bailey's gaze lingered on her for a moment, a small smile on her face. Aaron just stood and looked at her. Being this close to her again, having her with him, was still surreal. He had never thought he would see her again, let alone in these circumstances, but he was glad he'd had the chance. If only so he could take the opportunity to clear the air a little about what had happened between them. He hadn't betrayed her—he'd only done what he needed to keep her safe, and he had to make sure she understood that.

"I'm going back up to the cafeteria for some food," she said finally. "You want to come with me?"

It was the first time she had actually offered to spend time with him by choice—a good sign.

Aaron nodded at once. "Yeah, sure," he agreed. "You need a hand getting down there?"

"I can walk, Aaron," she replied bluntly. "It just hurts a little. I'm not an invalid."

"Point taken," he replied, holding his hands up. "Anyway, I've been working all day. I'm starving. Let's go get some food."

The two of them made their way back to the main building together, talking easily about his work at Warrior Peak. He told her about the outbuildings, about bringing in the horses. It was just like old times. He was amazed at how easily they slipped back into their old dynamic, like they had never been apart.

The sky was clear and the sun was shining bright. It was the kind of strikingly beautiful day that Aaron had come to look forward to here. It was hard to believe that there was still so much danger and drama hunting them, everything he thought he had left behind all those years ago.

But for now, as he and Bailey made their way back toward the lodge, he didn't want to dwell on all of that. No, all he could think about was how good it felt to have her right there next to him again. The woman he hadn't been able to get out of his head, finally back by his side.

It felt right. Even if the circumstances were far from ideal.

Chapter Nine

Bailey woke with a start, her heart pounding and her eyes wide as she sat up straight in bed. The dream that had just plagued her was still fresh in her mind. She could almost see them crowding around her, the four of them staring down at her, not knowing if she was going to be able to get away. The flash of the knife had played in her mind's eye, the shock and fear of it. She had closed her eyes, ready for the end, only to open them again back in her temporary bedroom in Warrior Peak, right where she had fallen asleep.

She rubbed her eyes and planted her feet on the ground, doing her best to pull herself back together. It had been nearly three weeks since the attack, and she had been having nightmares about it nearly every night since. When were they going to go away?

When she put those guys behind bars where they belonged. That was when the nightmares were going to stop. After just over two weeks here, she was still no closer to actually tracking them down and exposing them for what they had done, and it was driving her crazy. She couldn't just sit around doing nothing. Yes, she was healing, but her mind was a mess, and she didn't know how to sort through everything going on inside of it.

She got to her feet and wandered out of the small room

that had been assigned to her—nothing special, but it did the job. She was just glad to have somewhere to stay where she didn't have to be looking over her shoulder the entire time. This place was hardly ideal, though. She was surrounded by people she didn't know, still trying to figure out how many of them she could trust. But it was a place for her to rest, recuperate, and get back to full strength again.

Plus, Aaron was here, and they seemed to have finally started breaking down some of the barriers between them. There was so much history there that she knew it would be a while before they were anywhere close to normal, but she could work with that. At least he seemed willing to help her out with the crooked cops after them, if only to keep her out of trouble. She would take that.

She knew she could handle it all by herself if she needed to, but she was glad to have Aaron's help. She padded quietly along the corridors, toward the common room, where she knew there was a computer. She wouldn't be able to get back to sleep after that nightmare, and she needed something to keep her mind occupied until she could have breakfast. She had never been much of a morning person, but it turned out all it took was a terrifying encounter where she feared for her life to get her ass up and out of bed first thing. Who'd have thought?

She took her seat at the computer, which was set aside for residents to check emails and make video calls. It wasn't exactly high-tech, but she didn't need it to be. She just needed it to work. Before getting started with her search on Ziegler and the rest of the group, she sent her captain a message checking in and stating she needed a little more time before she returned to work. She had originally contacted him upon arrival after getting settled, feigning an unexpected emergency. He'd always been kind to her and agreed to her request as long as she kept him updated.

Once that was completed, she started to search for any information she could about Ziegler and his friends—anything at all that might hint someone else knew what she did. It was a long shot, but there had to be *something* out there. A mention in an article, an old report filed about them, any halfway coherent explanation as to how they had managed to get away with what they had for so long.

Nothing. There was nothing. She tried every search term she could, every approach she could think of, tapping in to every database she could imagine, but she couldn't find anything. An hour passed, and she gnawed on the inside of her mouth, trying to figure out the best way to get to the bottom of this.

What she really needed was interdepartmental information. Any notices that might have been passed back and forth between cops about what they were doing. She wouldn't be able to access them without arousing suspicion or even drawing attention back to Warrior Peak. Aside from the fact that'd be dangerous and risky, she didn't want to expose the people here like that. This was a sanctuary, a safe place for healing, and these people were kind and helpful. They didn't deserve that type of evil brought to their door. But if she could find someone who was already working within a department in some official capacity, who wouldn't look too strange delving into this stuff, it would be a start.

Maybe someone nearby? She started searching for sheriffs in the local area, trying to use her intuition to find one who looked trustworthy. Though, after what she had found out about the men she worked with, maybe she shouldn't trust herself on that front.

Eventually, she stumbled across the smiling image of a sheriff for the small town nearby. He was a little older, and his bio said that he had been serving the same small community for his entire career—over twenty years. Was that a good sign? It meant he had either earned the trust of the people around him, or he'd hung on to his position through more nefarious means. She wasn't sure. She would have to ask Aaron about it. He knew more about this place than she did.

All at once, she looked up and realized that sunlight had started to filter through the window in front of her. She had been so lost in her research, she had almost forgotten that there was still a day ahead of her. A few people were moving around upstairs, and she could hear one of the cooks humming to themselves as they passed by the common room on the way to the kitchen.

She quickly deleted her search terms and turned off the computer. For some reason, she didn't like the idea of anyone seeing what she had been looking for. Better to keep it to herself for now, until she was sure she could trust everyone around here.

She felt a little guilty for even thinking about them like that, when everyone had been nothing but kind and welcoming to her. By the sounds of it, everyone here had a story of their own, some of them probably a whole lot wilder than hers. Maybe she would get around to hearing them one day, once she had dealt with this mess of corrupt cops.

"Hey."

She whipped her head around as though she had been caught doing something she shouldn't. Cade stood in the doorway smiling at her, and she smiled back. Seeing him made her wonder if River was already around. She hadn't seen her in a few days and should probably touch base with her soon. River'd asked her to keep her updated on her therapy with Carter, and she needed to do that before she came looking for her on her own.

"Hi," she replied, her cheeks turning red. She didn't even know why.

"I see you're up early," he remarked. "I could use some help in the kitchen, if you're up for it."

She parted her lips, about to turn him down, but then she stopped herself. Everyone around here worked to keep the place running, and it would have been pretty rude if she'd just expected not to have to pull her weight.

"Sure," she replied.

He grinned. "Thanks."

"Is River up yet?" she asked as she looked around him. "I've been meaning to check in with her."

"Yeah, she's still at the cabin. She'll be down in a bit. Ready?"

"Yep. Put me to work." As she got to her feet and headed over to join him, he eyed her thoughtfully.

"What is it?" she asked, a little more defensive than she had intended to be.

"I just know that if you're up early, chances are it's not just because you're a morning person," he replied. "People get restless here. And I know a restless spirit when I see one. Come on, you're on bacon duty."

She followed him down to the kitchen, hoping he wasn't going to ask her anything too invasive about what brought her to Warrior Peak. Thankfully, he didn't seem interested in much more than setting her to work. As he chopped vegetables, he got her to man the stove, cooking pancakes and bacon until there was a heaping pile of them on the plate ready to be taken out to everyone.

"You've got a mean pancake-flipping arm," he remarked.

She laughed. "Hey, I guess you're never too old to learn new tricks, right?" she replied. She felt comfortable in his presence, which surprised her. She had been a little nervous around new men after what had happened, but Cade seemed to know not to go delving into her past. He had probably dealt with plenty of people like her over his time here, and the practice was obviously paying off.

"Okay, let's start plating up," he told her as people started to file into the cafeteria. The place was starting to fill with a warm chatter, and Bailey felt a million times more relaxed than she had when she had woken up. That seemed to be the magic of this place: It was meant to be a safe place for those who had nowhere else to go. Even though she had already stayed longer than she intended, she was glad to be here.

They began to carry the food out into the communal area, and she spotted Aaron sitting at the far end of one of the long tables. He grinned up at her when he saw that she had been put to work, and she couldn't help but smile back. God, it was still so strange to see him again, but she was glad to have a friendly face staring up at her among this sea of people she didn't know.

Once they had set out the food for everyone, she took a seat next to Aaron. Her mouth was watering now—all this cooking for other people had made her hungry. She hadn't been eating a whole lot since she'd gotten there, not wanting to take advantage of their generosity too much, but she tucked into breakfast like a starved animal.

"It's good to see you eating," Aaron murmured to her.

She glanced up, her heart flipping when she caught his eye. She couldn't stop thinking about what he had said to her the other day, when they had been out at the paddock together—that all he had wanted when he was back in Kings Mountain was her. If she had known back then that he felt that way, would it have changed things? Would she have made a move, or would she have forced herself to hold back because he was her superior? She didn't know.

"I've been up for hours," she replied through a mouthful of food. "Been looking into…well, you know."

He nodded.

"You should give yourself some time to heal," he reminded her gently. She knew he was just trying to help, but he must have been aware that she wasn't going to let go of it that easily. Maybe she could find some middle ground, instead of trying to shut him down again. They weren't going to make any progress if everything ended in a battle.

"Maybe we could go out to the paddock again today," she replied. "I'd like to see how Wheatie is doing."

"I'm sure she would be happy to see you," he told her, and she grinned.

She loved that horse. Heck, maybe she was starting to like it here more than she cared to admit. She never would have imagined she would feel safe anywhere after what had happened to her back in Kings Mountain, but she felt more comfortable in this place with each passing day.

As though he could see what was going on inside her head, Aaron leaned forward and lowered his voice. "See? It's not too bad here, once you get settled."

"Eat your breakfast," she said on a laugh, but he was right. This place had a lot to offer—and the longer she stayed here, the more she saw that.

Chapter Ten

As Aaron set about working on the cabin, he whistled through his teeth. Breakfast with Bailey was about the best way he could think of to start the day. Spending time with her stirred something inside of him he thought was gone for good. The reminder of how good it felt to be around her was bringing all sorts of emotions back to the surface. Feelings he'd pushed down long ago.

Plus, she seemed to be settling in a little better now, which made him happy. He was glad she was starting to see how good this place could be for her, especially after what she had been through. Nobody deserved to be assaulted the way she had been, but at least this was a safe space, somewhere she could heal and relax.

Even if she didn't seem very good at relaxing. She had never been good at it, actually—even when they worked together, she had always been looking ahead to the next case before the last one was even finished. It was something he used to tease her about, and she had always rolled her eyes good-naturedly and reminded him she was trying to make a name for herself.

But now? Now, things were different. This was about taking down the corrupt cops who had infected the department, not just handling a case. She would be even more laser focused on her goal than before, and he couldn't even imagine what that was going to look like.

He heard footsteps crunching on the grass behind him, and glanced around to see Bailey approaching. She was still limping slightly, but not as badly as she had been a week ago. She was healing fast, like her body was trying to prepare her for what lay ahead.

"Hey," he greeted her, straightening up.

"Hey," she replied. "What are you working on?"

"This old cabin needs some TLC," he remarked, nodding to the slightly dilapidated shack next to him. "I think it could make a good living space for someone once I've had some time to put it all back together again."

"Sounds like a heck of a job," she replied.

"It will be," he agreed. "But it's satisfying to see it all come together when it's finished."

She smiled but he could tell at once there was something on her mind. You didn't work with someone as closely as they had and not have an idea of what was going on inside their head.

"What's up?" he asked.

"Sheriff Willis," she replied. "You know him?"

"Yeah, he's the sheriff for the small town down the mountain," he told her, propping up his tools and turning to face her properly. "What about him?"

"You think he's trustworthy?" she pressed.

Frowning, he nodded. "He's never given me any reason to think he isn't," he replied. "Why do you ask?"

"I think he could be the contact I need in the force to dig up the information on Ziegler and his crew," she explained. "I can't use my own credentials—that'll make it easier for them to find me. But someone like him, he could."

Aaron sighed, leaning up against the shack. "You're not going to let this go, are you?"

"Of course I'm not," she replied, and she turned to head back toward the main building.

He took off after her. She was so focused on what she felt like she needed to do, she was going to walk herself straight into trouble if she wasn't careful. He knew he wouldn't forgive himself if something happened to her. She had already been through so much, and he wasn't about to let her walk into this mess without trying to deter her.

"Bailey, you don't want to start this fight," he warned as he matched pace with her.

She shot a look at him. "I'm not the one who started it, they are," she reminded him. "I'm just going to finish it."

She reached her truck and climbed in, wincing as she swung her leg in after her.

He stood in front of it, arms crossed. "I'm not going to let you go down there alone," he warned her.

She stared at him for a moment, as though daring him to try and stop her.

"You can either get out of my way, or you can help me," she replied. "Which one is it going to be?"

He paused for a moment, then let out a sigh, and gestured for her to get out of the truck. "Come on, let me drive," he told her. "Your leg's still healing."

She looked as though she was about to protest, but thought better of it. She climbed out and allowed him to take the driver's seat while she hobbled around and got in on the passenger's side. Being beside her again like this, it brought back a flood of memories. All those hours they had spent cruising around the county, talking, listening to music, and getting to know each other. In all the years he had been on the force, those had been his favorite memories.

Maybe he would be able to make some new ones with her before this latest mission was over.

They drove into town, and Bailey peered around, taking the place in with her incisive gaze. She had always been really observant, able to pick up on details that went over his head. It was one of the many things that would have made her an amazing detective, though he supposed he had shot her in the foot when he had written that report about her. He tried not to linger on the thought of it. He had done what he had to do at the time, and at least she was willing to let him help now, right?

They arrived outside the sheriff's station, and he helped Bailey out of the truck. Aaron didn't know Sheriff Willis particularly well, but he had met him a few times and the sheriff had always seemed capable and trustworthy. Reminded him of some of the cops he'd known when he was first starting out: Dedicated, focused, and committed to keeping the small town where he served a safe place for everyone.

Bailey led the way inside, where they found Willis leaning up against the reception desk. She smiled pleasantly at him.

He looked her up and down and extended his hand. "You must be new," he remarked. Aaron guessed he knew almost everyone in this town, which would make his job a lot easier.

Bailey took his hand, and nodded. She introduced herself. "I'm Bailey Masters. Nice to meet you."

"You too," Willis replied, and he nodded in greeting to Aaron.

"Sheriff Willis." Aaron returned the nod.

"So, what brings you in here today?" Willis asked, escorting them back to his office. "Nothing serious, I hope."

She grimaced. "I wish I didn't have to bring this to you, but I can't think of anyone else who can help," she explained. "Aaron told me you're a good cop, and we need more of those around. I'm really hoping you can help me out here."

She filled him in as quickly as she could on what had happened with the guys at Kings Mountain, and Willis paused to take it in, his eyes widening as the enormity of it seemed to settle over him. Though he had dealt with some big cases in his time, he had probably never had to work one that was aimed at his fellow cops.

"I'm so sorry that happened to you," he told Bailey, his voice quiet, as though he couldn't believe what he was hearing. "To think of our own people turning on us like that." He shuddered, shaking his head.

"It was an eye-opener for me, that's for sure." She nodded with a grim smile. "I never expected something like that from the guys I worked with."

"It's unthinkable," he muttered. "But I'm sure you understand where I'm coming from when I say I need a little more proof of your status. Do you have ID on you? Someone who can vouch for you?"

"Of course," Bailey replied, not missing a beat. She didn't seem offended at all. Aaron guessed she was just glad someone was actually listening to her and taking her seriously. She reached into her pocket and pulled out her ID, then handed it over. Willis inspected it for a moment, lifting it so he could compare the picture to her face. Satisfied, he nodded, and handed it back to her.

"Well, I hope I can be a better cop to you than those guys were," Willis remarked. "What exactly is it you need?"

"I need to get any information that has been passed around about them, what they've been doing, all of it," she replied. "There has to be someone who knows something and kept quiet, or someone who's passed something around the local departments, even if it's not much. I don't want to arouse any suspicion by going after it myself, but someone like you… they're far more likely to hand over what we need."

He nodded, leaning back against the desk.

"I'm not sure how much I'll be able to get," he warned her. "I'll look into what I can, but I don't know how much would have filtered down from Kings Mountain to here. I do have a few contacts around the state. They might be able to help out."

"Can you trust them?" Bailey asked.

Willis narrowed his eyes and nodded. "I'd trust them with my life," he replied firmly. "I'm happy to let you into the system, Bailey, but Aaron, you're not a cop, so I'm going to have to keep it in the business."

Bailey passed him a quizzical look. "Oh, but Aaron—"

"Of course, Sheriff," Aaron replied, cutting her off. He had never mentioned to Willis that he'd been a cop before, because he was worried it would bring up too much of his past that he didn't want to talk about. But the more he got to know the older man, the more he trusted him. Maybe he would start to come clean about some of his past when all of this was over.

If they could finish it, of course.

"But you might be better off talking to Lawson and Xavier about this," he continued. "They used to be CIA, after all."

Bailey spun around to face Aaron, her eyes wide.

"They *what*?" she demanded. "You never thought to tell me that?"

Aaron shrugged. He had his reasons. But he got the feeling he wasn't going to be able to keep them to himself for much longer.

Mainly because Bailey got the truth out of him, one way or another. He couldn't hide himself from her.

Even if that made him feel vulnerable in a way he hadn't for a very long time.

Chapter Eleven

"You think it's safe for us to be out like this?" Bailey whispered to Aaron, as they pulled the truck up to a restaurant at the edge of town.

He smiled at her, raising his eyebrows. "You have nothing to worry about," he promised. "It's just a little family-owned place. They don't ask any questions, apart from what kind of wine you want with dinner."

A smile spread over her face. "That sounds really good," she agreed, biting her lip excitedly.

Bailey and Aaron had spent the better part of the day with Willis, talking over everything that had happened and figuring out what their next moves were going to be. There was still a whole lot Willis needed to look into, and the best thing they could do for now was give him his space, and try to get some rest. Not that Bailey had been able to rest much, but he had convinced her to stop by this little Italian place on the edge of town before they headed home. The food was good at the lodge, but sometimes it was nice to get out and go somewhere fresh, especially when that place made the best garlic bread in the state.

Was this a date? She certainly wasn't trying to think of it like that. It was just a couple of old friends hanging out together, taking a chance to catch a breath after everything that had been going on. She might even consider him a friend again—or at least an ally. Yes, their past was messy, but they were working toward the same goal here, and that had to count for something.

The restaurant was quiet when they walked in, and they were led to a red-and-white-checked table at the far side of the room, next to the window. Trees swayed in the breeze beyond as the sun dipped behind the mountains. A single candle flickered between them. If it wasn't for the history between them, she would have said it was almost romantic.

"Why didn't you tell me about Lawson and Xavier being former CIA?" she asked as soon as they sat. Now that they were out of the sheriff's office and alone, she couldn't stop herself from interrogating him. She'd never been a patient person.

He shrugged. "I don't know much about it really. I do know that he and Lawson were in the military together," he admitted.

"You don't know much about it?" she replied, confused. "You've been living there for years now, right? It's never come up?"

"I guess I'm a bit of an outsider at the sanctuary," he explained. "I think it's because I kept to myself so much when I first arrived. I hoped that if I didn't ask people questions, they wouldn't ask me questions I didn't want to answer. I'm just the guy who fixes stuff, and I like it that way."

Her eyebrows drew together. "That's a shame," she remarked. "You think you could ask them about it? See if there's anything they'd be willing to do to help us?"

"Yeah, I think I could manage that," he replied. "I don't know them super well, but they don't like it when people are up to no good. There was some stuff that happened not too long ago with a gang that the sheriff asked for their help with. And if it's something that could possibly pose a threat to Warrior Peak, they'd definitely want to help."

"Hope so," she replied, as the waiter arrived with their menus. She turned her attention to the food options, and her stomach grumbled. She hadn't eaten since breakfast, too caught up with how much she felt like she had to do. She knew she needed to focus on taking care of herself, but at least Aaron was there to remind her to rest and eat.

"What's good here?" she asked, and he grinned.

"The garlic bread is amazing," he replied. "They make it fresh in-house. You have to try it."

"That sounds really good," she murmured, and her mouth started to water as some of the delicious savory scents came floating out of the kitchen. She began to relax as she cast her gaze over the menu, deciding what she was going to have. Her stomach had been in such knots when she'd first gotten here that she'd hardly been able to think about eating—now it was catching up with her.

They ordered a huge pile of food, until the table was practically quaking under the weight of it. She grabbed a slice of garlic bread first.

"Oh, my God, this garlic bread really is amazing," she hummed, as she took a bite of the cheesy, crispy, garlicky deliciousness that had just arrived.

He grinned at her. "See? I told you."

"I'll never doubt your opinions on Italian food again," she promised him. "You have my word."

Maybe it was the food, maybe it was the peace of the restaurant, or maybe it was finally getting a start on her mission, but she was really starting to relax now. They chatted about the sanctuary and about the small town they were in, Blue Ridge. It reminded her a little of Kings Mountain, except without the stress that was now tied to that place for her. She was amazed at how easily the conversation seemed to flow between them now that she was starting to let her guard down.

"You ever think about going back to being a cop?" she asked him with interest once they were waiting for their dessert.

He thought about the question for a moment, and then shrugged. "Sometimes," he admitted. "There's so much that's happened, I'm not even sure where I would be able to start. And I'd have to explain why I just walked away from it all those years ago."

"When people find out what kind of trouble you were in, they'll understand," she replied, catching herself off guard with how much she meant it. She'd had a hard time forgiving him for what had happened all those years ago, but knowing what she did now, she could better understand his reasoning.

"Plus, someone needs to bully the rookies until they harden up," she joked.

He laughed. "Hey, now, I was never a bully," he protested, shaking his head. "I just made sure they didn't get soft once they'd graduated training."

"Oh, yeah?" she fired back playfully. "And when you used to call them on the radio and send them to the middle of nowhere, that was part of hardening them up too, was it?"

"You were just as guilty of that as I was," he reminded her, and she laughed as their order of homemade tiramisu arrived.

She could still remember the way they practically rolled around the car laughing together when they played these little pranks on the rookies in the department. They were probably a little mean, but when they were in it together, it didn't feel that way.

"Yeah, and you were my superior," she shot back. "So

you're the one who'd have to answer for it. You were supposed to set a good example."

"I think I was setting a great example," he argued playfully. "Showing you how to let loose and have some fun for a change."

"For a change?" she protested, laughing. "You saying that I'm not fun?"

"I'm saying you were a rookie who took the work dead seriously," he replied, digging his spoon into their dessert. "And maybe you could use a little loosening up from time to time."

She stuck her tongue out at him, and he chuckled. She had always liked his laugh, how genuine it sounded, like he really meant it. There were so many guys who came across as so insincere—she had been on enough crappy first dates to confirm that theory—but he had never seemed that way to her.

It was starting to feel distinctly like old times, much to her surprise. When she had imagined seeing him again, she had never thought they would be able to talk like this. She had thought about chewing him out, giving him a piece of her mind, telling him off for what he had done to her, but never that they could sit around and laugh and talk about the past together, as though they were old friends.

As he looked at her, she felt the familiar flutter in her chest she had come to recognize when she was near him. And she knew that, no matter how much she might have wanted to tell herself otherwise, there was always something more than friendship between them.

"I guess we should be getting back to Warrior Peak," he remarked, once the waiter had cleared away the delicious tiramisu they'd shared.

"I'm not sure I can even walk, I'm so full," she groaned. "You're going to have to roll me back to the truck."

"Fine, as long as I'm driving," he replied.

"I can drive us back," she protested, but he held up the keys and raised his eyebrows at her.

"You're going to have to fight me for them."

He settled the bill, insisting on paying for it himself, and then they headed to her truck outside. She hadn't actually expected him to make her fight for her keys, but when she went to take them out of his hands, he held them high up over his head.

"I told you, I'm not letting you drive," he reminded her.

Her mouth fell open in surprise. "Aaron, it's my truck!" she protested, but she couldn't help but giggle. There was something about him when he was goofing around like this that just made her happy. He was normally so serious, or he had been back when he'd been at the station, apart from pranking the rookies. Knowing she got to see this side of him, this side he didn't seem to let many other people see, sparked something inside of her.

She stood on her tiptoes to grab the keys, but he was so much taller than her he could easily hold them over her head. She swiped for them, but she couldn't quite reach.

"You're going to have to do better than that," he teased her.

"Hey, no fair!" she argued, still giggling. He was acting so ridiculous, it was hard not to. And there was a spark in his eyes that reminded her of the old days—the days she had thought they had long since lost—but here he was, standing in front of her, looking at her like nothing at all had changed.

"I'm injured, this is practically bullying!" she continued, reaching up again.

He jingled the keys just out of her reach. "I'm sure you can handle it," he replied. "Besides, you shouldn't be driving on your injured leg, you know that."

"I can manage it," she told him, and he switched the keys from one hand to another, making it even harder for her. She hobbled around him, but it was too late. He was moving too quick for her, and it was clear from the look on his face that he was enjoying her struggle.

Or maybe just enjoying how close the two of them were to each other right now. Finally, he had lowered them just enough that with one more stretch she managed to lock her hands around the keys, and snatched them out of his grip.

"Got them!" she exclaimed, but as she lowered back down on to the balls of her feet, she was suddenly distinctly aware of how close the two of them were standing. Practically nose to nose, his eyes pinned to hers, the smile on his face shifting to something else as he looked at her. The warm light from the restaurant spilled out onto the sidewalk they stood on, the leaves blowing in the light breeze the only sound nearby.

She remembered, all at once, what he had said to her the other day, about how he had wanted her—and only her. Her old feelings, the ones she had tried to push down all this time, were starting to rise up again. She couldn't deny them any longer. He could feel the shift, too; she could tell by the look on his face as he stepped even closer. The chemistry was practically burning in the air between them, impossible to ignore.

He dropped his hand down to her face, and grazed his fingers along her chin, tilting her eyes up to meet his. Her heart hammered inside her chest as she looked up at him. How many times had she imagined exactly this? How many times had she longed for him to look at her the way he looked at her now? She couldn't count. But it was real, it was happening.

His eyes softened as he gazed at her, like it was the first time he had ever seen her. "You look so beautiful right now," he murmured.

Her breath hitched in her throat.

"I'm so sorry for everything, Bailey," he told her. "I never thought I was going to see you again, but I… I never stopped thinking about you. Not once. And I'm so glad you found your way back to me."

"Shut up," she said, a smile turning up her lips. "And just kiss me already."

And without any hesitation, he finally did.

Chapter Twelve

Aaron stared at the ceiling, listening to Bailey's breath settle back to normal again. A sheen of sweat on his brow spoke to the exertion they'd both just thrown themselves into. Even now, he could hardly believe it had happened.

From the moment their lips had touched back at the restaurant, he had known how he wanted this to end. He wanted to take her to bed, just like he had craved all those years ago. The desire and need were so strong he could hardly breathe, only this time, she wasn't his rookie. There was no reason to deny himself any longer.

They had driven back up to his cabin, his hand on her leg, the anticipation crackling in the air between them. How long had it been since they'd first met? And how hard had he worked to keep his feelings to himself? To finally do something about it felt electric, especially when he had never expected to see her again after what had happened between them.

They had stumbled through the door of his cabin and fallen into bed together, bringing to reality all the fantasies he'd had about her over the years. It had been so needy, so desperate, so full of all the built-up passion that they'd never been able to do anything about. It felt so damn right he couldn't believe it had taken them this long to finally make it happen.

He looked over at her, grinning, and she flashed him a smile. Her hair was a mess, her cheeks flushed, but she had never looked more beautiful to him.

"Good?" he asked her, reaching over to brush her hair away from her face.

"Oh my gosh, yes," she breathed, and she leaned over to plant a kiss on his lips. He couldn't get over how good they felt together, as though they had been made for each other. He knew he could never have done this when she was working as his rookie—it would have put both of their careers at risk. Besides, all that mattered was that they had this now. She was finally his, the woman he hadn't been able to stop thinking about, even after all these years.

She turned on her side and reached an arm over his chest, pressing her face against him and inhaling deeply, like she wanted to lose herself in his scent. He knew just how she felt. They had been apart for so long, it seemed as though they had so much catching up to do, so much of this passion to enjoy.

"I can't believe it took us so long to do this," she murmured, running her hand over his chest so she could feel the beating of his heart. He couldn't remember how long it had been since he'd been with someone—since before he came to Warrior Peak, at least—but he hadn't wanted anyone else, anyway. Only her.

"I know," he replied. "But you know the trouble it would have gotten us into if we'd done this before."

"Mmm," she agreed, and she closed her eyes for a moment. Of course, if they had done this before, he might not have been able to send her away when he needed to. It would have made his eventual betrayal of her—no matter how well-intentioned—hurt even more deeply than it already did. This was the right time for it, the time that made sense, and he was glad it hadn't happened before now.

"Yeah, everyone would have thought I was sleeping my way to the top," she remarked, grinning.

"Hey, if you're that good at it, it would probably have worked," he joked back.

She burst out laughing, burying her face into the pillow.

"Hey, glad you appreciate my skills," she said flirtatiously, turning to face him. A huge smile spread over her face as she looked at him, and he raised his eyebrows at her.

"What is it?" he asked.

"Nothing," she replied, shaking her head. "I just... I just thought about this a lot when we were first working together. I guess I had come to terms with it never actually happening, but...here we are."

"Here we are," he agreed, and he reached out to wrap his arms around her and pull her in close. Closing his eyes, he pressed his face into her hair, breathing in the scent of her deeply. Like her, he'd long since had to let go of the thought of something like this ever happening between them, but now it seemed like the most natural thing in the world.

He listened to the sound of her breathing as she began to doze off in his arms, and he just lay there for a while, enjoying the feeling of finally having her in his arms. After all this time, they were both right where they needed to be.

He wasn't sure how long this newfound peace was going to last. But he would take as much of it as they could before their pasts caught up with them again. If anything, this was only going to bring them closer together, make it easier for them to work alongside each other once more.

His eyelids started to feel heavy as he drifted off to sleep.

Contentment settled in for the first time in what felt like forever. All because of her.

Bailey.

Finally, they had cleared the air and were mending what he'd broken all those years ago. They had finally admitted their attraction to each other and were able to act on it.

They'd made their way back to each other, despite everything.

And now, they had to take on the corrupt cops who had driven them apart in the first place.

Chapter Thirteen

"Can you help me with these?" Hannah asked, holding up a bunch of flowers so big she could barely see out over the top of them.

Bailey couldn't help but smile at how ridiculous she looked, but she nodded at once.

"Of course I can," she replied, scooping a few of them from her hands. "Where are these going?"

"We're planting them up next to the paddock," she explained. "Aaron's done such great work there, and now that he's finished, we want to add a splash of color to finish it off."

"Sounds awesome," Bailey replied, perking up as soon as she realized it meant she was going to be able to see Wheatie again. And maybe Aaron, too. It had been only a couple of days since their night together, and she hadn't been able to stop thinking about him. But it wasn't the same confusing mess of emotions she was used to dealing with when it came to him. Instead, it was excitement, the thrill of a new romance, and the incredible heat of their chemistry.

She and Hannah headed out toward the paddock, where the sun was beating down on the fresh green grass sprouting up around the new fences Aaron had put up. They both kneeled down at one corner, laying out the freshly uprooted flowers, ready to replant them—or they would have been, had it not been for Wheatie cantering over to see what they were doing.

"Wheatie, no!" Bailey exclaimed as the horse dipped her head down to take a chomp out of one of the flowers. She chewed thoughtfully for a moment, as though trying to decide whether she liked them or not, and then dived in to take a few bites out of the rest.

"Shoo! Shoo!" Hannah yelled, waving her hands at Wheatie to try and chase her away. But it was no good—the horse had already decimated at least half of the flowers.

"Wheatie, go away!" Bailey told her, but she couldn't help but laugh at how ridiculous this situation was. Wheatie could fit her head easily through the fence, and as soon as she had laid eyes on the flowers, she had seen her lunch.

"Look, I'll try to lead her away," Bailey told Hannah, and she scrambled over the fence, trying to gently direct the horse out of the chaos she was currently causing, but Wheatie just politely brushed her off, as though she was nothing more than an annoyance. Hannah burst out laughing, shaking her head.

"I think it's a lost cause," she told Bailey. "Don't worry about it, we can get more flowers. We just need to have a better defense system against Wheatie next time around."

"She's…a lot to handle." Bailey laughed, shaking her head. "Maybe we could ask Aaron to put up something, a blocker of some kind, just a temporary one to keep her out."

As though she had summoned him with just the power of her words, she glanced around to see Aaron leaning on a shovel, watching the two of them. She felt a flush to her cheeks when she realized he had been staring, but she didn't mind.

"He's been watching you since you got out here, you know," Hannah said wryly.

Bailey raised her eyebrows. "Has he?"

"You didn't notice?"

"Nope," she replied, shaking her head. She felt like she would have been able to feel his eyes on her, but she had clearly been too distracted by Wheatie's mischief.

"Damn, girl." She laughed. "You should pay more attention when hot guys are checking you out."

"Hot guys?" she teased right back.

Hannah shrugged. "Hey, I'm not trying to jump in on your territory," she replied. "But he's cute. And it's clear he likes you."

Bailey shrugged. Aaron lifted a hand to wave at her, and she waved back. A flicker in her chest reminded her of just how attracted she was to this man. But she sure as hell wasn't going to go talking to Hannah about it. No, whatever was going on between them, it was just between them.

"The two of you have a history, right?" she pressed, her eyes widening with interest.

Bailey shrugged. "I guess," she replied, keeping it as vague as possible. Hannah was a really sweet woman, but it was going to take a long time for Bailey to totally trust anyone again.

Especially Aaron.

"Well, I think you should go for it," she told her, leaning forward and lowering her voice conspiratorially. "You don't want to leave him single for too long."

"Has he been dating other women? Since he got here, I mean?" she asked, hoping her voice was convincingly unbothered.

"Not that I've ever seen," Hannah remarked. "He's mostly kept to himself, actually. Nobody really knows a lot about what was going on with him before he got here."

Bailey watched Aaron as he headed back inside one of

the sheds to finish his work. That made sense. It would explain why he didn't know a huge amount about Xavier or Lawson, even after living on the property and working here for as long as he had. She felt a little pang when she thought about that—that he had been holding back so much about himself, probably worried it was going to put either him or her in danger. No matter what he had done to her, he didn't deserve to live looking over his shoulder every moment, unable to be honest with anyone.

"Right," she replied.

"But you guys…it's clear there's something going on," she continued.

"Why do you think that?" Bailey replied.

Was it really that obvious to everyone else? She had hoped she might be able to keep it under wraps, at least for a little while, but it looked like the secret was out.

"Because he's always hanging around," she replied, nodding over to where Aaron had just been standing. "Come on, you must have noticed it, too. He used to hide out in his cabin most of the time unless he was working, and we would just see him at meals. But I feel like whenever I'm with you, he's there, too."

"Maybe," Bailey replied, but she couldn't help but smile. Aaron had been looking out for her—just like he had done when she was a rookie. There was still so much of that dynamic between them, even if it had been twisted and nearly destroyed by what he'd done to her.

"He *likes* you," Hannah told her, and Bailey couldn't help but laugh.

"I'm not sure about that."

"Well, I am, and I'm never wrong about these things," Hannah replied matter-of-factly, and her confidence made Bailey giggle again.

Or perhaps it was just the thought of Aaron really liking her that had her all kinds of excited. She didn't know for sure what was going on between them right now, but she knew the night they'd spent together had been amazing.

"Aaron's a good man with a good heart," Hannah continued. "I don't know what happened between the two of you, but whatever it was, you shouldn't let it get in the way of whatever you feel for him now."

Bailey didn't reply, chewing her lip as she gathered what remained of the flowers before Wheatie made her way through them, too.

Hannah and Bailey headed back to the main building. Much to Bailey's relief, Hannah dropped the conversation about Aaron. Bailey wasn't sure how much longer she would have been able to throw Hannah off the scent, and the other woman didn't seem like she was good at keeping her mouth shut. Bailey could imagine her spilling the secret before she was ready, and it was hard enough to settle into this place without people wondering what was going on between the two of them.

Back inside the lodge, Bailey headed in for a quick shower. There was dirt all over her from the flowers, and she needed to clean herself off before she helped out with anything else. More importantly, she needed a minute to herself, because she was starting to feel all kinds of flustered about what was going on with her and Aaron.

She closed her eyes as she stepped beneath the rush of the warm water, letting out a breath she didn't even realize she had been holding. Her mind drifted back to their first kiss. The feel of his fingers skimming across her skin, the way he looked at her, the way he spoke to her like she meant so much to him.

She had craved that from him for so long. Craved his

touch, craved his approval, craved those precious words he had spoken to her. But it was all so wrapped up in their messy past, she wasn't sure how she was supposed to make it out the other side in one piece. Could she really forgive him? He had sent her away, and he had left those corrupt cops in the department without telling anyone. Even if he had had his reasons, even if it had been to protect her, it still didn't seem right.

But if she could end this—if she could expose those men, and bring a close to their reign of terror over that department—the past wouldn't be such a problem any longer. The problem right now was that they were still out there, and the danger was hot on their heels. Neither of them could relax and focus on the moment.

Well, maybe once. When they were lying in bed together the other night, she'd looked over at him and it had been like she was seeing him with clear eyes for the very first time. Like all their history had just vanished, and all that mattered was the man lying beside her—the man gazing at her like she was the most beautiful thing in the world. She couldn't think of anything that mattered more than the feeling in her heart right then, the warmth of it flooding her whole body.

She sighed as she stepped out of the shower. She wished she could go back to that moment, just for a second, just to feel the way she had felt then. One day, she would be able to. But for now? Until they could make their move on the dirty cops who had done this to them, they were stuck in this strange limbo, and she wasn't sure if she could handle it much longer.

Chapter Fourteen

"I think you should sit down," Xavier told Aaron, nodding to the seat on the other side of his desk. On either side of him, Cade and Lawson stood, flanking him like they were in formation.

"Yeah, thanks." Aaron sank into the seat and tried to gather himself. He had come here for a reason, and they were as aware of it as he was.

"So, what's going on? Why did you want to see all of us together?" Xavier asked, clasping his hands on the desk and giving him a serious look.

When Aaron had asked for a meeting with the other men earlier that day, he had known they could tell that something was up. He never tried to spend extra time with anyone here. Not that he didn't like them, but it just seemed safer to keep to himself.

But he needed their help. More importantly, so did Bailey. They had some serious skills if they were former military, then also adding Lawson and Xavier's former CIA experience. They could probably make good use of them in their quest to bring Ziegler and his crew to justice.

"I've been talking to Bailey," Aaron explained. "And we…a lot went on in our past. I already filled you two in on some of it." He nodded between Lawson and Xavier, and then looked to Cade. "To keep it short and simple, Bailey and I worked together before. I was a police sergeant for a town similar to here in Blue Ridge, and Bailey was a rookie at the time—training under my supervision. We were in a small department with a handful or so of other guys. We handled mostly small-town stuff, nothing too serious for the most part, but we kept on top if it."

Lawson and Cade exchanged a glance when he paused. Xavier nodded at him to go on. "And?"

Aaron filled them in on the rest of the story, how he had discovered some of them were corrupt, and they had beaten the hell out of him, and then threatened to come after Bailey if he didn't leave. The report he had written to get her removed, and the six years they had spent apart in the meantime. How she had come back, only to be faced with the same betrayal he'd been through all those years ago, and how she was determined to take them down.

The men fell silent for a moment when he was done, taking in the enormity of what he had just told them.

"That's why you've kept to yourself all these years." Cade hit the nail on the head with that one guess.

Aaron nodded in agreement. "I was really messed up from everything when I first got here, and just wanted to forget about it. Plus, I thought if I talked about it to anyone, I might end up drawing them to me somehow and something worse might happen. It just felt safer to stay out of the way and keep my head down."

"Now, I've heard a lot of stories from people who've ended up here," Lawson remarked, finally. "But that has to be one of the wildest."

Xavier chuckled, and nodded in agreement. "Yeah, but that doesn't mean we can't help with it," he replied. "Bailey's been leading the charge so far, right?"

"Trying to…so far," Aaron replied. "I've tried to get her to slow down, but she wants to finish this."

"I can't say I blame her," Cade chimed in. "Sounds like she's committed her life to the force, so of course she wouldn't want to let that corruption go."

"Yeah, but I don't think it's a good idea for her to be involved in this anymore," Lawson added.

Aaron raised his eyebrows. "You don't?"

Good luck telling her that.

She had never been good at hearing *no*, especially when it was a case she felt personally connected to. And this one was about as personal as they came.

"She's got too much on the line not to get distracted," Xavier agreed. "And besides, if she does want to get back to work eventually, she's not going to want to have a history of working with people off the books."

Aaron grimaced. He hadn't even thought of that. Bailey was so focused on dealing with this in the immediate, she hadn't thought about how it might impact her career in the future. She had so much potential, even after being stuck behind a desk for so long, and he didn't want her to risk putting all of that on the line.

"You're right," he agreed.

"We need to get all the details she has to combine with yours, but I think it's best if we handle it from here on out," Xavier assured him. "And of course, we'll keep the two of you updated every step of the way. But it's better for her in the long term if she holds back from this."

"We can find somewhere else for her to stay so she's not tempted to get involved," Lawson added.

Aaron felt a twist in his chest at the thought. Losing her again, when she had only just come back into his life? It didn't feel right. But their help would be invaluable to bringing this to a close, and Bailey would surely recognize that.

He hoped, anyway. And he hoped her leaving wouldn't put an end to what the two of them had just started to share after all these years.

"Yeah, I agree with these two. It's too dangerous and could cause more problems down the line if she's involved in this. We'll come to her for information, if needed," Cade agreed. "But she can't be involved with the actual operation. I'm sure she'll be safer somewhere else, too."

"Yeah, apparently they know I'm here," Aaron admitted, and Xavier jerked his head back in surprise.

"You could have told us that sooner," he replied. "If they know you're here, there's every chance they know she's here, too. We'll need to lock down any information coming in and out, make sure we don't have any leaks."

"Agreed," Lawson replied. "Aaron, we'll get started on this today and start working out a plan. You can tell Bailey what's going on and we'll get with you both later to confirm information. We'll also find somewhere else for her to stay as soon as possible."

"I'll talk to her and fill her in," Aaron confirmed. But he had a bad feeling about this.

He had made a decision for Bailey before in the past, and he was pretty sure some part of her still hated him for it. He doubted she was going to take this well, no matter how sensible it was.

"Uh, one more thing, guys," he said hesitantly. He hoped what he was about to say wasn't going to have a negative impact on anything they'd be planning. "Bailey and I spoke with Sheriff Willis the other day in town, and she filled him in on some of it, hoping he could search for information for her."

The guys all exchanged glances, sharing unspoken words within those looks.

"We'll check in with Willis and see if he's made progress up to this point. Let him know we're on it now," Lawson told him.

"We'll talk to you later today," Xavier replied, rising to his feet and opening the door for Aaron. "And Aaron, thanks for coming to us with this. We haven't known a lot about you or your past up to this point. We didn't want to push and make you feel like you had to defend yourself to stay here. We wanted you to know you were welcome, regardless of your past. You know you can trust us, right?"

Aaron nodded. "I know. And I appreciate it. I should have made more of an effort before to open myself up and get to know all of you, but I was...scared, I guess. That I'd bring trouble if other people knew, and I just wanted to forget it all and disappear. And I thought I was doing right by Bailey at the time. I didn't have time to think it all through properly. I never expected her to come back after everything that happened." He paused, suddenly thinking his words were getting too heavy. "Anyway, thank you. For everything." He nodded at them all, then turned to leave.

He meant it. He knew he needed to start putting more trust in these guys. They had been there for him when he had needed it most, even if he hadn't told them the truth about what had brought him to Warrior Peak until now.

Now, he had to go tell Bailey the news. And he got a feeling she wasn't going to take it well.

It was another beautiful day outside, and Aaron knew exactly where Bailey would be—out at the paddock, hanging out with Wheatie. The bond she'd made with the old mare was downright adorable to him, bringing out this softer side of Bailey she didn't always show. He hoped she would be in a good mood when he got there, something to soften the blow of the news he was about to share with her.

He followed the path out to the paddock, and sure enough, she was standing with Hannah and River, the three of them laughing as they tried to shoo Wheatie away from the flowers they wanted to plant there. He paused for a moment, and couldn't help but smile.

She didn't see him yet, and the way she was interacting with the other women reminded him of how well she was settling in here. She might not have come to this place under the best of circumstances, but it was clear she really belonged. He had never really had much of a chance to see her outside of work before, and this relaxed version of Bailey was one he was really falling for.

Hannah glanced up and saw him standing there, and gave him a big wave. He lifted his hand to greet her, and Bailey looked up to see him, too. A small smile spread across her face, and his heart twisted hard in his chest. He hated that he was going to have to give her bad news, especially when it seemed like she was having such a good day.

He made his way toward them, his mind racing. Well, he couldn't tell her in front of the other women, that was for sure. Maybe that would give him some kind of an out? He didn't want to outright ask River and Hannah to leave—that would be rude of him. That would also invite all sorts of unwanted questions and probably hurt their feelings. And he didn't want to dampen the mood, since it looked like they were having so much fun. He would have to wait until the two of them were on their own.

He finally reached them, and Hannah tapped the fence beside her.

"You're going to have to come up with something better

than this," she remarked playfully. "Wheatie and the other horses have been demolishing our flowers."

"Yeah, I think they've eaten a solid pound each." Bailey laughed, shaking her head. "I thought she was my friend, but Wheatie totally ignores me when the flowers are around. She's got a one-track mind!"

They all giggled, and Aaron grinned. How could he break this good mood with such bad news? He would wait a little while longer. He knew how badly he had let her down before, when he had written that report about her, and it felt like this would be an echo of that again. Sent away from the action, when she wanted to be in the middle of it.

"Maybe I can put something up so you can at least get them planted," he suggested, and he headed toward the shed where he kept his tools. A little guilt stirred in him as he thought about what he was hiding from her, but it was for the best.

At least, that was what he had to tell himself.

Chapter Fifteen

"If you hold the pallet up there…yes, that means she can't duck under it to get to the flowers."

Bailey instructed Aaron as Hannah and River went to work planting the flowers. Wheatie pawed at the ground, clearly a little annoyed that she couldn't get at her favorite snack.

Bailey reached out to pet her apologetically. "There's plenty of grass here for you, Wheatie," she reminded her. "You don't have to eat our flowers."

Aaron chuckled. "I'm not sure she's going to listen to reason," he warned her.

Bailey shrugged. "She deserves an explanation," she replied, smiling.

Today had been about as peaceful and perfect as she could imagine. She'd come out with Hannah and River first thing in the morning to get these flowers planted around the paddock. Now, Aaron was out with them, manhandling a pallet around to make sure the horses couldn't gobble them up before they were planted.

The sun was shining above them, and the horses were keeping them company, watching them as they tried to get their work done. Bailey was sure that they would descend on the newly planted flowers the first chance they got, but hopefully enough would survive to pollinate and actually get some color out in this part of the land. She could imagine how beautiful it was going to look in the summer, how striking and bright.

If she stuck around that long, of course. She had found herself thinking about the future here, which surprised her. It had been a last resort when she'd arrived, but as her body started to heal properly and her mind began to settle, she could see herself staying. It was like a little sanctuary away from the rest of the world. Even if she missed her work, she found purpose here, and it was a pleasant change of pace. This sure beat sitting behind a desk like she had been doing for all those years, anyway.

"I think that's the last one!" Hannah exclaimed as she got to her feet and dusted off her hands. Her knees were stained with grass and dirt, but she didn't seem to notice. Aaron lowered the pallet he held so he could see their hard work.

He nodded in approval. "Looks great."

As soon as he took his eye off the horse, Wheatie lunged forward again, but Bailey caught her before she could eat the flowers.

"Hey, you leave those alone," she scolded her playfully. "You've got to show some self-control, girl."

"I think I need to take a shower," River remarked, looking down at her grass-stained clothes. "Do you need a hand moving the pallets, Aaron?"

"No, I'll be fine," he replied as he hefted one up into his arms. The muscles in his biceps flexed slightly, and Bailey quickly averted her gaze. She was still getting used to seeing him out of his uniform, and she had to admit, there was something seriously sexy about him in a T-shirt and a pair of well-fitting jeans.

"I'll stick around and help," she offered without thinking.

Hannah shot her a look, and Bailey knew at once what was on her mind. She raised her eyebrows at her pointedly, as though daring her to say something, and Hannah grinned and followed River to the path back to the main lodge.

"You sure?" Aaron asked. "I can manage it myself—"

"You said you need to move them to the other shed, right?" she reminded him. "I can give you a hand with that."

"You sure you're feeling up to it?"

"Aaron, I'm fine," she told him. She knew he was just trying to look out for her, but she was really feeling so much better. Her leg still twinged every now and then, but the wound had healed well, thanks to the help of the women and the physical therapy.

"If you're sure," he replied, and they began to carry the empty pallets toward the outbuilding at the far corner of the paddock.

"I never tagged you for a horse girl," he remarked to her as they walked.

"I don't think I was," Bailey replied. "Until I met Wheatie, at least. She's just such a sweetheart. With the worst attitude ever."

Aaron laughed. "Yeah, I can see that," he agreed. "You think she's going to leave those flowers alone?"

"I think they're going to be gone before we even get back there," she replied as they carefully put down the pallets inside the other outbuilding. The shed still needed a lot of work done on it, but judging by the job Aaron had done on the other one, it wouldn't be an issue for him.

They turned to head back through the long grass around the paddock. The sun was just starting to dip a little lower in the sky, and a coolness had settled into the air. Their hands brushed against each other as they walked, and a jolt of electricity rushed from his fingertips to hers. She drew her hand away quickly. She still didn't know exactly where they stood, and she didn't want to confuse the matter any further.

Aaron cleared his throat. "I spoke to Xavier and Lawson today. And Cade, too. He's part of a tactical unit they train and run out of here."

Her eyebrows shot up excitedly. "You did? What did they say? Are they willing to help?"

"They are," he replied, but she sensed a hesitation in his voice that told her there was a *but* coming.

"Okay, good," she replied, frowning in confusion.

He sighed and looked down at her. "But they don't want you involved in the case any longer. They also want to move you to a safehouse while they get everything in order."

She stopped dead in her tracks. She must have heard him wrong. What was he talking about? She was the one who had been attacked by those guys! She was the only one who was still a cop, for God's sake! They couldn't expect her to just drop this, like it didn't matter to her.

"What did you just say?" she demanded.

He shook his head. "I'm sorry, I know it's not what you wanted to hear," he apologized.

She almost laughed at how ridiculous that statement was. Not something she wanted to hear? Yeah, you could say that again. She had been working behind a desk for so long to get where she was right now, only for him to turn around and tell her she couldn't be part of this mission? It was ridiculous.

"No way," she snapped at him. "No way. I'm not letting go of this. I'm the only one with the credentials—"

"Yeah, and that's exactly what they're worried about," he shot back. "They're worried that your involvement might put your future career at risk."

"And I won't even have a future career if these cops don't

get what's coming to them!" she protested. "I can't... I can't believe you would do this to me. You really think this is a good idea?"

"I think you're great at your job, and you would be an asset to any team," he replied carefully. "But this is dangerous. And you don't want to put your future on the line when you have people who are willing to handle it for you."

"I don't want them to *handle* it for me," she replied through gritted teeth. "I want to handle it myself. I don't see what's so hard to understand about that."

They stared at each other for a moment, and she felt the anger crackling in her system. After everything they'd been through, he was doing this to her again. He was pushing her out of something that mattered to her.

"I don't want you to get hurt, Bailey," he told her, and she tore her gaze away from him. Was he right? Probably. But that didn't make this any less painful, didn't make listening to this any easier.

"And what about how I feel?" she demanded. "What about what you did to me? What you're doing to me right now?"

She took a step closer to him, her anger getting the better of her. He stood his ground. He wasn't going to budge on this, she could tell. He had made up his mind, and he had decided this was what was best for her. She couldn't believe it, couldn't wrap her head around him doing this to her again, as though they hadn't been through enough already. They had found each other again and she had finally started to trust him, and then this. This betrayal. Again.

"If you think I'm going to let you stop me—"

"If you think I'm going to let anything happen to you, you've got another thing coming," he replied.

Their hands grazed again, but this time, the electricity

matched the anger in her body and morphed into something else entirely.

She pressed her lips to his before either of them could say anything else. She knew they weren't going to resolve this by talking, she knew she couldn't change his mind right now, and all she wanted was to find the one thing both of them could agree on. The feel of their bodies together, and the lure of this chemistry that never seemed to go away.

His hands tangled into her hair, and she kissed him hard, desperately—needing more, needing as much as she could have from him and so much more. His touch aroused her in a way nothing else did, and even though they were right out there in the middle of a field, she couldn't deny how much she wanted him.

Before she knew it, they were sinking down in the long grass together, and forgetting everything else but the intensity of this kiss.

Chapter Sixteen

"So, what have you got?" Aaron asked as he took his seat at Xavier's desk once more. This time, Lawson and Cade had pulled chairs around as well, a few pages of notes and screenshots lying out on the table in front of them. It was clear they had been hard at work, and Aaron appreciated the effort.

"I've been scouring the social media pages of everyone you mentioned to us," Xavier explained. "Most of them were smart enough to have everything on lockdown, but Benning was tagged in a few pictures with his ex-girlfriend. Looks like they were together until a few months ago and, judging by some of her posts after they broke up, it didn't exactly end well."

Aaron nodded. That made sense. It was hard to imagine someone like Benning in a good relationship—hell, any of them, really. With the subterfuge and lies they had to live their lives under, how could they ever really be honest with anyone?

"If we can get her to talk, we can find out what she knows about Benning and the others," Lawson added. "Seems like he'd be the kind of guy who'd have a hard time keeping his mouth shut, and he might have been flashing his cash with her in a way that made her suspicious. If we can get enough intel from her, it could be enough to get us a warrant and Bailey can take it from there."

"What are we waiting for, then?" Aaron asked as he pulled one of the screenshots on the desk toward him to take a look. Sure enough, there was Benning, his arm wrapped tight around a woman who looked more like she was grimacing than smiling. He couldn't help but feel sorry for her. She had been dating a cop, probably thought he would be the kind of stand-up guy she could trust, only to find out she had managed to land one of the worst of the bunch.

Xavier and Lawson exchanged a look.

"There's one problem," he replied. "It doesn't look like she's willing to…talk to any guys about this. Seems like the experience with Benning was enough to make her wary of men. Especially law enforcement types. So, we're going to have to find some other way to get to her."

Aaron leaned back in his seat, staring at the picture. He couldn't blame her for feeling that way. He had left his own life behind when he had found out the crap those men were tied up in. And being even closer to him? That would have screwed with her head in a big way.

But it posed a real problem. There was no way any of them could get her to talk without scaring her, and it was unlikely she would be willing to give them any useful information. They would need to find a woman to do it, but none of the women could know what was going on here. There was only one woman Aaron could think of who would fit the bill, but there was no way.

"I'll do it."

All four men looked up to see Bailey standing there, her mouth set in a hard line, her eyes sharp as she glanced around the room at them. She must have been listening at the door. Aaron hadn't told her about this meeting, so he had no idea how she'd found out about it, but it was clear from the look on her face that she wasn't going to leave.

"Bailey, what are you doing here?" Xavier asked, sounding annoyed. "Aaron was supposed to tell you—"

"I did," Aaron fired back. Bailey narrowed her eyes at him. In all fairness, their conversation had been cut off before they could come to any conclusions about what they were going to do. As much as he wished he could have convinced her, as soon as she had planted her lips on his, he had known he was done for.

"You need a woman for this job," she replied. "I'm a woman. And I know what I'm doing. I know what we need to get out of her to get the warrant—"

"How long have you been listening in?" Lawson demanded, but she ignored him, not taking her eyes off Aaron.

"I can do this," she murmured to him, her voice almost pleading, as though she was begging him to see her as strong and capable. He felt a tug in his chest, but he pushed it down. He couldn't let his emotions get the better of him. He had just gotten her back, and he wasn't going to let her get hurt or mess up her future if he could help it.

"No," he replied, getting to his feet and shaking his head. "Sorry, Bailey, but no. We talked about this, and we decided it's not safe for you. You know why."

"And you know you can't do this without me!" she exclaimed. She was getting heated. Aaron should have known their encounter the day before wouldn't be enough to shut down her usual stubborn, focused self. When she got something into her head, nothing was going to stop her, especially a bunch of men telling her she couldn't do something.

"You're staying here, where it's safe," he replied. "They already know the lodge exists. At least that's a known fact."

"No, I'm not," she snapped back. "You can't just make these decisions for me, Aaron. I'm sick of it!"

Her words hung in the air, laced with more meaning than

he cared to acknowledge. He knew he had to stop this. He didn't want Xavier and Lawson hearing all the ins and outs of their messy history, but there was nothing else he could do. She was going to make him have this argument right here, right now, in front of everyone.

Luckily, the guys seemed to realize this wasn't a conversation they should be sitting in on, and all of them made their excuses and hurried off. Bailey and Aaron were alone together again, but this time, there was none of the chemistry between them there normally was. No, it was just anger and all the feelings of hurt and betrayal.

"This is exactly what you did to me six years ago," she told him, tears rising in her voice. "I… I can't believe you think I would just go along with this again. Don't you know me at all?"

"I wanted to protect you," he replied through gritted teeth. "That's what I'm trying to do now. You know that, right?"

"You don't need to protect me," she shot back. "You didn't need to protect me then, and you don't need to protect me now—"

"Of course I needed to protect you back then!" he exploded at her. "They were going to hurt you, Bailey. You have no idea what they were capable of!"

"I know that they weren't capable of anything the two of us couldn't have handled together," she replied, her voice dropping. "You should have told me, Aaron. You know I would have helped you. Hell, I would have run with you, if you'd asked me to."

That stopped him dead in his tracks. He stared at her.

"You would have?" he murmured.

She nodded, her eyes dropping, a tear running down her cheek. "Of course I would have, Aaron," she told him. "I would have left with you. I was in love with you, I would have done anything you'd asked me to. *Anything*. As long as it meant we could be together. I would have chosen you over my career, my safety, anything. I just wanted you."

He couldn't bear to hear her say this. It hurt too much. If he could go back in time and tell this to his younger self, he would done things differently. He would have kept her close to him, supported her, maybe even worked with her to take them down.

But it was too late for that now. The damage was done. And he wasn't sure if there was anything he could do to put the pieces back together.

"I loved you, too, Bailey," he replied, his voice catching at the back of his throat. "That's why I did what I had to do. And that's why I'm doing this now. I can't live with the thought of you getting hurt because of me—not again."

He couldn't even finish what he was saying—the thought of it was far too painful. He couldn't bring himself to acknowledge the truth of what he had put her through, especially knowing how deeply she felt for him. It made him feel even guiltier, knowing how much he had hurt her without even realizing it. He hated himself for what he had done to her.

"That's not how love works, Aaron," she replied, shaking her head. "You don't take someone's choices away when you love them. You work with them. You talk to them. You tell them what's going on. You don't just throw them away."

He parted his lips to try and protest, but he couldn't think of anything to say. She turned away before he could speak, and headed for the door. When she got to the door, she paused for a second with her hand on the knob, like she might say something else, but instead she opened the door and left the room.

He listened to the sound of her footsteps down the corridor, the sound of her words ringing in his ears. She had loved him. She had loved him so much she would have given up everything to be with him. Instead, he had taken that choice from her. He had taken away everything she had worked for, everything she had dedicated herself to, and then left her alone, without the support of the man she had loved.

He felt like she had punched him in the stomach. This pain was worse than anything he'd ever felt before, worse than the beating he'd taken from Ziegler and his men. Because this was a pain he had inflicted on to her, a pain he would never be able to undo. The way she saw it, he was just doing the same thing he had done to her six years ago, and he couldn't even argue with her.

But he couldn't stand the thought of her out in the line of fire again. He wouldn't be able to live with himself if something happened to her, just like he couldn't have all those years ago. He could still remember when they had threatened her, when they had told him they would take her out if he didn't do what they said, and the sheer terror that had consumed him when he had been forced to confront the thought of losing her.

So much terror, he hadn't even thought about how she felt about all of it. He wished he could go after her, find the right thing to say to fix it, but the pain in her eyes when she looked at him ran deep. Maybe deeper than he would ever be able to reach.

He sank back down into the chair and let out a sigh. It was never easy with her. No matter what he did, no matter how he tried to look out for her, he always seemed to find some way to mess it up and hurt her in the process. How much longer was she going to let him keep doing this?

How much longer was she going to stay in his life?

Chapter Seventeen

As Bailey piled clothes into her bag, she dashed away the tears that had started to fall from her eyes. She didn't need to be emotional right now. There were more important things to deal with.

Like getting out of here.

She'd made the decision after her conversation with Aaron earlier in the day. She just couldn't stay at the sanctuary, not as long as he was there. She felt her old emotions rising up again, the attachment to him deepening faster than she could stop it, and she just couldn't let herself go through it all again.

He wanted to protect her, but what he didn't realize is that she didn't need him to fight her battles *for* her, she needed him to fight her battles *with* her. As much as she loved him, she couldn't be with someone who was going to make decisions for her and treat her like she wasn't capable. It broke her heart to leave so soon after they had found each other again and confessed their feelings, but she wouldn't stay to be treated like some damsel in distress.

She knew he had reasons for wanting her to sit this out and let him and the other men handle it, but it didn't feel good to be pushed out of a situation that was so important to her. And while she appreciated that he cared about her safety and her future career, she needed to be involved in taking these bad men down. She was the one who had nearly died at their hands, and she was expected to just... step aside, let someone else take care of it for her? No. That wasn't who she was. It wasn't who she had ever been, and she wasn't going to start now.

She'd seen the screenshots they'd had laid out on the desk, so at least she had something to work with. If they had been able to find this information on social media, there was a good chance she would be able to do the same thing. Once she figured out who this woman was, she could go talk to her and get any information she was willing to share. Hopefully, it would be enough to get a warrant.

And she could go back to the Bay, see if any of her friends there were willing to work with her. She had been too scared to even think of it before, but now it seemed like a pretty sensible idea. She could go to them, explain everything that had happened, and with the information she managed to glean from Benning's ex-girlfriend, they could make a move and end this corrupt circle for good.

Her mind had been racing all the way through dinner, where she had played nice with everyone, not wanting anyone to guess what was going on inside her head. She didn't want them to keep an extra watch on her. She was going to sneak out of there in the middle of the night, and then she could start out on her own again.

All on her own. A pang hit her chest hard, and she had to stop and take a deep breath to gather herself. How was she going to manage that? All alone? It just didn't seem fair or right. She had come here because she had wanted Aaron's help, and while he had given it to her, it had been the same kind of betrayal he'd done before. Even if he had his reasons, and even if she understood them to some extent, she couldn't let him do this to her again.

Once she had gathered a few supplies, clothes, and some food she'd snuck from the kitchen, she opened her bedroom door as quietly as she could and stepped into the corridor. She shot a look one way and then the other, making sure nobody was out there. It was just past midnight, and the physical work everyone did during the day meant they slept pretty deep. There was no reason anyone would be up and about at this time of night.

Which meant there was nobody to stop her.

She started to creep down the corridor, and something at the back of her mind silently wished someone would catch her doing this. Then she could make her excuses and stay. They didn't want her to leave, and she knew she was going to miss so much about this place—the views, the horses, and the women she had grown friendly with.

And Aaron, of course. Mainly Aaron.

He was going to be devastated when he found out she was gone—she wouldn't be surprised if he tried to catch up with her and bring her back. She hoped that he would just let her leave. She didn't have the strength inside to hold off against her attraction to him, and if he came for her, she might just go back with him.

No. She had to be strong, she had to be sure of herself. She couldn't let these ridiculous doubts get caught up in her mind. She padded down the stairs and to the front desk, where she grabbed a set of truck keys hanging on a rack behind the counter for one of the older vehicles on the property. She felt bad for stealing from them when they had been so good to her, but she didn't want anyone to immediately realize she was gone and track her truck. And she knew Aaron would do it, too. He'd follow her and try to convince her to come back. Besides, she wouldn't keep theirs forever, she'd bring it back when she was through with it. Her own had sentimental value and she'd want it back eventually. Hopefully, no one here would hold the theft against her.

She just had to bring down the dirty cops, once and for all. And she would—with or without help. She'd show them all she was capable.

Outside, the night was still. The only sound was the grass rustling around her as she made her way up the main path that led from the central building. Her heart was in her throat as she quietly unlocked the truck door and climbed in. She couldn't believe she was doing this. A part of her was screaming to turn around and go back. She could go back upstairs, slip back into her bed, and act like this never happened. Wake up tomorrow, go down to breakfast just like usual…

No, she couldn't do that. She pushed the key into the ignition, her eyes blurry with tears. Gritting her teeth, she felt the engine come to life beneath her. Glancing over her shoulder to back up, she put the rusty old truck into motion, her first step on her journey out of here.

Then, something caught her eye. For a moment, she thought she had imagined it—a tiny movement at the very edge of her vision. If she hadn't been so hyperalert, she might not even have noticed it. But she looked around and saw some movement at the top of the path that led through the forest and into the paddock.

"What the hell?" she muttered to herself, and she pushed the door open and slipped her feet back to the ground again.

It must have been an animal, something like that. She tried to soothe her panicking mind, and she was about to climb back into the truck to leave when a scent wafted by her on the wind. She sniffed the air. What was that?

Then her heart dropped. It was oil. That was the smell of oil.

Before she could react, the sky lit up in a flash of flames, and she could see the paddock in the distance bursting into a fireball. Her eyes widened, and she clapped a hand over her mouth. The horses had been moved to another paddock while the buildings were being finished up to be weather-tight, but if that fire spread, it could easily reach them—or the main building, if it was left long enough.

"Fire!" she screamed at the top of her lungs. "Fire!"

She felt as though she was frozen to the spot, trapped exactly where she stood as she tried to pull herself together. She couldn't just walk away from this. Someone was targeting them, she was sure of it. The fire was spreading unnaturally fast, and whatever accelerant they had used was clearly working exactly as they had intended it to.

Bailey leaned on the truck's horn and yelled for help. Within a few minutes, the residents of the lodge were pouring out onto the grass around her. Cade shielded River from the sight, and she pressed her face into his chest as though she couldn't believe what she was seeing.

"Get as many buckets as you can from the supply closet!" Xavier yelled, springing into action. "Hannah, get a hose hooked up and call the fire department—come on, we need to move!"

Everyone was rushing around a moment later, trying to stop the fire before it got any worse, but Bailey just stood there. She wanted to help, she did, but she felt trapped. She needed to make sure Aaron was okay before she left while everyone else was distracted by the fire. What if he had been out working late at the shed and been caught in the blaze?

"Oh, God."

She heard a voice behind her, and spun around to see

Aaron standing, ashen faced, a few feet away. He must have come from his cabin as soon as he heard the commotion. She breathed a sigh of relief as soon as she saw him, and she wanted to hug him, hold him, tell him how sorry she was. How she was sure this had something to do with her, his little piece of heaven torn apart by something he had tried to leave behind.

He rushed toward the rest of the group to help, but Bailey hesitated. Should she go after him? It was an all-hands-on-deck situation, that was for sure, and they would likely need all the help they could get.

But if she didn't leave now, she wasn't sure she would ever have the nerve to again. No, as awful as it was, she knew she couldn't stay here. She had to go. Guilt tore at her mind as she raced back to the truck, checking over her shoulder to make sure everyone was accounted for. She saw all the people who had helped her rushing to try and contain the fire. She wished them a silent goodbye, and a thank-you for everything they had done for her.

The tears flowed freely now as she reached the truck once more and climbed inside. Covering her face with her hands, she took a deep, shaky breath, trying to gather herself. She couldn't believe she was doing this when they were facing off against a ferocious fire, but she didn't have a choice. They couldn't help her. They wouldn't give her the justice she knew she needed, and she wasn't willing to give that up, not for anything or anyone.

Even Aaron.

She shot one last look at him in the rearview mirror, sprinting out of the building with a bucketful of water. She couldn't risk letting him break her heart again, not after how long she had been hung up on him before. Whether she liked it or not, it was all on her now—all on her to take down the men who had driven her from Kings Mountain for a second time.

It was time for her to bring Ziegler and the others down and she knew she wouldn't be able to do that if she stayed here. Aaron, Xavier, and Lawson meant well but ultimately, she needed to be involved and if they wouldn't let her do that, she needed to leave. With a final deep breath to steady her erratic heartbeat, she set her hands on the steering wheel and her eyes on the road ahead of her.

She put her foot down, set her eyes on the road in front of her, and took off away from the sanctuary as fast as she could. She felt the sobs rack her body, but she kept driving. All she could think about was him—the man she was being pulled away from all over again, the man she wasn't sure she would ever be able to forget.

Chapter Eighteen

Aaron could hardly believe what he was seeing as he stood there in front of the paddock. The whole thing was ablaze, and it was obvious someone had done this on purpose. But who? And why?

And where the hell had Bailey gone?

"Aaron, come on!" Cade yelled, gesturing for him to use the water in his bucket to put out some of the fire. Aaron blinked, reminding himself where he was, and then tossed the water over some of the flames in front of him. They had to work with what they had right now, and that wasn't much. Hannah was bringing over a hose, but that would only reach so far. In the main building itself, they might have been able to handle a fire of this magnitude, but out here, it was hard to imagine how they were going to deal with it.

He sprinted back toward the main building, the smell of smoke thick in the air. Everyone was up and working hard, most of them still in their pajamas, some even barefoot. This wasn't the kind of event where you could just take your time to get dressed before you dealt with it. No, it was a now-or-never kind of thing, and if they missed their chance, it would be a disaster.

It had been sunny for a few days, so the leaves of the trees in the forest nearby were basically perfect kindling. It would just take one swift breeze, and the whole thing could go up in smoke. And then the cabins, then the lodge…damn, this was bad. This was really, really bad.

He filled up another bucket as River raced past him, Hannah in tow. He could already tell that they were going to get the horses. They loved those beautiful creatures, and they would likely be freaked out by the fire, even if they weren't in the direct line of it right now.

Aaron filled the bucket up as quickly as he could, and rushed back to the paddock. A line of men was forming to pass buckets back and forth as fast as possible, but the fire was spreading faster than they could contain it. Lawson was in the midst of it, directing the buckets, and he had to cover his mouth to keep from inhaling too much smoke. He was going to need to be careful.

"Lawson, I'll swap out with you in five minutes!" Aaron yelled to him over the noise of the crackling fire behind him. Lawson shook his head.

"I'm fine!" he yelled back.

Aaron rushed to him and grabbed his arm. "The smoke!" he reminded him. "You have to take a break! Five minutes, okay?"

"Fine, go!" Lawson replied, gesturing for him to head back to the building. He did as he was told, filling another bucket and bringing it back to the scene of the crime.

Xavier just stood there, looking shaken. His eyes were wide as he tried to take it all in. Aaron felt for him—this place was his home, the home he had made for himself and other people who had struggled like he had, and it was literally going up in smoke right before his eyes.

"Xavier!" Aaron called to him, grabbing his shoulder. "You can't just stand there. You need to do something!"

Xavier blinked, and then seemed to come back into himself. It was important he was in the midst of it. He commanded the most respect at Warrior Peak, and if people saw him panicking, they would panic.

"You go to Hannah and River, help them with the horses," he told Aaron.

Aaron nodded and took off toward the barn where the horses had been staying that night. Thank God they hadn't been in there when the fire had broken out. He wasn't sure the women would have been able to handle it. Bailey would have been devastated.

Thinking of Bailey, he glanced around, trying to see her. She had to be back at the main building, right? Helping out with the water? Had she been the one to raise the alarm when this fire had started? And if she was, why had she been out of bed in the middle of the night?

But before he could linger too long on that thought, he heard a horse let out a startled whinny, and he forced himself to focus on the matter at hand. The women needed his help, and he wasn't going to leave them to deal with this alone.

"Hey, Wheatie, chill!" Hannah called to the horse, who had reared up on her hind legs as soon as she had caught sight of the fire. Aaron quickly caught River's arm and pulled her away before Wheatie brought her hooves down a little too close for comfort.

"It's okay, she's just freaked because of the fire," Aaron told them. "There are some reins in the barn, let's get them on the horses and lead them as far away from this as we can, all right?"

"All right," Hannah replied, and they rushed toward the barn to grab the reins.

Aaron could smell oil in the air, the thick scent telling him this had been a deliberate, calculated attack. The people who had done this hadn't just wanted to cause a scene or scare them, they had wanted to cause real, long-term destruction. They had waited for the perfect night to do it—dry with a slight breeze.

A few licks of flame had already caught on to some of the low-hanging branches near the paddock. The flowers that Bailey, Hannah, and River had planted had already been swallowed by the flames entirely, nothing but ashes now.

Aaron looped the reins around Wheatie's head, and she let out a snort in protest. He planted a hand on her neck, trying to soothe her.

"Hey, girl, it's going to be all right," he tried to assure her. He hoped his tone of voice would be enough to soothe her, even though she must have known something was wrong. Horses were incisive at the best of times, and it wouldn't take much for them to start to really freak out. If they did, it would be chaos—panicked horses galloping around on top of everything else would only add to how hard this was going to be for them.

He led Wheatie slowly but surely away from the fire, grabbing the reins of another horse as he went. Hannah and River were close behind him, each with another horse, Hannah talking to River as though doing her best to keep her calm and focused.

He could smell the acrid smoke in the air as they reached the far end of the other paddock. Tying up the reins of the horses, Aaron hardly waited before he bolted back toward the fire once more.

"Lawson, out!" he roared toward Lawson, as he saw him still standing by the edge of the paddock. His face was covered in ash—only his eyes peered out from the smudges across his skin. He seemed to know better than to argue with Aaron, so he quickly nodded and turned his back, allowing Aaron to take his spot.

Aaron wrapped his fingers around his sleeve and pulled hard, tearing away the seam so he could wrap it around his face. It wouldn't do much, but it might be enough to keep him from getting too badly injured by the smoke inhalation. He had attended a few arsons cases in his time, and he knew that the smoke was what really got people. He'd seen what it could do, and he wasn't about to let that happen to him.

Xavier was still at the far end of the paddock, directing people. A line was passing buckets back and forth quickly, and Hannah rushed toward Xavier, checking that he was okay.

There was only so much they could do on their own. Getting one side of the field under control was a start, but the fire had started to spread rapidly through the trees. A few burning leaves had dropped to the ground, and the dry grass was beginning to catch fire.

"We need buckets over here!" Aaron yelled to the crew, waving one of them over so he could try and handle at least some of the inferno. His own cabin was only a few hundred feet away, and it wouldn't take long for the fire to reach it if he didn't get it under control.

He grabbed a full bucket and dashed into the forest, splashing the water wherever he saw the flames. He couldn't do much about the trees above him, but if he could stop the fire spreading through the forest floor, it might do the job.

But soon, he ran out of water, and he had to return to grab another one. The paddock was completely consumed now, either in flames or in the ashen remains of what had once been the fence and the building he'd spent so long putting together. He hated seeing the work he'd done reduced to nothing, but he would have time to think about that later. Right now, all that really mattered was making sure he stopped this before anyone got hurt.

"I'll help you," River told him, grabbing a bucket and following Aaron back to the forest. But just as she reached it, someone called her name.

"River, watch out!"

Aaron spun around just in time to see a heavy, flaming branch crash down from a tree, nearly landing on River's head. She dived out of the way just in time, managing to aim the water in her bucket at the branch to put it out. Cade rushed over to her, then dropped to his knees to pull her into his arms.

"Are you okay?" he demanded.

She nodded shakily. "Go," she told him. "I'm fine. We have more important things to worry about right now."

Cade dropped a kiss on her head, and River followed him back to the main building to grab another bucket of water as Aaron went about putting out the small patches of flames catching on the scorched earth. It would take the forest so long to recover from this, so long to regenerate back to its former glory. If they didn't stop this fire, it would damage far more than just the forest. Hopefully they would hear sirens soon and could leave the firefighting to the professionals.

He finished dumping the bucket and ran out of the woods again, past an exhausted-looking Xavier. He was breathing hard, sweat sheening his brow as he looked out over the seemingly hopeless fire in front of them.

He caught Aaron's eye, and his face darkened. He gestured at the paddock, now consumed with the inferno that he wasn't sure they would be able to control.

"This wasn't an accident, Aaron!" he yelled to him.

Aaron nodded in unspoken agreement. There was no way to deny it. This hadn't been an accident. Someone had come here to make sure they knew they weren't safe.

But until they got the fire under control, they couldn't even worry about that yet.

Aaron covered his mouth from the choking smoke and ran back to the lodge, his legs burning and his lungs scorching with each and every breath.

And, in the midst of it all, all he could think about was how much he hoped Bailey was safe.

Chapter Nineteen

Bailey stared at the skyline in her rearview mirror. It had started to glow orange now from the intensity of the fire burning up the property she had just run away from. Even winding her way down the mountain and toward the town, she could see it. The whole damn county probably could.

She slammed her foot on to the brakes, cursing herself. She hissed through her teeth. How could she turn her back on them? On Aaron? What kind of person was she? She couldn't just leave like this. They needed all the help they could get right now, and she would be damned if she walked away from her friends when they needed her. No matter what happened, she couldn't leave them to deal with the fire alone.

She looked over her shoulder, and was about to throw the truck into Reverse when a van came out of nowhere and smashed into the side of her truck. She hardly had time to process being hit before the truck spun off the road, dipping into the ditch at the far side and then tipping over on to its hood.

She pressed her hands to the sides of the cabin to try and brace for impact, gritting her teeth and tensing her body. A vehicle like this was probably too old for airbags, so she didn't have to worry about being blasted by one of them.

Yet, that could end up being a bad thing, too. If the airbag had been there and deployed, it would have softened some of the abuse her body was taking now.

The truck bounced down the steep incline at the side of the road, crashing through a thicket of trees and bushes. Branches stabbed through the shattered windows, and one caught Bailey on the shoulder, digging into her flesh and leaving a deep gash through her shirt and into her skin. She cried out in pain, but the noise was lost over the sound of crumpling metal and the trees around her.

Finally, the truck came to a halt. Bailey breathed hard, the adrenaline coursing through her system. She could barely feel her fingers or toes, and she knew shock must be taking hold. But she needed to get out of the vehicle as quickly as possible. She didn't know what had been damaged in the accident, and she wasn't going to wait around to see. She needed to get out.

The accident. It felt wrong for her to even think of it that way, because she sure as hell knew it wasn't an accident. There wasn't much activity on this mountain road this time of night. There was nothing out this way except Warrior Peak Sanctuary. It wasn't like another vehicle wouldn't have seen her driving down the road, either. No, they must have been lying in wait for whoever tried to leave. Apparently, they didn't intend to let anyone escape tonight, blocking off their only route away from the lodge as soon as they had set the fire.

Once Bailey had managed to calm herself some, she checked around to see the best way out. The truck had landed on its side, so she would have to scramble out of the driver's side and climb up and out of the smashed window on the passenger one. She unclipped her seat belt, the wound in her shoulder throbbing, blood coursing down her arm to her hand. It was so slippery that it took her a moment to press the release button on her seat belt, but it finally sprang free.

Using her good arm, she pushed herself upright, then removed her jacket. There were a lot of glass shards still hanging from the broken window, so she'd need to use it to wipe away what was left in order to get out. She tied her jacket around her waist and then, using the steering wheel, dashboard, and driver's seat as a ladder, pushed and pulled her way through the truck to the window.

She suddenly thought she smelled gasoline, and paused to look around. She didn't see any flames, but if there was a leak in here, she really didn't have any time to waste at all. Clenching her jaw, she renewed her climb to the opposite window and wrapped her jacket around her fist to clear away the glass still clinging to the edges. She was already injured, but she didn't need to make it worse by getting broken pieces of glass embedded in her.

Bailey hoisted herself up to where she was hanging half in and half out of the truck over the window sill, and shimmied and pushed her way through. She braced for the hard landing as the ground suddenly came up to meet her. She lay on the cold ground for a moment, catching her breath, and realized there was nothing but dead silence surrounding her. She slowly sat up and looked around to check if the people who had done this to her were lying in wait. If they were, she couldn't see them anywhere close.

Taking a deep breath, she pulled herself up to standing, then started making her way back to the road, straining her ears for any noise of someone approaching. It was a slow process with her leg not completely healed, now aching more, and the throbbing in her shoulder and blood loss. She had to put pressure on the wound, but she needed both hands to help her balance and climb.

She also needed to get back to Warrior Peak, to make sure Aaron and the others were okay. She couldn't believe she had left them. She would never have ended up in that truck on the side of the road with a gash five inches long in her shoulder if she had just stuck around to help them fight the fire.

Reaching the road, she collapsed to her knees and leaned forward to rest her hands on the pavement as she caught her breath. With her new injury, how long would it take her to get up the mountain? She could already feel herself getting a little dizzy as she sat there. What if she couldn't make it back to the lodge? What if nobody noticed she was gone— or worse, what if they noticed she was gone but didn't come looking for her? Hell, someone might have seen her driving away from the fire and think she had started it. She hoped they wouldn't think that badly of her.

She tried to stand up, but it seemed like her body didn't want to cooperate. It took a couple of tries before she could successfully manage to get back on her feet. Her knees were trembling, and her hand was sticky with blood, but she grabbed her jacket and tied it around the wound as best she could, hoping it would do enough to stem the bleeding until she could get some real medical attention.

Looking back toward the dim glow of the fire on the horizon, she steeled herself for what was to come. She had to get back to Aaron. It might not be easy, but she had to do it. She had to make sure he was okay.

And she had to tell him how sorry she was for even thinking about leaving him and Warrior Peak.

But before she could start her journey, a sudden light blinded her. She lifted her hands to shield her eyes, but she could still barely see. Two headlights blazed from the other side of the road—the van that had hit her. Her heart dropped and her lungs seized.

She tried to take a step but her legs gave way and she crashed to her knees again, still hiding her eyes from the glare of the bright light in front of her. Her entire body was pumping with adrenaline and she felt sick. She tried to tell herself it wasn't going to be as bad as she thought. Maybe these guys were just here to help. That could be true, right? Maybe they had been rushing up to Warrior Peak to help with the fire, and this had really just been nothing other than a terrible accident.

Lifting her head once more, she managed to make out two figures coming toward her. Their silhouettes cut through the near-white light from the headlights of the van. Didn't they know she could hardly see? She tried to call out to them, but her tongue was thick and heavy, and she was so nauseous she was going to be sick. She gagged and coughed but no words came out.

They had to be here to help her.

She lifted a hand, pointing in the direction of the lodge. She needed them to understand.

"Warrior Peak Sanctuary," she rasped, her voice tiny as she tried to force sound out of her lips. "You need to call someone, get help. There's a fire…"

"Oh, we know."

The sound of that voice froze the blood in her veins. Her body responded before her mind did and she heaved herself to the side and vomited in front of his shoes.

"Damn it!" He growled at her and shoved her back.

Bailey's ears started ringing and black dots danced before her eyes. She knew who that was. She tried to lift her head to look at him, but her eyesight was blurry and she felt too weak. She could just see his dark figure towering over her, outlined against the headlights behind him.

The sliding door of the van opening reached her ears, then two more sets of footsteps approached. The others were coming, all four of them were here to finish her off. She tried to turn to crawl back down the ledge, but her entire body had seized up. She wasn't sure if it was the pain or the fear or a mixture of both, but she couldn't move. All she could do was sit there as she waited for this nightmare to come to an end.

All four men advanced on her now, just like they had the night they had attacked her in the bar parking lot. Back then, at least, she had been able to run—she had had somewhere she could run to. But now? Now, she wasn't so sure. With Aaron and the others at the sanctuary fighting the fire these men had started, no one even knew she was gone. She didn't even know if any of them would survive the inferno. Her truck was wrecked, she was injured, and felt like she was on the verge of passing out. She had no means of escape and nowhere to go if she managed to get away. Which in her condition, was unlikely. She was at the mercy of the criminals before her and she was all alone.

The man who had spoken dropped down to his haunches in front of her, inspecting her like a predator would inspect their prey. She recoiled from him, her hands sinking into the dirt at the side of the road, but she couldn't get far enough away. She could finally make out his face now, the hard smile that twisted his lips as he watched her with amusement. She tried again to push herself away again, but her body was done. Between the wreck, her injury, the blood loss, and the adrenaline crash, she had nothing left.

He grabbed her arm, the one with the gash, and she let out a loud groan of pain. She felt the throb of that agony racing through her whole system at once, her eyes rolling back as the shock of it took control of her.

"Good to see you again, Masters," Ziegler snarled, as he yanked her to her feet. She groaned again, stumbling as her body screamed in protest. She wanted to rip her arm from his grasp, but she didn't have the strength. All she could do was hang there like a rag doll and pray he finished her off quickly. Her body was utterly wrung out from everything she had endured. She couldn't even find the words to tell him what she thought of him and his cronies and what they'd done.

He leaned in close, a grin on his face that didn't reach his eyes.

"Thanks for making this so easy for us," he said, sneering.

With that, he shoved her toward the other men as everything faded to black, the headlights still burning the back of her vision.

Chapter Twenty

"Take the last of the buckets around to the other corner!" Xavier called to the group, and a few men hurried to take a couple more buckets full of water to the far edge of the paddock. Aaron breathed a sigh of relief as soon as he saw them douse out the last of the flames. It was over, thank God.

Everyone was shaken, but nobody was actually hurt, which had to count for something. The horses were okay, too, though it would take a while for them to fully settle again. The fire hadn't reached the main lodge, and the county fire services had finally arrived and managed to put it out at the edge of the forest. Everything was under control for the time being.

Aaron sank down to the grass for a moment to catch his breath, and unwrapped the sleeve he had tied around his mouth. Tilting his head back, he drew in a deep lungful of air. Not exactly clear yet, but the smoke was at least starting to fade now.

Everyone had backed off to a safe distance now that the fire was actually contained, and he scanned the group, searching for Bailey. He hadn't seen her since that brief moment when the fire first started, but she must have been out there helping, right? It was all such a blur.

But, as he looked around, his heart started to hammer

in his chest again. Where was she? He couldn't see her anywhere. He hurried toward the crowd that had formed near the front entrance to the main lodge, hoping she was just buried somewhere toward the back—she couldn't be missing. Not on the night of this fire. It would have been too much of a coincidence, and he knew she wouldn't have walked away from them right now unless she had a really good reason.

Or, unless someone forced her to.

"River, Hannah," he called to the women when he spotted them together.

They both turned to greet him.

"Hey, what's up?" Hannah called back. Her face looked drawn and worried, and he wondered if she had noticed that Bailey was missing, too.

"Have you seen Bailey?" he asked them.

They exchanged a look, and then shook their heads.

"Haven't seen her," River replied. "Why? Is something wrong?"

He shook his head, panic starting to rise. He needed to find her, right the hell now. He could feel it in his chest, how bad it would be if he didn't locate her. He couldn't let anything happen to her. Not after he had given up so much to keep her safe in the first place.

"You're looking for Bailey, right?" one of the guys asked. He was a relatively new arrival at the lodge, and Aaron didn't know much about him, but if he had some information about Bailey, he was going to hear it.

"Yeah, yeah, I am," he replied. "Have you seen her?"

"I saw her driving off a few minutes after the fire started," he replied, pointing down toward the road that led away from Warrior Peak. "In that direction."

Damn. Aaron's mind was racing. Why would she leave?

Had she done it willingly, or had she been forced? The last conversation they'd had was an argument, and he hated the thought of her fleeing so soon after their disagreement. He thought it was something they could work through, but maybe she felt differently.

"I noticed her truck still here. You sure she took off?" Xavier asked, cutting into the conversation. His brow was furrowed, and he looked concerned.

"Seems like it. I saw her a moment at the start of the fire, but haven't been able to find her since," Aaron replied. "She must have snagged a lodge truck so we wouldn't know she was gone." His eyes darkened. Looks like she was running away this time. That thought made his chest ache.

"Then you need to find out where she's headed," he replied. "It's not safe for her to be on her own right now. This fire starting out of nowhere can't be a coincidence, either. And so soon after you fill us in on your past and finding out dirty cops know of your location. We can only assume they know Bailey was here, too. It's got to have something to do with why she left. Maybe they contacted her in some way?"

Aaron nodded in agreement. That made sense. If Ziegler or one of the others had found a way to contact Bailey and made threats against Warrior Peak or even him, she would have left to protect everyone here.

Xavier tossed him a set of keys. "Here, take my car," he told him. "We'll be waiting. And call if you need backup."

"Thanks. I will," Aaron replied.

With that, he made his way toward the car, his mind running so fast he didn't know how to control it. As he climbed in and drove off, his thoughts were frantic, his entire system consumed with the fear of what might have happened to her.

He stared at the road ahead of him as he drove, willing himself not to screw this up—not to make more of a mess of this than he already had. He should have checked on her after what had happened the night before. He knew she was upset about the guys at the sanctuary wanting her to stand down and let them handle it. She thought they all saw her as lesser than, incapable. But she wasn't thinking clearly, letting her emotions override reason. They knew she could handle herself—that wasn't it at all.

With their backgrounds, though, they were protectors at their core and if they could stand between someone else and danger—they'd do it every time. The guys were also thinking of her future. If Bailey wanted to stay in law enforcement, she needed to be removed from all of this. Not have this black mark on her record where anyone could question her motives.

The road wound down the mountain, and he drove as quickly as he could without throwing the car off the side when he took the corners. He just needed to get to her. She couldn't have gotten far, right? She didn't know the area well—unless she had done her planning before she left, and made sure she knew where she was going. And she had never been the kind of woman who would walk directly into something without knowing what she was facing.

He gripped the wheel tight, his whole body rigid with tension. He would find her. He *would* find her. And if Ziegler and his crew had put themselves in the middle of this, he would take them all out on the spot and bring them down for good, as long as it meant she was safe. He would not fail her this time.

He had blown up his life to make sure she was okay—and blown up hers in the process. Both of them had given up so much, lost so much time with each other and the thought of losing more just because these villains couldn't just leave them alone… He didn't know what to make of it all. He and

Bailey were both out of the picture, no one else knew what they did, so why could Ziegler and the rest just not move on? Were they that far gone with their power and corruption that they thought they had to eliminate them permanently? He just couldn't wrap his mind around that.

Whatever their reasoning, though, there wasn't a chance in hell he was going to let anything happen to her.

And if she had left of her own volition? What then? If she was okay, he felt like he should be fine with it, but the two of them had something he didn't want to give up quite so soon. He wasn't entirely sure what their connection was, or if she would even want to pursue it after everything that had happened, but he knew he would do anything to make it work. He had waited so long before, and now she was finally back. How could he pass up that chance?

He rounded a bend in the road, and slammed on the brakes, taking in the scene before him. Down the embankment on the left side, near the tree line, was the lodge truck—it looks like it had flipped off the road, rolling and sliding nearly twenty feet before coming to a smoking stop on its side. His gut clenched at the sight. He quickly scanned the area but didn't see any movement near the crashed vehicle. He hoped Bailey made it out in one piece, or there'd be hell to pay. On the right side of the road, sitting at an angle facing the embankment with the headlights still blazing, was a van with a dented front bumper.

He turned off the car's headlights and quietly pulled behind the van, making sure his car was hidden behind the glow of the headlights. He didn't know what was going on here, but he wanted to make sure he had as much time as he could to work it out before anyone else spotted him. He got the feeling he was going to have to take every advantage he could.

He silently got out and looked around. It was pitch black out here, the only light coming from the headlights. If he stayed low and moved quickly, he'd be able to cross the road without being seen. Keeping his steps as soft as possible while hurrying, he made his way to the opposite side of the road and down to the crashed truck, praying she would still be inside. Even if she was hurt, he could get her back to the sanctuary and patch her up. But if she was gone, what the hell could he do about it? Would he even be able to get her back? He immediately shut that thought down.

If Ziegler and his crew were the ones to have caused this and had taken her to parts unknown, Aaron knew he'd move heaven and earth to find her and get her back to the safety of Warrior Peak with him, where she belonged. He wasn't giving up, no matter what he had to do or where he had to go. No matter how long it took, he'd find her.

The truck was empty when he peered inside through the windshield, but he did see blood. He took a moment and looked around to see if there were any signs to indicate she had managed to get away, but there were no visible clues as to where she went in the immediate area.

Looking back at the truck, he noticed a lot of blood smeared across the seatbelt and door handle. Seeing both, he knew Bailey was at least badly injured and he needed to get to her soon. The passenger side window, which was facing upright, was smashed, so she could have crawled out or someone could have pulled her out. Either way, she wasn't there, so she had to have at least survived the crash. He had to believe that. So where was she now?

He tried to think what he would do if this had been him, but his mind kept going back to all the blood inside the truck. Yes, the truck had tumbled down the embankment so he'd expect some, but not as much as he'd seen inside.

If that was any indication of how she was doing, Bailey needed him now.

Or else…

No, he couldn't even let himself think that. He wouldn't let his mind go there. He had to trust she had been able to find a way out of this, no matter how bad it might look. He knew he didn't give her enough credit for what a badass she was—none of them did. She could handle so much more than her small stature indicated.

Giving up on his search at the truck, Aaron quietly made his way back toward the road, keeping his steps light and his head down. That van had run her off the road, he was sure of it. There was no way she would have crashed without cause. She was a careful driver, even when she was under stress. And if someone had wanted to take her out like this, who was to say what else they would do to make sure she played by their rules?

He sank down by the edge of the road, looking back and forth, trying to figure out who was here and what they might have been doing. He didn't want to make his presence known until he had a better idea of what was going on. Nobody would be coming up to Warrior Peak unless they had a good reason to. Someone might have tried to play hero with the fire, but he doubted it. It was impossible to see anything down this far, apart from the smoke in the sky.

Around him, he couldn't make out anything but the usual sounds of the night. The van was still running, so whoever was out there was planning on using it for a fast retreat once they finished whatever they were doing. Since he couldn't find her below at the wreck, he had to assume the *whatever* had something to do with Bailey and why he hadn't seen her around. He wasn't going to walk away from this until he knew for sure what was going on.

He was about to move to a different angle when he heard it. The sound of a struggle—of voices. Mostly men, but he could also hear a woman saying something, protesting. Much to his relief, it sounded like Bailey.

He kept a watchful eye pinned to the van opposite him. He felt his heart pounding in his chest, and he took long, deep breaths, trying to settle himself before he freaked out too badly. He couldn't rush this. He had made decisions based on his emotions before, and that rarely ended well for him.

Suddenly, he saw a commotion near the van. Just for a split second, four familiar figures shoved Bailey toward the back. They were trying to kidnap her! God only knew what they would do if they managed to get her out of there, but he wasn't going to let that happen. He had to stop it.

He rose to his feet and took a deep breath. *Now or never.* If they got her into that van, it was over, and he wasn't going to let the woman he loved be lost to him a second time.

Without another thought, he went sprinting toward them, blazing with all the anger of a bat out of hell and ready to put these guys down. For good.

Chapter Twenty-One

"Let go of me!" Bailey yelled as she tried to yank herself away from Benning. He had her arm in a viselike grip, twisted up her back, and the pain was throbbing so badly from the gash in her shoulder she thought she might pass out. One of the men had ripped the tourniquet she had made with her jacket off her arm, probably wanting to cause her more pain. She felt the blood leaking down her arm again and dripping off her fingers onto the ground. If she didn't think of something soon, she wouldn't be able to put up much of a fight at all. She'd already lost a lot of blood and was feeling dangerously woozy. She didn't know how much longer she even had.

"You already tried that, remember? You're only hurting yourself more," Ziegler remarked to her, his voice laced with a mocking amusement. She tried to turn to him, her eyes dark with anger, but Benning had too strong a grip on her. She couldn't fight them off.

"Really, Bailey, you should leave the hurting to us," Moore added with a laugh, the others joining in.

Sheer terror took hold of her as she realized their intent. *I can't fight them off.*

Ziegler and Benning were pushing and dragging her toward the van, where Moore and Lee stood by the sliding door, waiting to help force her inside. What were they going to do with her when they managed to get her out of here? Her mind spun with all the hideous possibilities, and she couldn't stand the thought of letting them get to her like that.

She was shoved toward the van again, but the physical manhandling didn't seem to be enough for these guys. No, they wanted to really hurt her—they wanted to make sure she suffered. She hadn't even exposed them, she just hadn't gone along with their twisted plans. She didn't even want to think what might happen if they found out she had actually been scheming against them.

"You really thought you could stop us?" Ziegler said, sneering at her as he grabbed a handful of her hair and yanked her head around in his direction. "After you've been away so long? After your precious boyfriend sent you packing for desk work for years on end?"

She felt the tears blurring her eyes, and she tried to blink them back, not wanting them to see how much they were getting to her. *Aaron*. If they got her out of here, she would never see Aaron again, she was sure of it. Even though she had almost made the same decision herself tonight, she could clearly see now how much of a mistake it was. She couldn't let that happen.

"You're nothing," Ziegler continued, jerking on her hair, clearly enjoying her distress. "And your boyfriend is going to go down for this, too. We might have left him alone if you hadn't run crying to him."

The tears racked her body now. She had brought this to his door again, she had made it so he couldn't be safe. If she had just kept her distance, not been so stubborn thinking she could fix everything, it never would have gone down the way it had. She couldn't believe she had been so foolish. She—a rookie cop who ended up riding a desk for six years—thought she could end this, when Aaron—a sergeant on the police force, a seasoned officer, and the best man she had ever known—hadn't even been able to succeed. What did she think she would be able to do against these men?

As the fear and dread set in, all of this started to feel as though it was happening to someone else. Like she was watching herself as it happened, not in her own body. And, when she saw it like that, the anger was what rose to the top. All of this was so unfair. All she had ever wanted was to be a good cop, and they had taken that from her. They had taken her chance to live out the career she had wanted, the life she had wanted—with the man she wanted, too.

Before she could think it through, she spat at Ziegler. "You're never going to get away with this."

He smirked at her. "I already have," he replied smugly.

"I know you've managed all this time, but that was before you let me know about it," she continued. "You know how many people there are working on this case? Not just cops, either—former military and former CIA agents. There's so much crap coming your way, you don't have any idea."

They fell silent for a moment, and Benning and Ziegler exchanged a look. Both of them actually looked...worried. Like there was something to be really afraid of. A swell of pride filled her chest as she watched them. Yeah, they should be scared. They should be downright terrified at the storm that was coming their way. They might have thought taking her out would stop it, but it was only just getting started.

And she couldn't wait to see it rip them apart. If she was still around, that is.

But before she could continue rubbing it in, Benning pulled a gun from his holster. He pressed it against her side, and she tried to pull away from him, so then he leveled it straight at her head. She immediately froze, and time stood still. She wanted to shift away but all she could see was the black barrel looking back at her. Unflinching, unwavering.

She had never been on the other end of a gun like this. They had flashed a knife at her before, of course, but that had been different. This? This was the end. One wrong move and she would be dead. Of course, some part of her had known they were going to do this eventually.

Her life flashed before her eyes as Benning wrapped his other hand around the gun. The other men were dead silent, like even they hadn't been prepared for this to happen. The tears were gone now—she was too scared to cry. Her whole body was frozen in terror as she faced the reality of what was going to happen to her.

What had she even done with her life? All she'd ever wanted to do was be a police officer. After sitting behind a desk for six years, she had finally gotten back to where she felt like she could make a difference, and these men had taken that away from her. She had spent those years so angry at Aaron for betraying her, but she understood that he was only trying to protect her from this. This moment right here. And now that they had found each other again, she realized that he was the only man she'd ever loved.

That was what she had done with her life: She had loved him so much more than she had ever loved anyone else. Even when it had been hard, even when they had been apart all of those years, she had never stopped loving him. Being with him was what she had dreamed of since she first met him, and she was glad that she had let him know that she loved him. That was something, at least.

"You don't speak to us like that," Benning spat at her. She heard his voice shaking. Was he really willing to do this? Kill another cop? Maybe she wasn't even the first. There must have been other people through the years, other people who had dared to get close to discovering their secrets. Maybe they had just killed all of them off, like they were about to do to her.

The thought of it was enough to make her sick. She would never get to see Aaron again, she would never get to apologize to him. Maybe they had been right, maybe it would have been better if she had stayed off the case, because look at what was happening to her. She had basically led them right to him, and she wasn't sure if they would stop after they had killed her.

"I'm sorry," she whispered under her breath. She knew he couldn't hear her, but it didn't matter. She had to believe there was a way for him to know how she really felt. She had to believe she could take her leave from this life without fearing that he didn't understand how much she cared for him. She always had, even when she had also hated him.

"You bitch," Benning snarled.

Bailey inhaled a deep breath, bracing herself for what was about to come.

And then, the gun went off. She jumped, and waited for the blackness to hit her. She fell back into the van and squeezed herself into a ball so they couldn't take another shot. The pain would come any second now. Where had the bullet hit? She could still feel the throbbing in her shoulder, but...

She lifted her head and looked at her body. No fresh wounds, other than the ones she'd gotten from the crash. And no bullet holes, either. She slowly sat upright. Outside, through the ringing in her ears, she heard chaos. Shouting, banging, crashing, the low, heavy sound of punches being landed. What was going on? Had they turned on each other, or...?

She slid to the edge of the van, and her eyes widened

when she figured out what was actually happening. They were fighting—but not with each other, with Aaron. Aaron seemed to have already taken Ziegler and the others down, but Benning was still on his feet, holding the gun.

"Back off, Ward!" he barked at him. "If you know what's good for you—"

But before he could get out another word, Aaron lunged at him, dropping his head and slamming it into Benning's chest. The force of the impact knocked the gun out of his hands, sending it flying across the ground and into the tall grass. Bailey couldn't make out what happened after that, but judging by the sounds of their struggle, it wasn't going Benning's way.

When she got the nerve to peer around the van, she saw Aaron getting to his feet, wiping away sweat from his brow before he turned his attention back to her.

She felt herself collapse the moment before he reached her. All the emotion, all the fear, facing down death—it all fell away the minute he wrapped his arms around her, holding her tight, as though he never wanted to let her go.

"You're okay," he murmured to her, his voice soft in her ear. She knew they couldn't stay long. It was only a matter of time before the guys came to, and they needed to be as far from here as possible. But right now, all she wanted to do was press herself into his arms.

"Oh my God," she gasped, hardly able to think straight. The sound of the gunshot was still ringing in the air around them, and it was at that moment she remembered the gun.

"Aaron, the gun," she squeaked to him. "You need to get the gun—"

"This gun, you mean?"

Aaron spun around, protecting her with his whole body without thinking. She cowered behind him. She wanted to help, but she feared Benning might take the shot he had missed the first time.

"This little reunion is nice, isn't it?" he said, sneering at the two of them. Bailey heard such cruelty in his voice, she had no idea how she had been able to miss it before. All of it seemed so obvious to her now, the reality of what they had done, how far they had gone. That they would kill her and Aaron if they got the chance.

"Stay away from her," Aaron snarled, and Benning cocked the gun. The sound of the click echoed through the air around them, a threat.

"You going to make me?" Benning asked.

Before Bailey had a chance to hold him back, Aaron dived at Benning again, shoving him to the ground and picking up right where he had left off with the fight.

Chapter Twenty-Two

Aaron reached for the gun, managing to knock it out of Benning's hand for a moment. Lee was stirring next to him, coming back from the hit Aaron had dealt him to the back of the head with a rock he'd found on the road. He had to subdue them both, and keep them away from Bailey. He knew one thing for damn sure: He wasn't going to let them get away with this anymore.

"Damn," Benning snarled as he rolled out from underneath Aaron and scrambled back toward the weapon.

"Aaron!" Bailey yelled from the van, but Aaron held his hand up.

"You stay right there," he told her. "I can handle this."

He gritted his teeth, and repeated the same thing to himself. He *could* handle this. He just had to keep pushing forward, keep doing what he could to bring this nightmare to an end.

All he could think about was the way Bailey had been trembling in his arms. He didn't want her to feel that fear for another moment, and he would do anything to end it. She didn't deserve this, and the only way he could stop these men from hurting her again would be to take them out for good.

Lee was on his feet again, and Aaron rounded on him,

pushing him back against the van, next to Bailey. He crashed into it, still woozy from the blow he had taken to his head, and his entire body shuddered with the pain.

But he had a knife, and he reached for it quickly, pulling it out and flashing it at Aaron. Aaron sprang back, and Lee raised the knife, ready to swing down again.

Until Bailey swept his feet out from under him. Lee seemed to have forgotten she was there, and Aaron nodded to her in thanks. Just like old times, he knew he wouldn't have been able to do it without her by his side.

He turned his attention back to Benning again, his face tightening as he glared at him. Benning had managed to get the gun trained on him again, and Aaron ducked just in time to feel a bullet whizzing over his head. It hit the van with a loud clang, and Bailey let out a yelp of surprise. Aaron turned to make sure she hadn't been hit, but she was out of the van, her arms wrapped around Lee's neck as she held him in place and pushed the air out of him to subdue him once more.

She had him covered. Even though she was scared, and injured, she could still fight for herself. He lunged at Benning, who fired off another shot in a panic. There were only so many bullets in that magazine, and it wouldn't be long before he ran out entirely. And when he did, Aaron would make his move.

He dove into the tall grass for cover, making it so Benning couldn't see him to fire off another shot. His chest pressed to the ground, his whole body was rigid as he waited to make the next move. He didn't even know what he was going to do, but he had to do something.

He crawled along the ground as Benning paced around at the edge of the grass, trying to spot him. He probably would have just shot blindly if it hadn't been for the limited amount of ammo he had right now. He didn't have the support of the others, and he knew Aaron was well trained in how to handle himself and what he should do in these situations.

Only problem was, so was Benning. They'd likely been through the same training, and Benning was far more practiced when it came to a showdown like this one. Aaron shuffled through the grass, trying to make as little noise as possible, until he reached Benning.

He grabbed his feet and yanked hard, knocking the other man off-balance and sending him crashing to the ground. Benning let out a yell, but there was nothing he could do to fight it. His whole body fell like cement, landing with such a thump the air was knocked out of him.

Aaron used the moment he had before Benning got himself back together to dive for the gun and take it from him, then tossed it as far as he could into the tall grass behind them. He just wanted that thing away from him, away from Bailey. When he had seen Benning pointing it at her, that was the only thing he had been able to focus on.

Once it was gone, he scrambled away from Benning to get to Bailey again. She had Lee passed out at her feet, and she jumped up as soon as she saw him getting close. He threw his arms around her, pulling her in against him, pressing his face into her hair. He needed this. He needed her. He needed them together, no matter what he had to do to make it happen, no matter how hard it might be.

"You're okay, you're okay," he told her again. "I've got you. We can get you back up to the lodge, get you patched up—"

But before he could say another word, a sound rang out behind them. He stiffened—a gunshot. He could hear it burning in his ears. He should have kept the gun, but he had been in such a rush to get back to Bailey, he couldn't think about anything else.

And it might have just cost him everything.

"Aaron!" Bailey exclaimed as she pulled back. There was blood on her shirt, staining through, and for a second he thought somehow she had been shot. But then, as she reached out her hand to his torso, he realized that wasn't what had happened.

It was him who had taken the bullet.

"Aaron, get down," she pleaded, but he turned to shield her, refusing to let Benning take her down, too. The pain was starting to set in now, radiating through his body. He glanced down and saw the thick, wet rivulets of blood running down his jeans. He could hardly see straight, dark spots clouding his vision, but it didn't matter—he had to keep her safe. It was the only thing he could think of, regardless of what was happening to him. He wouldn't let anything happen to her.

If it was the last thing he did.

Finally, as the spots began to clear, he saw Benning walking toward them, limping slightly as though he was injured. But he had a grin on his face, as he advanced on the two of them.

And this time, Aaron didn't know if he had any more fight in him. If he could hold him off.

"Aaron," Bailey begged him, trying to pull him back down by her side, but he didn't move. He couldn't. It was as though his feet were rooted to the ground, every bone in his body telling him that the only thing that mattered was Bailey's safety. Just like he had done all those years ago, he would sacrifice himself to protect her.

"Get out of the way, Ward," Benning said, sneering at him. "You really want to leave her to die alone? Your shot was meant for her. Move so I can do her, too. That way, you can have your little romantic moment before you both go."

"Shut up," Aaron snarled back at him. "You're not getting past me." He never wanted to hear Benning talking about what he and Bailey had together. It was just for them.

He would never allow anything between the two of them to be sullied by what these monsters would say about them. Benning would never understand the love Aaron had for Bailey, anyway. Or the love she had for him in return. He was a man who scared women, a man who made them feel as though they weren't safe. He would never understand sacrificing everything for that person, doing anything to make sure they were protected and cared for.

"You sure?" Benning asked, cocking the gun again. How many bullets were left in there? Aaron eyed the barrel, contemplating his next move. But there was no way, no way he could win this. He was starting to feel woozy and tired from the blood loss. He wasn't going to make it much longer.

No matter all that had happened, though, Aaron had never imagined a cop would point a gun at him like this. Someone he was supposed to be brothers-in-arms with, no less.

But Benning clearly felt none of that for him. Benning had banded with a team like Ziegler and his cronies, men who would likely turn their backs on him the first chance they got.

That was something Aaron could take away from this, at least. Benning would never be happy. None of them would be. They had to live their lives looking over their shoulders, never able to rest, never able to slow down, never able to stop. Aaron had lived more than half a decade in peace, really finding comfort in himself and the choices he'd made— enough so that when Bailey came back into his life, he had been able to meet her and tell her how he really felt.

Benning pressed the gun against his chest. Then, a voice cut in from beside them.

"Wait. Let me."

Ziegler was on his feet again, standing there, holding out his hand for the gun. Even through it was clear Benning wanted to be the one to pull the trigger himself, he knew better than to argue with their leader, and he handed the gun over to him, pressing it into his palm.

Ziegler stepped forward and took his place in front of Aaron, grinning widely.

"I've been waiting for this for a long time," he spat. "See you, Ward."

Chapter Twenty-Three

Bailey didn't understand how they'd gotten here. They had gone from being in each other's arms, his voice in her ear promising her she was going to be okay, to this—to this man holding a gun against Aaron's head, ready to end him for good.

Bailey hid behind him, hanging on to him for dear life, arms wrapped around his waist and face pressed into his back. He would never let her take this bullet for him, that much she knew for sure, but she still didn't want to let him die without feeling her here with him. She loved him too much for that.

There had to be something she could do. As Ziegler took a breath and steadied up his shot, time slowed, spreading out before her and giving her a moment to gather herself. She had to make her move now, she knew that, but what could she do? She was right behind him. Could she make it out in time? She remembered what she had done to take down Lee, taking him out at the legs, and she knew she was going to have to pull the same thing again.

No time to think. Only time to act. And if she didn't move now, she and Aaron wouldn't be alive much longer.

She lunged out from behind Aaron, rolling down to the left, and caught Ziegler's eye, drawing his attention from

Aaron just long enough for her to drive a leg into his, sending him crashing to the ground. He squeezed the trigger, sending a bullet up above their heads, and Bailey rolled out of the way and under the van so it wouldn't hit her on the way down, crawling quickly to the other side.

A commotion had broken out around her again, and it took her a moment to realize that it wasn't Ziegler and the others causing it. No, this time, there were people here on their side. Xavier and Cade rushed past her, followed by Lawson, and a few men from the tactical team at the lodge. She scrambled to her feet, only interested in one thing: Aaron.

He had managed to make it to the back of the van, leaving the other highly trained people to take down the corrupt cops who had done this to them. Bailey checked on him, and found his face pale, his eyes distant.

"Here, put some pressure on this," she told him, linking her hands through his and pressing them into his wound.

And then, she heard Xavier yelling for help. When she turned, she saw Ziegler scrambling toward the gun where he had dropped it on the ground. She sprang up and dived toward it, kicking it out of his reach, and then grabbed it and let off the rest of the shots into the ground. She didn't want anyone else using this tonight.

She sank to her knees as the guys took down the cops, subduing them one by one until there was no fight left to be had. Xavier came over to her and offered her a hand, helping her up to her feet.

"How did you know?" she asked, and he shrugged.

"When Aaron went looking for you and didn't come back, I figured something was up," he remarked. "And then when we heard the gunshots, we knew you must need our help."

"Thank you," she whispered softly to him. The words

didn't feel strong enough for how grateful she really was. If it hadn't been for him, and the rest of the guys from Warrior Peak, she would have lost Aaron, and she knew she would never have been able to live with that.

She made her way back to the van, where Aaron had managed to prop himself up. He looked a little better now—his face wasn't quite as pale. Maybe the wound hadn't been as bad as she first thought.

"Bailey," he breathed, and he wrapped his spare arm around her and pulled her in close, pressing his face into her neck. She sank into him. It was over. It was really over. After everything that had happened, everything that they had been through, it was done. There was no way Ziegler and the rest of them were going to get away after this. They didn't stand a chance. Whatever they thought they had been capable of, they were wrong.

She could finally relax and just be with Aaron. She knew he was going to need some serious patching up—a bullet wound wasn't the kind of thing you messed around with—but he was alive. She could feel the slow rise and fall of his breath as Ziegler, Moore, Lee, and Benning were handcuffed and put into trucks, ready to be dropped off at the sheriff's office when they were done here.

"I thought something had happened to you in the fire," Aaron murmured to her, and she pulled her head back.

"Nothing happened to me then," she assured him, but she was certain he'd have more questions. Like why she'd left while everyone else was distracted with the fire. She wished she had a better answer for him than the truth, but she didn't see any way around it right now.

"I… I was just leaving," she admitted. "I thought I could go after them myself, I thought I could take them down. I didn't want to be pushed out of it again. I saw the fire, I let everyone know what was going on, and then I left."

He tensed.

"But I can see how wrong I was," she assured him. "They drove me off the road—that's why I crashed the truck. And if it hadn't been for you, they would have killed me."

She inhaled shakily as the reality of that hit her. Yes, they really would have killed her. If it hadn't been for him throwing himself into the fray the way he had, she would have been dead. The thought chilled her to the bone. She squeezed him tighter.

"And they told me...they told me they came looking for you because of me," she confessed. "And I'm so sorry for that, Aaron, I never meant for that to happen."

"Hey, you have nothing to apologize for," he told her, brushing her tears away. "I know how hard it's been for you. I know how much you wanted to take them down. And I know you probably could have done it yourself. I just wanted to help you. The only thing that matters to me is that you're all right."

She nodded, but she wasn't sure she totally believed him. Could he really be that quick to forgive her, after everything she'd done? She didn't know. She wanted to believe it, but she knew she had some explaining to do.

"I didn't want to go," she admitted to him. "I never did, Aaron. I just... I didn't want either of us getting hurt again, not after what happened before. And I thought if I made the decision for you, it wouldn't be something you had to... something you had to do for yourself, at least this time."

"That was one of the hardest things I've ever had to do," he murmured, shaking his head, eyes misty as though he was remembering it at that very moment.

She cupped his face in her hands. "I'm never going to

be apart from you again," she told him fervently, surprising even herself with how sure she was of that fact. She scanned his face, eyes wide, needing him to understand how much she meant it.

"That sounds good to me," he agreed, and he drew her in for a kiss. Even with the slash in her shoulder, her body filled with pleasure at his touch. Here he was, the man she had wanted for all these years, the man she loved, and there was nothing in the way of them being together. It was finally just…them. Their pasts left far behind for once, a history they never even had to think about again. No matter what happened next, she could hold on to him, and she wanted that more than anything in the world.

She wrapped her arms around him and buried her face into his shoulder again, a wave of emotion crashing through her. He held her to his side, and she knew he was feeling everything she was right now. The two of them were together again, no matter what had pushed them apart, no matter what had landed them back in each other's lives. All the fight in her was gone, all the anger forgotten. Their pasts didn't matter now.

No, the only thing that mattered now was their future. And that they got to spend it together.

Chapter Twenty-Four

As Aaron held Bailey, he tried to let himself relax. She was safe. The guys were dealt with. Even though this bullet wound wasn't exactly making him feel fantastic right now, he knew it could be treated. He would have been dead by now if it was lethal.

"Hey, Aaron."

Lawson stood next to the van, waiting for them to break from their embrace. Aaron winced as he turned around to face him, doing his best to keep the pain from his face. He didn't want to worry anyone.

"We're going to get one of our guys to drive you down to town," he explained. "Xavier let Willis know what's going on, and they've got emergency personnel standing by at the hospital for you and Willis will meet you there. Cade and I will make sure this scum gets to the station to be locked up, once and for all. Bailey, you need medical attention, too." Lawson pointed at her. "You look about as bad as he does."

"Not quite." Xavier walked over and chimed in. "But you lost quite a bit of blood, too." He nodded at her shoulder. "That needs to be cleaned and treated as soon as possible."

"Thank you," Aaron replied, his voice coming out weaker than it had before. He could see those dark spots at the side of his vision again, and he tried to blink them away.

"Aaron, are you all right?" Bailey asked, the worry evident in her voice as she pushed away some of his sweat-soaked hair from his face.

"I will be," he replied, and she offered him an arm to help him to his feet. He leaned on her heavily, and she draped one of his arms over her shoulder to help guide him to the car waiting to get them out of here.

It was carnage out on the road. Truck parts were scattered everywhere from the wreck, and Lee was making a scene, fighting hard to try and break free. He didn't stand a chance against the people around him, but he had never known when to give up.

Bailey managed to get Aaron into the car, and laid him out on the back seat. She climbed in behind him and put his head on her lap.

"It's going to be okay," she whispered to him, though there was some doubt in her voice. How bad was it? He planted his hand on the wound as the driver pulled away from the chaos around them, driving them the rest of the way down to the small town at the bottom of the mountain.

Aaron looked up at Bailey. For the first time since he had seen her on the side of the road, he noticed there was a mark on her arm—a wound, actually. Then he suddenly remembered the blood smeared in the overturned truck. She had been injured, and he was just recalling it. Getting to her, keeping her safe, taking down the guys... All of it was running together. But now that the adrenaline was leaving his system, he was remembering the rest. He couldn't believe he'd forgotten that she'd been hurt, too. He lifted his head to look at it, and when she noticed him staring, she shook her head.

"It's nothing."

"Did they hurt you?"

"I just got a few scratches in the crash."

"A few scratches?" Aaron exclaimed. "That looks worse than a few damn scratches—"

"Please, Aaron, you need to rest," Bailey begged him, gently pressing on his shoulders to guide him back down to the spot he had been in before. He was going to make sure they were done and out for the count. He was going to do everything in his power to make sure they never got out of jail. Never had the chance to do something like this to anyone again.

His head pounded with anger, almost distracting him from the pain rushing through the rest of his system. He wanted to tear them apart, limb from limb. He wanted to make them pay for thinking they could dare lay a hand on the woman he loved.

"It's okay," she promised him. "I'm fine, really. I'll healed up in a few weeks. It'll be like it never happened."

His jaw was still clenched, his body still tense at the thought of them doing that to her.

"Aaron, it's over," she reminded him gently, still running her fingers through his hair. "There's more than enough now to put them behind bars for good. They won't stand a chance after this. They're going to have to face the reality of what they've done, and you know how hard cops go after their own."

He nodded. She was right. When people found out what they had been doing, they would put them away for a long time. It would only be a start when it came to finding justice for the people who had been hurt by their crimes, of course, but it would be something. After so long fearing them, so long wondering if they were going to come after either him or Bailey, he never had to worry about that again.

"I know," he breathed back, and she leaned down to plant

another kiss on his lips. He reached over to grip her hand tight, never wanting to let her go.

He settled his head back against her lap. He still felt the pain, but he could also feel himself starting to relax, feeling so tired…

"Aaron."

Bailey spoke his name again, and he could just about make her out through the fog enveloping him right now. He was exhausted all of a sudden. Maybe just the rush of adrenaline he'd needed to survive tonight, or maybe something else entirely, but his eyes were starting to droop.

"You need to stay awake," she told him, shaking him slightly. He managed to half open his eyes again, his gaze landing on her above him.

"I know," he mumbled.

"It's not going to take us long to get there," she promised him. "We just passed the restaurant we had dinner at, remember?"

He smiled at the memory. That was when he had kissed her for the first time. When they had told each other how they really felt, and slept together for the first time that night. No matter what happened next, he knew he would always be glad he got a chance to share that with her. He never wanted to forget how it felt for her to tell him to kiss her, just like he had imagined a million times over the years.

"I remember," he replied, but his words came out a little slurred. She tightened her grip on him slightly, and he felt her starting to panic. He didn't want to scare her, but he wasn't sure how much longer he could stay conscious. He knew he shouldn't fall asleep—he didn't know how much blood he'd lost. But with every passing second, he felt himself shutting down.

He needed to focus. He needed something to focus on

that would fill his mind the way he needed right now. He squeezed her hand again, letting her know he was still there.

"Tell me about us," he murmured. "Tell me how you feel about us right now."

She took a deep, shaky breath. She looked out the window for a moment, as though pondering his question, before she responded.

"I thought about us all the time," she murmured to him, looking down at him and even managing a smile. "Even when we were apart, I thought about us. I just couldn't forget you, no matter how much I wanted to, no matter how much easier it would have made my life if I did. If I could have just left you behind, I could have started a new life for myself. I could have moved on…"

She trailed off, then shook her head.

"But that was never going to happen," she confessed. "Even back then, I knew I loved you. Even thinking you'd turned on me. I used to wonder if there was something more to it, because the man I knew…the man I knew would never have done that to me."

She took another breath, closing her eyes for a moment, as though bringing it all back to mind again.

"And I never thought I could live without you forever," she went on. "I always wanted you back in my life. And then, when Ziegler and the others turned on me, there was only one person I could think of to go to for help."

She smiled down at him. "You."

He tightened his grip on her slightly. His vision still wasn't entirely clear, but the sound of her words cut through the confusion around him completely. He couldn't deny how much he loved her, not even if he wanted to. He felt the same way she did, and he was glad to hear her say those words, even if the circumstances were far from perfect.

When he was better again, he would say all of this back to her, make sure she knew how much he cared for her. Just as soon as he could string a sentence together without slurring again.

"And I know I haven't always made it easy for us, you know, since we've been back together again," she continued. "But I think I was just scared. Scared that something was going to pull us apart again. I couldn't have lived with that. It was why I left. I know it doesn't make sense, but it just seemed safer to get out of there before either of us got too attached, especially with Ziegler and the others on our tail."

She shook her head, her face dropping.

"And I wish I could have come back to you without bringing them with me," she whispered, her voice cracking.

He reached up to cup her face, even though his body cried out with every movement. "You didn't bring them," he murmured. "They were always going to come find me. I'm just glad you trusted me enough to help you when you needed it most, even after what happened. I would do anything to protect you. You know that, right?"

"I know that," she replied. "I can see it now."

He smiled, dropping his hand back down to his side with a wince.

A silence hung in the air between them. The only sound was the wheels of the car bumping over the road. And then, he spoke again.

"And what about…our future?" he asked her. "You've covered our past. And our present. What do you think's going to happen now?"

She parted her lips, trying to find the words to express what she wanted to say. Maybe it was unfair of him to ask her so soon after they had taken down the men who'd been chasing her. But he wanted to know—he wanted to be sure she saw the same future for them that he did. Up until an hour or so ago, they hadn't been able to think past the immediate threat. But now? Now, they could do just about anything they wanted.

"I want to join the force again," she replied firmly. "And do everything I can to make sure people like them are weeded out of whatever departments they're infecting right now. I can't stand the thought of more of them out there, and more people who are working with them and don't even know it. If they hadn't tried to pull me into it, I would have just worked with them without knowing. I'm never going to let that happen again."

He could hear the certainty in her voice, and it made him proud. She had come so far since she had been a rookie, but she'd had the same determination and certainty since day one. She had always been ready to take on the world, and now she would. He could tell. And he wanted to be there to support her every step of the way.

"And what about the lodge?" he asked her, his voice weaker.

"What about it?" she replied, looking down at him and brushing another strand of hair away from his face.

"You think you'll stay?"

She smiled slightly, cocking her head at him. "Hmm," she murmured, tapping her finger against her bottom lip. "I don't know about that. Would have to be some pretty good reasons to stay, right?"

"Wheatie?" he suggested, and she laughed.

She leaned down to kiss him again. "I can think of a few other reasons," she murmured against his lips before she pulled back. "And there's plenty of work I can do here. You said Sheriff Willis is a good guy, right? I'm sure he'd be willing to help me with a job."

He gazed up at her, hardly able to keep the smile from his lips. It was exactly what he'd wanted to hear, what he'd needed to hear.

The car pulled to a stop.

"We're here," the driver called to them.

"You're going to be okay," Bailey murmured as she helped him out of the back seat of the car.

"As long as you're here, I will be," he agreed.

But as he stood, he slumped against her, and the last thing he heard was Bailey scream for help as the whole world went black.

Chapter Twenty-Five

Bailey paced back and forth through the hospital waiting room, still bleeding some from her arm. She had too much nervous energy to sit down even though she was exhausted.

As soon as Aaron had passed out in front of the hospital, nurses and doctors had whisked him away on a gurney and straight into surgery to remove the bullet from his torso. She had run alongside him until she wasn't allowed any further, shooing away the nurses who were trying to fuss over her injuries.

"I'm fine," she had insisted. "Go take care of Aaron, please."

The surgeon had come out to tell her that the bullet had been successfully removed from his torso and that if the bullet had entered just a millimeter to the right, he wouldn't have been so lucky.

Lucky.

As it was, Aaron was still unconscious. Recovering from surgery, blood loss, and a gunshot wound just shy of hitting important internal organs. She knew the doctor meant to be encouraging, but right now, things didn't feel so *lucky*.

The doctor had also said that all she could do now was wait. Wait there in the same room she'd been in since they had arrived, wait for Aaron to wake up, wait to see what his long-term recovery looked like.

She decided she was done waiting.

She marched up to the closest nurses' station and put on her best charming smile even though she knew she must look crazy—bleeding and disheveled—from what she'd been through.

She took a calming breath. "Hi, I need to see my friend. We came in together. He was shot and just got out of surgery, and I need to be with him when he wakes up."

The nurse looked a bit shocked but quickly regained her composure. "Ma'am, you seem to be injured as well. Can we have a doctor look at you?"

"No," Bailey replied forcefully, "I just need to see Aaron Ward."

The nurse smiled patiently. "Okay, I can take you to his room, but maybe you could let someone bandage up that shoulder once you're there."

She nodded in agreement and the nurse led the way down the maze of identical hallways to the room where Aaron was lying, still unconscious, from his surgery.

Just seeing the rise and fall of his chest eased some of the anxiety in her stomach. She let out a relieved breath as she walked across the room to his side.

"I'll send someone in to look at your shoulder and any other injuries," the nurse said before closing the door behind her.

Sure enough, a different nurse came in a few minutes later to clean up, stitch, and bandage her injured shoulder, and look her over for any other injuries. Once that was done, she sat in the chair next to Aaron, holding his hand and waiting for him to wake up.

Her eyes started to get heavy as she listened to the rhythmic beeping of the heart monitor. She decided to climb into the bed next to Aaron and close her eyes, just for a few minutes. She knew she shouldn't—she was filthy, after all— but she just wanted to be close to him right now. She'd rest a few minutes and then she'd wake up before he did and be the first thing he saw when he opened his eyes.

She curled up next to Aaron's uninjured side and dozed off thinking about how thankful she was that they were both alive. And she realized that at that moment, lying next to Aaron, *lucky* was exactly how she felt.

Bailey woke to the feel of someone's fingers running through her hair, and it took her a moment to figure out where she was.

The smell of antiseptic filled her nostrils, and she sat up. Oh God, she remembered now. She had insisted on being let into Aaron's room after his surgery, and had fallen asleep lying in the hospital bed next to him.

He had collapsed just outside of the hospital, and the panic that had run through her veins in that moment was unlike anything she had ever felt before. She blamed herself for getting him involved in this situation and she was furious at the crooked cops who had hurt them both so much, both physically and emotionally.

But, as she opened her eyes, she saw that he was awake and smiling at her. She threw her arms around him and hugged him tight, emotion rising up inside of her.

"You're okay," she gasped.

"Well, I feel like I just got shot." He grunted at the impact of her attack, but she could hear the smile in his voice. She sprang back, eyes wide.

"Oh, I'm so sorry," she blurted out, realizing she had applied pressure to his fresh wound.

"No, it's okay," he replied. "It feels a lot better than it

did when I passed out. Sorry for giving you that scare, by the way."

"Yeah, you should be sorry," she joked, swatting him playfully on the arm as she shook her head. "You scared the hell out of me!"

"My bad." He smiled, and she grinned back.

"How are you feeling?" he asked her, nodding to the bandage on her shoulder. She had wanted the nurses to focus on Aaron instead of her, but she was thankful they had taken care of her wound as well. She'd hardly been paying attention to it, ordering the nurses to focus on him instead, but she was thankful they'd ignored her.

"I'm fine," she replied. "Better than ever, actually."

And even though Aaron was waking up in a hospital bed today, it was the truth. She and Aaron were alive and they would both be okay, though they'd need some time to heal and get back on their feet. But, this time around, they weren't going to have to look over their shoulders the whole time for fear of someone coming after them. Ziegler and his cronies were behind bars, and there was already an ongoing investigation into what they had been up to. They were going to spend a long time in prison for what they had done.

"Have you heard anything about Ziegler and the others?" he asked.

She nodded. "Yeah, I spoke to Willis while you were in surgery and it sounds like they've got plenty to work with just in the van—unregistered weapons, stuff like that."

What she left out was the shovel, rope, and plastic wrappings they had found in there, too. The shovel was no doubt going to be used to dig her grave if they had succeeded in finishing her off. The rest, she didn't want to think about. She'd already be having nightmares for a while to come. She didn't want him knowing about that part, either. It just didn't seem fair to put him through that when he was the one who had taken a bullet.

"And the fire?" he asked.

"There were a few empty gas canisters in the van," she explained. "It seems like way too much of a coincidence for something like that to have happened on the same night they were there on the road to Warrior Peak, so they'll most likely be charged with arson, too."

She paused for a moment before asking quietly, "How bad was the damage to the lodge?"

Nobody had given her a straight answer yet, like they knew she would find a way to blame herself. And of course she did—it was because of her all of this had happened. If she hadn't come to the sanctuary, the guys would never have tracked her down there. In her mind, she was at fault as much as the men who had started the fire.

"It wasn't as bad as I thought it was going to be," he replied neutrally. "There's still plenty of work that needs to be done in the paddocks to get them right again, but it will be summer soon. Things will start growing back quicker than you think."

She smiled at him. That was a relief, and she hoped he was being totally honest with her. Warrior Peak Sanctuary was such a beautiful and peaceful place, she couldn't stand the thought of it being ruined.

"And what about the horses?" she asked. They had been on her mind ever since she had left.

"They're okay," he replied at once. "River and Hannah helped me get them out of the way of the fire. Wheatie was pretty freaked, but I think she'll calm down when she sees you again."

"I think you vastly overestimate my horse-wrangling skills." She laughed, squeezing his hand. She sat up and stretched as much as she could while yawning. She could have slept for a week and not felt rested. After everything she had been through in the last few days, she shouldn't be surprised about that. She hadn't expected to come out alive, but now she was here with the man she loved, and she couldn't imagine anything else that mattered.

"You going to come back to the sanctuary with me?" he asked, and she nodded at once.

"Everything I said last night, I meant it," she promised him. When he had asked her about their future, it hadn't taken her long to realize what she wanted. When it came to him—when it came to them—she had to give it a chance. She wanted to find out what lay ahead for the two of them. They could finally let go of all the stress and fear, and find out how they would be as a normal couple.

Well, after all that had happened, she doubted that the two of them would ever be a normal couple. But they could be a happy one. And that was all she cared about.

"I want to go back to the sanctuary with you," she continued. "And I want to help you in your recovery. You've got some of the best people around you to help with that, and I know Xavier and Lawson want to do everything they can to get you back on your feet."

"Just so I can get to fixing fences again." Aaron chuckled.

Bailey shook her head. "You should give yourself more credit than that," she told him. "They really like you there. I know you've mostly kept to yourself since you got there, but this could be your chance to open up and get to know people and let them get to know you."

Aaron nodded. She could see it made sense to him. He had been avoiding putting down roots because he had been scared of his past catching up to him, but he didn't need to fear that any longer. He could put that all aside now, and just let himself be the person he wanted to be.

"You're right," he murmured, skimming his thumb over her knuckles. "I've already done a little of that, but I think it'll be easier with you around."

"That's not the only reason I'm staying," she promised him softly. "I... I really want to try and make things work between us, Aaron. God knows what we've got is complicated, but I want to give it a try. When I'm with you, I feel... I feel something I've never felt before. I want to see where that takes us."

"I don't think it's complicated at all." He smiled. "I think it's completely straightforward. I'm in love with you, and I want to spend every day of the rest of my life proving to you just how much I mean that."

"Oh, Aaron," she breathed, and she leaned over to kiss his lips. She was just so overwhelmed with emotion, she hardly knew where to start in sorting through it. But the one at the top of her list, the one that most stood out to her, was sheer and utter gratitude. Gratitude that despite everything that had happened, the path to their future finally seemed clear.

"I love you, Aaron," she murmured to him. She would never get tired of saying those words to him, she was sure of it. When she looked at him, she just wanted to tell him over and over again.

"I love you too, Bailey," he replied.

She closed her eyes for a moment, letting the sweetness of this moment linger. She couldn't wait to get back to Warrior Peak with him, so the two of them could settle into their new life together—whatever that happened to look like. As long as they were together, she didn't care at all. Whatever she did next, as long as it was with him by her side, she would be happy.

Chapter Twenty-Six

"You want to go feed Wheatie?" Aaron asked Bailey, as she grabbed an apple from the breakfast table. She always picked up a piece of fruit when she wanted to see her favorite horse. She never felt like she could visit the mare without some kind of treat, and the horse was never going to turn her down.

"You read my mind," she replied, looping her free hand into his arm. "I'm not keeping you from anything?"

"I'm all good," he replied, slipping an arm around her waist. "I've got the day off. Got physical therapy with Carter."

"Ah, of course," she said. "How's it going?"

"I really don't think I need to be going anymore," he grumbled slightly. "I'm totally better. It's been more than six months since I got shot."

"Yes, well, better to be safe than sorry, right?" she told him.

He grinned at her. "I know better than to argue with you," he replied.

She laughed. "Damn right you do," she agreed, tossing up the apple and catching it in her hand again as they stepped out of the door. She'd actually finished her own physical therapy sessions not long ago and got a clean bill of health.

Between the knife wound in her leg and then her shoulder, she'd had some work to do of her own to heal up properly.

The sun blazed down, a late fall day alive with the gold and red of the trees. More than half a year after the attack on Warrior Peak by Ziegler and his men, things were finally starting to get back to normal, and he couldn't have been happier.

In fact, the day before he had spent most of the afternoon planting rows of flowers and grass in and around the paddock. Bailey had offered to help him, but he knew she had an appointment with Willis to talk over some more of the evidence that had come to light, and he didn't want to keep her from that. Besides, it was a chance for him to get back to reality, a chance for him to forget about all the limitations that had been on him as he had been recovering from getting shot.

Of course, they hadn't felt like limitations with Bailey around. She had been there to help him out every step of the way, literally. He had struggled with walking for the first couple of weeks, the pain sometimes getting to be too much for him, and she would patiently take him over to the cafeteria for breakfast without a word of complaint. After that, she helped with his physical therapy on the side, learning the best exercises for him to do and making sure he always got them done. She liked to crack the whip, but he was thankful for that. It kept him on track. He had finally been allowed to get back to doing some work the month before, though Xavier and Lawson had both tried to talk him out of it, and they wouldn't let him do everything he was doing before he got shot.

"You don't need to push yourself," Xavier had tried to warn him. "You don't want to do too much and have a setback with your recovery. The work will still be there when you're ready."

"At this point, I think I'm putting it back more by not getting out there and doing something," he had protested. "I need to feel like I'm doing something useful. You guys get that, right?"

"You're resting," Lawson had told him. "Sometimes, that's the most useful thing you can do."

"Besides, it's not like you haven't been busy helping out with the case," Xavier had pointed out—a fair thing to bring up.

Aaron and Bailey had been working with Willis and a few other cops across the state with the case against Ziegler and his crew. Not that it was actually going to court. At the moment, it looked like they would each be taking a plea deal. It wasn't ideal, and Aaron would have preferred to see them made an example of, but he got it. The information they handed over might have been enough to get to the bottom of a few cold cases, and those victims deserved justice.

And at the end of the day, he didn't care how they went away, as long as they were out of his life, and Bailey's life, for good. It had taken a long time for Bailey to recover emotionally from what she had been through, and even now, he sometimes found her awake after a nightmare. But, these days, he could usually coax her back to bed and hold her until she fell asleep.

She'd even recently agreed to meet with Sarah, the counselor at the sanctuary. He had finally shared with her about how he came to be at Warrior Peak all those years ago. How messed up his head was, paranoid of being tracked down or worse, and how Sarah had helped him overcome some of the worst of the nightmares. After listening to Aaron voice the details so similar to her own, she'd decided it might be good for her, too. Just to round out her healing, and Aaron couldn't have been more proud of her for that.

Bailey had settled in at Warrior Peak amazingly well, and was working with Willis down in Blue Ridge to help put the pieces of the case together. She had even dropped in a few mentions about working with him long-term, and Aaron truly hoped she would. Blue Ridge wasn't all that different from Kings Mountain, and it would give her a fresh place to start over.

They arrived at the paddock, where Wheatie was already working her way through some of the flowers Aaron had planted there the day before. He had done everything he could to help erase the damage caused by the fire.

"Hey, you!" he called to the horse.

Wheatie lifted her head long enough to snort in their direction, and then went right back to eating the flowers.

He sighed and shook his head.

"I told you this would happen," Bailey teased him. She had—she'd reminded him of how Wheatie had gone through the flowers before, and suggested putting up some new fences before he started work on replanting, but he hadn't listened.

"This is supposed to be where the plants are regrowing," he reminded Wheatie as he reached the fence. "You're not going to let that happen as long as you keep eating them."

"Hey, leave her alone," Bailey protested, reaching over the fence to pat Wheatie on the nose. She and Wheatie had such an amazing bond. Wheatie lifted her head to stop eating for a moment to greet her friend.

"Here, I brought you an apple," she continued, offering the fruit in her hand. Wheatie carefully wrapped her lips around it and then snapped it up, making Bailey laugh.

"And now you've just rewarded her for eating my plants," Aaron pointed out.

Bailey shrugged. "You can't blame a horse for horsing,"

she replied. "She deserves it. She worked very hard supervising you, you know."

"I should have known you would take her side in an argument over mine," he replied, but he couldn't help but grin. This side of her, this softer side, was one he was falling more in love with every day.

"Yeah, I always will, sorry," she replied, tossing her hair over one shoulder and flashing him a playful grin. "Come on—let's take a look at the flowers, and see if there might be anything to salvage, huh?"

She slipped her hand into his and guided him toward the other side of the paddock. Thankfully, Wheatie had done less damage over there, and it looked like there would be enough for them to work with.

"Well, I guess it's something," he muttered, and she leaned into him.

"It's going to be overflowing with green again soon enough," she promised him. "You've done a great job here. And I know it's not going to be long until you start to reap the rewards."

"Oh, I think I've already got plenty of those," he murmured, and she smiled as he leaned his head down to hers to give her a kiss. He meant it—she was a greater reward than anything he could ever have asked for. Sometimes, their closeness didn't even feel like it could be real to him, but it was. It was as real as the sun beaming down on them from the sky above, and just as warm.

They headed back to the main building to help with preparing dinner. It was a ritual they had gotten into doing a few times a week, spending some time together and helping Cade and the others make some delicious food. One of the new arrivals had even started a vegetable garden, giving them fresh produce to use. It was these quiet, domestic times they spent together that Aaron loved the most. It made him imagine what living with her in a real house would look like. He was in no rush to leave the sanctuary, not for a long time, but getting to picture her in a home of their own made him smile.

They served up dinner for everyone, and the core group crowded around the center table. Xavier, Lawson, and Hannah on one side, Cade and River on the other, along with Bailey and Aaron.

"This looks great," Hannah remarked as she went to serve herself up a generous helping.

"Hey, leave some for the rest of us," Lawson teased, nudging her, and she raised her eyebrows at him pointedly.

"First come, first served!" she retorted, and everyone laughed.

While they were all eating Lawson asked, "You had a meeting with Willis yesterday, didn't you, Bailey?"

"Yeah, I did." She nodded.

"How did it go?" Xavier asked. "How's the case coming along? Anything they need us to give them a hand with?"

"I think they're okay for the time being," she replied, smiling down at her plate. "But, uh, there was something we got to talking about. I wanted to tell everyone when we were all together."

Aaron's heart leaped in his chest, and he reached over to squeeze her hand beneath the table. She shot him a slightly nervous look, biting her lip, but he nodded at her to go on. He could tell everyone was on pins and needles, waiting for her to share her news.

"I asked him if there were any positions open in the Blue Ridge police force, and he said yes," she explained. River drew in a sharp breath, and Hannah clapped her hands together.

Aaron could hardly believe it. He thought she would have come to him first about this, but from the look on her face, he could tell she wanted to be sure before she told him anything. She never liked to get his hopes up without good reason, and this was about the best one he could imagine.

"That's amazing!" Hannah exclaimed, jumping to her feet and rushing around the table to give her a hug. Bailey smiled and hugged her back; the two women had become close in her time here. They, along with River, could often be found walking in the forest together.

"Yeah, I know it's not exactly what I pictured for my career," she continued, once Hannah had released her. "But I can work really closely with him on the case against Ziegler and the others, and maybe work my way up to a bigger agency from there."

"But that means you're going to be staying for now, right?" Hannah asked enthusiastically.

Bailey nodded. "Yeah, it does."

"Then this meal is a celebration!" Hannah exclaimed, grabbing her glass and lifting it up. "To Bailey. And her first year at Warrior Peak!"

"First of many, I hope," River added, and Bailey flushed excitedly. She glanced over to Aaron, and Aaron could do nothing more than smile back at her.

"To Bailey," Lawson announced, and everyone echoed him, their words overlapping as their glasses tapped together.

"Thank you," Bailey replied, lowering her head in gratitude. "It means so much to me that you're all happy I'm staying."

"Of course we are!" Hannah replied, but Aaron knew one thing for sure. As much as everyone here was happy she was sticking around—nobody was more excited about what this meant than him.

He leaned over and brushed his lips against her ear. "I love you. And I'm so proud of you."

Chapter Twenty-Seven

Bailey woke up slowly to the feel of Aaron rubbing her back lightly. She rolled toward him with a sleepy smile on her face.

"Good morning, beautiful," he said softly, giving her a quick kiss.

She beamed. "Good morning, handsome."

No matter how many times she woke up next to him, she was always so happy that he was the first thing she saw when she opened her eyes every morning. She still felt giddy when he kissed her, and got butterflies just from looking at him. She didn't think she would ever get over how thankful she was that they had found each other again.

"It's your first official day of work today at the Blue Ridge Police Department. How are you feeling about it?"

That was one thing she loved about Aaron—he was always so thoughtful and he cared about her feelings. "I'm excited," she replied. "A little anxious, too, if I'm being honest. The last first day I had at a police department didn't go so well." She shrugged a shoulder.

He tucked a strand of hair behind her ear. "That's true, but just remember that Blue Ridge isn't Kings Mountain, and there are more good cops out there than ones like what we dealt with from Kings Mountain."

She sighed. "I know you're right. I'm excited to be part of the department here. Willis has been such a big help with our case."

"You have a lot to offer the BRPD. I've always known you were a good cop, even before I fell in love with you," Aaron said.

Bailey smiled. "Right back at you, Ward."

Aaron laughed. "Want to make some breakfast together before you have to get ready to go?"

She sat up and swung her legs off the side of the bed. "Yes, that sounds great."

They made their way into the tiny kitchen of the cabin where they lived. Even though it was a small, cramped space, it was sentimental to Bailey because it was their first place together. She knew that someday they would need to find another bigger place, but for now, she was happy right where they were.

They worked together like a well-oiled machine. Bailey brewed the coffee and set the table while Aaron scrambled eggs and made some toast. Then they sat down to eat breakfast together, like they did almost every day. They chatted comfortably about the sanctuary, their friends, and Aaron's plans for the day while Bailey was at work.

After they cleaned up their dishes, Bailey took a shower and got dressed for work. She looked at herself in the full-length mirror—it almost felt strange to be wearing a uniform again after everything that had happened. It felt good, though. Being a police officer was what she was meant to do. She'd never been more sure of that.

She walked out of the bedroom and into the small living room where Aaron was, and did a flirty little spin like she was a supermodel at the end of a runway. "What do you think?"

Aaron whistled. "Hottest new cop I've ever seen in Blue Ridge," he said, linking his arms around her waist.

She swatted his chest playfully. "You probably say that to all the new cops."

He tipped his head back and laughed. "I can assure you, I definitely do not."

She went up on her toes and kissed him. "I love you. I'll see you tonight."

"I love you, too. You're going to kill it today, and I can't wait to hear about it when you get back."

Bailey smiled as she walked out the front door of the cabin to her truck. She couldn't wait to see what the day had in store for her.

BAILEY DROVE DOWN the mountain toward the town of Blue Ridge, thinking about the accident she'd had on that very road just a few months earlier. Although it was a scary, horrible, painful situation, ultimately it was what had allowed them to arrest Ziegler and his band of crooked cops, and get justice for the people who had suffered because of them.

She pulled into the parking lot of the small-town police department and took a deep breath, gathering her courage. She knew Willis and had met many of the other officers while working the case to put the corrupt cops behind bars. It was also part of living in a small town—almost everyone knew each other in some capacity, even if the only interaction they had was a friendly wave when their paths crossed at a local store.

She realized that she enjoyed small-town life more than she thought she would. When she thought back to her time working behind a desk in a small beach town and how much she wanted to get back to Kings Mountain, she couldn't believe how her life, and desires, had changed. She didn't need fast-paced and dangerous. She was perfectly content to make sure that Blue Ridge stayed the safe and quiet little town it was. Of course, Aaron being in the safe and quiet little town had a lot to do with her change of heart as well.

With one last calming breath, she stepped out of her truck and walked toward the front doors of the police station. Once inside, she walked up to the front desk, where a pleasant-looking older woman sat.

"Hi, I'm—" she started.

"Bailey!" the woman exclaimed, her face lighting up with a smile. "I know who you are, honey. Sheriff Willis is waiting for you in his office. Do you want me to show you the way?"

Bailey couldn't help but smile back at the kind woman. "You don't have to do that. I know the way."

The woman nodded. "Okay, dear, but let me know if you need anything. My name is Evelyn." She leaned in conspiratorially. "I keep these officers here in line like they're my own children. You be sure to let me know if anyone gives you any problems."

Bailey's smile widened. "Thank you, Evelyn. I'll be sure to let you know."

"See that you do," Evelyn replied, waving her off toward the sheriff's office.

Bailey was still smiling from her interaction with Evelyn as she walked down to Willis's office, finding the door open. He was on the phone but motioned for her to come in and have a seat in one of the chairs in front of his desk. She looked around the room while he finished his phone call. On the walls were awards and certificates, and on his desk and credenza behind it were pictures of his wife, kids, and grandkids. She smiled at one particular picture of a little boy, face smudged with mud, holding up a tiny fish and grinning broadly like it was his prized possession.

Sheriff Willis said his goodbyes to the person he was talking to and hung up the phone. "Sorry to be on the phone when you first arrive, Bailey."

"No apology necessary, sir, I know you're a busy man," she replied.

Willis nodded his thanks. "I take it you met Evelyn out at the front desk?"

"Yes," she confirmed. "She seems very nice."

"Oh, she is," he replied. "Just don't get on her bad side. One time I tracked mud through the lobby after I had been walking through the woods in the rain for a case. She was so mad that I had to bring her that fancy coffee she likes every morning for a week before she would forgive me."

Bailey chuckled. "No to mud, yes to coffee. Noted."

"I think you're going to fit in here just fine," he said with a smile. "Do you want to go meet the others before I show you the ropes and give you the whole introductory spiel?"

Her stomach flipped but she nodded confidently. "Yes, that sounds great."

She followed behind Sheriff Willis as he led her out to the bullpen where the officers' desks were.

"Everyone, this is Bailey," Sheriff Willis said over the din of the busy environment. "Bailey, this is everyone." He swept an arm around the room.

Bailey smiled and waved awkwardly. "Uh, hi, everyone."

"You'll have a chance to learn everyone's names and get to know them personally soon," Sheriff Willis promised.

Throughout the day, almost every single person found Bailey to talk to her and kindly welcome her to the department. Some of them asked questions about how Aaron was doing or how things were going with the rebuilding of the parts of the sanctuary that were damaged in the fire. She realized that she had no reason to be worried about these people being like the guys she had worked with in Kings Mountain. Aaron had been right—they were good cops and good people. She was excited to be a part of this group of officers.

By the end of the day she was tired but happy. Some of the officers invited her to grab a beer at the local bar after their shift, but she declined, promising to join them next time. She didn't say no because she was worried about a repeat of what had happened at the bar in Kings Mountain, but because all she wanted to do was get home to Aaron and tell him about her day.

She got in her truck and drove back toward Warrior Peak. She waved at Hannah and River, who were taking a walk, as she drove by but didn't stop to talk. She would give them all the details about her first day on the job tomorrow. Right now, the only person she wanted to talk to was Aaron.

When she pulled up in front of their cabin, she paused for a moment, taking in its charm. Sure, it was small and rustic and the hot water didn't always work, but if home was truly where the heart was, then this was definitely home. At the end of a long day, that's all she could ask for.

She got out of her truck and walked into the cabin to find Aaron cooking dinner. He turned and smiled when she came in.

"Hello, officer," he said with mischief in his eyes. "I promise I'm not doing anything illegal."

She tried to look stern, playing along. "I sure hope not, or else I might have to handcuff you."

He waggled his eyebrows. "Is that so?"

She nodded solemnly. "Yes, and I was given my department-issued cuffs today, so you better watch it, buddy."

He laughed. "Let's save that for later. First, let's eat and you can tell me all about your day."

"That sounds like a good plan," she said. "I'm starving and whatever you're making smells delicious."

They sat down and ate together, and she told him all about her day. The people she'd met, how kind they'd been, and how much she looked forward to working for the department. Aaron listened and asked a few questions, then told her about his day. He'd had some physical therapy and then worked on some small projects that he had convinced Lawson and Xavier to let him do.

"Sounds like we both had a pretty productive day," Aaron said.

Bailey nodded in agreement. "Are you ready to do it all over again tomorrow?"

"I guess so," Aaron replied. "But first, I have some other plans for us tonight."

"Do you?" she said coyly, standing up from the table.

He stood, too, and grabbed her around her hips, lifting her off the ground. "I sure do. Let me show you."

She wrapped her legs around his waist as he walked them into the bedroom, and couldn't remember a time she was so content in all areas of her life.

She was finally where she was meant to be.

Chapter Twenty-Eight

Aaron looked around the cabin that he and Bailey shared and sighed. Things were quiet now that she worked and wasn't around all day. He was so incredibly proud of her, but he missed her when she was gone. He had gotten used to slow mornings, midday walks to visit Wheatie and give her treats, afternoon coffee on the tiny back porch of their cabin, and cooking dinner together every night.

They could still do those things sometimes, just not every day like they had been. It didn't help that he wasn't fully back to work, building and doing other physical jobs around the lodge grounds. He could admit that he was a little envious of Bailey being able to put that uniform on each morning and go to work helping people. While he didn't want to be a police officer anymore, he did want to do something that mattered.

He felt like what he did at the sanctuary mattered. Now, if he could just convince Lawson and Xavier that he was healed up enough to go fully back to his job. He'd been consistent with his physical therapy and going to all of his doctor's appointments. He felt strong and capable of returning to work. He decided he was going to go talk to Lawson and Xavier about it right then and there.

He made his way to the main building, stopping to

pet Wheatie and give her an apple. Even though Wheatie seemed happy to see him, she looked past him as if she was searching for Bailey. When she didn't see her, she turned doleful eyes back to Aaron.

"I know you miss her, girl," he said softly to the horse, stroking her silky head. "I do, too, but she'll be back this evening and I know she'll want to come out here to see you."

Wheatie nudged him gently with her nose and snorted like she understood what he was saying. With one more pat, he left Wheatie in the paddock and continued toward the lodge. He was a little bit nervous about this conversation with Xavier and Lawson, because not only did he want to talk about fully returning to work, but he also had something else important that he wanted to ask them.

When he stepped through the doors of the lodge building, he saw Hannah.

He waved at her. "Hey, Hannah, have you seen Lawson and Xavier? I was hoping to have a meeting with both of them."

Hannah's brows shot up. "Yeah, I think they're both in Lawson's office. Is everything okay?"

"Yep. Everything is great," he replied reassuringly.

Something like relief passed over her face. He knew she worried about everyone after the fire and the other things that had happened that night.

"How is Bailey liking her new job at the police department?" she asked. "I feel like I haven't had much of a chance to talk to her about it because she's been so busy."

"She's really loving it," he said with pride in his voice.

"I'm so glad to hear that." Hannah smiled. "Hopefully, I'll catch up with her soon. But for now, I'm going to let you go track down the guys, and I need to head to town for some supplies."

They said their goodbyes and Aaron continued down the hallway toward the offices. When he reached the outside of Lawson's office, he knocked twice.

"Come in," Lawson called.

Aaron opened the door and poked his head in, where he saw both Lawson and Xavier, just as Hannah had predicted. "Hey guys, I was hoping to have a conversation with you. Do you have a few minutes?"

Xavier and Lawson exchanged glances before looking back at him. "Sure," Xavier said, gesturing to a chair next to him. "What's on your mind, Aaron?"

Aaron took a seat and a fortifying breath before jumping in. "I'm ready to start working again."

Lawson looked confused. "You have been working."

"No." Aaron shook his head. "I mean, like my real work. I want to get back to building and all of the things I was doing before my injury and surgery. Not the easy little odd jobs you've been creating to make me feel useful."

"Aaron," Xavier started. "You were shot only a few months ago. We just want you to have a chance to heal up before you're back to climbing ladders and doing all of the other things you do."

Aaron made eye contact with each of them. "I am healed up. My doctor cleared me and he said I can go back to my life—and work—as usual."

The men smiled genuinely. "That's great news, Aaron," Xavier said. "Just promise to let one of us know if something is too much or if you start to feel like you need to take a step back again."

"I will," Aaron promised, and excitement bloomed in his chest.

"Was there anything else you wanted to talk to us about?" Lawson asked.

"Actually, yes, there is…" Aaron trailed off, trying to decide how he was going to bring up this next topic he wanted to talk to them about. "It's about Bailey and me."

For the next hour, Aaron, Lawson, and Xavier talked through logistics, asked questions, and Aaron showed and explained the plans he had.

"Bailey doesn't know any of this yet, though," he warned. "I would appreciate it if you could keep this between us for the time being."

Lawson and Xavier agreed.

By the time Aaron left Lawson's office, he was so excited and relieved. And for the first time in a long time, he was looking toward the future, instead of dwelling on the past. He knew exactly who to thank for that.

With Bailey by his side, he knew there was nothing they couldn't accomplish together.

Forever.

Epilogue

Bailey edged the car to a halt at the edge of the path, letting out a long sigh as she pulled her hair from her ponytail and shook it loose. No matter how long the day, no matter how hard the case, she was always glad to come back to this place. It was home to her. But more importantly, it was home to Aaron, and she couldn't wait to see him.

She climbed out of the front seat and locked up the car, then tucked her keys into her pocket. She'd been given her own cruiser a couple of months ago, and she was still proud to drive it. A reminder of how far she had come, and how well she had done in earning Willis's trust.

It had been nearly a year since she'd arrived at Warrior Peak Sanctuary, and the difference between her then and her now was almost staggering. When she'd gotten here, she'd been a scared little girl, on the run for her life. Now, she was a self-assured woman who had a thriving career and a reputation for bringing down the shadiest cops in the business.

The relief of knowing that the men who had tormented her and Aaron were behind bars was immense to her, even more than she thought it would be. They had each been put away on plea deals, and a handful of cold cases had already been solved based on evidence they had obscured or destroyed, with a few more well on their way to the same end.

She had been working with the victims directly, doing what she could to restore their faith in the police after what they had been through. She could only imagine how hard it had been for them, and she was able to relate to them based on her own experiences with Ziegler and his gang.

She made her way up the path to the cabin where she and Aaron had been staying for the past year. It was small, but it wasn't like they needed much space from each other anyway. He had been teasing her since they had first moved in together that he had been keeping her flexible through his physical therapy, and she supposed with their bedroom antics, he was kind of right. A flicker of a smile passed over her lips as she looped the final corner to their cabin.

Aaron was sitting out on the back porch, in the chair he'd grabbed from a dump and started to fix up in his own time. It was something he had really gotten into over the last few months, restoring old furniture. Most of it, he donated to local charities, but some pieces they had kept for their place. It was starting to feel like a real home, and she found herself craving something even more like that.

He looked up from his lap when he saw her coming over. It still felt a little strange to be in uniform and him not, but when he looked at her with such appreciation in his eyes, nothing else mattered. She made her way up the steps to the porch, and looked down at what he was working on. Spread across his lap was a blueprint, covered in small pencil strokes here and there.

"What's this you're working on?" she asked, and he lifted the blueprint from his lap and patted his leg, indicating for her to come take a seat.

"Just working on a building design," he said.

She draped her arms around his shoulders. "Talk me through it."

"Well, this is going to be the entryway," he explained, tracing his finger along the paper. "And this is going to be the living room. Through here, the main bedroom, and down this hallway, a nice kitchen with a big window looking out over the mountains..."

"Wow, this place looks amazing," she murmured. "What is it for? Is the sanctuary opening up new places to stay, or something?"

He glanced up at her, a smile on his face, and shook his head. "Nope, it's not for Warrior Peak," he replied.

She furrowed her brow, confused. "Then who is it for?"

"It's for us," he replied simply, and her eyes widened as she looked down at the page.

"You're designing this for us?" she whispered in shock. She had seen him working on these pages a few times, but she had always figured it was something for the sanctuary she would find out about eventually.

But a home? For them? It made her head spin with the possibilities.

"Yeah, I want to give you a real home," he replied. "A place we can live. A place with room to start a family, if that's what you want."

"Oh, Aaron." She sighed and leaned down to kiss him. She couldn't think of a damn thing in the world more romantic than what he had just said to her.

"I would love that," she added, brushing her nose against his. "And where exactly is this palace going to be?"

"I already spoke to Xavier and Lawson," he replied. "To see if they'd be willing to give up a little bit of the sanctuary grounds for us."

She gasped. "And what did they say?"

"They said yes," he replied with a grin.

She squealed and wrapped her arms around him even

tighter, pushing her head into his shoulder. "That's the most amazing news," she breathed. So she could stay here with Aaron, continue her work with Willis, and they could start putting down real roots. Just like the grass that had regrown to cover the paddock and the flowers around it, they could settle here and find a place to bloom. A family? He had said something about a family, and her heart fluttered at the thought.

"I love you so much, Aaron," she told him, and he ran his hand along her back, a small, simple gesture that made her whole body tingle.

"I love you, too, Bailey," he murmured back.

For a moment, they just sat in the silence. The birds were chirping in the trees around them, the same songs they had been singing when she had first arrived, but her future looked a whole lot brighter than it had back then.

And she could hardly wait to see what else was in store for her.

* * * * *

COMING SOON!

We really hope you enjoyed reading this book.
If you're looking for more romance
be sure to head to the shops when
new books are available on

Thursday 15th January

To see which titles are coming soon, please visit
millsandboon.co.uk/nextmonth

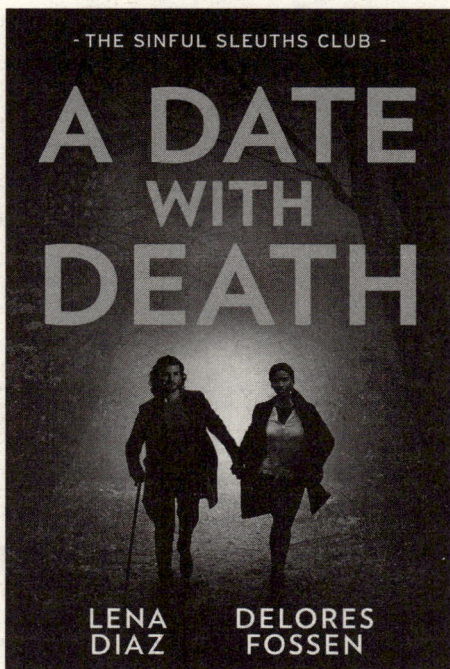

FOUR BRAND NEW BOOKS FROM
MILLS & BOON MODERN

Indulge in desire, drama, and breathtaking romance – where passion knows no bounds!

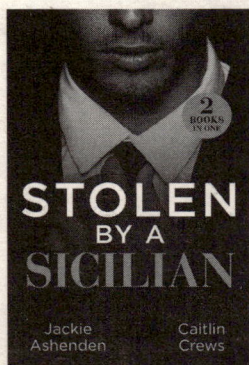

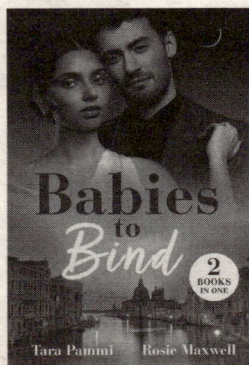

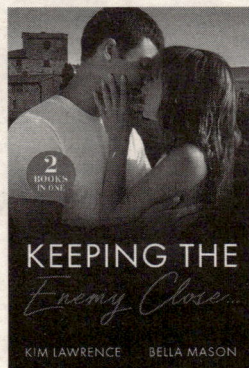

STOLEN BY A SICILIAN
2 BOOKS IN ONE
Jackie Ashenden
Caitlin Crews

Babies to Bind
2 BOOKS IN ONE
Tara Pammi
Rosie Maxwell

TO HIRE AND TO HATE
2 BOOKS IN ONE
Michelle Smart
Annie West

KEEPING THE Enemy Close...
2 BOOKS IN ONE
KIM LAWRENCE
BELLA MASON

OUT NOW

Eight Modern stories published every month, find them all at:

millsandboon.co.uk